THE LOST SOULS

THE LOST SOULS

SHANNON LEE

Bindi

Contents

Contents ~ vii

First Printing, 2021

I would like to express a huge thank you to those who believed in me, encouraged me, and allowed me to follow my dreams.

To my spouse, Kevin, son Joshua, and daughter Sierra. With your faith and understanding in me throughout the past five years, I thank you from my heart.

My mom, who read this book before she passed, always telling me that I could do it.

My grandmother for telling me stories of her life. It's from you, I get my writing abilities.

My beta readers: Lisa, Julie, Kyle, Cassandra, Lois, Becky, McKenzie, Kristin, Amy, Laura, JoAnne. Your patience and suggestions were appreciated.

To all the others I forgot to mention. Just listening to me, and giving me hope. You'll never know how much that has meant to me.

1

Syn

The hardware store just outside of Summerville, South Carolina, was his final stop before he headed back to the house. It was late, and the store was vacant. That was good. He liked it when there were fewer people around to notice him. Paint and paint supplies were the last things he needed to complete his task. He wasn't picky about the color. All he needed was a dark shade to cover up the big windows facing the road. He quickly grabbed a cart and headed to the back of the store, where he picked up what he needed and headed to the checkout.

This is the last time I will ever have to do this. He thought. *Ever. After this gig, I will have enough money to quit doing his shit.*

He could not get the blonde girl out of his mind. She was perfect and came from money. Just what he needed to finish his career. Since the day they met, he had been watching her and following her daily. He was getting to know her friends and her daily routine, slowly coming up with the perfect plan. This plan had taken him years, but she was worth the wait—every single minute of it.

When they first met, she was sitting next to him on a first-class flight from England. He had just finished up with some business there and was on his way home. She was coming from London.

She had told him all about her visit and that she was traveling alone for the first time. She wanted her parents to be confident in her capabilities of making the trip alone. She told him of her plans to study abroad during her last few years of school. She talked about her father, his banking career, and how his money allowed her to travel everywhere.

She sure was grown-up. Anyone could see that was the message this stranger had conveyed to her. The more this man seemed interested, the more she wanted to share her life's story with him.

She smiled as she told him every detail of her life. Where she came from, why she was in London. She told him what her father's name was and what he did for a living. She rambled on about all the plastic surgeries her young mother had. There was a lot of information shared with him in that nine-hour trip across the ocean. He listened to every word as the young blonde talked. The man could tell that she was young and naive, like most of his encounters. He would allow her to talk uninterrupted as he memorized every bit of her story.

The man thought of many ideas and scenarios as he listened to the girl talk. Some being so complex, they would take years to plan out.

What else do I have but time? He thought. *This has become my life. So far, it has been working out very well.*

Over the next couple of years, he had become more focused on this well-laid-out plan.

* *

He made his way to the checkout, pulling his hat down to

shadow his eyes. He unloaded his things onto the belt, handed the clerk the exact cash, and grabbed his bags. He learned at an early age to keep covered, avoid eye contact, and above all, no small talk. His ultimate goal was to remain invisible and forgettable. He learned the least amount of time he spent interacting with the public would aid him in staying unnoticed. He had done this successfully for almost all of his 28 years. The most recent five years have been in the US, where his research became more accessible. The money here was abundant. His life in the US was about to enter its final chapter.

The final years of his research into Harper Bengston's life were coming to a close. The blonde didn't remember him or their conversation from all those years ago.

But he remembered every word.

The girl told this stranger all about her father's career and how he wanted her to go to London to study. She felt that her best friend somehow needed her to get through the last couple of school years. He remembered her saying that she would be leaving just before her Sophomore year of high school.

With school starting in the fall, he needed to finalize his plans soon.

By the time he pulled up to the house, it was late. Like many times before, he would go quietly around the block once. Making sure no one noticed him. There was a faint flickering light of a TV behind a curtain from a house just down the street. When he felt safe, he slowly rolled into his garage, with his car lights turned off.

Once the garage door was fully closed, he worked hastily unloading his supplies in the faint light coming out of the car's trunk.

His priority was to darken the front room windows so no one could see what was going on inside the house—making it sound-proof and escape-proof before the first group of girls arrived.

Finally finished, he sat on the couch to admire his work. He started to think back to where he came from and how far he had gotten.

The image that came to his head was his first real memory of his childhood. Russia.

* *

His mom called him Syn-it was the Russian for the word for son. She raised him the best she could in the red light district of southeast Russia. Not knowing who his father was, the boy almost looked Asian. His almond-shaped eyes were a slate gray, and his hair was jet black. His skin turned a beautiful copper color from the sun.

The boy and his mom kept on the move, ahead of the law. The two of them dodged the 'polisiya'-Russian police. They traveled from city to city, constantly crisscrossing the border into China. It was easy for the boy to blend in, and his mother knew most of the pimps running the girls here. The money was hard-earned, and the pimps took most of it. The rest of it, his mom spent shooting up heroin. It was how she dealt with things. A vicious cycle that never seemed to have an end. Young Syn grew up in the middle of this nightmare.

It wasn't long into his short life that Syn's mother lay dying on a filthy river bank. Going around, collecting various pieces of trash that had washed downstream from the latest storm, Syn worked hard at making her a small shelter, keeping her out of the elements. Weak and starving himself, he never slowed down.

Syn tried his best to keep his mother dry by wrapping her up in anything he could find. She was all he had ever known in his young life, and now she was fading away. He knew that soon he would be alone. He would keep himself busy to stop himself from crying. Crying was a sign of weakness, and his mother would disapprove of it.

Over the past few days, Syn noticed a growing stench coming from his mother. It was getting harder and harder for him to stay beside her. She spent most of her last days sleeping. When she was awake, she would cry and scream out in pain. Syn began to distance himself as much as he could.

Crying, she reached out for him with her thin, frail hands. She was shaking, grabbing onto him. Her touch was as cold as ice, her arms covered in sores. She would pull him close to her. Reluctantly, he dropped down next to her, resting his head on her chest. He could feel her bones heaving against his cheek. He remembered listening to her heart faintly beating inside her hollow chest. She stroked his black curls and began to gasp.

With a weak voice, she whispered into his ear.

"Syn, you will be on your own soon. Remember everything I taught you. Do not trust anybody." Her heavy breath across his cold cheek stank of rotten flesh. Her stomach was rotting. A tear rolled down the boy's dirty face, leaving a wet trail to his quivering chin. He closed his eyes. He could hear her heart getting weaker. *Lub-dub... lub-dub... lub...dub.* Her chest now had a rattle, becoming louder with every breath. She was too weak to struggle anymore. Syn's mother was dying.

Syn laid with his mother, hugging her tightly. He closed his eyes more tightly, his head moving with the steady heave of her chest. The young boy shivered.

Syn must have dozed off when a loud gurgling jolted him awake. He sat up, staring at his mom for the last time, holding her weak hand. He whispered, '*I love you, mother,*' before he turned around and ran off for good, not back.

Syn's mother's last breath was taken alone in a makeshift shack, on a riverbed, on a cold Russian night. She tried to cry out several times, each call getting weaker. Hoping her son would come back and hold her just once more. But, he never returned.

Syn again was on the run. This time he was all by himself.

****

Syn always traveled the backwoods to Charleston. He would memorize and map out all the routes he may need to take someday. As he passed a driveway he had many times before, he noticed a large gray van parked along the road with a sale sign in the window. It was in excellent condition for the price. Syn slowed to a stop and got out, looking over his new find with excitement.

This is it! He smiled with excitement. *This van would be perfect! Some rust, a flat tire, all fixable!* Syn hopped back into his car. Maple trees and white fencing lined the driveway that eventually opened up to a large yard. A beautiful white farmhouse with a full front porch sat along the edge of a field. There were several kids, a dog, and various other small animals running about the yard. A middle-aged man covered in blood walked out of a massive red barn towards Syn's car. Syn froze in fear.

'Remember what I taught you,' Syn could hear his mother's words echo in his head. An intelligent man, one with little human contact. Syn needed to be on his A-game.

The farmer motioned for the kids to get on the porch as he wiped his bloodied hands off on an old towel. Slowly he began to approach the car. Syn kept his sunglasses on to keep his eyes covered.

"Hello. Are you lost, boy?" The farmer asked, now looking into the car window.

Syn took a deep breath, still nervous about rolling the window down.

"I-I was just l-looking a-at the v-van out by the road." Syn, a little nervous, replied through the now opened window. He glanced over the bloodied man's shoulder, seeing a large cow hanging by its back feet off the front end of a loader bucket just inside the barn. Half skinned. This man was butchering a cow. He took a deep breath, opened up the car door, and stepped out.

"Is this your van? The gray one by the road. Is this for sale? Some friends sent me here to take a look. We are interested and have enough in cash." Syn reached into his suit pocket and pulled out an envelope full of money.

"I am going to the local University, and we could use it for our fraternity. We have been looking for a big van like this for a long time." He smiled. "How does it run?"

The farmer looked at the man's hand filled with hundred-dollar bills.

He smiled. *A taker!*

"I forgot that I had put the van out there. She runs pretty well, and I just put a new brake job on her. She leaks a little oil, not enough to worry about, though. The tire has a slow leak. If you want to take her for a ride, I will air it up. I wanted five thousand for her. But, if yer paying with cash, I'll drop the price to forty-five hundred." He turned towards the children sitting on the covered porch.

"Go get yer ma and tell her to bring out the paperwork fer the van."

One of the older girls jumped up the stairs and quickly ran into the old farmhouse, yelling for her mother. The girl was tall and thin; a long skirt covered her legs. She had long blonde hair rolled up into a bun on her head, her eyes a soft blue. Her younger siblings stayed back, sitting on the steps, watching Syn with curious eyes. All of them looked somewhat alike.

Syn counted out the money and handed over the cash in turn for the paperwork and keys to the van.

"I will be back as soon as I can. I am not sure if it will be today. Is that going to be an issue?" Syn's deep voice almost sounded local. He was proud, as he had been practicing. "I have to get one of my fraternity brothers to drive it back to the city."

"Not at all. Take yer time," The farmer said. "That'll give me time to air up that tire again for ya." The man turned and walked back to the barn.

Relieved that the interaction was over, Syn quickly jumped into his car. Two boys playing frisbee darted behind him, chasing a large yellow dog.

Man, Syn thought. *There are a lot of kids around here.* Noticing another group of kids hanging from the apple trees, he drove out of the driveway. *These people have way too many kids. I wonder if they would notice if one of them went missing? They could easily part with just one.* He chuckled as he pulled out of the driveway.

The next day, Syn picked up the van from the end of the farmer's driveway. He didn't bother going up and letting him know. He didn't want any more interaction with the man than he already had. Less was good. He scanned around for the pretty young girl with the long wavy dress.

On the way back to the house, Syn drove slowly by a playground, where several children lined up to go down the long, silver slide.

Syn's memories went back to the first city he stopped at after his mother had died. There was an aluminum slide similar to this one. It was his favorite thing on the playground. Syn loved to climb to the top. There he had a complete 360-degree view of the world! It's where Syn found some peace.

****

Alone and on the run was how Syn spent most of his teenage years. One particular night, he had decided to go back to an abandoned playground. He was very familiar with the area. He had been going there every night for a few weeks straight. It had been the longest time he had ever spent in one place. He loved the view at the top of the slide! Syn wanted to stay here for as long as he could. He didn't think anyone had noticed him hanging around there at night, so he decided to stay here a little longer. Besides, he loved the weather, the pickings were plenty, and he was getting tired of constantly moving around.

The choice proved to be a huge mistake. One night, as Syn settled on the top of the slide, he glanced around to admire the nightlife around him. That's when he noticed three dark figures approaching the playground. He froze in fear, hoping they would not see him.

A moment later, they stopped and pointed directly at Syn.

"There he is! I told you I wasn't making this shit up!" Crackled the voice of one of the boys. To this day, thinking of that voice still made the hair on Syn's neck stand on end.

There were three of them, carrying clubs, chains, and knives. They started to run after Syn. Little did they know, he was fast. He had to be; that was how he survived. He ran. Syn ran faster than he had ever run before. His advantage was that he planned his escape route every time he entered the playground. Before the boys got to the slide, Syn disappeared into the shadows, running as fast as he could, not looking back.

That was too close now you need to move! Idiot! His mother's voice echoed in his head.

Syn immediately packed up his things and left before daybreak. Angry at himself for almost getting caught. Syn learned that he could never frequent any one place twice. So, he was back to dodging through the Russian peninsula, occasionally crossing into China, as his mother had taught him. Syn learned to speak the two languages fluently. He blended in, disappearing from the people around him.

Very few people knew or cared about Syn's existence. He preferred it that way, though. Sometimes he would go weeks without any human interaction. Syn was alone in a crowded world. He would stop and listen to people talking and interacting with one another. Syn was brilliant and self-taught by just observation. He still lived by his mother's rules every day, by trusting no one and always watching his back. It was only him and her in his short life. Since she died, it had been only him.

By fifteen, Syn's income mainly came from running drugs. He vowed he would never use. Remembering what drugs did to his mother every day and seeing the dark path she went down. How men she was with would beat rape and torture her and Syn.

One night in particular. His mom and her client had been together, high all day. They had just finished having sex when the man began gasping for air. Foam poured out of his mouth, he reached out for Syn. Tears were coming from his bloodshot eyes. He was slowly dying while Syn watched, silent in the corner. Feeling relieved inside, knowing this man would never hurt him or his mom again.

For many years following, Syn would wake up in a cold sweat.

At seventeen, Syn had enough money saved to move into the bigger city. His first stop was Beijing, China. Far away from everything familiar to him. Syn believed this would be a great fresh start.

It was in Beijing where Syn first learned about human trafficking. It brought in more money and danger. So the first year, Syn only observed, studying how things ran. The drugs and sex were always around him, and everyone from children to adults had used. Everyone, except Syn., that's what gave him the advantage. He stayed sober. He liked working with a clear head.

WhenSyn took his first victim; he realized it was easier than he ever imagined. He made triple of the amount he would have made that entire month! It didn't take long before Syn became hooked. He thirsted for more.

For years, Syn collected young girls (and sometimes boys)selling them on the black market. He eventually compiled a list of wealthy clients who would pay good money for young escorts. Syn always had girls available to those people. No questions asked.

Eventually, it became too dangerous. Syn decided to leave Beijing and never return.

****

Syn had done his usual slow drive around the street before he pulled the van into the garage. Once the garage door was down, he started to transform the van. He worked hastily on it for most of the night. It turned out perfect. A darker shade of gray and even darker windows. He had even fixed all the rust spots. Happy with how it turned out, Syn retired to the house for something to eat.

The online groups that Syn created were his source of girls. If someone asked to join, he would research them thoroughly before accepting their request. He was very good at researching. He memorized each profile on all the popular social media platforms. Keeping everything straight would be difficult for an average person, but Syn had the gift of excellent photographic memory. He kept in contact with girls from all over the United States. Before he reached out to any of them, he would research them thoroughly. Finally, sending a friend request, exchanging numbers, then texts. He learned, he studied, and he planned. All the girls had one thing in common. They were desperate for someone to listen, so Syn taught himself to be a good listener. He became the best.

Then there was this one girl. Carmen Potter. She had sent a request to join one of his groups. How fortunate for him. After careful research, Syn could see that she was friends with the girl he met on the plane many years ago.

He accepted her request.

2

James Cavalier

At 35 years old, James Cavalier thought he had his life all figured out. He was born and raised in the small town of Sandpoint, Idaho. After high school, Jim went on to study forensic science in Seattle.

After graduating from college, Jim moved back to Sandpoint and married his high school sweetheart, Kristy. They planned on settling down and starting a family. Following in his father's footsteps, Jim became a detective at the local police department. Kristy got a job teaching history at the local high school. Everyone who knew them liked them. The couple did a lot of volunteering for local events and helping out at their local church events. Their life was simple and perfect.

It changed when Jim and his partner Tom received a call about a missing girl from the Coeur d'Alene.

When it was slow at the Bonner County Station, Jim and his partner Tom would help out at the department in Coeur d'Alene. Coeur d'Alene was a bigger city fifty miles or so south of Sandpoint. Sometimes they would have a crime surge or an investigation that

THE LOST SOULS - 13

would need some extra help. Jim had proven perfect for those jobs. He was an intuitive thinker and could point out the smallest of details that others often overlooked. Those qualities made him valuable to the Sandpoint *and* Coeur d'Alene departments. It also made Jim's dad incredibly proud.

Jim had the missing girl's file spread out on his desk. He had gone through every detail so far. It seemed this case had grown cold before he even had a chance to investigate it.

He did this kind of shit all the time. Jim thought.

He decided to put a call out to his buddy Rob in Chicago. Rob would know what to do.

As Jim was flipping through the paperwork on his desk, he knocked a picture off his desk. It was a picture of him, his dad, and his best friend, Rob. The boys were about nine years old at the time. Jim was standing with his father in front of his squad cars, holding up a shiny badge. Rob was sitting cross-legged on the hood with a kitten on his lap. Jim's dad was in uniform, standing proudly, hands on his hips.

Jim remembered that day like it was yesterday. They were the most fantastic kids in town that summer! The station had even got the boys their very own junior badges!

****

At an early age, Jim showed interest in detective work. Each visit to the station with his dad was a different adventure. He knew from the beginning that he wanted to become the next great detective, like his dad.

All the officers had come to know Jim and his friend Rob quite well. The men loved entertaining the two boys. The officers would let the boys take turns calling out on the CB radio, checking in with each squad car out on patrol.

While Jim was at the station, they got a call about a kitten someone had seen stuck up in a tree over by the local church.

"Wanna go out on a call, boys?" Jim's father looked over at the two boys, who were jumping up and down with excitement!

This call was their first real one. The boys could hardly contain themselves. Jim's dad pulled up to the fire truck. Its lights were flashing, with the ladder had been extended up into the tree. One of the men was on his way down with a tiny kitten tucked safely inside his jacket. He handed the scared little kitten to Jim. She was so small and so frightened, she wouldn't stop meowing. Jim and Rob calmly took turns holding and talking to the tiny kitten all the way back to the station. No one ever called to claim her, so at the end of the day, Jim's dad let him take her home. He called her Siren, and he shared her with Rob.

✳✳✳✳✳✳✳✳✳✳✳✳✳✳✳✳✳✳✳✳✳✳✳✳✳✳✳✳✳✳

Jim placed the photograph back in its spot and leaned back in his chair. He refocused back to the case he had been working on for the past week. He had no genuine leads. It seemed that the girl just vanished into thin air.

Last week, the young teenage girl disappeared while out walking her grandma's dog. About an hour later, the dog came home alone with no collar, no leash, and no sign of the young girl.

Jim and his partner were assigned to investigate the area. The only witness they had at that time was grandma's standard poodle.

Where could she be? Jim thought. *Who would have taken her? It had to be someone who the girl knew. But who? Did she have a secret boyfriend? Was she a runaway? If only the damn dog could talk!*

"Dammit, Rob!" Jim impatiently muttered out loud. "Call me!"

Jim's phone finally rang. It was Rob.

"It's about damn time!" Jim picked up the phone.

"You okay, Buddy?" Rob's voice came over the line.

"I'm sorry I haven't gotten back to you until now, but I've been busy trying to wrap up a homicide here before I head out." Jim was on speaker in Rob's car. Jim could always tell when Rob called from his car. The whooshing of the engine made it difficult to hear Rob.

"That's okay, buddy. I know you're busy." Jim let out a sigh.

"I've been working on this dead-end case of a thirteen-year-old girl who vanished without a trace south of here. I'm at a loss with it, and I need to bounce some ideas off of you. I have nothing to tell the family."

"She's a runaway." Rob's voice shot back.

Being in Chicago, Rob worked on a lot of runaway cases.

"I'm not sure you are right this time. This girl is a straight-A student, she belongs to all the academic clubs at her school, and she loves staying with her grandparents." Jim shot back. There was a long pause on the other end of the line.

"If she planned on running away, why would she be taking grandma's poodle for a walk?" Jim asks, his voice cutting in and out.

Rob took Jim off of the car's speaker and put the cell to his ear.

"So, she was walking a dog and came back with no collar or leash?" Rob inquired.

"That's right. No collar, no leash, no girl." Jim replied.

"Well, Jim. You need to go back to the crime scene and look harder. Find that collar. It's gotta be there somewhere. If the dog slipped it, it should show up. Besides, all teenagers nowadays have cell phones. Look for that. It has to be somewhere. Ask the local phone carrier for her last cell ping." Rob pulled up to a drive-through and ordered his dinner. He continued to talk to Jim as he drove across town toward his apartment.

"You need to find out where that dog was. Go back and walk

around the area where the girl was last supposed to be. Take the metal detector. It might help you find that collar.

"I've already reached out to the cell phone company," Jim answered. "I'm waiting for their info to come back. In the meantime, I'll go back and take another look around."

"You'll probably get most of your answers once those cell-phone records come back." Rob implied.

"Don't forget the metal detector. They sometimes find some weird shit. Remember, the smallest details can be the key to solving any crime. Walk the sides of the highway with that thing and see what you can find. You never know. If this girl were out walking the dog, maybe the clues would be on the side of the road. It could be right in front of you, man." Rob hung up.

Jim sat his phone down and ran his hands through his thick, dark hair. He remembered that he was overdue for a haircut. *I better make an appointment for the barber sometime before we go on his trip.* He thought.

Kristy loved his curls; she hated every time he came home from the barbershop.

"*Just let it grow, honey.*" She would demand. "*I would love to run my hands through your locks.*" Jim smiled. His heart skipped a beat, thinking of her. He loved Kristy from the beginning.

****

Kristy was just as much in love with Jim. It was the typical high school sweetheart romance. She was the cheerleader, and he was the ballplayer.In the last semester of her freshman year, Kristy had moved to the area after Rob moved to Chicago. But, it was her Sophomore year when she had joined the pep club and became a cheerleader. That's when she got to know Jim. He was the captain of the football team. Kristy had fallen head over heels in love.

Jim and Kristy started dating seriously just after homecoming that year. Jim was voted in as king, and Kristy, the queen. From that point on, the two of them did everything together. After graduation, they both went off to grad school in Washington.

****

Jim reached into the drawer to grab the keys to his cruiser and headed over to his partner's desk.

"Let's go out to the scene once more, Tom," He noticed that Tom was on the phone.

That man was always on the phone. Jim sighed and motioned to Tom that he would be outside.

Tom gave Jim a nod. *If Tom didn't hurry his ass up, they would never be back before the end of the shift.* Jim headed to the cruiser.

"Ok." Tom's deep voice rang out as he headed towards Jim. "Time to go, Pard?" He put on his sunglasses and smiled at Jim.

"Yeah, I would like to get one more look in the area with a metal detector before I call it a day." Jim opened the car door and slid into the driver's side.

"I called my buddy Rob in Chicago, and he said to go check the ditches and roadsides better with a metal detector."

"I don't know what the big hurry is," Tom muttered. "It's not like the shit is going to disappear overnight."

"Don't you wonder where this girl is, Tom.? Or who took her? Or do you think she just ran off with her boyfriend? Then again, maybe she is dead in a ditch somewhere. Maybe she was hit by a car. A drunk driver, maybe." Jim sounded a little frustrated.

"I would like to get to the bottom of this case already. You do remember that I'm leaving in a couple of weeks to go on that vacation with Rob, right? I just need to see if maybe I am missing something out there. I hate to leave you hanging with nothing to go on."

"Shit, that's right!" Tom exclaimed, throwing his head back into the seat. "I forgot all about the mighty moose hunt," He motioned his hands over his ears to represent moose antlers.

"I can't believe you forgot about it! I've been counting the days out to you for a month! You know how much I love hunting! Especially since the reconnection with Rob every year is another adventure!" Jim paused.

"Stupid me. I forgot. Ya know, you're damn lucky I am willing to cover for you, partner."

They both chuckled as they headed towards Coeur d'Alene.

Twenty minutes later, they were driving past the grandparent's driveway. The grandma's poodle barked in the yard as they drove slowly past the house. Jim continued cautiously down the shoulder of the road. All that he heard was the crackling of the gravel as they pulled into an abandoned roadside park.

How did they miss this little parking lot? Jim wondered.

Tom gave Jim a strange glance.

"How in the hell did we-----" Tom stopped mid-sentence.

"Cause no one looked in this direction," Jim interrupted, pulling in to park the car.

"No wonder she disappeared unnoticed. You can't see the road from this parking lot." Tom remarked as Jim stopped the cruiser in front of a trash can overgrown with weeds. The parking lot was small and grown in as well. Some weeds were bent over, showing evidence of a recent disturbance.

"I just want to walk this road from here to her grandparents' house one last time. I'll go as far as I can tonight, then come back tomorrow if I have to." Jim said as he got out of the car and walked towards the trunk. He reached inside and pulled out a metal detector.

"I would love to find something."

Tom followed Jim down the side of the road

"Maybe......"

Jim put his hand in the air, interrupting Tom. All his attention was still on the ground. He swayed the sensor over the area several times until he could zero in on the item. He reached into the weeds and pulled out a round piece of metal.

"Just a rusty washer." He said, disappointed as he flicked the piece further off the road.

Within the next fifteen minutes, the detector went off a half-dozen more times. Finding an array of lost items, including an old set of keys, a gun shell, and some bottle tops.

Then, the detector went off with a different sound. Jim looked at Tom, puzzled. He reached under the beeping disk to find his prize. Not exactly what they were looking for, but it got Jim's attention.

Jim proudly held up a dime. "Do you know what finding a dime on your travels means?" He looked over at Tom, who was looking confused.

"Well, it means that someone in Heaven is thinking of us." He smiled, holding the tarnished dime up into the sunlight like it was a holy symbol. For Jim, it was sacred. His grandpa would have agreed.

****

The first time Jim had heard about the dime thing, he was helping out his grandpa in the garden. They were getting ready to plant a row of peas. Jim's grandpa had tilled up and fertilized the day before. Jim pushed the seeder while his grandpa walked behind him, covering the seeds with the rich, dark soil.

Jim was looking at the ground, making sure that he planted the seeds in a straight line. He noticed something sticking halfway out of the soft dirt. Jim came to a sudden stop bending over to pick up his treasure. His grandpa bumped into him just as he grabbed the dime, toppling Jim over. Sitting in the dirt, wide-eyed, he held up his find.

"Well, I'll be!" Jim's grandpa shouted out. "Ya found yer first dime! Today, someone in Heaven is thinking of *you*. It's *your* special day!"

That same dime still sat on top of a special box on the mantle in his house. Inside the box were many more Jim had found throughout the years.

Jim had always believed in the supernatural. When he was a young boy, he could see and hear things that he could never explain, nor even begin to understand himself. He was extremely close to his grandpa Cavalier, who lived with them.

Jim's grandpa loved to take him out for car rides. He would drive around town and talk to Jim about the afterlife and his experiences with the supernatural. Jim would sit for hours listening to his grandpa telling stories. He would memorize every detail of those stories, pretending he could talk with those same spirits. Jim had an array of imaginary friends that his parents dismissed. In his teen years, Jim would experience unexplainable encounters with the afterlife. Then, as he became an adult, he brushed them off as coincidence, afraid he would get laughed at or committed to some psych ward for being crazy.

But the dime-thing. That story was exceptional. Jim's grandpa had told him about coming across dimes, and he would never have lied to him. Besides, Jim had found some of his dimes in the most unusual places. Every one of them, he kept. When his grandpa found out about Jim's collection, he helped Jim build a wooden box for them.

As Jim's grandpa got older, he promised Jim that if he died before him, he would come back to visit him, to prove that there was an afterlife. Jim never saw his grandpa's ghost, but every once in a while, he would come across a dime. Invariably, when he wasn't looking or paying attention. Every time they made him smile.

'If you find a dime in your path, a loved one from Heaven is thinking of you.' His grandpa would say. 'You cannot just look for a dime. It'll find you when you least expect it.'

* *

"Haven't you heard that saying?" Jim asked as he put the prize in his left chest pocket, close to his heart.

"No, I can't say I have." Tom furrowed his brow.

Tom's wife, Jenni, was the daughter of a Nez Perce medicine man. She was always calling to the spirits. They would guide her on her journey. But Tom never heard about the dime-thing. He shrugged his broad shoulders as they continued their walk towards the grandma's house. Jim waved the detector back and forth across the ground in front of them.

After walking silently for quite some time, Tom started to get impatient.

"I hate to say this, Jim, but I think this is a waste of time. All we found so far was a dime and some junk." He grumbled, kicking at the dirt.

Ignoring Tom, Jim stayed focused and kept walking, slowly waving the detector back and forth across the weedy ground in front of them. They were in sight of Grandma's house when the sensor started beeping a series of strange beeps. Excited, Jim handed the detector to Tom and quickly parted the dried-up matted weeds. A plastic floral case laid shattered on the ground, and next to it was a faint shine of dirty shattered glass. As Jim parted more weeds, he found a tiny circuit board, some more pieced of glass, and a flat piece of metal. It was the remnants of a cell phone! Tom reached into his front pocket and grabbed his camera to take some pictures.

Jim reached down and slowly plucked each piece out of the weeds and laid them on a white cloth.

"I can't believe what we just found!" Tom continued to take pictures as Jim approximated the pieces. As they both looked up, they realized how close to the grandmother's house they were, giving Tom goosebumps.

"What balls! This guy drove right by the grandma's house!" Tom uttered.

"We don't even know if this is a phone, let alone if it belongs to our girl," Jim said in an oddly calm voice. "If the cell does belong to her, how in the hell did she disappear this close to the house, unnoticed?"

They both gathered as many of the pieces as they could, took a few more pictures, and headed back to the station. They needed to call the forensics team to examine the parts and confirm where they had come from. Maybe even brush them for fingerprints.

Jim and Tom brought the pictures to the family, who positively identified the pieces to be the girl's cell phone. It was determined when they got her phone records back that she had contacted someone. They were supposed to meet at the nearby park. The same park that Jim and Tom had parked in the previous day.

Now, most importantly, they had a contact number! If they could pull some pictures off the circuit board, maybe they would have their person.

Over the next few days, information was unlocked from the girl's social media accounts and text messaging. The girl's parents had kept a close eye on her friends and often checked all her accounts. At least the ones that they found. The girl's mother was shocked and not easily convinced that her perfect little girl had more than one account for each social media platform. Those accounts ended up being the ones she had been using to talk to men. It was a high probability that this man knew where the missing girl was.

They needed to figure out who this man was.

"We need to get back to the playground and look for more clues. Maybe there is something we missed when we went through earlier," Jim ordered as he headed out of the station with Tom in tow. It was almost like Jim had a sixth sense about him. Noone questioned his intuition now.

It was mid-morning when they arrived at the park for the second time that week. Just like the last time, the park was empty. It almost seemed like it belonged in a ghost town. There was no sign of activity at the playground since Tom and Jim had been there.

Jim followed his old tracks in and parked next to the trash can to park the cruiser.

Jim jumped out as soon as he put the car in park. He hurried over to the swing set and looked around. Noticing some scuffled tracks in the sand, but the weather had pretty much made them undetectable. He turned and slowly started to comb over the grounds back to the squad car. He grabbed the metal detector from the trunk.

Tom walked over to the trash can and peeked inside. It had some fast food bags and soda containers. The flies and stench came billowing out at Tom, making him gag. He slammed the cover and walked over to sit on the top of the picnic table. He ran his fingers over the carved letters on the sun-bleached wood. It was nastily overgrown with weeds and cobwebs. He waited patiently to see if Jim's intuition was correct.

"Nuttin' Hunny?" Tom mocked Jim.

Jim stopped and looked over at Tom, who was still sitting on top of the picnic table. Ignoring Tom, Jim slowly walked towards the slide, sweeping the detector back and forth, listening for the slightest clue. His focus was intense. That was what made Jim so good at his job—ignoring what was around him and focusing on the little things hidden in plain sight.

"Why don't you get off your lazy ass and help your partner out?"

Jim said sarcastically back, brushing the sweat off his head with one arm and holding the heavy detector in the other.

Tom chuckled and jumped to his feet. He started to walk towards Jim when something caught his shoe, causing him to fall flat on his face into the overgrowth.

Startled, Jim quickly spun around, seeing his partner, face first in the weeds. Jim laughed out loud.

"You don't need to put your face that close. That's what this detector is for, buddy!"

Tom looked up from the ground, spitting out some sand and dried grass. He was not impressed with Jim's joke.

As Tom tried to pull himself to his knees, something was holding his right leg back.

"What the...." Tom grumbled out loud as he turned to see what it was that made him fall. "God-damned weeds are..." He stopped, freezing in his place. He slowly reached for the toe of his shoe and slid a dog collar off of his foot.

He was holding the collar in his hand. Tom looked over at Jim, who was already standing next to him.

"I see it," Jim calmly said as he watched his partner pick up a camouflage dog collar and leash still tied to the picnic table. Tom held the name tags closer to his eyes so he could get a better look. They belong to grandma's poodle.

"The girl was here!" Jim excitedly grabbed the collar. "She must have tied the dog to the picnic table at some point!"

"Holy shit, Jim," Tom exclaimed. "Another lead!" They untied the leash from the picnic table and headed back to the police station.

Over the next few days, Jim talked with the girl's parents, holding a vigil at the grandparent's house. They were in denial as they heard what Jim had to say. There was no way their daughter would have hooked up with any stranger. They continuously checked her accounts, making sure they knew what friends she was in touch with and who she was texting. They lectured her all the time not to talk or give strangers information. But this time, they were wrong, very wrong. Their daughter had befriended someone and met them at the playground next to her grandparents' house. She had told no one about him. Now, she has disappeared without a trace. The only lead was an old Tracfone number and an abandoned social media account.

According to the girl's cell records, the man had contacted the girl on the internet. He then gained her trust, eventually asking for her number. She willingly gave it to him. They had been texting each other almost constantly for about two weeks. In the texts, the girl gave him details about her parents leaving on a trip. She told him she would be staying with her grandparents on the outskirts of Coeur d'Alene. She even gave him their address. This person said that he didn't live too far from there and would like to meet her. According to the texts, she agreed to meet up. No one has seen or been in contact with her since.

3

<svg>flourish</svg>

Detective Robert Jackson, Chicago

Robert Jackson was at the top of his game. Now newly divorced, he could invest more time into the department. The amount of time he had spent at the station, had been the main topic of his marriage for years. But Rob loved his job, more than anything else in the world. He loved the crimes, bringing closure, and getting the bad guy. Rob had given his life to the department.

His now-second ex-wife would concur.

Rob left work and headed to his apartment just outside of downtown Chicago. On the way, he returned a phone call to his buddy Jim, who seemed to be struggling with a case he had been working on.

We better not be canceling this trip! Rob thought to himself. *These trips we take are what keep me sane!*

****

Growing up on the same street, Rob and Jim were childhood friends. Rob didn't talk much, and Jim didn't care. Without exchanging words, Jim knew what Rob was thinking. They seemed to have a bond no one understood.

The doctors told Rob's parents that he may have some form of autism. But no one had an exact diagnosis. Rob was extremely talented, he just could not communicate.

When it was slow on Sundays, Jim's dad would bring the two of them to the station with him. The boys helped with keeping the station clean and organized. They became glorified office boys, with candy and sodas for payment.

When Rob turned ten, everything changed. First, his dad had died of a stroke. Then, his mother got remarried. Jim comforted his friend the best way he knew how. He explained to Rob what happened to people when they died.

"Your dad's soul went to Heaven," Jim would repeatedly remind his friend. "Someday, you will see him again. He will be waiting for you. But for now, you have to stay here with your mother and watch over her and your sister."

Rob gravitated towards Jim listening to his reassurance. Trusting in his friend. The two became inseparable.

Rob's mother was struggling with the realization that she was now a single mom. She was doing her best to raise a special needs child in a cruel world that didn't understand him. So, it wasn't long after the death of her husband, she married Stan.

Stan was a lawyer. They had met in their grieving group. Stan's wife had committed suicide just about the same time Rob's dad died. They both were drawn towards each other.

Stan had no children, and it wasn't long into their marriage, Rob's mom realized how much he hated them.

Stan also was an alcoholic. When he was drinking, it became

more difficult for him to understand or communicate with Rob. That's when he took out his frustration with the poor boy. When Rob's mother was at work, Stan would call him terrible names and slap him around. It had become so bad that Rob was afraid to be alone with Stan. He would beg his mother to bring him to work with her, and when she turned him down, Rob called up Jim crying. The Cavaliers never said no to Rob coming over.

Once school began, Rob stayed at Jim's until a call would come in from his mom saying it was safe to go home. There were some nights that Rob's mom never called. It was then that Rob would spend the night at the Cavaliers. Rob never minded. It's where he felt the safest—often pretending that he and Jim were brothers, that this was his family.

There were some days that Stan would make Rob come home. As Rob feared, those days ended up bad. Stan would be drunk waiting for Rob to walk through the door. He would beat Rob and degrade him for hours until passing out on the couch.

Rob learned the hard way early on not to ask questions or to have Stan repeat himself. Anything to piss the man off meant a smack to the side of the head. Often, so hard that Rob's ear would ring for hours.

Rob's mom and sister would hide in their bedrooms when those conflicts happened with the television blaring. Too terrified themselves to help Rob.

Rob struggled to understand Stan and his abuse. He wondered why his mother stayed with this man. Rob missed the gentleness and kindness of his real dad.

Many nights the young boy would cry himself to sleep.

As Rob got older, he got braver. One day after school, he decided to walk past Jim's house, heading straight home instead. Rob came through the front door and caught Stan on top of his sister, holding her down half-naked. That landed Rob in jail and his stepfather in the ER.

Rob's mom denied everything Stan did to Rob's sister that day.

Stan turned the story around. Saying that he caught Rob with his sister, and Rob got violent. Since Rob was different, and his stepdad was a lawyer, most people believed Stan.

The fabrication made Rob even more distant.

In the last big fight, Stan accused Rob of taking money out of his wallet. Stan could not remember using it up on whiskey the night before. Rob's stepdad ended up pulling a gun on Rob, and both of them went to jail.

Rob finally convinced his mom to get the help she needed and divorce his stepdad. After the divorce, Rob's mom packed them up and moved to Chicago to be with her parents.

Rob took the move hard, not that he wanted his mom to stay with Stan. He just didn't do well with change. Rob was an outcast wherever he went. His only friend was Jim, and Jim was now over 1,700 miles away.

Attempting to keep a long-distance relationship hadn't been easy for the boys. They wrote and called each other when they could. Jim's family even flew him out for a visit. They vowed nothing would come between their friendship.

Then one day, the inevitable happened. The calls stopped, soon after the letters quit. Life had moved on, distancing the young men and their friendship.

The first couple of years in Chicago had been brutal for Rob. Once the calls stopped coming in from Jim, Rob focussed a new passion. Forensics.

Rob's fondest memories were of him playing with Jim at the station in Sandpoint. So, in the summer of his senior year, Rob enrolled in forensic science at the local university. His obsessive personality made him excel, and he graduated at the top of his class.

His proficiency made him the best forensic detective Chicago ever had.

****

Many years later, Rob received a call from Jim. He was getting married and wanted Rob to be his best man. Rob reluctantly accepted the offer, unsure if he wanted to return to his hometown and face the raw emotions from the years of abuse.

Rob decided to come home. He stayed at Jim and Kristy's house. The two of them reminisced every night about their childhood days at the station while Kristy listened. Their hunting stories were the best. It was like they had never been apart.

From that point on, Rob and Jim made a promise to set up an annual hunting trip. No phones, no family. Just Jim, Rob, and the woods.

It was that time of the year again, and this year's hunting trip was going to be unique.

4

Besties

Carmen Potter and Harper Bengston had been best friends since kindergarten. Harper was the daughter of Bradly Bengston, the CEO of two high-end banks in Myrtle Beach. Her mother was an accountant for the city. They lived in a beautiful home located in an upper-class neighborhood on the east side of town. Harper's mom had family in London, so they sent Harper there for her undergraduate studies.

The two girls were inseparable. Harper loved Carmen, and Carmen loved Harper. They got each other. Carmen, on the other hand, did not come from money. Her mom was single, working two jobs just to make ends meet. As the girls started their teenage years, Carmen's ambitions changed. Her interest became different from Harper's. Carmen was drawn towards the older boys while Harper was busy with her studies.

Harper's flaw was her loyalty to Carmen.

Harper didn't understand Carmen's infatuation with men. She would notice Carmen always reaching out to strangers on the internet, making "friends" with men she didn't even know. Harper tried to discourage this, but it fell on deaf ears. To the point, the two started to drift apart. Now that Harper wasn't around as much, Carmen withdrew more into her social media status and finding male friends online. She was slowly traveling down a dark path.

A dark path that led to him.

****

There was this one guy that Carmen could not get out of her mind. She met him on one of her social media platforms, under her secret spam account. Soon after, she gave him her number, and they began to talk.

Before any personal contact with this guy, Carmen crept on his page. It seemed like he was an ordinary guy doing usual guy stuff. The pictures of him were cute. He attended college and had a car. He told Carmen that he was having some problems with his father. Their conversations went on nightly for weeks, both complaining about their lives in general. It started as just innocent chatting. He was such a good listener. Carmen felt she could tell him anything. Her deepest secrets were safe with this guy, and he always knew all the right words to say. His advice was comforting, and best of all, he talked sweetly to Carmen. No one ever spoke to her as this guy had.

The man started calling Carmen his beautiful Podruga; it was the Russian word for friend. She adored the name. It made her feel special, and it was working. Carmen was falling for this boy.

Falling deep.

Carmen had no one that she could share her feelings. She wanted to tell her best friend Harper all about him, but he wouldn't allow it.

"Not just yet," he told her one day on the phone. "Let's keep us a secret for now. Let's get to know each other a little more, first.

Then, you can tell your friend. Someday, I would love to meet her. She sounds amazing!"

"Besides, people with money and parents who are not divorced wouldn't understand us."

He was right, Carmen thought. *Harper was leaving in the fall, and she already had no time for me lately.*

"Isn't that how we got together?" The guy questioned Carmen. "Didn't you need someone to listen to you? That you and your best-and-only-friend were drifting apart? Why tell her now?"

Carmen began to think that this guy was right. This fall was the beginning of Harper's College prep years. Soon she would be leaving. In the meantime, she would have her nose stuck in a book, studying. She had no time for Carmen. Harper was leaving for London, and Carmen was staying as a sophomore at Myrtle Beach High.

The man was getting Carmen to think. He was making her feel alone and that he was the only person who cared.

The man also made Carmen promise to keep their relationship a secret from her mother for now. He told Carmen that he was afraid her mother would not understand nor approve because he was not a US citizen. He said to her that for now, he wanted to get to know everything about her. Carmen reluctantly agreed. She didn't want their relationship to end. She finally felt like someone loved her for who she was.

It was just a little secret. Carmen thought. *Besides, she never met up with him in person.*

Not yet.

After a couple of months, Carmen got the much-anticipated text that she had wanted! Her guy had finally decided that he would like to meet Harper. Maybe go on a double-blind date.

He told Carmen that he had a single friend and was interested in going out as well. He made Carmen promise to keep it a surprise until he came up with a plan. Impressed that he wanted to make plans, she never questioned him. All she wanted was to meet this guy.

What a sweetheart. Carmen thought. *A little surprise for me as well!*

Carmen knew that Harper loved surprises just as much as her.

This weekend was going to be one of the hottest fall days on record and one of the last few days the girls would be able to hang together before Harper headed to London. So, Carmen thought, what a perfect way to spend time with her best friend, *and* meet her guy! Carmen was sure this was going to be the best double-blind date on record!

The man asked Carmen if she would like to meet in a public area like the beach. Someplace safe. The beach was going to be packed with vacationers and locals soaking up the last of the fall sunshine. She immediately agreed and was excited to share with Harper part of her plans. She left out the role of meeting some men there. Carmen and Harper texted each other about going to the beach all morning long.

HURRY UP!!! Came to a text from Carmen

ALL THE BEST SPOTS WILL BE TAKEN!

I WILL BE THERE IN A FEW, JUST GRABBING SOME THINGS BEFORE I LEAVE! Harper replied.

"Geeze," Harper grumbled, tossing her cell phone in her backpack. Thinking it was unusual that Carmen was so antsy to get to the beach. She blew it off to it being the last weekend they would be spending together for a long time.

Harper finished packing her things and quickly headed out on her bike to the little store on the corner where she was meeting Carmen.

Carmen, bursting with excitement, was standing on the sidewalk outside. Her long wavy dark brown hair fell past her waist. She pointed to her imaginary watch and waved her arms in the air when she saw Harper pulling up.

"I've aged while waiting for Your Highness to arrive!" Carmen yelled out loudly.

"Well, I'm here now, aren't I?" Harper winked and smiled back at Carmen as she parked her bike and proceeded into the store.

"Let's go inside and get something to drink and snack on. I plan on making a whole afternoon out of this!" Harper pulled a wad of money out of her pocket and waved it in front of Carmen's face.

"Let our destination bring us to a lot of hot, sun-tanned bodies to chose from!" Carmen stated enthusiastically.

"You're a maniac!" Harper shook her head as they walked into the store, straight to the chip aisle.

When the girls arrived at the beach, Carmen's eyes scanned the area. They parked their bikes, and Harper began looking for a spot close to the water. Carmen, with her mind on other things, looked anxiously for any familiar men.

As they approached an open area, a little boy was crying, as two others were walking up from the ocean with buckets full of water spilling everywhere. They stumbled through the soft sand, spilling it right where the girls planned on setting up their towels.

"No freakin' way that I am setting up down here, Harper," Carmen growled. "Number one, we will be covered in mud, number two, I hate kids, and three: THERE ARE NO AVAILABLE GUYS IN THE FAMILY AREA!"

She turned and stomped up the beach with her nose in the air, passing two young men setting up their towels. They smiled, staring at the girls as they passed by. Carmen paused, not looking back.

Her heart did a flip. *It was the guy she had been chatting to on social media! The one she was supposed to meet up with today!*

She turned her head, smiled, and gave a little wave as she led Harper to an open piece of beach just far enough away that she would not get suspicious too soon.

"Here we go. Perfect!" Harper stared at Carmen as she began to pull off her shorts and top. She smoothed out the sand with her foot and placed her bag gently on the towel so as not to get sand inside of it.

"What?"

"This close to those creepy guys?" Harper looked over at the two men sitting on their towels, staring at the girls.

"Why not?" Carmen looked over at the men and smiled. "They are hot, and they seem interested."

"They are *not* creepy." She put on her sunglasses. "You are just weird, Harper. Get over it." Carmen sat carefully on her towel and started to put sunscreen on.

Harper rolled her eyes and plopped on her towel next to Carmen. It was hot, the beach was packed, and she wasn't going to argue with Carmen today. It was their last long weekend together, and Harper was going to make the best of it. Besides, this day was just too beautiful to spoil with a stupid argument over some harmless guys on a packed beach.

The two girls eventually made their way to the ocean's edge to cool off and play in the waves. The guys watched the girls for a while from a distance. Carmen flaunted herself and occasionally smiled towards them. The guys kept their distance for quite some time that Harper thought they were gay or taken. In the back of her mind, she was hoping for either one of those. There was just something about them that seemed to make her uneasy.

After quite some time in the ocean, the girls made their way back to their towels.

One of the men could not keep his eyes off Carmen. She, too, would look towards them every so often. She was hoping that he liked what he saw.

"I have to use the bathroom," Harper stood up, wrapping a towel around her waist.

"Wanna come?" She looked at Carmen.

"Nah, I'm fine for now. I'll watch our stuff. You never know on a day like today if someone might take off with something."

Harper sighed. She never liked to use the public restrooms alone.

"Come look for me if I don't come back in a few minutes, then." She walked away, passing by the two men, relieved as they pretended not to notice her. Somehow, they seemed to be more interested in Carmen, and that was fine with her.

As Harper left the restroom, she could see that Carmen had gravitated over to the men. Carmen saw her approaching and grabbed her by the arm.

"Let's go swimming!"

Moments later, the young men joined the girls in the waves. The four of them splashed, body surfed and laughed together. Harper started to feel bad that she did not trust them earlier. She, too, began to think that the guys were kind of cool and it would be fun to hang out.

As the men walked back to their towels, Carmen questioned Harper about them again.

"They seem decent, I guess," Harper told her as she floated around on her back.

"They are so sweet!" Carmen reassured her friend. "They want to go out on a double date to the movies tonight!"

Harper sighed and rolled her eyes.

"C'mon! Harper. It's the final fun thing to do before the end of summer! You'll be leaving for London, and we need to make some memories!" Carmen straightened out her swimsuit.

"Besides, I gave them our numbers!"

Harper's heart sank.

"You did WHAT?" Harper's voice was shaking.

"We exchanged numbers," Carmen repeated in a slower tone. "What's so wrong with that?"

"WHY?" Harper stood up in the water. "Why MINE?"

Carmen shook her head and rolled her eyes.

"You need to chill and enjoy life before daddy sends you away." She started walking back toward the shore.

"It's only a phone number Harper, and I'm going with or without you!" She shouted back over her shoulder. She made one final bikini adjustment before laying down on her towel.

Harper thought, standing alone in the water, thinking about what Carmen had just said. She was right. She did need to get out more and enjoy her youth before she was off in another country where she would know no one.

Besides, it was only one night. Harper walked back, laid on her stomach next to her best friend, and started to draw in the sand with her finger.

"Alright. One last hoorah." Harper breathed out a deep sigh. She was looking over at the guys. They both smiled. She half-smiled back. "They don't look so scary; besides, they are kinda cute, and it is only the movies. What could go wrong?" She looked over at Carmen and smiled. Carmen put both her hands in the air with a big thumbs up.

Harper was running her fingers in the sand when she felt something. It felt like a small seashell. She dug in with her finger and pulled it to the surface.

It was a dime.

She plucked it out of the sand and tossed it into her beach bag.

Lucky find, she thought.

The midday sun was beating down on Myrtle Beach, and the sand was almost too hot to walk on. The sun started to take effect on them.

"Let's go home and get out of this sun before we burn." Harper stood up and started to put her things away.

"Besides, we need to come up with a plan for tonight." Harper stood up and started to put her things away. She looked over towards where the two men were. They had left.

"You are right!" Carmen began to pack up her things. "I can't believe we are going to do this! We are going to have so much fun! Eeek!"

Giggling, they both walk back to their bikes, coming up with a plan so Harper's parents would let her go. Usually, when Carmen's mother was working, the rule was Carmen had to come to Harper's house.

Harper's phone vibrated with an incoming text. She stopped to look. It is from an unknown number. It was one of the men:

I HAD A GREAT TIME TODAY! CAN'T WAIT TO SEE YOU TONITE!

Goosebumps traveled up her spine. Looking over at Carmen who was elated, it was something that Harper had seen in her in quite a while.

She began to type a response.

CAN'T WAIT ;) Harper sighed and hit send.

It's only one night. Harper kept telling herself. *She was leaving Next week for London. How bad could this be?*

Harper would be lying to her parents for the first time. To her, this was a big deal. Because once she left, there would be none of this. None of Carmen's antics. She decided she was going to live on the edge just this one time. Reassuring herself, it was only one night and that this was going to be fun.

So, what's the big deal? Harper thought. *What could go wrong on a simple double date with your best friend to the movies? It's not like someone was going to die.*

When they got to the little store, the girls parted ways back home. The plan was to tell Harper's parents that they were going to the movies, and then Harper was spending the night at Carmen's.

It was their last weekend together, and they wanted to make some memories. Harper's parents didn't even deny the girls their plan. Movies at 9, home by 11:30.

SEE YOU AT BAREFOOT LANDING AT 9 PM. Carmen's text went through to her guy. BOTH OF US WILL BE THERE! SO EXCITED!!

The girls' plan fell into place. Tonight was going to be perfect!

It surprised Harper that her parents didn't question the plan. They told her that they just wanted her to have fun and be safe about it. Harper's parents adored Carmen. They thought of her as the second daughter they never had. So, they wanted the girls to enjoy their last weekend together.

WELL, THE PLAN WAS GOING WELL! THEY SAID I COULD GO! :) :) :)

Harper took a quick shower and packed her clothes. She always packed an extra set for Carmen to wear.

AWESOME! I CAN'T WAIT! :) :) :) Replied Carmen.

Once she was all packed, Harper walked into the sitting room where her mom was reading.

"Are you all ready, Honey?" Her mom asked.

"Yes, mother." Harper trotted over and kissed her on the cheek. "Carmen and I are getting ready at her house!"

"Enjoy your night out! Don't forget to call when you get back from the movies, so I know you are safe."

"Of course, mother!" Harper smiled. "The movie starts at 9 and runs for about two hours. We should be home around 11:30. I will call you around then." She turned towards the door and paused.

"Love you, mom."

"Love you too, Sweetie," her mom called back over her shoulder.

ON MY WAY, FRIEND! Harper texted Carmen as she pulled her bike out of the garage.

Harper's phone buzzed almost immediately with a text. She looked to see who it was.

It was unavailable.

HOPE YOU ARE WEARING SOMETHING SEXY. The text read. Harper shivered a little.

Carmen said they were decent. Harper sighed. *It's just the movies.*

OF COURSE. She responded and slipped her phone into her pocket.

Harper pulled up to Carmen's house. She was sitting on the porch. Her hair rolled up in a towel.

"I figured we would put our makeup on together."

"Same," Harper replied. "I also brought some outfits." She smiled a devilish smile.

"Well, then let's get ready." If this movie starts at 9, we should probably get there a little early." She shoots Harper a wink and trots into the house.

On Their way to Carmen's bedroom, they pass Carmen's mom eating supper on the couch in her nursing uniform. She looked exhausted. Too many double shifts lately have taken their toll on her.

Carmen's mother had just stopped home to rest, eat a bit, and head back to the hospital. This weekend was going to be a long one for her.

As it always had been lately.

"Hello, girls." She said, looking up. Her eyes were bloodshot from the many hours she put in lately. "I hear you are going to the movies at nine and will be back at 11:30 or so?"

"Yes, ma'am," Harper answered.

"Well, enjoy. Oh, and Carmen? Shoot me a text when you are back home, so I know you are safe." She forced a tired smile.

"Of course, mom." Carmen winked at her and blew her a kiss. "Will do. Love you!"

They continue to the bedroom. Carmen had several mirrors and lots of lighting propped up and ready to go. Perfect for makeup application.

Wanting to look decent, Harper brought all her best name brands. It was the girls' last night on the town together.

Carmen started shuffling through all the makeup. "Awesome!" She began organizing the colors.

"What are you wearing?" Harper asked Carmen.

"I'm not sure. What did you bring?"

Harper held up two shirts. One pink, one white. "I have these. We can each wear one."

"Great! Thanks!" Carmen grabbed the pink one. "I love the keyhole front in this one."

Looking down at her phone, she reads her text.

"OK. The guys are going to pick us up at Barefoot Landing."

"They are excited for tonight." Carmen's phone kept going off with incoming texts.

"What is he saying?" Harper asked, sounding a bit concerned.

"They are picking up something to drink and heading out." She replied, keeping her eyes on her phone. "Are you as excited as I am?"

"Sure," Harper tried to sound sincere.

The girls reached the landing and sat on a park bench. They were anxiously waiting. Both excited and nervous. Little do they know what waited for them.

A few minutes later, a large dark gray van pulled up. It was the one from the beach, dark gray with black windows.

It was the van from the beach. Harper's stomach did a flip.

Harper nor Carmen had ever done something like this in their lives. They hear other girls talk about it in school, meet guys, go out to the movies or parties.

How bad can this be? Harper thought. *Our friends all have done it, and they survived, so why can't she and Carmen have a little boy fun?*

Cautiously, the girls walked up to the van. The passenger's window rolled down. In it were the guys from the beach.

"Hello," the driver greeted them as his dark eyes moved up and down Carmen's body. As Carmen got closer, he reached out and ran his hand through Carmen's hair. "Beautiful as ever."

Carmen shuddered, tingling down to her toes.

"Looking good, girls!" The driver stated in a deep voice. He seemed older than Harper remembered from the beach. But then again, the boys their age were immature, so it was hard to compare.

These two were real men. College men! What a story this was going to be on the first day of their Sophomore year!

"Jump in, and let's go." The driver welcomed the girls into the van.

"Popcorn and soda await!"

What the girls didn't notice was that his eyes nervously scanned the park.

The van door slid open, and the girls eagerly got inside. The van was immaculate.

The door shut behind them, and the van drove off.

5

Vacation Mode

Jim and Rob had a "bucket list" of trips planned every year. The one coming up was the biggest so far. Almost a year of planning and reservations went into this hunt. Then a couple of weeks before they were to head out, a missing girl case came in.

It took Jim and Tom a lot of convincing the chief that Tom could cover for Jim, that he finally decided to let Jim go.

It was the day before his vacation started, and Jim was doing a once-over with Tom on the reports he had from the kidnapping case. There hadn't been anything more than what they initially had found.

They were assuming that the girl was just a runaway. They couldn't find a trace of her or her body so far. The case was growing cold. Fast. The hardest part was seeing the girl's parents rally search parties throughout the area of Coeur D'Alene. The family believed someone had taken their daughter. Jim and Tom had nothing to disprove their theory.

Nearing the end of his shift, Jim's cell phone went off. Jim looked at his cell phone. It was a text from his buddy Rob. He was just as excited as Jim was to go on this hunting trip. His flight left in the morning for Bonners Ferry.

ONE MORE HOUR LEFT-I CAN'T WAIT!

"The longest hour ever!" Jim set his phone back on the desk.

****

Detective Robert Jackson looked more his age than Jim. Years as a Chicago detective had taken their toll on him. The stress showed in the deep lines on his face. He only took one or two weeks off per year and always kept his phone on him. The department could not run a day without him, let alone a whole week. Rob put his heart into his work, he was a true hardcore detective inside and out, and the department reflected on that.

But this trip was going to be different. It was the first time Rob was going to be off the grid. The department would not be able to bother him with work issues.

Rob's latest case was a murder of a young college student from Chicago's north side. She had been raped and choked to death and was found naked in a barn just southwest of the city in a little Amish community. Leather reins wrapped around her neck, and she had been covered in whip marks and bruises.

Rob wanted to solve this case before he went on this hunt with Jim. An Amish elder owned the barn, which made the investigation more difficult. The man removed the body and covered it up before he was able to notify authorities.

He said he was protecting the children from seeing such a macabre massacre, and Rob had to be extra careful to balance his investigation and respect the Amish community.

It seemed that the girl never made it to the class one Friday morning. Then a month or so later, she was found hanging over some hay bales inside the barn.

Was it suicide? Was she depressed? Did she know someone in the Amish community? Rob ran these questions over and over through his head.

He needed more answers, but he had to wait for the coroner to return his final report. In the meantime, Rob's attempts to question one of the Amish elders had become a futile effort. The man was in ill health, and his sons were protecting him.

Who the hell could have done this? Rob thought to himself as he put the girl's files into a box and locked them up in his file cabinet.

Rob turned his attention to his phone as it buzzed with a text notification from Jim.

JUST FINISHING MY DAY, AND I'M DONE!

Rob smiled and took one last look around his office, locking up his file cabinets and making sure his desk was clean.

Get me the hell outta here! His mind started to change gears.

Rob reached under his desk and pulled out his briefcase. He slid his office chair up under his desk and grabbed his phone. Everything was in its place.

He can't remember when he took this much time off work. Excited, Rob does a little hop.

****

It was just after 4 pm when Kristy pulled up the driveway. Kristy usually got home before Jim, but not today. He was out in the garage when Kristy pulled up.

She waved to him and smiled as she entered the house. She stumbled over Jim's hunting stuff that laid scattered about the foyer.

"Men," she mumbled, half kicking at the pile as she walked into the kitchen to prepare dinner.

Jim had packed a few days before the trip, and then he would go through the pile one last time before he left. Moving everything closer to the door as he did.

It was an annual tradition, he once told her. *I will never forget anything if I do it this way.*

Jim finished cleaning out the Jeep when he came through the front and stumbled over his hunting pile.

Kristy moved it over just a bit to confuse me. Jim chuckled to himself. *I bet she tripped over it as well, and now she's trying to prove a point.*

Jim closed his eyes and inhaled deeply. The smell of dinner immediately took over his attention. He could hear his wife singing. A song he heard many times before. All of this deliciousness was coming from his kitchen. Jim smiled a devilish smile as he approached the kitchen.

Kristy was standing in front of the stove with her apron on, preparing dinner. Jim swiftly snuck up behind her, wrapping his arms around her waist.

"Oh, honey," He whispered in her ear as he kissed her neck.

Kirsty froze, only for a second, then she melted into his arms.

"Mmmmm!" Jim said seductively. "Two of my favorites!"

They embraced deeply into each other's arms, forgetting the world around them until the smoke alarm went off. Both of them giggled as Jim waved a towel at it until it stopped beeping.

After dinner, they casually enjoyed a glass of wine.

"Wait until you see what I got for your dessert!" She took the glasses and replaced them with a bowl of fresh strawberries.

It was the best dessert! It had consisted of whip cream, strawberries, and sex. THE best sex Jim remembered having in a very long time. He laid in bed watching his beautiful wife sleep, thinking about what had just happened. He couldn't imagine loving anyone else as much as he truly loved her. How she always made him feel warm and happy inside.

He melts into the moment and closes his eyes.

* *

The annoying ringtone on Robert's phone was a cross between a wounded rabbit and a pack of howling coyotes. It worked, and that's what it was supposed to do. He looked at his phone. 3:30 am. Just like a kid on Christmas morning, Rob jumped out of bed and into the shower. By 4:15, he was on his way to the airport. After going through security and checking in his bags, Robert grabbed himself a latte.

His change was a dime. He chuckled as he put it in his pants pocket. He, too, had heard Jim's grandpa talk about the dimes and their link to the afterlife.

Taking a sip of the hot sweet intoxicating liquid, Rob got into the boarding line.

Life was good.

* *

In the morning, after breakfast. Jim and Kristy slipped into the shower together, having sex one last time before Jim had to leave.

Kristy admired Jim as he came down the hallway pulling his t-shirt over his head. She loved how in shape he was. Jim had a six-pack and the waistline to go with it. Every time she saw him without his shirt on, she got butterflies in her stomach.

Jim went through his list and his luggage as he placed each item into the Jeep. After packing, he walked back to the house one last time to say goodbye.

"I guess I'll be heading out." Jim approached Kristy, who was standing just inside the doorway.

"Remember now. I will not have any cell service once that bush plane takes off. I'll send you one last text before we leave."

They embraced in a long goodbye kiss.

"I miss you already," Kristy whispered as she buried her face in his neck.

"Keep that thought." Jim kissed her forehead. "Love ya."

"Love you, too."

Jim got into his Jeep and pulled out of the driveway. Checking his rearview mirror, he could see Kristy standing on the porch, waving. Jim waved back until Kristy was out of sight. Something they did every time he left on a trip.

God, I love that woman! Jim thought, watching his beautiful wife fade out of sight.

* *

Rob's plane landed on time. He quickly headed to baggage claim to grab the rest of his stuff. As the luggage passed through the unloading dock, Rob could not see his suitcase. For a moment, he began to panic. His eyes frantically searched the carousel, hoping his luggage hadn't gotten lost.

Relieved, when he saw his suitcase and bag, Rob quickly grabbed them and started across the airport looking for his friend. As he reached the center, a familiar voice came from behind him.

"Hey, Mr. Jackson? Detective Robert Jackson from Chicago? Is that you?"

Rob began to smile and turned around. Standing in front of him is his best friend, Jim.

"Hey, buddy! How's it going?" Rob made his way toward Jim and hugged him like he hadn't seen his friend in a hundred years.

"Ya know? It just got a whole lot better!" Jim replied enthusiastically.

Rob instantly inhaled the fresh air when they walked outside.

"The fresh air here is amazing compared to the oil, gas, and raunchy air of downtown Chicago." The two of them loaded up Rob's stuff, jumped into the Jeep. They began to head out across the parking lot.

"Let's go grab something to eat," suggested Rob. "My belly button is touching my backbone!"

They both laughed as Jim pulled the Jeep out on the highway.

"I know of a place that is a short trip to some of the best grub you'll ever have."

Just a mile up the road from the airport, Jim pulled into a gravel parking lot. The restaurant looked a little run down.

"Oh, my Gawd! I can't believe this place is still up and running! I remember hanging outside here when it was a drive-up place." Rob's eyes lit up. "We used to come here after the movies on Saturdays, remember?" Rob's stomach growled. "Told you, I was hungry. They don't give out food on airplanes like they used to."

"You remember Tom and Jenni Mason? They bought this place for cheap. It was pretty run down. Kristy and I helped them to gut the place and remodel it. Wait till you see it on the inside!"

"Christ, it was a run-down shack when I lived here," Rob stated as he jumped out of the Jeep.

"Well, Jenni wanted to share her heritage with the community by serving some of her favorite Native dishes."

Jenni's great-grandmother was full-blood Nez Perce. Before she died, she taught Jenni everything about their native diet and how to prepare it.

Jim pulled open the front door. There was a fluorescent OPEN sign in the window.

Inside, Jenni, Tom's wife, greeted the men. She was in a leather dress. Feathers and beads adorned it like a young Native American maiden. Her beautiful black silky hair was in one long braid down the middle of her back.

Rob always had a little crush on Jenni.

"Well, look at these two handsome men!" Jenni exclaimed. Her contagious smile revealed a dimple on her left cheek.

Dang, she still is gorgeous! Rob thought to himself.

"Hello, sweetie," Jim kissed her on the cheek. "Thank you for allowing Tom to cover for me so that I could go on this trip. I owe you one."

"I can't wait for some girl time with Kristy," she giggled. "Tom is just changing. He'll be right out," She grabbed two menus.

"Follow me."

As soon as they finished ordering, Tom came out from the back and sat next to Jim. The three of them caught up until their meals arrived.

"So, Rob, do you have any interesting cases you're working on?" Jim took a big bite out of his salad. He always felt that whatever Jenni put in it was the same stuff growing in his backyard, but he never had the nerve to ask. Part of him didn't want to know.

"Well, there's one I still have lingering on my desk, believe it or not."

Rob began to tell Jim about the girl found in the Amish barn. How the girl was missing for a month before being found in the barn.

"I have no clues on her, no copycats, no serial-type cases in that area. This case had me at a total loss for the first time in many years." Rob picked at the greens on his plate. "But, it was Amish country too. They had tampered with the evidence before we got there. I don't think they were involved. This group is peaceful and keeps to themselves. I can't even figure out how this could have happened there without any witnesses."

"If there is anything that I swear to do before I die, it is fucking solve this murder," Rob grumbled. "It's starting to make me look bad!"

Rob described in detail the girl's background. How she never partied or got into any trouble. It made her disappearance even more puzzling. Her circle of friends was shocked when they heard about her death. Jim listened intently. He loved Rob's stories.

The missing teenager case that Jim and Tom were working on was the first significant thing that happened in their jurisdiction for quite some time. Jim was struggling as the case grew cold. It almost seemed like she just ran away. But her family denied any thought of her leaving. The longer this girl remained missing, the less likely it was that they would find her.

After lunch, the two of them ordered some desserts to go. They jumped into Jim's Jeep and headed North.

They were turning left on Highway 1 towards Porthill. Only 13 or so more miles until they reached the Canadian border. For miles, they passed trucks hauling massive trees. Single and double pups each filled to their capacity, everyone making their last big run before winter slowed them down.

"Jesus, they are hauling out some huge logs!" Rob commented as one of the trucks blew by them, shaking the Jeep.

Jim stayed silent, listening as Rob told him about his divorce and latest fling. For an instant, Jim drifted into Rob's life. Imagining himself as a well-known big-town detective, having any woman he wanted, and all the freedom in the world.

BANG!!!

That's when it happened.

The accident.

In an instant, it changed many lives.

Especially Jim's.

After the deafening bang and sudden stop, everything turned silent. Jim slowly started to regain consciousness. Through the ringing in his ears, he could hear a faint cry of a baby. A few seconds later, the ringing became louder. He could hear sirens blaring in the distance, getting louder as they approached.

Jim opened his eyes, and everything was a red blur. He could make out that the redness was blood. It was everywhere! That's when he realized he couldn't move his head.

Where am I? He thought. His brain felt jumbled.

The burning rubber and gas started to enter his lungs. Every breath he took felt like hot acid. He coughed, but that caused piercing pains in his head. He could feel bits of glass grinding around in his mouth. He tried spitting the pieces out. It was then he realized that it was not glass at all but broken teeth. His. Mostly, the front ones by what his tongue could tell. But, strangely, he felt no pain, just numbness. The pressure in his head made him feel like he was deep underwater. Unable to move and unable to see or hear clearly, Jim was frightened. He gasped for air. The burning acid feeling spread its way down into his throat and his lungs. All he could do was cough.

It was then that Jim heard a soft moan from the back seat.

Rob? Jim recalled driving. *No! Holy shit, it can't be!*

Jim tried to look to his right. The front passenger seat where Rob had been sitting was gone! A log had pushed it into the back seat.

Where is Rob then? Jim panicked. *This can't be good!* The pressure began to get worse in Jim's head!

OH, MY GOD!

Jim realized the moaning sound coming from the back seat was his best friend!

Jim couldn't turn his head enough to get a good look at Rob's mangled body. It was probably a blessing. Impaled by a log splinter the size of a two by four, Rob's body lay motionless.

"No!" Jim's voice was garbled. "Rob!" Jim tried to yell as the moans in the back seat became silent. Jim started to panic, he felt a sharp pain jolt across the left side of his head, and he began to black-out.

Jim fought to keep conscious. He could hear the muffled distance of the sirens getting louder.

Hurry! Please, hurry! He thought, feeling helpless.

Jim tried to move his arms. The only one cooperating was his right. But, every time he moved it, it felt like it weighed a hundred pounds. He was trapped in his crumpled Jeep, next to his best friend, who was dying. Jim could hear a faint cry of a baby. It would silence to a sob, then start to cry again.

Tears began flowing down Jim's face as he realized what was happening to him. He, too, felt himself fading away.

This was it. He tried to comprehend. *This was what it felt like to die.*

Goodbye, Kristy. I love you. Jim closed his eyes.

That was when he felt a hand on his shoulder and heard a muffled gasp.

"Oh, this was bad." The muffled voice rang in Jim's head.

Jim attempted to look around, but his vision was so blurred, he could only make out a bright yellow figure.

Jim tried to tell the paramedics to help his friend, Rob. He was not responding to Jim anymore. Little did Jim know, Rob was not in much better shape. He started to cough up blood, the burning in his lungs, the jolt of pain shooting through his head. Once again, Jim passed out.

* *

That was when he first saw it with a clear vision.

It was the light. The one that everyone that ever had a near-death experience talked about right before crossing over. It was so amazing. There were no words that could describe it.

But here it was, right in front of him.

Jim noticed a figure in the distance. It slowly moved toward the edge of the bluish light, and as it began to appear closer, Jim recognized it as Rob. He lunged after it and tried to yell out. But he was unable to move.

He has to recognize me; Jim thought as he stood watching his friend, trying to wave his hands to get his attention.

But Jim was frozen in time. He was watching Rob, who was staring straight ahead, in a trance. Standing in front of Rob was his dad.

Rob slowly began to walk toward the beautiful light. What happened in the next few moments was indescribable! The feeling of peace became so overpowering that any confusion or fear either of them had, was gone.

Jim got a glimpse of Heaven.

The Shack

Harper's blood-curdling scream woke Carmen. Feeling dazed, she slowly attempted to gain composure. The last thing she remembered was getting into a van and driving off with the guys from the beach. She recalled them driving away from the park, the guys offering them a drink. It all became blurry after that.

The van had stopped in the woods, and Carmen could see Harper standing outside with one of the men. Her blood-curdling shrieks echoed through the damp forest. Carmen tried to get her bearings. She felt like she was moving through quicksand. She tried to struggle to her feet. Almost instantly, she was pushed back into the van's seat, slamming her head against the window ledge. The blow to her chest knocked the wind out of her. All she could do now was lay still and gasp for air.

"NO!" Harper's terrified voice screamed out.

The scream startled Carmen as she once again tried to focus. Her head was pounding like never before. Her chest and lungs ached. She laid sobbing and helpless on the seat in the back of the van listening to Harper's pleas.

"Where are we?" She heard Harper ask several times.

The man's foreign voice shouted at Harper to shut up. Carmen then heard them struggle, occasionally bumping up against the van. Helpless and fearing the worst, her heart started to race.

"My dad has money, lots of it! He will give you any amount you ask for, as long as my friend and I return home safely." Carmen could hear the fear in Harper's voice.

"Please! Think about what you are doing! My dad has lots of money. He will find you and lock you up for a very long time! But, if you let me and Carmen go uninjured, he will let you live."

"Please. Please. LISTEN TO ME!"

There was a grotesque sound like a wet, dull clap, a thud, then silence.

Carmen listened for a while, shaking with fear. She fought to focus, but whatever drug they gave her was still affecting her ability to do anything.

"Harper?" Carmen's voice shook as she sobbed out Harper's name.

Silence.

What was I thinking! Carmen's mind began to think back. *What have I done!*

"God help us! I wanna go home. Me and Harper. I wish we had just gone to the movies!" She sobbed out loud.

It was getting dark, and the air outside the van felt cold and damp. Between the cold and fear, Carmen began to shiver.

Harper was jolted awake by dragging her up the porch steps. She noticed a sheet still covering her lower body. That was when Harper realized what was happening. Her scared eyes were scanning the area. She tried to struggle free, but the effect of the drugs was too strong in her system.

Harper felt a lump in her throat as she had recognized one of the men from the beach earlier that day.

"Oh my God!" She shrieked. The pines surrounding them eventually soaked in the sound, making the forest dead quiet once again.

"You said you loved me!" Carmen's voice was shaking. "I believed you."

They were in the middle of nowhere. The man she met online had Carmen standing in front of a shack hidden by overgrown grass and trees, abandoned for a very long time.

"Well, that was your first mistake. Bitch." He growled at her as he pulled her towards the porch.

Harper's arm started to ache as the man pulled her inside and shoved her onto the mouse-eaten sofa.

The smell coming off of it was putrid. It made Harper gag as she gasped for fresh air. One of the men laughed.

"What? Not what you're used to, 'Queen Whore'?" He grumbled as he stood by the door, as his partner walked in dragging Carmen. He slammed her onto the sofa alongside Harper. Stunned, Carmen sat still, seemingly calm. She looked over at Harper's bruised face. Blood was coming out of her nose and one of her ears. Her platinum hair, stained pink with blood.

Carmen gasped.

I'm so sorry. Carmen mouthed to Harper. Tears were rolling down her cheeks, making her eyeliner run in long black streaks.

Harper looked into Carmen's eyes, her eyes puffy and bloodshot from crying. She, too, was shaking, sobbing, and had the look of disbelief in her eyes.

"Why?" Screamed Harper. "Why did I listen to you, Carmen! Why did we get into that fucking van? WHY?!?!"

Harper felt a sharp blow to her head. It was so powerful that it knocked her off the couch and onto her knees. Her head bobbing, she tried to steady herself. It would take every ounce of energy she had to stay upright. She sat, wavering back and forth, trying to comprehend what was going on.

"Stay there, whore, if ya know what's good for ya," One of the men grunted as he stood over her. He was strong and very muscular. He was the roughest of the two, almost like he enjoyed slamming the girls around.

Stunned, Harper could not respond. She stared straight ahead, slowly blinking, trying not to pass out.

Carmen silently watched the men as they walked over to the kitchen area and started talking in a foreign language. She was still in disbelief. These guys had seemed so sweet earlier at the beach.

How could this be happening to us? Questions began running through Carmen's fuzzy mind.

Carmen tried as hard as she could to hold back her sobs. Looking over at Harper, still staring ahead, almost seemed zombie-like.

Suddenly, Harper's attention had moved towards the open front door. It was opened just enough to see the moonlit porch that led to freedom. She decided to make a run for it!

At this point, what did I have to lose? She thought as she jumped up, not looking back, and ran. Before the two men knew what was happening, she flung open the front door and took off outside.

Carmen let out a shriek.

"You are not leaving without me?!?!" She tried to stand up. Her knees were still shaky. As she struggled to stand, she was knocked back onto the couch by one of the men as he chased after Harper.

Carmen rolled over onto her back. The man paused, looking down at her for a moment. Realizing Carmen was unconscious, he joined his partner in the pursuit of Harper, who was running at full speed towards the woods.

Harper almost made it to the trees when a fist connected with her back, knocking her down. As her face pushed into the damp ground, Harper could taste dirt. She coughed as fresh blood began, running down her throat. She was pulled to her feet and was now looking directly into the man's dark, angry eyes.

Harper recognized the guy from the beach. The man Carmen had finally told her about earlier this week. The 'sweetheart' that she had a video call with many late-night hours. The man that seduced them to get into the van.

"What do you want from us?" She sobbed. "What did we ever do to you?"

Harper remembered Carmen telling her that he was the one she was in love with, who understood her, listening to everything she said. She was the reason they were here right now, missing from their families, without a trace.

"Why are you hurting us?" His face blurred as tears filled her eyes. "Carmen said you were a nice, sweet person, so why this?"

"Shut up, you little Whore!" He screamed at Harper, punching her in the face and knocking her out.

Once Harper was secure, the older man returned to the shack and dragged Carmen's limp body to the back bedroom. He placed her wrists in shackles and locked her up. Little did she know, this room was going to be her prison for the next few months.

Harper started to wake up again. She was back in the shack and propped up on the couch. Her legs were tied this time. Unable to move, she sat silently, dazed and confused.

The younger man pulled his phone out of his pocket and made a call.

****

He called his boss, Syn.

"We got the two girls you wanted!" He spoke in an unknown language. Harper could tell that he sounded excited. She only wished she knew what they were saying.

There was a pause as he listened to the voice on the other line.

"They are fighters! One almost got away!" He continued in his native Russian language, so Harper could not understand him.

"We should separate them," Syn responded." "It'll make it much easier to handle them once they are apart. I will contact her father for the ransom. Since you two can't do a fucking thing right. I cannot risk anything happening to those girls. They are worth a lot of money to me right now."

"Ok, man," the man replied in a sheepish voice, still talking in his native language.

"When and where do you want to pick her up?" He glanced over at Harper. She was sitting on the couch looking at him. Her head was still bobbing on her thin frame. Her eyes were puffy from crying. It was hard to tell if she had them open or closed. She was listening and trying to comprehend what he was saying. Even though she could not understand the language, she realized that they were concocting another plan.

This cannot be good, she thought.

"I will take her immediately. I will pick her up at the spot where I have the barrels. You can put her in one of them. Make sure you have her bound up well and seal the top. I'll get her from there." Syn was still keeping his identity a secret. The men had never seen his face. The fewer people that saw him, the less they would recognize him in the future.

Syn trusted no one.

The man turned and walked out the back door, still talking to

Syn on the phone. Harper heard the screen door slam shut, and now only muffled sounds were coming from that direction.

They were talking about Harper and Carmen's future. A slight change in plans.

Harper was terrified, not knowing what was going to happen to her. She had a gut feeling that this was not going to end well.

What have they done with Carmen? Harper thought. *Did they kill her? And why did I say my dad was rich? WHY?* Her brain was fuzzy, and she barely had the strength to sit. Holding her head up at this point took great effort.

I thought I could scare them, that's why. Harper thought as she began crying. At this point, her whole body ached.

Still, on the phone, the man came back into the shack. He handed the phone to the other man and walked over to Harper. The conversation continued in their native language, preventing Harper from understanding him.

Harper had had no clue what happened to Carmen. She was completely out of it when she was brought back into the shack.

Maybe she got away. She hoped. *Lucky.*

It wasn't long, and the two men were on the move again. They had given Carmen a larger dose of sedative. She wouldn't be waking up anytime soon.

They grabbed Harper's arm and pulled her out the front door of the shack. Her head pounded, and her legs felt weak. She was still fighting consciousness as they pulled her up to the side of the van. Then, they wiped her face off and took several pictures, forcing her to smile.

Harper never felt so terrified. For all she knew, she was now alone with the men and didn't want to imagine the horrors that may happen to her. She started to panic but was too fuzzy to attempt another getaway. Running was not an option for her anymore.

After taking some pictures, the men pushed Harper into the van.

One of the men grabbed a sheet from the back and wrapped her up in it. She screamed, trying to struggle free, but it was no use. No one could hear her anyway. They were out in the middle of nowhere, alone.

Her voice was just a silent, muffled echo in the pines.

With her entire body bound in the sheet, she lay crumpled on the van's floor. One man jumped into the van's driver seat and started it up. The other man said something and quickly jogged towards the shack. After a few minutes, he came back holding a pistol and waving a joint.

The older man jumped out of the idling van. The two of them started smoking the joint. Harper could hear them talking. They were talking about her, scaring Harper more than ever. Being bound up, she felt so helpless.

"Yeah, we could just keep them here. No one would know. Not even Syn." The man from the beach said. "Syn doesn't know about this place, does he?"

"Man, Syn knows everything!" His partner shouted back. "Are you brave enough to cross that psycho?"

After getting high, they both climbed back into the van.

What were they going to do with me? Where were they bringing me? Harper's heart started to race as the van pulled away from the shack.

We are leaving again, but where to now? Why not stay here? They're taking me away and plan on doing bad things to me! Harper's heart raced even faster!

As the van started to drive off, Harper could feel herself starting to panic.

Harper knew that she needed to break free!

With her heart beating out of her chest, Harper started to kick! Her hands were bound, and the sheet was tight around her body. But this didn't stop her from trying one last time to escape the horrors of what laid ahead. She was fighting now on pure adrenaline!

The more Harper kicked, the more she felt the need to be free. At first, the driver ignored her and continued to pick up speed along the narrow gravel road. Harper's anxiety increased as she began to kick harder, trying to break free.

She continued to kick and scream, getting louder and louder. The driver began to get irritated. He punched down on the gas as the van increased speed down the rough, gravel road. Just as he was rounding a sharp corner, the van's front tire hit a pothole. The movement had jerked the wheel out of the man's hands. At the same time, Harper gave one last big kick to the van door. To Harper and the driver's surprise, it popped open!

I am free! Harper took a joyous breath!

Within a split second, she felt a jerk on the sheet. Another second later, the sheet pulled tight as it ripped Harper violently out of the van. She felt a sharp pain on the side of her head and pressure in her chest.

Another sharp pain shot through her heart, then nothing.

****

A moment later, Harper opened her eyes.

Where am I? Harper's thoughts passed seamlessly through her mind. She squinted as the prettiest of blue lights seemed to blind her. *What are these lights? What happened to me, and why don't I feel any pain?*

Harper walked toward the bright lights. Looking down, she noticed she had a greenish-yellow aura around her. It was then that Harper froze. She was next to a man she didn't recognize. But she wasn't afraid. This man seemed like he needed her help.

Later. I'll go to the light later. Harper's thoughts were clear now. *First, I need to help this man. He seems lost. I need to help him.*

As she stood next to the man, Harper could tell that he was focusing on someone else.

Who is this beautiful stranger? He is warm and calm but filled with sorrow. He makes me feel safe, and I want to help him. Harper studied the man. There was a very faint orange aura around him. *I wonder why his aura is so faint?*

Trying to recognize her, the man stared at Harper for a while. She smiled as he turned his head and looked away.

Why isn't he smiling at me?

The man next to Harper turned his focus to another figure approaching two others, their auras becoming brighter with every step. So bright that Harper had to shadow her eyes with her hands. The men were smiling and talking to one another like they hadn't seen each other in a long time. Harper realized they were family.

The man next to her started to move forward, calling out to his friend.

I don't wanna leave him! Harper's mind was racing as she moved in sync with the man. She was watching the trio's auras grow and meld into the beautiful iridescent lights until they were gone.

Harper could feel the man next to her was extremely sad. So she comforted him in his sadness.

That was when he noticed her presence. Staring into her large blue eyes, he smiled. She felt peace and harmony as she smiled back. Green and orange, their auras meld together.

They have bonded.

****

Shortly after, Syn would receive another call.

6

Death and Revelation

Once the ambulance arrived, things were loud, and people rushed around. Everything Jim heard sounds muffled. His left eardrum had filled with blood, and the pressure in his head was unbearable, feeling like lightning bolts shooting behind his left eye. He kept trying to move to see if Rob was okay. Something was pressing into the left side of Jim's face.

It was a large log, and it was pressed so hard into Jim that his head was being pushed sideways into the back of the seat. There was blood everywhere.

Jim couldn't hear Rob anymore, making him panic; he needed to see if Rob was okay. Jim could only move his eyes, looking and searching for his dying friend. A red blur was all he could make out.

Hearing the familiar rev from the Jaws of Life, Jim's attention turned to the outside of the vehicle. The EMS workers had to cut the mangled car apart to get to the injured men. Jim could feel the pressure coming off his head as the workers slowly pulled the log away. Eventually, Jim felt the pressure release off his legs. The paramedics worked swiftly removing parts of the vehicle until they could reach the men. There were sharp pains-the only pains Jim could feel-shooting through his head.

Oh, my head! Jim thought.

Jim spit out more bits of shattered teeth. As he did this, the lightning-sharp pains streaked through his left temple. The constant sound of sirens and motors increased the pounding in his head, and now, the ringing in his left ear became intense!

Just make it all stop! He passed out.

Once the top of the Jeep had been pried open, the EMS workers started moving at a faster pace around Jim. They were busy stabilizing his neck, starting IVs, and assessing his injuries. Jim rolled his eyes open. He tried to speak but could only moan.

"Hello there, we are trying to help you. You have been in a bad accident, and we are going to take good care of you." Came a deep, familiar voice from outside the vehicle.

Jim looked up, relieved to see someone familiar. The EMS crews had gone on many calls with Jim. But, the man did not smile. He worked diligently, focused on Jim.

"Can you tell me your name?" He asked, but everything was so muffled, Jim could barely make out what this guy was saying. Jim looked at him, confused.

"Your name?"

"James Ca...Ca...," Was all Jim could convey.

Jim tried to talk louder, but he was unable to. His mouth was too swollen, and every time he tried to speak, a jolt of pain ran across the left side of his face.

"Rob." Jim managed to mumble. He kept trying to turn around. Looking for Rob. Jim noticed the EMT looking over his shoulder toward Rob. His face was like stone. The EMT sighed, shaking his head as he looked straight into Jim's eyes. Jim knew Rob was gone.

"We are doing our best to save you." He stabilized the safety board behind Jim's upper half, and ever so slowly, the team pulled his broken body out of the mangled Jeep. As Jim could feel them working on him, he started to feel weightless. Again, Jim faded away. Feeling numb, he couldn't fight anymore. The workers continued to stabilize Jim on the side of the road.

The emergency lights and sirens continued to warn oncoming traffic of the unimaginable scene that awaited beyond their bumpers. Logs were spread out everywhere, which made approaching the area difficult. The gawkers were holding up cell phones, eagerly plastering their newsfeeds with videos and pictures of the horrifying accident on Highway 1.

Jim drifted away. The EMS workers lifted him onto a stretcher and loaded him up into the ambulance. The crew started working more frantically on him as he began to go into shock. The workers were getting the defibrillator ready, slapping the electrodes onto his chest.

Seconds later, Jim coded.

* *

"Hey there!" Jim heard Rob's voice in the distance! Jim opened his eyes to see his friend Rob standing tall on what seemed to be a hill of white in front of him. This amazing blue incandescent light surrounded him. There was a beautiful blue-green aura spinning and dancing like a magical cloud around him. It was so bright, Jim squinted and shaded his eyes. Jim was no longer in a crumpled-up car but standing in a soft whiteness. Jim and Rob locked eyes for a moment. Each was coming to grips with what was happening.

Who was he waiting for? Jim thought. *Me?*

Jim felt peaceful, almost like he was weightless and numb. There was a static charge traveling up his arm. It felt like the ones you had on dry days in the wintertime. The ones that made your skin tingle and hair stand on end. That's when he noticed a young girl standing beside him holding his hand. Jim wondered who she was and why she was smiling. Her green aura was as bright as Rob's. Jim looked away, turning his attention back to Rob.

"I just wanted to tell you something before I go," Rob's low voice echoed in Jim's head. Rob's lips were not moving. His voice sounded peaceful.

"Please tell mom that I love her and that I am sorry for any trouble I may have ever caused her." Rob smiled and slowly started to walk away. He paused, looking over at Jim.

"Please tell her that dad and David are here. They have been waiting for me. They told me that they knew I'd be coming today! They look amazing, Jim. Tell her that dad and David look amazing!"

Rob again started his journey toward the light. Right before he entered, he turned one last time. His eyes turned into a bright blue light, burning Jim's eyes.

Jim felt a static charge enter his body, this time through his eyes. He closed them. The girl next to him mirrored his movements exactly, their auras melding together in smoky swirls of green and orange.

Jim remained still, slowly opening his eyes and trying to process what was happening. He watched Rob, Rob's dad, and David all rejoice inside the blue lights. Time had stood still.

This must be 'the light' everyone talked about. Jim thought, realizing that Rob was leaving. *I am witnessing Rob crossing over.*

Jim's mind was trying to process what he was observing.

"Wait!" Jim yelled out as he reached for his friend. Rob ignored him as he walked with his brother and father toward the light, disappearing. Jim squinted as he started to lose sight of Rob. Jim reached out towards the light. He suddenly stopped, feeling a lightning bolt travel through his body.

Oddly, there was no pain, only a slight pause.

Stop it! Let me go! I'm losing him! Jim jerked his arm back. Static surrounded his body as he again felt the jolt inside his chest.

Jim tried to walk toward the men, but his legs began to feel like lead. He was unable to move. Someone was pulling him back.

As Rob continued into the light, a bright blue wisp quickly darted at Jim and the girl. Their auras intertwined in a beautiful green and orange mist wrapped in hues of bright blue. Harper's figure slowly melded around Jim, disappearing with a shock of blue. Three souls became one. This moment of death was called a trifecta.

Jim's Rob's and Harper's souls had melded together forever.

Only God could decide who became one.

On this occasion, one soul survived. A single soul bound together from three. That soul went back to Earth. James Cavalier defied death and Heaven to help the lost souls on Earth live.

"It's not your time, buddy," Rob's voice was ringing through Jim's ears.

Jim stopped fighting and began to feel the warm flush feeling of peace. Jim drifted through the memories of his childhood with Rob. Their boyhood, their pre-teen years, and finally, their adult life. Their last lunch together at Tom and Jenni's cafe, laughing at Rob's stories. Past events flashed through Jim's mind. Each memory was faster than the previous!

Jim opened his eyes. The light was so bright; it burned them. The feeling of peace started to flow through his body. Jim felt a tingle of electricity engulfing his hand. He glanced over, seeing the girl holding it.

Rob told Jim her name was Harper.

She smiled again; this time, Jim smiled back. Their auras were swirling together, constantly intertwining.

As hard as Jim tried to stay focused, everything started to fade. He was leaving Heaven and coming back to Earth, to his battered, aching body.

Heaven was not ready for James Cavalier, and this was the beginning of Jim's purpose.

* *

The EMS team continued to work aggressively on Jim as they sped off to the hospital.

"We're losing him!" It was that familiar voice from the accident. It sounded faint and muffled.

Jim was drifting in between Earth and Heaven. In and out of consciousness, pain-no pain. Death, then life. He finally coded.

"Charging to 300 joules!"

"Clear!"...........................Jim felt the lightning bolt going through his body.

"Again! Clear!"................Lightning bolt!

"We can't lose him! Another dose of EPI!"

"Again! Clear!".............Fading.......The light..:.......Drifting..............Rob........Harper.......

As the ambulance pulled up to the little hospital, the entire emergency room staff eagerly awaited, not expecting to see what they did. The hospital's emergency room wasn't equipped to handle such a critical trauma. The team did their best to make Jim as comfortable as they could. They worked diligently to stabilize him for the medi-flight ride to the trauma hospital in Spokane. They all moved together, like a well-oiled machine.

Unfortunately, Rob was unable to be saved, and it was his time to go. That's what was supposed to happen, and Rob knew it. Jim felt his presence through everything that was going on. It felt comforting, so Jim embraced it.

Harper never left Jim's side. He felt comforted by her presence, embracing it.

Jim remained unconscious after the accident. As his body continued to fight, Jim could feel the EMS and emergency room physicians tirelessly stabilizing him. He heard them talking about his injuries and Rob's untimely death. His thoughts went to Kristy, hoping Tom was with her to help her through. He thought about the girl again.

Harper. How do I know her? Jim drifted into peacefulness.

7

The News

Kristy decided to clean after Jim left. With Jim being gone for seven whole days, she thought that she might as well start it off with a clean house.

She went into the hallway closet and pulled out the candles that Jim hated so much.

As she lit the candles, she inhaled the sweet scent. It reminded her of when she was a child, and her dad would buy her rum-flavored caramels. She paused, reminiscing back to her childhood.

And she smiled.

Kristy was looking forward to a relaxing quiet week. She got caught up in all her love stories. She had books and movies lined up for the week. All were long overdue for her attention.

She was blasting her 80's playlist on the soundbar. Housework had always moved quicker when she could dance around the house.

With the music echoing in the hallway, Kristy was in her shorts and tank top, bouncing from room to room. She didn't hear the telephone ringing, nor the answering machine.

Looking down, Kristy saw the notifications blowing up her phone. She picked it up and opened it up to see what the buzz was all about.

People were sharing pictures and posts on her feed of an accident on Hiway 1. In the photos, she could see the logging truck, its overturned pup, with all its contents strewn across the road.

Oh no! She thought. *It looks like traffic will be jammed up for hours! I hope Jim and Rob got past that.*

Kristy's phone began to ring as she was thumbing through the photos of the accident.

It was Tom. Oh my god, it was Jim's Jeep!

Kristy was now shaking and slid her finger over the screen to answer the call.

"Kristy?" Tom's voice came on.

"Yes." Kristy's voice was shaking.

"Where are you?" Tom's voice sounded strained.

"Home. Tom. Why?" Kristy asked. Afraid she may not want to know the answer.

"I have to talk with you." Tom was driving quite fast out of town, towards Jim and Kristy's house. "Don't go anywhere. I'll be there in a few." Tom hung up and sped down the highway.

Kristy felt numb. Her legs felt heavy, making it difficult to move. She knew it had to be bad news. She couldn't bring herself to look at the rest of the posts.

She just sat silent, waiting for Tom to come through the doorway. She could not possibly prepare for the news that would change her life forever.

Oh, God. Please let Jim and Rob be okay. Kristy prayed.

Minutes seemed like hours. Then came that dreaded knock at the door. Kristy was still on her knees, trying to hold back the anxiety she felt at that moment.

Maybe, she thought, *if I didn't answer the door, he would go away. Perhaps this is all a practical joke.*

Tom opened the front door slowly, peeking in. He was in his uniform.

"Kristy?"

Kristy couldn't answer. She cringed at the sound of Tom's troubled voice.

Go away, Tom. She thought, covering her head with her shaking hands.

If Tom never came over, maybe this awful feeling would go away. She thought. *Then, possibly there would not be any bad news.*

Tom continued through the front door. Kristy was in a daze. She looked through him like he wasn't even there.

Tom hurried across the living room and approached Kristy on the floor. He knelt in front of her and put his arms around her tightly. She buried her head into his chest and cried. He sat, silently holding her for a few minutes.

"I'm so sorry, Kristy." Tom gently released his grip.

"There has been an accident. The ambulance is bringing Jim and Rob to the hospital," He paused, "The accident was pretty bad."

Kristy started to sob out loud.

"I have seen some posts." Kristy started to have a meltdown.

"This couldn't be happening!" She screeched, looking at Tom. He stared pitifully back into Kristy's eyes. He placed his hands on Kristy's shoulders as his stare stiffened. He took a deep breath. He began to tell Kristy what he knew about the accident.

"The accident was just a few miles south of the Canadian border. There was a logging truck heading south on Highway 1 when he lost control and dumped his load. The logs sprayed across the centerline and struck Jim's Jeep." Tom tried hard to keep his composure. This part of his job was never easy, especially today.

Kristy stood up and slowly walked over to the counter. She

leaned on the edge, her arms wrapped around herself. She was in shock. Tom stood and walked over to the front door and shut it.

"Let me know when you are ready, and I'll take you to the hospital.

"Yeah, I'll be ready as soon as I get changed." Sobbing silently, she headed toward her bedroom. Tom could hear her. His heart ached. He knew he had to be there for her, no matter what.

A few minutes later, Kristy came trotting back down the hallway, grabbing her purse, keys, and cell phone.

"Grab your charger," Tom advised. "Batteries go dead quickly in those damn things."

He was right; Kristy's phone never stayed charged long anymore. She grabbed the charger and shoved it into her purse. Tom escorted her to his cruiser.

Maybe you should call Jim's parents." Suggested Tom.

"What?" Kristy's mind was racing, thinking of Jim and Rob. Of what she might see. She had forgotten about Jim's parents.

"Maybe you should call Jim's parents."

"Oh my Gosh, you are right." Kristy started searching through her purse, looking for her phone.

"I don't know, Tom!" Kristy began to panic. "I can't find my phone!" With each second passing and each hand turning up empty, Kristy was starting to become more frantic. It wasn't long, and she was hyperventilating.

Tom continued to watch Kristy from the corner of his eye. She was shaking and crying the entire time, moving the contents of her purse around, searching for her phone. She kept coming up empty-handed.

"I just want to see Jim and Rob and talk to the doctors!" She blurted between sobs.

Tom pulled up to a stoplight, reached inside Kristy's purse, pulling out her cell phone, and handed it to her. She looked at his hand, and she slowly pulled the phone from it. Through teary eyes, she called Jim's parents. Thankfully, it was Jim's dad who had answered the phone.

"Hello, Frank." Kristy's voice was thick with emotions.

"Kristy? Are you okay?" Frank instantly sensed the fear in her voice.

"I am. I am calling to let you know Jim and Rob were in a bad accident," She paused, trying to keep her composure. She broke down and started to cry.

The phone was silent for a few minutes.

"Oh...MY..." Frank gasped. "They just left today, didn't they? Jim? How's Jim?"

"He is alive, and I don't know much beyond that. The accident was pretty bad, I guess." She stammered through her words. Everything seemed to be going in slow motion. "They were bringing them to the hospital. I am with Tom Mason. He is driving me to the hospital right now." She took a deep breath, waiting for Frank to respond on the other end of the line.

Frank was standing next to the phone jack on the wall. He stared blankly out his kitchen window. He was trying to comprehend everything Kristy just told him. Jim's mother walked into the tiny kitchen. She froze when she saw the shock in Frank's eyes. The tears were running down his leathery face. Kristy could hear him tell Jim's mother what had happened.

Jim's mom let out a scream as his dad dropped the phone.

Tom's squad car was approaching the hospital. He pulled up under the canopy outside of the emergency exit. He had done this many other times in the past. But, this time was different. It was personal.

"Thanks, Tom," said Kristy as she jumped out of the car. She quickly rushed through the emergency room doors.

The unit clerk looked up and immediately recognized Kristy. She was her history teacher in school. That's when it dawned on her, who they had just brought in by ambulance.

The hospital was small. The usual patients had the flu or a broken arm. Something this horrific was practically not heard of, and this was the young clerk's first time dealing with something like this. She forced a smile.

"Hi, Mrs. Cavalier, may I help you?" Her voice stuttered a bit as she tried to stay composed.

"I'm here to see my husband, James Cavalier. He was brought here by ambulance." Kristy responded in an anxious, shaking voice.

Without questioning Kristy again, the unit clerk picked up her phone and paged someone from the back.

"She's here. Mrs. Cavalier. She is asking to see her husband." The unit clerk hung up the phone and looked into Kristy's eyes, not blinking for fear she might start to cry.

"They will be right with you if you want to have a seat." She walked around the desk and escorted Kristy to a small waiting room off to the side of the emergency room. Kristy paced the small room hugging herself.

In the small waiting room. There was a table, and some chairs, nothing else. The wait seemed like forever, with each exchanging few words. That was okay with Kristy. She needed time to process all of this. Tom was there for Kristy. If she wanted to talk, he would listen. She didn't need to explain this to Tom. He already knew.

"Would you like for me to get you something to drink?" Tom finally broke the silence. "It may be a while before you have the opportunity to get something." He placed his hand on her shoulder. She shuddered and again started to cry.

Kristy turned her head just a bit towards him, still looking at the floor.

Tom didn't push the question again. He just got up and left the room, heading down the hallway looking for a vending machine where he could purchase a couple of waters. When Tom heard the staff talking about the accident and the death of Rob, the details, everything, he was glad Kristy stayed back in the waiting room. She did not know about Rob. He wanted Kristy to hear this information from the doctors.

Tom took a deep breath to clear his throat. They all jumped, looking startled.

"I am looking for a vending machine or somewhere I can purchase water for my friend." He kept his voice stern. Making the staff realize that this was not the time or place for such a conversation.

Today was Kristy's story that they were gossiping. This disappointed Tom.

One older lady stood up. She was relatively short and stout.

"Follow me," she said sheepishly. "I'll take you to the kitchen, where you will find what you need." She headed off down the hallway, Tom in tow.

They got to the kitchen, and she turned to Tom.

"I am sorry if you heard any of that conversation." Her face turned a little red. "We just"...

Tom held his hand up and interrupted her.

"I am the victim's partner and good friend. I am here with his wife, also my friend. She does not know about Rob's death. If she had heard that conversation, she would have lost it. I understand why you all are discussing the accident, but take it where no one can hear. That's all."

He forced a smile.

"It's been a long day for all of us." He walked over to the vending machine and purchased two bottles of water. "It's not going to be over for James and Kristy Cavalier for a long while." Think about that when you go home tonight.

He passed the nurses' station on his way back to Kristy. It was silent, and everyone avoided looking his way. A doctor walked from the back room and asked the clerk where Kristy was. She called out to Tom as he passed by the desk.

"Sir, this is Dr. Schaati. He would like to talk to you and Mrs. Cavalier." She motioned to the doctor. He nodded and approached Tom holding out his hand.

"Hi, Dr. Schaati, ER physician taking care of Mr. James Cavalier." The doctor was a very tall, thin man with long, skinny fingers. He had a firm grasp. "Are you with Mrs. Cavalier?" He asked.

"Thomas Mason, I'm Jim's partner and a close family friend. Kristy, his wife, is waiting in the little private room. I just went to get her some water." He looked up at the doctor, who was at least 6-6 or so.

They both headed to the little room where Kristy was anxiously waiting.

Tom opened the door slowly, seeing Kristy sitting silently, just like he left her. She was rocking back and forth. He hands her the water.

"Thanks," she said as she noticed the doctor standing behind Tom. She jumped up, tossing the bottle at Tom.

"Hello, doctor!" Her heart was beating so hard, she could feel it in her throat.

"Hello, Mrs. Cavalier." He reached out with his long arms and shook her petite hand. "I am Dr. Schaati. I am taking care of your husband, James." She pulled away and wrapped her arms around her body. She felt herself starting to shake.

"The accident was pretty bad. A logging truck heading south on Highway 1 just out of Porthill when it lost its load. It happened at the same time your husband and his friend were coming around the corner heading north. They didn't see it coming. They couldn't have avoided it. It happened way too fast."

Oh, my God, Kristy thought as she closed her eyes. *Those trucks haul massive loads.*

For a moment, she had forgotten about Rob. She started to feel numb. Here came the news. She was sure it was not going to be good.

That was why they put me in this damn room! She thought

Kristy tried to swallow, but the lump in her throat made it difficult. Her head began to spin. She felt faint.

Breathe in, breathe out. Kristy reminded herself. Her eyes were still closed as she imagined the accident in her head.

"When the logs hit the blacktop, some of them had split, one went through the passenger's side, hitting Robert Jackson, killing him almost instantly." He looked at the floor. She gasped out a scream and covered her mouth with her hands.

"OH MY GOD, NO!!!" She started to cry.

Dr. Schaati looked Kristy in the eyes.

"I cannot guarantee the driver will live, but we are doing our best to stabilize him." He placed his hand on Kristy's shoulder.

"Rob was like a brother to Jim." She exclaimed. "We both love him dearly."

"I am sorry to be the one to tell you the news." He composed himself and finished his story.

"A log also pierced through the driver's side window and pinned your husband into his seat. He has a lot of head trauma and lost most of his front teeth from the impact. He also has a broken femur and several broken ribs from the dashboard. We are not sure how much brain, nerve, or spinal damage yet." He paused to let her absorb all the information.

"He's pretty broken up, Mrs. Cavalier. He needs to be flown out of here if he stands a chance to live."

She envisioned her husband and Rob laughing and talking about the big moose they would be bagging up in Alaska.

This horror cannot be happening! Not to them, they were too good for this! Kristy imagined. *They were going on their dream hunt!*

"Can I see him?"

"We are stabilizing him for the medi-flight helicopter to bring him to Sacred Heart in Spokane, Washington. He will get the best treatment for his injuries there, as they are the trauma specialists." He placed his cold hand on her shoulder.

"Again, I am truly sorry to be giving you such terrible news. My team and I are doing our best to get your husband stable enough so we can get him out of here." He turned toward the door and left the room.

"I will have my nurse come and get you in a few minutes."

Once again, there was silence.

This time it was Kristy who spoke.

"What happens if he doesn't make it, Tom? What will I do?" Her voice was shaking.

Tom handed her a tissue and hugged her tightly. He could not bear to imagine his life without Jim in it.

"Have Faith in God," He felt her trembling body against him. "Jim is a healthy, tough guy. A true fighter. He will be back to himself in no time. You need to stay strong for him. He will need you now, most of all."

"Rob was tough, too. Look what happened to him!"

"The doctor said he didn't even have a chance, Kristy. Jim got lucky. It wasn't his time yet," Tom tried to console her.

She dried her eyes. Still sobbing, she took a deep breath. "I'll have to call Rob's family, too. My God, how much can one person take?"

"If you want me to, I could call Rob's family." Tom looked into Kristy's watery, bloodshot eyes. "You will have enough to deal with for now, and I do this all the time. It's the least I can do to help."

"You are right, and I appreciate everything you have done for me so far. Jim and I are lucky for you to be in our lives." Kristy replied. She pulled up her contacts on her phone.

"I have Rob's sister's number on my phone. She was the closest to Rob. If you want to call her, that would be great. I'll call Jim's parents to update them on the accident and Jim's condition," Kristy moved away from Tom.

They both hung up their phones at about the same time. Just in time, the nurse peeked her head into the room.

"You can come and see your husband now, Mrs. Cavalier." The nurse stood in the doorway. "Follow me, please," She turned to Tom. "You can go now, Officer Mason. We will take care of Mrs. Cavalier now."

Kristy grabbed Tom's hand. "Tom is mine and Jim's best friend. He can come with me."

All three left the little waiting room.

On the way to Jim's ICU room, the nurse explained everything to Kristy and Tom.

"Please try to remember, he has a head injury, and it is important not to stimulate him at this time. His brain is very fragile right now. So, please try to keep your composure. We believe he *can* still hear you. Sometimes this makes people in his condition unable to handle stimulation. It will cause their brain pressures to go up. We don't want that to happen. Because that damages healthy brain tissue." She looked stoned face at Kristy to make sure she understood.

Kristy nodded.

"We are trying to keep James stable by putting him in a medically induced coma. It will help him rest while his body heals. He will have a lot of machines and tubes connected to him, he is very swollen, and there is still blood on him. Right now, we will not clean him up. Our priority is getting him stable." She continued. "So, please be aware that we are still working on this for the flight. The first twenty-four hours are very critical."

She approached Jim's room and opened the door.

Jim laid motionless in front of Kristy. A large tube stuck out of his mouth. The monitors were beeping and buzzing all around them.

Kristy could see his chest rise and fall with each forced breath the machine made for him. Kristy began to sob. Nothing could have prepared her for what she was seeing. Tubes were protruding from his head, arms, and chest. Jim's swollen face was beyond recognition, still covered with some blood. Kristy and Tom approached the head of the bed.

The nurse touched Kristy's arm. "I will be just outside of that door if you need anything," she whispered.

Kristy nodded and turned towards Jim. She was shaking, scared to death.

Jim's body was swollen, bloody, and bruised. At least what she could see of it. He laid lifeless. Helpless. His eyes were taped shut.

"I barely recognize him," Kristy turned away and started to sob quietly.

Tom pulled her into his arms. She buried her face into his chest and cried. A tear ran down Tom's face as he held Kristy and looked at her broken husband. His best friend. It was worse than he imagined. What if she was right and he didn't make it? Tom closed his eyes and tried not to imagine the horror. They held each other tight.

Kristy released her grip and turned back to Jim.

She began to wonder. *How am I going to take care of Jim if he survives? I don't know how I will ever be able to stay strong for him and Rob.*

She took in a deep breath and held it.

"Jim, I love you." She whispered, putting her hand on Jim's.

His hand was warm and soft.

Jim heard a familiar voice. Kristy's

He could not move. Kristy was here somewhere. He could hear her crying.

Where is Rob?

Kristy?!? Jim tried to call out to his wife.

A blond-haired girl was standing quietly in the corner of the room, no one could see. Her aura was now a bright green.

Harper? Jim could see her. It was like he was floating above his hospital bed.

One of the monitors started to go off with a series of low beeps, and the nursing staff entered the room quickly.

"I'm sorry, Mrs. Cavalier, you'll have to leave for a minute while we figure out what is happening." The nurse whispered as she walked by Kristy and attended to Jim. Tom escorted Kristy out of the room as more staff entered the room. Dr. Schaati gave orders to the nurses. The beeping finally subsided. They all walk out of the room.

"He's stable once again." The nurse told Kristy and Tom. "He's been like this for a while. As I said, he's in very critical condition," She touched Kristy's arm. "We will not give up on him here. He is a powerful man. He was always such a caring person when he had to come here with a patient. All the staff around here like him."

Kristy thought about that for a moment.

She had forgotten how much Jim got around with his job. He must have known everyone around town.

Kristy and Tom started toward Jim's room.

"Please, no talking and no touching this time," The nurse re-minded them. "I think that's what set him off. We need to try and keep him quiet and stable until that flight gets here." She turned and walked down the hallway toward the nurse's station. They both took a deep breath and entered the room again. The breathing machine and monitors were all quiet this time.

Tom and Kristy just sat in silence and stared at Jim's lifeless body. Kristy noticed a single tear fall from Jim's eye. It trailed through the dried blood on his temple. Through sobs, she said a little prayer. Her lips motioned out words in complete silence.

About half an hour later, the nurse came back into the room. She motioned to Kristy and Tom, calling them out of the room.

"The flight is here!" She whispered. "We have to get him ready for the move. You will need to keep out of the way. The flight team moves fast!"

As they left Jim's room, the flight staff lined the hallway with their belongings. Each was holding a different monitor. They were all cross-checking and preparing their equipment.

"Mrs. Cavalier?" It was Dr. Schaati's voice.

"We are preparing for the flight. There will be a short ride to the airport in the ambulance. You and James will fly to Spokane," He placed his hand over his heart. "I pray for you that your husband pulls out of this."

Just as Tom and Kristy began to walk towards the exit, Jim's parents entered the emergency room, asking to see their son. They didn't even notice Kristy standing in the waiting room entrance. She stood still, unnoticed, as they rushed by her with the nurse. Kristy stayed her distance as he escorted them to Jim's room.

They do need to see their son before he leaves. It may be the last time any one of them sees Jim alive. Kristy started sobbing again; her head was pounding with every heartbeat.

"I am sorry, Mr. and Mrs. Cavalier," Dr. Shaati joined Jim's parents as they hurried down the hallway. "But your son is very critical. Like I told your Daughter-in-law, this is going to be touch and go for a while."

"I just want to see my baby before you take him," Marlene demanded. "I will make it quick. I just want to tell him how much I love him." She tried to whisper. Her voice was hoarse from crying.

Dr. Schaati led them into Jim's room. Monitors were going off as the nurses were moving swiftly around the room. They were working quietly on the monitors, IV lines, and intubation tubes. They were transferring everything from their equipment to the portable stuff the flight team brought in. When they saw Jim's parents, they all tried to move aside and let them have some time with Jim.

"My God, Jim," his mother whispered. "You will pull through this,

I pray. You are tough like your father! I will pray hard for you. I love you, son." She kissed his cheek. Jim's dad stood back quietly, rubbing her back.

Jim could hear his mother's pleas, but he still was unable to move. He would give anything to hug her right now. To tell her everything will be fine.

If I could just move my arms and open my eyes, you would see that I am okay. Jim's heart rate started to climb.

"I am so sorry, but we need to move James soon." Dr. Shaati broke the silence. "He needs to get to Sacred Heart so that they can save him."

Jim's mother noticed Kristy standing with Tom by the Emergency Room entrance. She walked towards them, her husband's hand around her waist. To Kristy, they looked so old right now.

"Only one person can go on the flight with Jim," The nurse explained to them.

So, they decided that Kristy would go with Jim to Spokane while his parents drove out after they went home and packed. Tom would have Jenni pack up some stuff for Kristy and send it with Jim's parents.

Tom followed the ambulance to the airport. Its lights and sirens were blaring. Barely letting the car come to a complete stop, Kristy quickly jumped out. She glanced into the ambulance where Jim was lying on the gurney. He looked so helpless to her.

The staff cautiously pulled him out of the ambulance and into the waiting helicopter.

Kristy climbed in and sat next to the pilot. He smiled at her and handed her a headset and earmuffs. She put them on immediately.

"Can you hear me?" He asked her.

Kristy nodded her head.

"Great." He explained, "We are heading to Sacred Heart in Spokane. The flight takes just under a half-hour."

The emergency staff quickly settled in with Jim and all the equipment.

Kristy could not hear what was going on in the back, as he could barely see Jim. The seat belt held her securely. She could listen to the pilot and his conversation with the tower. She just sat there in silence. She was looking at the colorful land below, thinking to herself how much Jim would have enjoyed this if he wasn't so sick right now. Fall was his favorite time of year.

8

Sacred Heart

In just under half an hour, the medi-flight landed on the rooftop of Sacred Heart Memorial Hospital. There was another set of staff waiting for Jim's arrival. They quickly moved into position and waited for the helicopter to land. They immediately whisked Jim away without giving Kristy a chance even to see him.

A social worker from the hospital's trauma unit had an armful of papers and a 'welcome kit.' She waited patiently for Kristy to exit the helipad.

She showed Kristy around the trauma unit and where she was going to stay. There were rooms for patients' families just down the hallway from the ICU wing. It had a rec room and a small kitchen area.

Kristy was thankful, but all she wanted to do was see Jim. He needed medical attention immediately, and they wouldn't let her in his room until he was more stable. So, the social worker escorted Kristy to her room at the end of the hallway. She also had highlighted a map to make it easier for Kristy to get around.

Kristy looked at the map. First, she needed something for her headache, so she decided to go to the hospital gift shop to see what they had.

At the gift shop, she bought pills, water, and some protein bars. She brought them back to her room, ate a protein bar, and took much-needed pills. She slammed the entire bottle of water, flopped face-first in her pillow.

I don't think I'm strong enough for this. Kristy cried to herself. *What in the fuck am I supposed to do?*

After crying for quite some time, Kristy finally mustered the energy to get cleaned up and see what was happening to Jim.

The social worker was waiting at the nurses' station. She updated Kristy on Jim's status.

"The doctors have been working to keep Jim stable since he arrived. They have decided to keep him in a drug-induced coma," The social worker communicated. "It was for the best, as Jim's brain needed to rest so it could heal."

Kristy looked through the glass at Jim. The social worker's voice was trailing off. Every once in a while, she would get a glimpse of Jim's lifeless body between the nurses as they worked together to keep Jim alive.

There was so much blood. Kristy thought.

"Kristy?" The social worker's voice broke Kristy's trance.

"I have a personal identification number, or what we call a PIN for you. Now, you can know where your husband is at all times." She pulled James' name up on her computer and wrote the number on a small card. She handed it to Kristy.

"You can use this number on any of the computers throughout the hospital. How to log in is on the back of the card. Try to keep it in a safe place. Through our website, you can access your husband's patient portal. This app will tell you where your husband is if he is gone for tests. It will also tell you what time to expect him back to his room. We have free internet for families of patients staying here. The password is on the back of that card as well. If you have any problems, call the number on the bottom of the card, and someone from our IT department will help you." She smiled at Kristy.

She's a cute girl. Kristy thought.

"You have any questions?"

Kristy shook her head. She was looking at the card, skimming over the instructions.

"Good luck, hun. If you need me, my number is on the board in your room.

Kristy hurried back to her room to load the hospital app on her phone, so she could find out what was going on with Jim.

Kristy fell asleep playing with the app on her phone. When she awoke, it was way before daylight. Kristy had forgotten to shut her blinds, but the sky was still dark. For a moment, she had no clue where she was. Then, her heart sank as she slowly relived the past 24 hours. Kristy quickly got up and put on her clothes and headed towards the nurse's station. All she wanted to know was how Jim was. A different young lady was standing at the desk. She seemed to be in her mid-twenties and had long curly red hair. Her eyes were a beautiful hue of green.

She was rearranging her desk and filing papers. "Good morning." She stated in a cheery voice.

"How may I help you so early today?"

Kristy approached the desk. "My name is Kristy Cavalier. My husband James is on this unit. He was admitted to this unit last night, and I would love to see how he is doing." She forced out a small sleepy smile.

"Of course!" Exclaimed the young redhead. "He's over in trauma room two. Just right there." She pointed over Kristy's shoulder to James' room. "Did someone give you a card with his PIN on it? It can tell you everything from any computer in the hospital."

"Oh, I forgot about the card and PIN," Kristy replied. "Last night, he was having a bunch of tests, so I didn't get to see him. I went to my room and must've fallen asleep. I just woke up and decided to come and make sure he was okay and maybe see him before I get cleaned up and grab some coffee." She started toward his room.

Kristy got to the door and hesitated for a moment before she entered. The housekeepers had tidied up from the night before. Most of the blood was gone, and clean bedding covered his battered body.

Kristy slowly walked up toward the head of Jim's bed. He laid motionless, with only the heaving of his chest from the ventilator. The monitor's soft beeps and the breaths from the ventilator filled the quiet room. Fighting back the tears, Kristy sat quietly and stared at Jim's battered body. He was extremely pale, and his face was so swollen; he was unrecognizable.

Silent. Breath. Silent. Beep.

Suddenly, a Middle Eastern doctor entered Jim's room. He walked towards the opposite side of his bed and looked at all the monitors. He pulled the paper from one of the machines, held it up, and examined it closely. He typed something into one of the computers, walked to the foot of the bed, pulled the covers off Jim's legs, and placed his hands on Jim's ankles. Kristy noticed the large pieces of metal tenting the sheets over Jim's left leg. His swollen feet looked like sausages.

How much fluid can one person hold? Kristy thought.

The doctor walked towards Kristy and smiled.

"Come with me for a moment." He whispered to Kristy in a thick Indian accent. He motioned his hand towards the door.

Kristy followed the doctor into a small room across the hallway. He slowly shut the door behind them.

"You must be Mrs. Cavalier?"

Before Kristy could answer the doctor, there was a slight knock on the door. The redheaded receptionist poked her head into the room.

"I am so sorry to bother you, doctor. But Mr. Cavalier's parents are here."

"Perfect timing! Bring them in; they also need to hear what I have to say." He said as he shuffled through the pile of papers in front of him. He began to type on the computer.

"That way, I do not need to repeat myself," He smiled at Kristy.

The nurse opened the door wider and let in Jim's parents. They looked like they hadn't slept a wink. The stress from the accident was already showing on their faces. They took a seat and anxiously looked over at the doctor. They were silently waiting along with Kristy to hear about Jim's prognosis.

"Hello, my name is Dr. Ambudahl. I am overseeing the care of Mr. Cavalier." The doctor looked around the room, connecting with each person.

"He came to us a very injured man last night. He coded twice on us since his arrival. He has kept my staff very busy through the night." He stared into Kristy's teary eyes. "By this morning, I think we may have finally gotten him stable. He is a fighter!"

Dr. Ambudahl continued to go over all of Jim's injuries and update his condition. He explained to them the plan and expectations. He then reminded them that things were never a guarantee and could change quickly for the good or bad. The only thing that gave them a definite answer would be time.

Dr. Ambudahl walked out of the little room, leaving Jim's family to process the information. It would push them to their limits. Their strong faith in God would carry them through.

"Do you think he will let us see Jim?" Jim's mom asked Kristy, her eyes tear-filled and bloodshot. "I need to see him! I need to touch him!" She looked directly into Kristy's eyes.

"I need to know that he's still alive. I need that hope! He's my only baby, for God's sake!" She started to sob uncontrollably.

"Just, please try not to stimulate him too much until we stabilize him more." Dr. Ambudahl answered, startling them.

"Once he is more stable, we will encourage you to talk and interact with him. He needs to know he has something to fight for. But right now, we need to keep him quiet. At least until we get that blood drained off his brain and some of the swelling under control."

"You have to trust that we are doing our best to help your son. Every hour he makes it through without any setbacks is very promising," Dr. Ambudahl walked back into the little room.

"You can go in and see him for a few more minutes while we set up for the next procedure. Then we will be asking you to leave. Remember, the sooner we get this done, the better James will be."

Kristy and Jim's parents all stood up at the same time. They filed out of the little room and walked across the hallway into Jim's room. He looked so pitiful. The rise and fall of his chest and the heart monitor beeping in a steady tone was almost too much for Jim's mom to take. Kristy's eyes started to fill up with tears.

"I love you. It will be alright," Kristy stated. Her whisper was barely audible. She stood at the head of Jim's bed, allowing Jim's parents to be close to their son.

Jim's parents walked up to his side. His mom just stared pitifully at her broken son. Sobbing, she reached out and placed her hand on Jim's. His dad pulled up a chair for her so she could sit close, leaning over him. She did not say a word as she studied her son's battered, swollen face. She tried to hold back tears. Frank placed his hand on her shoulder. He, too, had tears welling up in his eyes.

Within a few minutes, Dr. Ambudahl and his crew walked back into the room. They were pulling a large cart with instruments wrapped in blue paper. One assistant was busy rearranging the packages while the other stood over a computer, entering data. Dr.

Ambudahl walked up to Jim's bed on the opposite side of his family. He looked at the paper coming from the monitor once again. Then, he typed something into the monitor, turned to Jim's family, and nodded.

"I am sorry, it is time to leave. We need to start this procedure." He whispered.

Jim's dad tugged at his wife's arm. She kissed Jim's limp hand and set it back on the pillow next to his lifeless body. Kristy blew Jim a kiss, and all three walked out of the room. Heads hanging on weary shoulders. The assistant walked over and closed the door behind them.

They all stood in the hallway for a moment in silence.

"I don't know what you two want to do while they are working on Jim, but you are both welcome to come back to my room to rest," Kristy broke the silence. Her speech slowed with exhaustion.

"I need to take a shower and get into some clean clothes."

"I think we will go in and register at one of the Hotels nearby. Then, go and get a bite to eat. Sweetie, why don't you join us?" Jim's mom placed her hand on Kristy's arm.

"I have your bag in the car," Jim's dad added. "Jenni packed some things for you. Why don't you come and grab it? Then, you can go back to your room and rest. You look tired."

Kristy agreed and followed them down to their car. She grabbed her bags, hugging them both, then headed back to her room.

When she got back to the room, Kristy opened her bag and grabbed the pill bottle. She popped two pills in her mouth.

Then, she decided to take a much-needed shower. She went into the bathroom and turned on the water. She stood in the shower, letting the hot water run on her weary body. It felt good. She closed her eyes, remembering their last morning together—the incredible sex in the shower.

Kristy began to sob.

After her shower, Kristy slipped into her clothes from home. The familiar smell comforted her. She laid on the bed, thinking of her and Jim's last day together.

Kristy's stomach began to growl, and she remembered that she needed to get some food in her. She decided to walk to the kitchen and see what was available.

As she walked into the kitchen, Kristy's phone began to ring. She looked at the number and quickly answered.

"Hello?"

"Kristy?" The voice on the other line was the redhead at the nurses' desk from this morning. She had that classic Southern accent.

"This is her," Kristy replied, scared of what the young lady might have to say.

"Dr. Ambudahl is finished with James' procedure and is waiting to talk with you and your in-laws." She stated.

"That was quicker than we thought. I'll be there in one minute." She quickly hung up her phone and began walking over to the nurses' station, leaving her toast in the toaster.

Dr. Ambudahl was standing in the doorway of the little room. Jim's parents were just arriving.

"Hello, Kristy. As I was just telling your in-laws, we successfully took out a fairly large hematoma from James' head. It has brought the pressure in his brain down a bit. That is the best news I have for you so far." He took a deep breath. "This should stabilize him even more. Hopefully, he will start making progress. We still do not know the extent of his head injuries. We will only be able to tell if or when he ever wakes up."

Kristy took in a big sigh. "At least he is stable for now."

"That's good news," Jim's mom also exhaled a big sigh of relief.

"Yes, in a way, it is good. But, he is still not out of the woods. Not yet." The doctor looked around the table, shifting his glance between the three of them. "Every time he has a code, it is a step in the wrong direction. Hopefully, we are now going in the right direction, and his brain can now start healing."

"I want to see him," Jim's mom stood up. Her voice was trembling.

Dr. Ambudahl immediately got up from the table and led the three of them once again across the hallway to Jim.

Kristy entered the room first, followed by Jim's parents holding hands. Jim's mom was holding back sobs. Dr. Ambudahl stood at the doorway as the three of them walked up to Jim's bed.

Kristy sat next to Jim's bed, mindlessly fixated on the rise and fall of his chest. Her mind drifted back to Rob. His beautiful smile, his hazel-brown eyes, and muscular build. All of it was gone. Just like that. Life as she knew it had changed. Forever. Her husband laid in a hospital bed, a helpless frail man. His body was bruised and swollen from injuries. He, too, was circling the edge of death.

Kristy once again started to cry. She leaned over and rested her face in her hands to muffle her sobs. She cried silently for some time, unaware of anyone else around her. The monitors kept beeping in the background.

Jim's parents stood at the foot of his bed, watching and praying that their son would wake up soon. They were eager to put this all behind them. They didn't realize it yet, but this was just the beginning of a very long, uphill road.

9

The Jeep

Tom stopped off at the car garage to where they had towed Jim's Jeep. He talked to the owner and explained why he was there this time.

The owner knew Jim and Tom quite well. They frequently would come by and investigate wreckage from previous accidents. He gave Tom his condolences as they walked over to the crumpled Jeep.

"I was in shock when we got to the accident and saw how mangled the vehicle was." The man stated, "Then when I was told it was Jim's, it shocked me even more. I didn't know if he had survived or not. I kept looking in the paper for something about the accident. Then you showed up. How is Jim? Is he alive?"

Tom told him the details of the accident. How Jim's friend didn't make it, and how critical Jim's injuries were.

When they get to what's left of the Jeep, Tom's heart sank. It was truly amazing that anyone could have survived such a crash. The wrecker had just dropped it off in the back, and no one had been around to go through it yet. They told the garage not to touch it until Tom got here. He needed to grab some of Jim's and Rob's belongings.

Tom got a pit in his stomach, knowing that he was the first one to go through it. But Tom also knew that if the tables were turned, Jim would have done the same thing. Without hesitation. That was what true friends and partners did for each other. They had each other's backs.

The Jeep was pretty mangled. They cut the top off, exposing remnants of the front dashboard. There was dried blood and shattered glass everywhere. A log had pushed the passenger's seat into the back seat, still coated with dried blood and pieces of flesh.

Rob's. Tom thought. *It was where he had taken his last breath.*

Tom had remembered meeting Rob a couple of times when he came home to visit Jim and Kristy. He thought Rob was a cool guy. He had lots of stories of big-city detective work.

The dashboard was almost to the driver's seat. The airbags had deployed, but there was a massive hole from the log that pinned Jim. The steering wheel had been bent up and twisted into a pretzel. Tom had noticed a foul odor coming from inside the Jeep, making him uncomfortable and nauseous. It was the aging stench of blood and flesh.

Tom went to the back end of the Jeep where Jim and Rob's belongings were. Tom was unable to open the hatch, so he decided to smash out the window. Tom unloaded the duffel bags, suitcases, and guns. The last thing was Jim's big green tote. Tom hesitated before he picked it out of the back.

Jim packs like a woman. Tom thought as he tugged as hard as he could pull the heavy trunk out of the window.

He then looked around inside the Jeep one last time. That's when he noticed a dime where Rob's seat was. It had dried blood on it. Tom picked it up and put it in his pocket, remembering Jim's story about the dimes and Heaven.

Maybe Rob's spirit was with Jim, Tom prayed.

On his way out of the junkyard, Tom stopped to thank the owner once again. Then slowly, sadly walked to his squad car and drove off.

When Tom got home, he walked into the house where Jenni was waiting eagerly for his return. Jenni was a native American and belonged to the Nez Perce tribe. Her father was the medicine man and had taught Jenni everything he knew about the native spirits and the many herbs that guided them on their journeys. She was sitting at the table, burning some strange-smelling incense. It was a scent Tom hadn't smelled before. Jenni's dark brown eyes were bloodshot from crying. Somehow, she knew he was coming home with bad news.

"Sorry I'm late, honey." Tom apologized as he walked over and hugged his beautiful wife. He broke down and started to cry.

"I knew it was bad. I have felt it," Jenni looked up, trying to hold back her tears. "I have had the incense burning to help guide their spirits."

"How is Kristy holding up?" Her eyes looked concerned. "My God, she must feel terrified and so alone."

"She will be alright," Tom answered. "She is strong, Jenni. I just hope Jim pulls through this. He is in rough shape. They had to fly him out to Sacred Heart in Spokane."

"I went to Jim's Jeep and picked up Jim and Rob's belongings. I got it all out in the car. I figured Kristy and Jim will want to go through this stuff once they are home, that's if he makes it home." He turned back towards the front door and headed back to his car.

Tom unloaded the squad car, brought the stuff into his basement, and set it in his office. Safe for now. He went up into the living room, where Jenni was now sitting. He told her the details of the accident. Jenni started to sob.

"Jim and Rob seemed so happy and in good spirits at the restaurant today. They kept talking about who was going to get the bigger moose," She wiped away her tears.

"My spirit visited me. It has told me that Jim and Rob's souls have joined," She hugged Tom tightly. "Rob is now Jim's *Weyekin*, his Spirit Guardian. This is rare."

10

Touch and Go

The next few days felt like an eternity to Kristy. Jim was still in a coma, and the doctors wanted to keep him that way for now. They told her that it was to let his body heal and his brain rest. The news brought Kristy down.

She tried to call Tom every day with some kind of report. But in the last couple of days, there was not much change. Jim was stable. Not better, but not worse.

The doctors told Kristy that there were no signs of him waking up anytime soon. Since they took the blood off his brain, he had remained stable. To Kristy and Jim's parents, this was good news. But Kristy somehow thought he would start waking up shortly after this. Now, they told her they didn't know.

Dr. Ambudahl reminded Kristy that it was best Jim remained in a coma until his body had time to heal. If he stayed stable all week, they would bring him back to the operating room and stabilize the fractures in his leg. His jaw fracture didn't displace and was beginning to heal, so they thought of leaving it go. The same went for his ribs.

At this point, Jim's parents decided to go home for now. His mom needed to get her pills filled, and his dad had a doctor's appointment. Besides, they needed to rest in their beds. There was nothing more they could do in Spokane at the moment, and Jim was stable.

As time passed, the lacerations on Jim's body slowly became scars. The bruises faded, and Jim's facial swelling finally started to subside. He was now at least beginning to look like himself once again.

Jim's room started to fill up with cards, letters, and little prayer tokens from family, friends, and coworkers from back home. The flowers were not allowed in the ICU rooms, so Kristy kept them in hers. She would read aloud to Jim every get-well card that came. It made Kristy realize how much everyone around Jim missed and loved him.

Kristy sat at night in Jim's room writing out thank you cards. She read those aloud as well, so Jim was aware of how thankful they were. She couldn't wait until he was awake so she could share all the well wishes with him again. Dr. Ambudahl seemed hopeful that Jim was on the right track to recovery. Kristy respected Dr. Ambudahl and his judgments as he had been upfront and honest with Jim's care so far.

It was almost the end of the week, and Jim had remained stable. As Dr. Ambudahl predicted, they would be bringing him back to the operating room to fix his broken leg the following day. Another step forward in Jim's recovery.

Tom and Jenni decided to come by and visit Kristy while Jim went into surgery. It's just the thing Kristy needed. She had missed seeing her friends back home.

"So, this place is pretty big," Jenni stated, looking around.

"Yes, it took some getting used to. Along with a map in the beginning." Kristy giggled. "But, this hospital runs amazingly. All the staff has been wonderful to us."

Dr. Ambudahl informed Kristy that Jim had made it through the surgery and was being transferred to the recovery room. Once he stabilized, he would be brought back to his room. The first of many surgeries were over.

"Jim is still a very sick man," Dr. Ambudahl reiterated to an anxious Kristy. "He had a minor setback during the operation," He paused. "Jim is still very critical, and we need to remember that. My team and I are doing our best to keep him going in the right direction. But, it is also up to Jim. Please remember that. We can only do what we can do. He needs to fight as well."

Kristy hung up the phone and started to cry again. She relayed the message to Tom and Jenni through sobs.

"Why did God do this to good people? I just don't know how much more I can take." Kristy sounded emotionally drained. Tom walked over and hugged her tightly.

"Jim is strong, Kristy. *You* are strong. You will both get through this. One day you will look back on this day and reflect on all your emotions. Respecting those who are going through the same thing." Jenni walked over and joined Tom and Kristy's hug.

"He will pull through this. My spirit guide has told me this. He has Cavalier blood flowing in his veins. They are strong fighters; he will be fine." Jenni's reassuring voice comforted Kristy. "Unfortunately, this will be your new normal for a while. But Jim will come around, and he will heal. I know this."

Jenni was right. It had become Kristy's 'norm.' The surgeries, the setbacks, the ups, and the downs. But, Kristy was kept busy with visits from friends, coworkers, and Jim's parents.

11

Alternate Plan

Harper laid crumpled and motionless in the mud. The sheet that wrapped even more tightly around her body was now cutting into her and saturated with blood. The two men stood over her lifeless body in shock, staring and hoping she would move.

"Holy fuck, man! What in the fuck did you do?" The older man shouted out in disbelief. "We need to call Syn! He's gonna be pissed! He's gonna fucking kill us!"

The younger man, ignoring him for a moment, reached down to feel for a pulse on the girl's bloody wrists. He felt nothing. He put his shaking hand over her chest, trying to feel her chest rise—still no sign of life. The girl was not breathing. She was dead.

"FUCK!" He shouted, his voice ringing through the thick woods.

Syn's phone rang. It was one of his men from the shack out west.

The man sounded hysterical. He was trying to explain what happened to the blonde girl. Syn began to rage, his face turning a bright red.

"What in the fuck do you mean the blonde girl is dead? You stupid fucks! She was my money out of here!!!" Syn roared. His voice was barely audible.

There was a long pause.

Finally, the man tried again to explain. "We were loading her up in the van. The bitches kept trying to run! I had to hit one of them pretty hard to keep her still. We finally got the blonde into the van and were leaving. That's when that stupid bitch decided to kick the van door open! It all happened so fast. She just flipped out and slid under the wheel before I could stop! There was nothing we could do!" The man's voice was shaking, and Syn could tell he was scared.

Good. You should be scared. Syn thought. *I should just kill you instead!*

"We did get some good pictures of her before we left the shack, though. It's still possible to pull it off, man."

"Nobody needs to know she died." He reassured Syn.

Syn took a deep breath. *How in the hell am I going to pull something like this off?* He thought.

He had no choice. The rich girl was gone. He could still try to get the ransom, somehow. Maybe by selling the other girl?

He was right. No one knew the girl was dead.

Syn had to figure out a way to fool her parents and get the damn money. At this point, all he wanted to do was get the hell out of America and not look back.

"Let me think about this, and I'll call your dumb-fucking ass back."

Syn hung up the phone and threw it across the room. It bounced off the couch, landing on the floor. A young girl who was sitting on the sofa looked up at him, terrified. She was tied and gagged. She wasn't going to be alone for long. Syn had more girls coming in over the next few weeks. He was busy making arrangements with a ship that was leaving port next month.

The ship would pick up some shipping crates, and Syn had his loaded with precious cargo. Girls. Syn had a quota to fill. The last one before he disappeared off the face of the Earth.

But now Aziz and his buddy had fucked that one up.

The plan had been to get the rich blonde to the meeting point where he could collect the ransom. Now, the girl's untimely death had ruined that.

The initial plan had been to get that ransom money. Now, with the girl dead, Syn had to come up with an alternate plan.

The good thing was that the ship wasn't due at the port for another couple of weeks or so. It gave Syn time to continue collecting more girls. Once this deal was all said and done, Syn would have his money and be gone. Out of this lucrative business for good.

But the rich girl wasn't supposed to fucking die. Syn grumbled to himself. *We will need another girl, one who looks like that blonde.* He thought. *At least they got some pictures of her before she died. If anything, that may buy us some time.*

Syn pulled a phone out of his pocket. He started going through its contacts. Until one caught his eye. He opened her profile information. She was someone not too far away from where the shack was. She was a girl he had been in contact with for a few weeks. She was his closest match, looking a lot like that rich blonde. With her, he might be able to pull this ransom off yet! After purchasing her father's van, he usually liked to groom them longer, but this could not wait.

This one was going to be a little riskier, though. Having been homeschooled, the blonde rarely went anywhere and had very few friends. Her only friends and contacts were within her church community. Syn kept watching her, though. Just in case he needed her. He would wait for the perfect opportunity.

Today, that opportunity had come. The girl had informed Syn that her mother had just given birth. It meant she would be alone, watching over her siblings and taking care of the house chores. Now that he needed her, Syn kept a closer watch. If he wanted to take this girl, he would have to make his move within the next 24 hours.

Weeks earlier, the blonde girl had lost her cell phone at the park when she was there with her siblings. Their mom had a prenatal appointment with her midwife at the hospital. It was supposed to be a home birth, but the baby was breech. The midwife wanted her to come in for some tests and talk about a cesarean section. The blonde promised her little brothers and sisters that she would bring them to get some ice cream and go to the park while mom was at her appointment.

Syn happened to be driving through town simultaneously and recognized the family playing in the park. The pretty blonde girl sat at a picnic table on her phone, watching her siblings play on the monkey bars. He decided to pull over and observe them. Study them.

Her mom had come out of the clinic entrance and called for the children. They all went running back to their car, including the cute blonde, without her phone. Lucky for Syn, she had left it on the table where she was sitting.

Syn waited for them to drive off before he walked up and grabbed the phone. It was a simple cell phone, straightforward to collect the information he needed. He then added himself as one of her church group contacts before he returned it to her.

After looking everywhere for the phone, she finally found it lying between the counsel and the car seat.

It had been perfectly placed by Syn the day before.

A week went by before Syn decided to contact her. The girl was stressed out and feeling all alone. It was perfect timing for Syn. She needed someone to talk to, someone who listened to her without making judgments. She quickly replied to Syn's text. Soon after, they began to chat on the phone. She mostly talked as he listened. Syn was a good listener. You could even ask Harper if she was still alive.

This new blonde was yet another lost soul Syn was about to collect.

Never questioning who he was, the girl could see he was a member of her church's extended congregation. They had teen group chats just for this type of situation. So, it was not unusual to seek counsel from a member from across the country. That was what kept this congregation so close.

Not in a million years, she would have ever believed that the young college student who purchased her father's van for his fraternity brothers contacted her. It would be the farthest thing from her mind. But, a congregation member reaching out to talk was not abnormal. Their church was huge, and its members were all over the country. This boy could have been someone she had met on one of their missionary trips. The contacts in the phone were put in by the elders and monitored. So this boy must be safe to talk with. Or so she thought.

She doesn't ever remember meeting Syn, but he remembered her. Apparently, at a church convention some time ago. Syn had stolen a name from her contacts and made it his number. Lucky guess. This boy had met her this past summer at a bible camp in Ohio. He told her he remembered her as the cute blonde. Quiet and shy. He liked that about her.

How long would it take before her family would miss her? Syn thought.

Once Syn had filled his quota of girls, he no longer needed this blonde. But, he did take a liking to her. She could be his.

Why risk something like that? Syn decided to stop all contact.

But, it was the girl who continued to call and text Syn. *She* wouldn't stop. So, after a couple of weeks of silence, she decided to send out one last text to Syn. Again, perfect timing.

Her luck had just run out.

Syn replied.

It didn't take long, and his phone rang. It was the blonde girl.

"Hey." Her voice cracked on the other end of the line.

"Hello, pretty lady," Syn chuckled. *If you were smart, you wouldn't have called me back. But now I know you are desperate.*

"I need to talk to you," The voice on the other end sounded like she had been crying. "Can we meet somewhere so that we can talk? Face to face?"

Syn could not believe what he was hearing.

"Of course, where would be the easiest place for you? Remember, I live a couple of hours away," He responded anxiously.

There was a long pause on the other end of the line. Syn started to panic.

"Want to meet at Mount Pleasant Pier tomorrow night?" She finally whispers back in a shaky voice.

Syn could feel her voice trembling, and this made him smile.

"Absolutely, doll. What time?"

12

The Connection

Jim couldn't move. He kept looking into the bright blue light for Rob. With Harper at his side. He searched, trying to look past the light, ignoring the girl. The light was so bright that his eyes started to burn.

"*What 'cha lookin' for?*" Rob's voice rang in Jim's ears. Jim spun around, searching for Rob.

"*Rob? Where are you? Where am I?*" Jim could hear his voice, but he didn't open his mouth. *Was this just a thought? I don't even feel myself breathing. I don't feel the vibration of my voice leaving my lips. What was this? Am I dreaming? Am I dead?*

"*Where do you think we are?*" Rob's voice again rang out in Jim's head.

"*We were in a bad accident, Rob.*" Jim looked ahead. The white, blue, and green lights seem to be endless. "*I have a feeling this was the light we've heard about.*"

"*You are right, buddy. It is where Heaven starts.*" Rob's familiar shape manifested out of the brightness. Jim focused on the beautiful blue and orange mist of the auras surrounding Rob.

Jim smiled, happy to see his friend.

"Why are we able to talk to each other without moving our lips?" Jim asked, confused. *"Am I dead?"*

"No, buddy, you are very much alive and will live a long life. But my life ended today, my friend." Rob walked close to Jim; his eyes were a blinding blue. *"But, as you live on, you will need to fight for your life. You are strong, Jim, and your will to live is just as strong. HE has told me so. You have a job to do back there on Earth. My job is to stay here and help you. Jim, your soul has been chosen by Him to bond with ours. Our souls had been lost and needed your help. Harper and I are now your spirit guardians. You see, Jim, when our souls left our bodies, they joined with yours. Somehow, this bond was meant to be."*

"He has a plan for us."

"But you, my friend, are not ready to go. You fought too hard, showing Him that your soul is powerful. Are you familiar with the beliefs that your grandfather taught you? They can be very beneficial. You proved to Him that you were able to handle those special powers He has given you. Powers so strong, very few have understood them. Remember how your grandfather talked to you about the afterlife? He taught you how to listen with your heart, and this has made your soul strong with Him."

"You can help the lost souls up here, Jim. You have seen all that is here. You know all that is here. You know things that will help you and others on Earth. You will be able to tell their stories. You have given the lost souls here a chance to be found and, finally, be put to rest. Every soul deserves to rest."

"You will have to learn how to channel each other's energy." Jim noticed the girl was still standing alongside him. She looked up at him and smiled. Her aura melded into his, like liquid smoke dancing over a fire.

"Remember, I will forever stay inside you. Our souls have bonded.

Harper and I are forever with you. Jim, you must learn from us. Listen to us. I will be there in your heart, helping you." Rob tapped the left side of his chest over his heart. Orange aura rings drifted off his chest and around his fist.

"*I have been chosen for you because you guided my life's soul on Earth. Now, it's my job to guide you from Heaven. It is my purpose.*" Rob's voice trailed off as he turned and walked away, disappearing into the bright light.

"*You still have more to do on Earth. You have more purpose. I will be there to help you.*"

"*And who is this girl?*" Jim asked.

"*Harper,*" Rob replied. "*Somehow, she needed you first. I can feel her trying to tell you this. Listen, Jim. Listen with your heart and open your soul up to hers. But first, you need to get better.*" Rob's voice began fading away.

"*It's time to start fighting, buddy!*"

13

Awakening

Kristy had been in her room watching the news when a flash came across the screen. It was about the two young girls missing from Myrtle Beach and how they had disappeared around the same time as Jim's accident. One of the girls had been the daughter of local millionaire Bradley Bengston. No one knew where they were. They were supposed to go to the movies and never made it back to the girlfriend's home.

The girlfriend's mother was working a busy midnight shift at the hospital. She didn't know they were missing until she got home and found that there had been no sign of the girls. The story had captivated the entire Nation's interest.

Kristy had tuned in every day to see if there had been any leads. It had kept her mind off of her situation. There were people out there like her, suffering their tragedies.

The bulletin stated that one of the girl's phones had been found! They were not saying much about the find at this point. Kristy hoped it contained some information that may give them a break in the case! The authorities were now going to find out which girl's phone it was and who she had come in contact with. This find could be a significant lead in a month-long investigation.

The following day, Kristy's phone rang quite early. It was Dr. Ambudahl. Kristy picked it up immediately and slid her finger over the glass to answer it.

"Good morning, Kristy," Dr. Ambudahl greeted her in a cheerful voice. "I am calling you with some good news. The best news I have given so far!"

Kristy reached over and hit the mute button on the TV remote.

"As you know, we have backed off on the medicines that were keeping Jim in his coma," There was a slight pause. "Jim is waking up, Kristy. Soon we will know more about how he is recovering."

"Oh my God," She exclaimed excitedly! "I will be right down!"

Dr. Ambudahl's voice echoed in Kristy's head:

"Now remember, Jim has been in a coma for over five weeks. His short and long-term memory may be jumbled. He may not remember you. Don't expect him to hold a conversation with you. He may not be able to talk for a while. He is going to have to learn how to do that, along with walking and eating all over again."

Kristy tried to understand. She knew it would be a long recovery once Jim woke up, but nothing could prepare her for what lay ahead.

The social worker had talked to Kristy about some cases where patients have woken up from a coma. How they behaved, and how the families dealt with it. To prepare Kristy for what to expect. But this was Kristy's story. Kristy's husband. It was their life now and their future together in sickness and in health.

"So, you're telling me, he may be like a child again?" She asked.

"Yes." Dr. Ambudahl answered, escorting Kristy to Jim's room. "We won't know the extent of his brain damage-if any until he fully awakens and begins to communicate."

For over four weeks, Kristy had walked the hospital halls in

Spokane, Washington. She had memorized every picture and knew every worker on the unit's schedule. She would sit for hours every day looking at Jim's sleeping body and watching his chest rise and fall with every breath the machine took for him. His cuts started healing, the bruises fading, and the broken bones mending. Coming in every morning, sometimes noticing a tube or machine absent, knowing his time asleep was coming to an end. She was praying that he would remember her.

That time had come today, October 11th. His new birthday, the day God gave Jim his life back.

Kristy slowly entered Jim's room and quietly walked to the head of the bed. Most of the machines are gone now. The only thing remaining was his IV line and heart monitor.

Jim's eyes were closed, and he was resting quietly. Kristy just stared, waiting for Jim to wake up and strike up a conversation with her. Dr. Ambudahl did tell her that he may never be able to talk or communicate again. She had to prepare herself for that as well.

But, what if when he sees her, he just strikes up a conversation? What if he asks her how her day was? Or her week? Or a month? Kristy prayed. *Please wake up and talk to me, Jim.*

Jim slowly opened his eyes. He stared forward, not noticing Kristy standing beside his bed. He just kept staring ahead. As if in a trance.

Kristy's face lit up when she noticed Jim.

"Hello, honey!" Kristy said quietly, grabbing Jim's hand. Happy tears started to roll down her cheeks. She tried to blink them away.

Jim turned his head towards the voice. He rolled his eyes slowly until they met with hers. Jim looked tired. He didn't blink or show signs of emotion. His glare fixated on Kristy's. Neither move for some time. It was almost like time stood still.

"It's your wife, Kristy," She broke the silence. "You have been in a terrible accident. I miss you. I love you, Honey. Jim?" She was in a full cry now. She struggled to stop. She held his hand, and buried her head into their hands, and cried.

Jim closed his eyes and took a few deep breaths. Then he again opened his eyes and studied her face. Still, there was no emotion. He took another deep breath. His toneless glare fixated on the blonde-haired girl standing behind Kristy.

Harper?

Kristy's voice broke the silence once again.

"I've been here by your side, waiting for you to wake up. The trees are starting to drop their leaves. Fall is here! Your mom and dad have been coming up to see you once a week. They will be happy to hear how well you're doing."

She took a deep breath, remembering Rob. She would keep that from him for now. She wanted to let him absorb where he was, who she was, and what had happened. He was still healing, both mentally and physically.

Dr. Ambudahl walked in with one of the nurses.

"He has been awake off and on since I first checked in on him at 6 am," The nurse reported. "He has not spoken yet, but he seems to be able to track us as we move around his bed to check his vitals and IV," She stated. "He does not seem to understand any commands. He may have some hearing impairment. It's too early to tell."

"I will put in an order for speech, OT, PT neurology along with an audiology consult. We will need to come up with a care plan once we find out how much he can communicate and understand."

"Welcome to Sacred Heart in Spokane. I am Dr. Ambudahl." He smiled at Jim. "You have been in an accident and have just woken up from a coma. You have been asleep for almost five weeks."

Dr. Ambudahl looked at Kristy. "Does he seem to recognize you?"

"No," Kristy shook her head, wiping the tears away. "He just stares at me."

"Yes, this is what I told you might happen. We never know what to expect from patients when they wake up from a coma. Each case is different. No matter how long they are out, days, weeks, or months. It is all a guessing game," He typed something into the computer. "Jim will need extensive therapy. We will figure out what he can do with these upcoming evaluations I have ordered. In a few days, we will sit you with the therapist, neurologist, and physiatrist. We will come up with a plan. He will start therapy right away and plans to move him to a rehab facility closer to your home will be made. Then, you will be able to get back to your life at home. You can start to make plans to prepare for his homecoming," He smiled. "He will be home sooner than you think, Kristy."

Kristy took a deep breath and held onto Jim's hand.

"That is good, hey Honey," Kristy turned to her husband and attempted to force a smile.

Jim looked up at her with no facial expression, no answer. Tears were still fresh in her eyes. She was just happy that he was awake and making forward progress.

"Tom and Jenni send their prayers," Kristy informed him. She hoped that by mentioning their names, Jim might start to remember something. "You have a lot of people back home who are worried about you. People have been calling and sending cards, gifts, and letters. There is a prayer chain at church," Her stare didn't leave his blank eyes. "I will read them all to you," She began to fight back the tears. "I hope you know what I am saying and remember who I am, Jim. It has been a long time here, and I would like to bring you home soon and get our lives back on track." She reached for his hand.

"Please, Jim, squeeze my hand if you understand me." She anxiously held his hand and waited. Jim stared at her for a long time, emotionless.

Jim ever so slightly squeezed his wife's shaking hand. She gasped, and tears started flowing down her cheeks again.

"I love you, Jim," She sobbed.

'*Harper.*' Jim replied in his mind.

14

Jim's Future

Over the next two weeks, Jim was moved from the Trauma/ICU unit to step-down, then over to the medical floor, where he remained for the rest of his stay.

Dr. Ambudahl briefed Kristy on Jim's progress daily, and she continued to pray with Jim. Jim just stared at Kristy as if he had never seen her before.

Kristy had an appointment scheduled with Dr. Ambudahl and his medical team by the end of the week. That was the moment she had been waiting for for weeks! A plan to go home!

As Kristy entered the little room off the nurses' station, she noticed the social worker and Dr. Ambudahl reviewing paperwork. As she took a seat, she listened to the staff talk amongst themselves about Jim's progress and what was expected before he left. After a few minutes, a therapist had entered the room and took a seat.

"Okay, everyone is all here," The social worker introduced everyone to Kristy, and they quickly started the meeting.

"The first thing I want to remind you is that Jim is a very, very lucky man. He has survived a horrific car accident and is awake from a 5-week long coma." Dr. Ambudahl began. He picked up a stack of papers and started thumbing through them. "Jim's CT shows that he had some facial trauma around his left eye and jawbone. I am glad to say that in comparison to the previous CT, he is healing amazingly well." The doctor looked up at Kristy. "I am not sure how much he can see out of that left eye. But it seems that Jim is responding well to visual aids and speech. Jim entered this journey a strong, healthy man. It was a good thing that he had been as active as he was. It may have saved his life. Jim's determination so far was incredible. He is getting stronger every day. All which are promising signs that his stay here will be coming to an end."

"They have decided not to fix Jim's fractured jaw as it has healed nicely in a good position. He will need dental implants to replace the teeth he lost. Eventually, the scars will fade even more." The doctor looked up from his paperwork and peered over towards Kristy.

"As I said before, he is one lucky man."

Dr. Ambudahl pulled Jim's MRI up on his laptop and reviewed it with Kristy. He pointed out a spot on the scan. "The brain is the most sensitive part of the human body," he explained. "See this tiny spot on the sensory cortex? I'm not sure what it is, but we need to keep an eye on it. It was the most damaged part of Jim's brain," Dr. Ambudahl expressed his concern. "Jim has come a long way but also has a very long road ahead of him. He will need you, Kristy, on this challenging journey." He closed his laptop.

"I will order another scan of his brain before Jim leaves. I will send the images on a CD with you, so you can follow up back home. We will not know how much it has affected him until Jim starts to communicate more with you and the therapists." Dr. Ambudahl encouraged Kristy to talk with Jim. "Try to get him to respond by giving him simple tasks or asking him simple questions. Like where he is or who you are. Little things like that. It might take time, but you will be surprised one day. Jim might just answer you!"

Kristy tried to be positive, up to this point, there had been no response to questions. The only thing was the slight squeeze of Kristy's hand a couple of days ago. She was even starting to think that was just a muscle reaction.

"Have you been reading Jim's cards to him?" Dr. Ambudahl asked Kristy

"Yes. He watches me, and I assume he is listening. I explain who each card is from and how he knows them."

"Perfect, that's what you should be doing!"

Kristy was elated at the news. She could not wait to get Jim back home. The team decided that once Jim was stable enough to start inpatient physical, occupational, and speech therapies, they would transfer him to a rehab facility closer to home. They had great support from family and friends in the community. Bringing Jim home may help stimulate him to remember more and more about who he was.

Dr. Ambudahl reminded Kristy that Jim would probably suffer from some form of post-traumatic stress disorder caused by his accident. He also mentioned that Jim might have nightmares or even act out with fear or rage. Anything might set him off, and with brain injuries, no one knew when or if these outbursts would happen. The doctor warned her that Jim might not understand what was happening and that her attempts to calm him may become a difficult task. The team educated Kristy on how to handle certain situations if, and when Jim presented them. She was reminded that this might be too big of a burden to take on alone. But, Kristy informed the doctor and medical team that they had support from their family and friends.

"All this is good news, so far," Dr. Ambudahl stated, pleased with

Kristy's answers. "Let's give him another week and see how he progresses. We will meet here in a week and decide from there."

As everyone left the room, Kristy stayed trying to absorb what the medical staff had just told her about her husband. Even after six weeks, it still all seemed surreal. She decided to stop by Jim's room before heading to hers. Tonight, she needed to make a few phone calls and update Jim's parents and their friends.

"Hello, handsome." She greeted Jim as he lay motionless, staring at her as she walked up to him. She forces a smile, leans in, and kisses his forehead.

"The doctors say you are ahead of progress and might be moving to Bonner Rehab soon. Doesn't that sound great?!" She peered deeply into his steel-blue eyes. His lips moved slightly into a smile.

"Jim? Do you understand me?" She pushed the table out of her way and sat on the side of his bed. She locked her stare with him, her eyes filling up with tears. He stared back. Like he was studying her. There seemed to be something different in his stare, almost like he understood.

"Do you want to go home?"

Again, the corners of Jim's mouth slightly twinge upward. It was small but still a smile. Kristy started to cry.

"We have been here so long. I want to go home and sleep in my bed." She grabbed his hand. "I want you to come home and sleep in our bed with me."

His grip tightened around her hand. It was still slight, but enough so Kristy felt it. She tightened her grip as well. There was a long moment of silence. Each unable to look away. Jim smiled again. This time it was a little bigger. Kristy knew he understood!

* *

Kristy decided to eat lunch with Jim, updating him on everything happening at home. She informed him that his parents finally sold their house and were busy moving into their condo.

"Being in town will be so much better for them."

"Oh, and Tom and Jenni were busy with their restaurant. It was a popular place in town now for dinner. Weekends were by reservation only. They had a special dinner waiting for you when you get well enough to eat out."

Jim just stared intensely at Kristy's sandwich as she told him story after story about the past six weeks in between bites. She finally realized that he hadn't moved his eyes off her sandwich.

"I bet you would like to have a bite of my sandwich, huh?" She asked, waving what wain ts left of it in the air. "Chicken breast sandwich with American cheese and lettuce." She described it, knowing that this was one of his favorites. Jim licked his lips, almost like he understood.

"That's what I thought." She smiled at Jim. "We will ask the occupational therapist when he comes to feed you when they plan on removing your feeding tube," She finished her sandwich. "When you are ready, I will make you the biggest, freshest chicken sandwich you can ever imagine!" She smiled again; Jim smiled back. His front teeth were gone.

Kristy decided to gather some more cards and letters from friends and family at home. She figured the more that she read to Jim, the more he would find the determination to get stronger so they could go home. She stopped by the kitchen for a soda and headed down to Jim's room. The patient portal said he was done with his MRI and back in his room.

She entered the room. Jim was sleeping. She quietly shuffled through the cards, carefully arranging them in the order she would be reading them to him.

Dr. Ambudahl entered the room. He motioned for Kristy to come over to him so he could speak with her. She immediately jumped up and headed towards the door. They go into the little room across the hallway.

"Jim has made amazing progress." He informed Kristy. "I think we will progress him slowly to oral food. Maybe now is the time to arrange for the oral surgeon to start the dental implants before he leaves here."

"Let's get this done. We are both getting a little homesick."

The two of them walked out. Kristy headed back to Jim's room, Dr. Ambudahl over to the nurses' station to schedule a consultation with the oral surgeon.

As Kristy entered Jim's room, he was now awake. He smiled at her as if he recognized her. *That was a good sign,* she thought to herself.

"Hello, honey. I just spoke with Dr. Ambudahl. He was pleased with your progress. He ordered a consultation with an oral surgeon. He will fix your teeth, so you will be able to eat real food." She pointed to her front teeth.

Jim's eyebrows lifted. He understood more today. He smiled and slowly brought his hand up to his mouth. He was feeling the emptiness where he once had teeth.

Kristy sat next to Jim and started reading the letters. After reading a few of them, she turned to Jim, looking at her with enlightenment. Kristy got closer to Jim's face. She stared into his eager eyes.

"Can you talk?" She asked.

There was a long moment of silence.

'Can you talk,' Jim slowly processes her words...*Can I talk?* No one has asked him yet. Can I *talk?*

Jim opened his mouth. He struggled to say something.

"Aagrah" was all that came from his mouth.

Kristy pulled away from Jim. She was shocked, and tears automatically started to flow.

"Oh my God, you can understand me! You are trying to speak!" She gasped.

15

Farewell Sacred Heart

The past week seemed to fly by quickly. Much faster than Kristy thought it would. Jim had his dental implant screwed in place and was now starting on oral foods. The therapist worked with Jim very hard so he could go to Bonner Rehab soon.

The days went by fast now that Jim was awake. As each day passed, Jim became more and more alert. He slowly started to recognize Kristy and the staff that worked closely with him.

"Hello, friend," Dr. Ambudahl walked into Jim's room and sat on the edge of his bed. "You are the one person we here at Sacred Heart will be talking about for a very long time. You, my friend, have cheated death and have jumped hurdles in your recovery here," He smiled. "I hope you have a full recovery back home. You have a wonderful wife that loves you dearly," He stood up and turned back to Jim. "I trust that you will be in excellent hands at Bonner Rehab. They will be in close contact with me, and if there is anything I can do to aid in your recovery, I will do my best to assist. Good luck on your path to better health."

Before he broke into tears, Dr. Ambudahl turned and walked out of Jim's room.

Jim sat in silence, looking around the room. Bright signs, banners, and cards of every size and color filled the walls. There was a card on the corner of the corkboard that caught his eye. It was in the shape of an angel's wings. He stared at it intently. He wanted to know who sent him that card and what they wrote on the inside.

When the beautiful woman who called herself his wife came back, he would try to tell her about that card. By the time she entered the room, told him her name, and kissed him, he had forgotten about the card. She made him feel good, and her touch left him with butterflies in his stomach. Whatever that meant, it was a damn good feeling!

Jim waited for Kristy to come every morning. He longed for her kisses. Sometimes she kissed him on the forehead, but sometimes it was on the cheek. That was when he got a warm feeling tingling into his belly. Jim's heart skipped a beat with her soft touch. He especially liked it when she read the cards to him and explained who everyone was.

He wished she would read the one with Angel's wings on it if he could only tell her. He thought.

Jim closed his eyes and listened to Kristy's voice telling him How the guys at the station couldn't wait for him to return. She talked about their close friends, Tom and Jenni, and how they wished him well. Jim started to drift off to sleep.

That's when he heard Rob's voice for the first time since he woke up back on Earth.

We need to talk, buddy. There are things I need to tell you. It's about Harper and Carmen. Then, just like that, all of a sudden...A flash...A man screaming.....A loud bang!

Jim screamed, opening his eyes wide just as the therapist entered the room holding a cup of water. He jumped back, spilling it all down the front of his shirt.

"Are you okay, Jim?" He asked, brushing himself off. "I am Adam, your therapist, and you are at Sacred Heart, Spokane. It is Thursday at about noon. You have been in a car accident. I am helping you learn how to eat and communicate." He walked over to Jim's bed and pulled up a table.

Haven't I heard all that before? This guy, Adam, repeats himself daily. Jim thought.

"Today, I have some yogurt for you. Kristy, your wife, said this is your favorite flavor." He held up the container.

Blueberry. Jim thought.

"Blueberry, with fruit on the bottom, all it was missing was the granola on top. Adam loaded a spoonful and offered it to Jim. He slowly reached for the spoon.

The therapist sat with Jim helping him eat his yogurt. He tried to sit up more in his bed; he was feeling stronger. Pretty soon, this bed will not keep him contained.

"Do you want to get up, Jim?" The therapist asked as he prepared his gait belt around Jim's waist. I can help you. The therapist helped Jim sit up on the side of his bed. Feeling a little dizzy, Jim closed his eyes.

"Take your time, Jim." The therapist reiterated. "We are in no hurry to go anywhere."

The therapist helped Jim slowly attempt to stand. His legs began to wobble as he kept his head held high and back straight. He was being coached by the therapist the entire time. Jim felt himself starting to blackout with exhaustion and sat back onto his bed.

Kristy watches in the doorway.

"You did awesome work today!" The therapist was elated.

He stood on shaking legs while the therapist stood alongside him. 'Stand tall, chin up high' was all he heard. It was a quick second and back on the bed. But Jim had done it.

As Jim slid back into bed, beads of sweat appeared on his forehead. Jim was exhilarated and exhausted, all at once. After the therapist settled him back into his bed, Jim pushed his head into his pillow and closed his eyes. He was gasping to catch his breath.

Kristy had tears in her eyes. Her husband stood!

Each day after that, the therapists work intensely with Jim. He was getting stronger; he was listening eagerly and following verbal cues well.

One morning while waiting for Kristy, he looked over at the corkboard. It was empty. *What happened to all the cards? Did I imagine them? Like I sometimes imagined seeing Rob and that little blonde-haired girl, Harper?*

The cards were real. The one with the angel wings in the corner was real, too. Jim knew this because Kristy read them to him. But she never noticed Rob and the little blonde girl standing by his bed.

So, what did this all mean? Jim thought. All this left Jim feeling very confused.

* *

The morning of Jim's last day was finally here, and there was so much commotion. His room was empty. Kristy worked hard for two whole days packing things up. Jim was excited to go to Bonner Rehab. Soon his life would be getting back to normal.

"Hello, honey." She smiled. "Are you ready for the big move to Bonner Rehab?" She grabbed his hand. "Everyone is ready to see you! They can't wait to come to visit you!"

"Yes," Jim responded slowly. He knew this was a good thing. Jim squeezed her hand and smiled. He was ready for the next step in his journey. As ready as anyone who had been through the same thing would be.

When Dr. Ambudahl walked into the room, he was pleased to see Jim sitting on the side of his bed, getting ready for his discharge. He walked over and stood directly in front of Jim.

"Jim, you have been one amazing patient here. You seem to understand more and more every day. I wish you well on your journey to a complete recovery," He smiled.

"Here are his discharge papers," Dr. Ambudahl handed a thick pile of papers to Kristy.

"I am giving you some pills to help you relax, Jim." He held the cup up to Jim's lips and dumped them into his mouth. He then handed Jim a glass of water. Jim took it and washed the pills down.

"We are happy to see you come such a long way. We hope you and your lovely wife have a beautiful, long journey together," He paused. "Take care of yourself, and if you are ever in this area, please stop by. I would love to see you!" He took Jim's hand and shook it.

Jim looked up at the doctor and took a deep breath.

"Thannk yyyyyou." He stuttered softly.

Dr. Ambudahl looked a little shocked. "My God, you are one amazing man! It has been my pleasure to take care of you. Again, please stop by if you are ever in our area, I would love to see how much progress you will make." He turned and walked out of the room.

The nurse entered shortly after and handed Kristy Jim's discharge paperwork to sign.

"You guys are all set to go!" She announced. "Karin, the social worker will follow you out to your car.

Kristy wheeled Jim out to the carport with the therapist and social worker at their side.

"It has been one helluva roller coaster ride, Andy. Thanks." Kristy hugged the therapist and kissed his cheek. "You are an amazing therapist, and I am glad you were on our team."

Kristy turned towards the social worker. She forced a smile as tears built up in her eyes.

"Karin, I feel like we have become good friends. I will keep all of you updated on Jim's progress." She gave the social worker a tight hug. It felt so bittersweet to them both.

The ambulance drivers loaded Jim into the vehicle. The doors slowly closed, and they drove off. Jim and Kristy waved until the hospital was out of sight. Karin and Andy waved back. Ther home was now just over an hour and a half away.

16

Bonner Rehab

Jim's parents and the small staff welcomed his arrival at Bonner Rehab Facility. Kristy was pleased to have Jim only half an hour's ride from home now. Jim's parents met Kristy in the Emergency waiting room. They were just as excited as Jim and Kristy.

Once Jim was resting comfortably, Jim's parents gave Kristy a ride home. Their home where she hadn't been since that dreaded day of Jim's accident. She was anxious to get back to a somewhat normal routine.

The ride seemed shorter than Kristy remembered. But she didn't care. Kristy walked up to the front door and slid her key in the lock, happy to finally be home. Slowly she opened the front door and inhaled the familiar smell of home! A scent she hasn't experienced since the accident. It brought back a lot of memories. She started to cry as she entered her home. Alone.

Kristy walked over to the kitchen table. Stacks of mail littered one end of her bar top.

My God, Kristy thought. She had forgotten all about the mail. *Hopefully, someone has been going through it.*

Jim's mom's attempt was organized by Junk mail, bills, and notices. Kristy was thankful for Jim's parents. They kept things together at home while Kristy could be with Jim.

That night, Kristy went through most of the mail and filed what she needed to. She wrote checks for what bills had come in.

When she finished, she put the radio on low and sat at her bar drinking a glass of wine. Being the first glass since before the accident, it tasted amazing. She remembered the last night she drank, how tipsy she had gotten. It was the last night she and Jim made love.

Kristy closed her eyes, reminiscing about their last night in the house together. She finished the first glass and immediately poured herself a second one. It hit her pretty hard. Afterward, she shuffled off to bed to call it a night. She sank into her cotton sheets, burying her head into her pillow, inhaling the familiar smell that comforted her. The bed had never felt so good!

The following day, Kristy relaxed, watching the news drinking coffee in her favorite recliner. She was happy knowing that Jim was just a half-hour drive away. So close to home, it seemed unreal.

The news had something brief about the missing teens from Myrtle Beach. It had been over a little over a month, and there were no new leads. Right now, the only information the news was giving out was that the two girls never made it to the movies. They may have met up with someone that they met at the beach the day they went missing. Their bikes were found in a bicycle rack at a local park, undamaged. There had been no obvious signs of a fight.

Kristy grabbed another cup of coffee and sat in front of the TV. She couldn't imagine how the girls' parents felt right now. The story had taken Kristy's mind away from what she had been going through. At least she still had Jim. The girls' parents may never see their daughters ever again.

How sad was that, she thought.

The local news team had gathered outside of The Bengston's home. They were trying to leave their home as a reporter approached them asking questions about their daughter and friend. The mother had been crying. Her makeup was running down her face.

The father put his hand up and turned toward the cameras.

"I'm sorry, we cannot tell you anything just yet. I will be talking to reporters later this week about what we have found out regarding the cell phone." He stepped into the black limousine. The driver shut the door and pulled out of the driveway.

What about the other girl's mother? Kristy thought. *Was she suffering alone?*

Kristy noticed that the news never showed or mentioned her, only a few times in the beginning. No one knew much about Carmen other than a few pictures of the girls together.

How sad, Kristy thought. *That poor mom must be scared to death.*

Kristy got up and got ready to go to the hospital. She was anxious to see how Jim had done during the night. Her routine at Sacred Heart was to visit him right after breakfast. She wondered if he would be expecting her. At least, that was what she was hoping.

As Kristy entered the hospital rehab unit, the smell of breakfast was still in the air. Eggs, toast, bacon, and the sweetness of maple syrup filled the halls of the hospital.

She headed towards the nurses' station. This morning there was an older receptionist at the desk. She looked up at Kristy immediately.

"Good morning," She greeted Kristy with a smile. "Who have you come to visit this fine morning?"

"Hello, I am here to see my husband, James. He was admitted here yesterday afternoon from Sacred Heart in Spokane."

"Oh, of course!" The receptionist motioned towards Jim's room. "The nurse is in there now. He just finished breakfast and is waiting for the therapist to evaluate him."

Kristy peered into Jim's room. She could see him sitting upright in his bed, wiping his face with a washcloth. The nurse was straightening out his pillows and giving him his medications. Kristy could hear her talking to Jim about the weather and what her plans were for the weekend. It made Kristy feel good. She knocked lightly on the open door and entered the room.

Startled, the nurse jumped and turned around.

"Good morning, Kristy," She smiled as she took the washcloth from Jim's hands. "I was talking about the weather with Jim. He is quiet this morning, but I hope he will come around a little more once we get him up and out to the therapy room. He had a really good night's sleep, and we even had to wake him up for breakfast." She turned to Jim. "Ain't that right, Mr. Cavalier?"

Jim nodded and smiled when he saw Kristy. He was happy to see a face that he recognized. She was the cute blonde who called herself his wife. He also remembered her kisses, how they made his belly tickle. His smile grew. He struggled to say 'hi', but the medications kept him drowsy.

Kristy approached him and kissed him on the cheek.

The butterflies in my stomach are back, he thought.

"Good morning, honey," She smiled at him. "Remember me?" Jim smiled and nodded. Kristy's eyes started to fill up with tears. "You do?" She questions him again. Jim nodded again.

"Hi, b-beeeeuuutiful," he said proudly. Kristy let out a shriek and reached over to hug him.

Jim's determination and willpower were strong. He needed to be strong for this journey. Both physically and mentally.

17

Going Home

The last couple of weeks were a blur. Jim's progression was going better than planned. He was walking short distances with a walker and now talking in complete sentences. His words were a bit slow yet, but he was communicating better each day. He had relearned most of the things he had lost. It wouldn't be long before he could function at home.

One of the last steps before he would be released home, Jim had to go back to Sacred Heart for his permanent dental implant surgery.

The procedure went well. While Jim and Kristy were at Sacred Heart, Dr. Ambudahl came and visited them. Jim didn't remember him at all, but that didn't matter. Dr. Ambudahl and his staff were amazed to hear that Jim had come so far. He had lots of company during his short stay.

The day had finally come! Jim was getting discharged home from Bonner Rehab. After almost two months in two hospitals, James Cavalier was well enough to go home! Just in time for the Holidays.

Kristy had so much she was thankful for. This Thanksgiving was going to be extra special.

"I. Can't. Wait. To get. Home." Jim expressed to Kristy.

"Well, once we are done signing all this paperwork, then we will be off," Kristy reassured him.

Once the last of the paperwork was signed, Kristy handed the nurse the pen and walked around Jim's wheelchair. She started pushing him towards the exit.

"Let's get you home, honey," She leaned into his right ear. "You deserve to be home."

As Kristy turned into the driveway, a banner strung across the front of their garage door.

WELCOME HOME, JIM!

"I guess I do have people that love me."

"Of course you do, sweetie," Kristy put her arm around him. "We all love you."

"I want to try and walk into my house on my own," Jim demanded. His speech was slow.

"Wait one second," Kristy replied.

As Kristy hopped out of the car to get his walker, Jim had the door of the car open and was attempting to stand. Unaware, she continued to struggle with the walker. When she finally freed the walker from the trunk, Kristy noticed Jim standing halfway to the house. He was looking back at her with a shit-eating grin on his face. She gasped and cupped her hands over her mouth. It was something that she never thought would be possible just a few weeks ago. Tears began to fill her eyes.

Steadily, one step at a time, Jim made his way to the front door. Kristy caught up to him and continued to walk at his side. He stopped just before the front door. He stared at the doorknob, trying to process how to open the door. Kristy reached around Jim, turned the knob, and pushed the door open.

"WELCOME HOME!" Came many familiar voices from Jim's life. Jim looked around the room. Tom, Jenni, his mom and dad, and some staff from the department were there to watch Jim walk into his home. They were all shocked at how far his recovery had come. None of them expected Jim to be standing in front of them!

"Jim can't remember names just yet," Kristy said, looking around the room into everyone's teary eyes. "He knows what love feels like, and this is it. Our friends and family are here right now to welcome us home. Thank you, everyone! It means a lot to us!"

Everyone gathered in the kitchen for cake. There was some talk about Jim's stay in Spokane and Rob's untimely death. Everyone had cake and coffee before filtering out, knowing that Jim needed his rest.

After the crowd died down, Tom, Jenni, and Jim's parents were all that was left.

Tom sat next to Jim, finally seeing Jim, one on one for the first time since the accident.

"How are you feeling, buddy?" Tom asked, looking deeply into Jim's tired eyes.

"Ok," Jim sighed. "I get confused. I struggle to find the right words."

"Well, that will come in time, my friend." Tom put his hand on Jim's shoulder. "I will be here for you every step of the way," He smiled, fighting back the tears. "I love you, man. I am so happy you are finally home and on the road to living life again. We have a lot of catching up to do."

Jim smiled back. "I'll be back to myself in no time. And back to work."

Jenni approached the table and placed a hand on Jim's other shoulder. He felt a warm rush through his body.

"Tom is right. We will be here for you and Kristy anytime you need us," She looked over at Tom and winked. "We should get going, so you can get settled in and rest for the evening. There will be plenty of time to catch up again soon."

Tom and Jenni headed to the door.

"Call if you need anything, okay?" Jenni hugged Kristy.

"We need to go, too," Jim's dad spoke up, a little out of breath from having pneumonia.

"We will be back tomorrow to see you, honey." Jim's mom kissed him on the cheek. "I love you," Her voice crackled as she held back tears.

"We will see you sometime tomorrow," Kristy replied, slowly closing the front door.

She noticed Jim was in a stupor, staring blankly at her.

"What are you thinking about?" Kristy asked.

"I'm just glad to be home, that's all." Jim smiled.

Kristy walked to the refrigerator and poured herself a glass of wine.

She sat on her recliner.

"All I know for now is that I am so happy to have you home with me. Right before the Holidays was a perfect gift," Kristy finished her wine quickly and headed to the fridge for another glass. Tonight, she needed two.

As they got ready for bed, Jim walked past Kristy and headed into his bathroom. She watched in shock! He grabbed his toothbrush and paused, looking up at her, confused.

"Wow, Jim! Do you remember our bedtime routine?"

"I feel a little like I do. Maybe I'm just going through the motions right now,"

After brushing their teeth, Jim walked towards the bed.

"Not tonight, honey," Kristy reluctantly grabbed him by the hand and walked him towards the spare bedroom.

"Someday, Jim. When you are better," She tucked him into the spare bed. "For now, it's this."

News Flash

Jim continued to make dramatic strides in both occupational and physical therapy. One day while going through his regular therapy routine, the therapist decided to test Jim's memory. There was a story the therapist wanted to talk to Jim about. To see if Jim had remembered any details of it.

The therapist told Jim how he had helped his family find his missing dad several years ago. Memories of that day flooded into Jim's mind. Like lightning bolts through his head, Jim saw flashes of that memory, plus some additional information no one else would have ever known.

So, Jim began to tell the story:

"I remember that you had lost his father a few summers back, right?" Jim asked, making sure he was on the right track.

"The man had been diagnosed with dementia, and he was deteriorating quickly. One early morning, your mother had called you in a panic. Your father had walked away from home, and she could not find him anywhere. I remember searching with a team for a few days straight. Nothing showed up, so I decided to go back to the house, talk again with your mother, and search for clues. This time, we started where we thought it was the beginning of the story—your dad's bedroom.

"That was where we discovered the final clue." Jim reminded his therapist.

"That summer, the weather was unusually cooler than average. Some of the days almost felt like fall weather. Your dad kept telling your mom that he was going to get his hunting gear ready. She didn't pay him any mind, as his dementia was getting so bad, he barely recognized her some days.

"Upon further inspection, your dad's hunting clothes and rifle were missing. That was when I decided to look in one of the most obvious spots. His deer blind, at the end of the road and across the neighbor's field. That same spot where he had taken many trophies over the past 50 years, "Jim continued his story, his therapist listening in awe.

"That's where Jim found your dad. He had died of exposure, doing what he loved," Jim paused. "What I know now is that your dad had a moment of memory relapse while sitting in his blind. That moment he knew where he was and what he had done. But, instead of getting up and going home to your mom. He thought about his life. How beautiful his family had become. He reminisced for many hours before his mind went blank again. He knew that he was becoming a huge burden on you and your mom. So, he decided to stay in the woods. He had come to peace with his life," Jim looked over at his therapist. The young man's eyes welled up with tears.

"I know you took it very hard. But your dad died happily. Content. He loves you with everything he has in him. I was breaking his heart to see you and your mom stress out every day dealing with his dementia."

A tear ran down the therapist's cheek as he sobbed, looking at the floor.

"Go to that blind on the edge of the woods today after work. He left a note scribbled on some scratch paper under the seat cushion, you'll see."

The therapist nodded and smiled. "Thank you, Jim."

"You bet," Jim smiled back.

"Do either of you mind if I turn on the TV?" A young lady asked. "I've been following this missing girl story for about two months now. The FBI finally has a new lead, and they are supposed to announce the breakthrough on this morning's news."

"Sure. I think my wife has been watching that, too. Sometimes I hear the TV on in her room late at night." Jim replied.

The news camera showed a bunch of reporters around a beautiful brick mansion. The therapist recognized this house.

"It's the Bengston home."

Jim recognized the house as well, but he was unclear why.

They were showing some pictures of two teenage girls.

That one girl. The platinum blonde. She looked very familiar. How could this be? Jim thought as he emerged into the story. He was blocking out everything around him.

The reporter briefed everyone who had just tuned in.

She talked about the disappearance of two teenage girls on Labor Day weekend, just over two months ago, how the two girls vanished without a trace from a small park in the middle of Myrtle Beach. One of the girls was Harper Bengston. She was the daughter of millionaire banker Bradley Bengston. The local FBI decided to offer a reward to anyone who had seen anything in the area of Barefoot Landing that night of their disappearance.

The breaking news today was about the backpack that investigators had found. It had some personal belongings in it, including the cell phone of one of the girls.

The reporter turned to a well-dressed man and his wife. They were pleading for their daughter's safe return.

"Harper is our only baby. Please return her safe! We beg you," The well-dressed man pleaded. His young wife was clinging onto his arm, staring away in a trance. "We know she didn't run away. This was not like her. Harper has many plans for her future."

Then, a pre-recorded video of a woman came on the TV. She was disheveled in nursing scrubs. She, too, was pleading for her daughter's safe return.

"Please, please bring back my daughter. She is all I have to wake up for in the morning," The woman began to cry. "Carmen, if you see this, honey. I will never give up on you! I know someone is holding you against your will. I will always be looking for you! I promise!"

The reporter came back on the screen.

"We know the two girls have disappeared together. A local sheriff's office found their bikes abandoned together at the Barefoot Landing area of Myrtle Beach, South Carolina. The girls are best friends, and neither of them ever have gotten into trouble before. The consideration of them running away was skeptical at best," The reporter concluded. "The cell phone that we found had recent pictures of the girls on the beach. Some of those pictures might have some clues into their disappearance. We will put them up after this commercial break."

Jim broke into a sweat. "Those girls looked familiar! I have seen them somewhere!"

"It's just because their pictures have been plastered all over since your accident. Maybe you heard someone talking about them or seen them on the news and just didn't realize it was them," Jim's therapist tried to calm Jim down.

"No. I have seen the one girl with blue eyes and white hair! She was standing in my hospital room. She was wearing a white shirt with a small pink rhinestone heart on the pocket and jean shorts!" Jim feels his heart race in his chest.

The news flash came back on with new pictures of the girls at Myrtle Beach. Some selfies, in the waves, and on beach towels.

Jim froze in shock. "Oh, my God, it is them!"

"Wait. How did you know what the one girl was wearing?" Asked the therapist, confused.

Jim's eyes rolled back into his head, and he passed out.

* *

"Hey, buddy. You okay?" It was Rob's voice. Jim was again standing at the light.

"Where the hell have you been? Am I dead?" Jim asked.

"I've busted my butt to start all over with eating, walking, and remembering my wife! You have no clue how hard it's been! I just remembered who

she was and realized she was terrified of me! You know how hard that is?!?" Jim spun in circles looking for his friend.

"I do, Buddy. I needed you to do that part on your own. You needed to prove to Him your strength and determination. I could not intervene. But you did it. You did it in amazing strides!" Rob steps out of the light.

"You have made Him proud." He smiled, looking at Jim and the girl who was again standing at his side.

"Now that you are remembering, you need to get back on track and go to the station and talk to Tom. You need to get him to believe what you have been seeing." Rob motioned to the blonde girl standing silently next to Jim.

"Harper here needs your help."

Jim looked at the girl, confused.

"She doesn't even talk to me. How am I supposed to help? And how do I know her and her friend?" Jim looked at the girl. She smiled at Jim. *"Why in the world does she only smile at me? Why does she not talk?"*

"Because she is afraid."

* *

Jim awakened, feeling woozy. He was in the hospital again. His eyesight was slightly blurry as he tried to focus on his surroundings.

Kristy was at his side.

"It's okay, honey." She rubbed his arm. "They think you had a seizure and passed out." She informed him.

Jim looked into Kristy's eyes and took a deep breath.

"I saw Rob again," he said in a slurred voice. He looked around the room. He seemed confused. Blinking, he couldn't get his eyes to focus. Kristy did not respond to what he had said. She began to shake.

"I recognized those girls on the news!" He started to get agitated. "I have *seen* Harper! She was with Rob!"

"Jim, honey. You've had a seizure and are recovering from a brain injury. You probably don't remember, but you were in a bad accident. So, please calm down..." Kristy said in a shaken voice.

Jim's first trigger. The news. Anxiety and post-traumatic stress. Having been told by Dr. Ambudahl and his therapist in Spokane that this may eventually happen, could never have prepared Kristy for this. She began to panic and reached for the nurse's light.

Jim grabbed her hand. But luckily for her, he was still relatively weak, and Kristy pulled free.

"Listen to me! I have seen Harper! When I was in that accident!" He began to raise his voice. "She was standing with Rob and me, just before he went into the light! She is dead too! I have seen her cross over! Now, when she comes to me, her aura is a bright green. Rob is here too! DON'T YOU UNDERSTAND???."

Kristy took a few steps back towards the door. "Your right. Rob didn't make it, Jim. He died in the accident. Who is Harper?"

Jim gave Kristy a confused look.

"The girl in the news you have been watching! I have seen her in my hospital room! The men ran her over! But the other girl, Carmen, is still alive! I know this! We need to save her!" Jim tried to explain through slurred words and jumbled sentences.

"I know where they are! I need to find her!"

My God, these are the two missing girls! But how would Jim know about them? Kristy finally understood what Jim had been talking about. *But, how could he possibly know where they are? How did he know that Harper was dead?* Kristy thought as she started to cry as she left the room toward the nurses' station.

An older nurse walked around the desk and assisted Kristy to a chair. "What can I do for you, ma'am?"

Kristy looked up with teary eyes.

"Are you OK?"

Just then, there was a loud crash in Jim's room. He started yelling as a nurse ran out the door, looking back at him.

"Help! I know what happened to Harper! Carmen needs our help! Kristy! HELP!" Jim was in a full-on panic.

The nurse looked at the unit clerk. Another nurse ran towards Jim's room. The unit clerk picked up the phone and called out a page for help.

Another nurse started toward Jim's room. She yelled over her shoulder to the unit clerk. "Get Dr. Jones here! HURRY!"

Kristy could hear Jim hollering and the nurse trying to calm him. Pretty soon, there are several hospital staff heading into his room, one being Dr. Jones. After a few minutes, silence. They all started to filter out of Jim's room. Kristy was standing in the middle of the hallway, crying and in shock.

"What happened?" Dr. Jones approaches Kristy. "Has he done this before?"

Kristy looked up at the doctor through blurry, teary eyes.

"No, this was his first episode!" She sobbed, shaking her head. "He was in therapy earlier. I had gone to get some coffee as I always do. When I got a call, Jim had an 'episode,' and they were admitting him. I rushed here to find Jim drugged up, lying in bed." She pointed to Jim's room. "He was talking nonsense, so I was going to try to keep him calm and press the nurses' light for help. He grabbed my hand and started talking about a girl he had seen, but he kept saying she was dead! Then he started to talk about his friend Rob, who died in the accident. I pulled away from him and went out to the nurses' station, and he went berserk!"

Kristy straightened up, "What is going on, Dr. Jones? Dr. Ambudahl warned me he would have PTSD. Was that what this was? If so, I'm scared of him! I don't know if I can handle him at home if he does that again?" Kristy started to panic.

Dr. Jones gave Kristy a concerning look.

"I am not sure what that was, maybe some PTSD. I will adjust some of his medications before we send him home." He forced a smile. "Do you know who Harper and Carmen are?"

Dr. Jones looked at Kristy. He could see the fear in her eyes.

"I think he was talking about the missing girls from Myrtle Beach." She explained.

"But, how would he know them?" Dr. Jones questioned. "It would be impossible for him to know them. Wouldn't it?"

"I don't know," Kristy replied. "I have only seen them on the news. I doubt Jim would know them. He hasn't watched TV since his accident, let alone seen the news. I don't know if he even knows what is going on in his head sometimes." She started to cry again.

"Well, we will get him evaluated and see what we need to do before we let him leave here," Dr. Jones said in a comforting voice. "I am going to talk with his therapist to see what triggered him and what happened after that. I just can't figure out why he would focus on those girls. But for now, he is sedated, and we will keep a close eye on him. You should go home and get some rest. I will call you once I get some answers." He patted her shoulder and walked off towards the therapy room.

Dr. Jones entered the therapy room. Jim's therapist was sitting at his computer documenting some of today's therapy sessions.

"Hello, Don. How was Mr. Cavalier's therapy session today? What happened with the TV?

The therapist told Dr. Jones about triggering Jim's memory in therapy with the story of his dad. Jim was doing great, and his memory was coming back a little bit. It all had seemed promising.

Then, Dr. Jones mentioned what had happened in Jim's room with Kristy. How he kept saying he had seen the two missing girls.

"Maybe we should call the police," The therapist proposed.

"I will give it a couple of days, then I will see. Remember, this is patient confidentiality—no repeating this to anyone. We will eventually have to go to the police, but for now, let Jim rest. He may even be making this up. Who knows for sure with his type of head injury." He walked out of the therapy department, back towards the hospital.

18

Spirit Guardian

After spending all day with Jim at the hospital, Kristy decided not to go home. Instead, she drove up to Tom and Jenni's. Kristy needed someone to talk to, and Tom and Jenni knew her and Jim better than anyone. Right now, she needed someone who understood. To make Kristy feel like she was strong enough to take care of Jim.

As Kristy approached the front porch, Jenni opened it. She was in her beaded leather Native American dress. It was the first time Kristy had seen Jenni dressed like this in a long time. Jenni guided Kristy to Tom, who was sitting at the kitchen table. She noticed the strange aroma of incense burning. Tom smiled. It seemed almost as if they were waiting for her.

"Welcome. Jenni said she thought you would be stopping by," He greeted Kristy. "I don't know how she knew it. That always amazed me about her. When I woke up this morning, she already had her Native dress on and had this incense burning. She proceeded to tell me that you were going to stop by and ask questions about Jim.

Jenni has been trying to come up with a way to tell you about what Jim sees and knows."

Kristy took a deep breath. The incense had a sweet, familiar smell to her. She began to feel as if she was afloat on a cloud. The aroma seemed to help her relax.

Jenni offered Kristy a seat at the table. She then sat across the table, next to Tom.

"I had a vision last night," She began immediately. "I saw Jim was having some difficulties since his accident. He saw Rob cross over into Heaven and become his Weyekin."

Kristy started to cry.

"Is Jim going crazy? Is he being possessed by this 'Weyekin? What exactly is it? A ghost?"

"No, Jim is not crazy or possessed. He has been blessed with something so beautiful. Something I've only heard my elders talk of it. No one has witnessed this for many generations!" She looked Kristy directly in the eyes. "A Weyekin is a spirit guardian. A person is considered lucky if their soul has been chosen to join with a spirit, and Jim has two! His protector, his advisor," Jenni continues. "Jim has seen things not many living people ever see. He knows things no living person should ever know. When two close spirits enter Heaven simultaneously, sometimes they join just before they cross over. Somehow this time, Rob and Harper ended up crossing over, and Jim was brought back to Earth.

"Time stands still in Heaven. In the time Jim had spent there, it was like an eternity on Earth. Jim has seen a lot of things from the present to the beginning of time. Those things-all that information-he may not understand or remember it all. Because he has seen stuff, his mind cannot comprehend. Right now, it is too soon to try and figure all this out. That will come in time. Someday, when his brain is ready, he will start to understand all of it. Only then will he be able to communicate it better. Different scenarios might trigger certain things. For now, he is scared because he only sees bits and pieces. Jim is now armed with some amazing knowledge. The kind of knowledge that could become dangerous. For Jim and those around him," Jenni took Kristy's hands into hers. Their eyes lock onto one another's. Jenni's were dark brown like the soil, and Kristy's a pure blue like the sky. Both of their eyes filled up with tears.

"I...I see another spirit," Jenni whispered to Kristy. "A young blonde-haired girl," She squeezed Jenni's hand tightly.

"She is Jim's second Weyekin? *Three* spirits melded! This was unheard of!"

19

Carmen

The room was dark and cold. Sometimes it was hard to tell if it was day or night outside. The windows had been either boarded up or painted black. Carmen hadn't seen the light in days. She didn't even know how long she had been captive. Carmen was thinking about it for at least a month or more. She had her period when she first got here, but nothing since. That didn't mean anything, though. She was starving, and her body wouldn't have regular cycles because of that.

She was so cold and hungry. The cool fall nights were almost un-bearable. Every day she cried, wishing she wouldn't have convinced Harper to meet with these guys. She wished she didn't step into that van. Carmen just wanted Harper back with her.

What happened to her friend Harper? She thought. *Why won't the kidnappers tell her anything?*

She curled up, shaking on a dirty, mouse-eaten mattress on the floor. It had been her confinement since day one. The stench coming from the pail in the corner was enough to make anyone sick to their stomach. The ammonia smell of urine and feces was horrid. Carmen had become immune to this. The cold had settled the stench a bit.

Carmen's hair was tangled and dirty. Her skin felt like it was covered in sand. She hadn't showered since she had been abducted. Just a quick, cold-water dip in a washtub after her period, and that was it. She hadn't brushed her teeth. They had felt like something was growing on them. What she wouldn't give right now for a toothbrush and a hot bath. She was still wearing the clothes that she was taken in. They were filthy and ragged. Her shorts were useless in this cold, and her pink shirt was so dirty you couldn't even tell what color it was anymore.

Carmen stood up, her knees buckling a little as she tried to straighten them. She walked over to the corner where a five-gallon bucket was. When Carmen sat down, the rim dug into her butt cheeks, but she didn't care. Her stomach ached. She wasn't sure if it was from the lack of or the quality of the food. This had become her life. The kidnappers only entered her room with a small amount of food every couple of days, sometimes smelling rotten. She always cleaned her plate. What little she ate was keeping her alive. She was beginning to wonder now if this was all worth it.

She Could Hear voices from just outside the door. So, she walked over to listen. She watched the crack on the bottom of the door. She noticed a shadow moving closer to her door. She slowly stood up and put her head against the wall to hear.

The muffled voices were still barely audible.

"I know we should text it again!" Muffled..."The wrong fucking phone, dammit."

Why did the wrong phone matter so much? Carmen thought. *Did they leave behind the wrong phone? Hers? She had both the men's numbers on her's. Harper only had one and no names. But why would that matter? The men could have lied about their names and everything else! But there was a SIM card! That held all of her contacts! Maybe the police will look them up and find out who this guy was! Maybe they would find her and Harper!*

"Ok," came the voice from the other side. "...One more time, but not here." The man had an odd accent Carmen couldn't figure out.

"I will drive out past the border road tomorrow and send out a text." He said, his voice getting clearer. He must be standing just outside her door. "He will be coming to take her and sell her on the international market."

Carmen sat with her back stiffened against the wall.

Holy shit! She thought! *Was I going to be sold to another country? I will never be seen again!* She started to sob silently. *Why didn't I listen to Harper?*

She wondered where Harper was and what she was doing right now. *If she was in the same house, was she being treated the same way? Or was she already gone, sold to another country. Why did they separate them?* Carmen headed back over to her mattress and cried herself to sleep, shivering uncontrollably as the air outside got cooler.

As she drifted off to sleep, she began to dream.

Carmen could hear waves crashing on the shore. The sun felt warm on her skin. She heard a laugh in the distance. It was Harper! She had two ice cream cones, and she was walking across the beach kicking up the golden sand. Carmen sat up. She and Harper ate their ice cream while watching the waves crash on the shoreline. They were the only ones on the beach. The sun was so bright it hurt Carmen's eyes.

"Carmen," Harper looked into her squinting eyes, "I want you to know that no matter what, I am here with you." Harper smiled her beautiful perfect smile.

Harper stood up, walked into the ocean, and disappeared. Carmen got up and ran towards Harper. That was when the first wave hit her. The water was cold! Harper stood up, walked into the ocean, and disappeared.

Carmen gasped as she was jolted awake from the cold water that the man dumped on her. One of the men was standing in front of her. She recognized him as the guy she had met online. He was unshaven, and his face was full of scars from years of abuse. His eyes were dark and evil as he looked at her in disgust. She sat up and let out a blood-curdling scream.

"SILENT!" The man's voice screamed back. "You stink like a whore!" His rugged voice was one of disgust. "You will not be worth anything looking or smelling like that!"

Carmen froze with fear. She just sat on the mattress staring at the man. She was afraid that if she moved, he would do something terrible to her. Over the past months, she had been starved, beaten, and tied up. She had learned to keep quiet and stay low.

"Quit staring at me, you whore!" The man with the funny accent screamed.

Not realizing that she was staring, she immediately looked down. The cold was settling in again. She started to shiver out of control. She wondered what she had done to make someone so mean.

It was the same man that had been so nice to her before all this. How could he have faked all that? What did she do to deserve this? She thought back to all the texts they had shared about their 'wonderful' future.

She knew what she had done wrong. She stepped into a stranger's van.

The man walked out of her room and slammed the door behind him. She could hear him locking it all up again, five clicks in all. The room once again was dark. She laid on the corner of the mattress, where it was dry. With no blankets, and now, her clothes and mattress were wet. Carmen could not get warm. She began shivering, almost to the point of convulsions.

Again, she was alone and cold. Carmen cried herself to sleep. This time, she did not dream.

20

Therapy Session

A day later, after having no more incidents, Jim was sent home in stable condition.

Kristy pulled into the driveway. Jim's parents were waiting at the front door of the house.

"Oh, Jim. Look, your parents are here waiting for you."

"Good, I have not seen them in a few days," He replied.

"Hello!" Jim's mom called out loudly. "It's good to see you home again!"

Jim's dad smiled proudly and patted Jim on the shoulder as he stopped in front of him.

"I'm glad you and mom could make it."

"We are happy you are back home, and hopefully you can stay home this time," Jim's mom stepped forward and gave him a big hug. Jim, at first, did not know what to do. Slowly, he hugged her back. She began to sob.

"I worry about you, Jim. I don't like it when you are in the hospital."

"I'm okay now mom," Jim held his mom while she sobbed.

"Let's go inside and have some dinner," Kristy opened the door to the house.

Jim's mom helped Kristy with dinner. They all sat and ate, talking about Rob and the good times he and Jim had growing up together. They talked about some of the shenanigans the two raised around town in their teenage years, up until Rob moved to Chicago.

"Those boys weren't innocent by any means," She informed Kristy.

"So, it looks as though Jim's therapy is going well," Jim's dad spoke up.

"Yes, it is," Jim replied. "I feel stronger and stronger every day." He smiled and looked over at Kristy. "I've had a lot of good help."

"Good. I always knew you would bounce back from this. You are strong like your grandfather," He replied.

Dinner was filled with stories of what was happening around town. After all the dishes were put away, and everyone had their fill of dessert, Frank and Marlene finally said their farewells and good night's wishes. They promised that they would check in tomorrow to see how Jim was doing.

The house was once again quiet. Kristy turned to Jim.

"Do you feel like you are progressing like you would like to be? Do you think the therapy is causing you setbacks, or do you think they are helping? Because I sometimes feel that you get agitated," Kristy paused. "It scares me, Jim."

"I-I feel like I am slowly improving," He answered as he felt the tension rising off of Kristy. "I feel bad that my actions the other day landed me in the hospital. I know I have to try to control them better. But, it is hard to do once my mind begins to race. When I black-out, I see so much I do not understand. I see everything all at once. I don't know if I'm dreaming or awake. When I see Rob, he comforts me," Jim paused, trying to find the right words to say. "I just wish you could understand what I see. Hopefully, some of these new pills will keep my brain a little better focused," Jim looked at Kristy, studying her beautiful features.

She is so beautiful, Jim thought. His heart skipped a beat.

"You make me feel numb when you kiss me," He whispered. "I feel my stomach tickle. I don't know what that means, but I like to feel that way. It makes me happy."

"It is getting late," Kristy stood up. "We have another day ahead of us tomorrow. A good night's sleep in our beds will help us get a good start to the day."

Kristy guided Jim to the bathroom to help him get ready for bed. They both went to their sides of the vanity and got ready for bed. Their routine was the same as before Jim's accident. The only difference was Jim still slept in the guest room. They both decided that it was safer that way. Kristy made it part of her new routine to settle Jim into his bed in the guest room. She would make sure he had his water and night light. She would then turn on the monitor to keep an eye on him if he were to start to get restless in the middle of the night.

The morning came fast. Kristy woke up to a familiar smell. A smell that she hadn't experienced in months. She sat up in bed. Now, fully awake. The aroma of freshly brewed coffee made her intoxicated with pleasure. Could she smell breakfast beyond the coffee scent?

Jim? How could this be? She thought.

She climbed out of bed and started trotting towards the kitchen. Jim was standing at the stove preparing eggs and toast. He had on his favorite blue plaid pajama bottoms. Shirtless. Handsome. He turned to her and smiled as he flipped the eggs. Tears fill her delicate blue eyes. His bare chest was still fresh with scars from the accident. She walked over to her cup, picked it up, and smelled delicious coffee. She tiptoed over to her handsome husband, leaned into him, and gently kissed his cheek.

He closed his eyes as he felt the delicate buzz of butterflies in his stomach again! He took in a deep breath, catching her sweet smell. He remembered the smell.

"Mmmmm," She muttered as she put the warm cup up to her eager lips. Staring into Jim's eyes, she took a sip. It was strong! A big smile crossed her face, and her heart skipped a beat. Jim loved super-strong coffee.

"So, you remembered how to make the coffee strong as you liked it?" She asked as she took another sip of coffee.

"Nope," Jim answered politely." I read the directions on the back of the can. It seems that I remember having done that once before," He winked. His smile made Kristy fall in love all over again.

"Thank you for breakfast, honey," Kristy walked over and poured herself another cup of coffee. She had a million emotions running through her mind right now. "I was thinking of going out and doing some shopping. Maybe next week we could start putting up our Christmas decorations," She turned towards Jim. "Would you like to join me? Maybe we can find a special ornament for us this year." She finished her coffee and headed towards the sink with their dishes. Jim got up from his chair and followed Kristy to the sink.

"I would love to! Like a date. Maybe dinner at Tom and Jenni's place."

Kristy smiled. "That sounds like a good plan."

"I am going to take a shower and get ready." She hurried to her bedroom. She could feel Jim staring at her.

Jim walked over to the couch and turned on the TV. It was the news. There was a blurb about the missing girls and how their families were trying to cope with the Holidays coming up. The reporter stated that tomorrow night she was going to be interviewing the girls' parents.

He was intrigued and hypnotized. He sat on the edge of the couch and listened carefully. Knowing Kristy might be listening, he tried not to get too excited. He remembered that was what landed him in the hospital last time. Jim stared into the TV screen until a commercial break broke his trance. He came to, sitting in a cold sweat like he had seen a ghost. He shuts the TV off.

That was enough. Jim thought.

Jim began to stare off into space. That was when he heard a soft, clear voice.

"*Hey, buddy.* Jim was startled, it was Rob's voice! *You're looking good.*"

Jim looked around the room until he saw Rob standing in front of him. Hues of blue and orange were lifting off his body.

"*I feel okay.*" Jim didn't have to speak to have Rob hear him.

Rob walked over and sat in Kristy's recliner, leaning toward Jim.

"Harper and *I have been watching over Carmen. Harper and we are worried about her. We do not know how much longer Carmen can take. She is starting to break, Jim. She's starting to give up.*"

"*I don't know how I can help, Rob. I can barely cook breakfast at this point. I want to do what I can to help, but I am still so weak.*" Rob stood up and walked towards the living room window.

"*You are the only one we have that can help find this girl! I hate to tell you this, but there are many more where she is.*" Rob turned towards Jim, staring into his eyes.

"More of what?" Jim asked aloud.

"What? Who are you talking to?" Kristy walked into the room. She noticed Jim was sitting in his recliner. He was staring oddly at the front window. She felt a coolness in the room as goosebumps bounced alive up to her arms and into her neck.

"We need to leave shortly for therapy. Are you okay, Honey?" Her voice was shaky with fear.

Jim slowly turned around to see Kristy standing alongside him. He didn't respond. He just stared at her.

"Jim, you are scaring me."

Jim blinked a couple of times and was back into reality. He flopped back in his chair, taking a deep breath.

"I need a minute." He whispered, sounding exhausted.

When Jim and Kristy finally arrived at therapy, his therapist was waiting for them. Kristy mentioned that she would like to take Jim out to the shopping mall for a quick trip and maybe out to dinner. The therapist agreed that this would be a good thing. It would help to see if Jim was okay coping with crowds and stimulation. So, Jim tried his hardest in therapy to prove that he could handle a mini date with his wife.

Jim flew through the therapy session. He did not mention what had happened at the last visit. The therapist said Jim could go, as long as Jim promised not to overdo it. When Jim felt tired, he should go home and get some rest. Jim and Kristy agreed. It would be his first outing with his wife in a very long time.

There was a little Christmas gift shop in the corner of the mall that had special handmade items. Kristy found the perfect ornament. She had it personalized with 'Jim and Kristy 4-ever' on a deep red heart-shaped piece of wood, all hand-carved. Angel wings with the year on the other side. It was perfect!

After the mall, Jim started to look tired, like he needed some rest. Kristy knew it was probably time to go home.

So did she.

"Let's go home, honey." Kristy proposed.

"Yeah, I agree," Jim replied in a tired voice.

They went home to a simple dinner that night with fast food tacos on paper plates and a fountain soda. But to Kristy, it was everything. This night had been a long time coming. Perfect time to give thanks for her Christmas miracle, she thought as she stared into

Jim's eyes. He glanced back at his beautiful wife and smiled wide. The accident was making her and Jim closer than ever.

Yes, she thought, she's very thankful!

21

Earhart & Lindbergh

After dinner, Jim and Kristy made their way to the living room to sit and relax. Fall's chill was in the air, it was warm during the day, but the nighttime frost would blanket the ground, cooling it for winter's freeze. Kristy lit a fire and turned the TV on to the history channel. She wanted to avoid the news altogether.

There was a documentary about missing people's cold case files. This particular episode was of the two most famous aviators of the 1930s. Charles Lindbergh, and Amelia Earhart.

That got Jim's attention. He sat and listened intensely, unaware of his surroundings.

Jim's eyes fixated, unblinking at the television. Kristy was watching his reaction as the first story unfolded. Frozen in fear, remembering what Jenni had told her about what Jim may have seen in his near-death experience.

As the film's Narrator stated:

'Charles Augustus Lindbergh Jr., the famous aviator's child, was kidnapped on the evening of March 1st, 1932. The boy was just 20 months old. There was a ransom request left on the ledge of the 2nd story window. But who would have taken little 'Lindy?'

'Thirty-nine-year-old Amelia Mary Earhart disappeared July 2nd, 1937, with an attempt to fly around the world. She was going to be the first female to complete this journey. Her plane vanished without a trace. Her body was never recovered.

'These two stories have been unsolved for over 75 years. There have been many theories and stories written about these two mysteries, but no one knows the truth to what happened.'

Commercial break.

Jim snapped out of his trance and glanced around, finding Kristy staring at him. Her eyes were watering from not blinking. Her face was still frozen. He tried to bring himself back into reality. He was in Heaven...no. Jim was in his living room in Sandpoint, Idaho. His wife, Kristy, was sitting alongside him with a terrified look on her face.

Shaking, Jim took a deep breath and stood up.

"Would you like water, Kristy?" He asked, wiping his sweaty palms on his pants as he headed towards the refrigerator.

"I would love a glass, please," She replied. Holding her stare at Jim, still in shock. She debated turning the channel while he was not looking. But then, she decided against it. Instead, she reached over and picked up the remote control and placed it in her lap.

Just to be on the safe side. Kristy thought.

She also made sure her phone was within arm's reach. Jim's reaction to the show was, nonetheless, interesting. Almost intriguing.

What did he know about these two cases? Kristy wondered. *Was Jenni right about him seeing all this stuff when he had his near-death experience?* Kristy was curious.

Jim returned to the living room with two glasses of ice water. He put the glasses on the coffee table between their chairs.

"Thanks, honey." She said to her husband.

"You are so very welcome, Kristy," He pleasantly responded.

Now back to the story.

'Baby Lindberg was put to bed around eight o'clock in the evening of March 1st, 1932, by the family nurse, Betty Gow.

Mrs. Lindbergh, seven months pregnant, had finished her evening bath at about 10 pm. She entered the baby's bedroom to check on him and give him a goodnight kiss."

'But, there was no baby. Mrs. Lindbergh began to scream. Nurse Betty came immediately from her bedroom, and Col. Lindbergh, who was in the living room, quickly headed towards the baby's bedroom as well. There, in the middle of the floor, was Anne Lindbergh on her knees, screaming, crying, and motioning towards little Lindy's empty bed.'

'They both run over and look for themselves. There was no sign of the baby. They then begin to search in all the rooms. Behind doors, under furniture, and in closets. Anne Lindbergh, crying hysterically in the middle of the bedroom floor, frozen and unable to move.'

"Run outside!" Jim broke the silence. Kristy jumped at first in fear until she realized he was speaking to the TV. She knew very little about the Lindbergh baby story.

What was he talking about? She thought. *What did he know?*

'There was an envelope on the upstairs window. The window was half open as it often stuck when closing. The envelope contained a ransom letter, $50,000, and the safe return of little Lindy.'

Commercial break.

Jim again regained a sense of his surroundings, took a long drink, and headed towards the bathroom. Kristy watched, in silence. She was wondering what he was thinking. Hoping he will not get out of control or have another seizure. She took a deep breath to slow her heart rate and calm herself. She picked up her glass and finished her water.

Standing in front of the bathroom mirror, Jim cupped his hands under the cool water and splashed his face. He looked deeply into his eyes, trying to make sense of it all. There was a green glow just behind him. Jim quickly spun around just in time to see a face, a blonde-haired girl with ice blue eyes staring at him! Her face brightened to light and disappeared.

Jim gasped for air like he had held it in that entire moment.

I need to get a grip on this. Jim tried to bring himself together. *Maybe at the end of the show, it will all be there, all the answers. Then I wouldn't sound so crazy!*

Jim headed back to the living room and quickly sat back in his chair. He looked over at Kristy, who was doing a crossword puzzle under the soft glow of the floor lamp. Unbeknownst to Jim, she was trying to keep herself calm.

The story began once again.

'The second and third ransom letters mailed to the Lindberg's demanded even more money for the safe return of baby Lindbergh.

This made Jim wonder. *Why would anyone ask for money when there was no baby? He was dead. The nurse knew that the kidnapper had accidentally killed him! But, did anyone else know that?*

'When the police arrived, they searched the surrounding areas. The only suspicious finding was a makeshift ladder that was hidden in the bushes behind the back shed. It was broken into three pieces. The police looked at everything that was out of place that night. The tire tracks and footprints in the melting snow were difficult to decipher who they were or where they came from.'

Commercial break.

"Silly people," Jim broke the silence. "The crappy ladder broke with the weight of both Bruno and the baby. This caused them to fall to the ground. The baby's head struck a rock very hard. He let out a small cry. Bruno carried the baby, barely alive at this point, to his car, hid the ladder in the bushes, and drove off. That is the true story."

He turned to Kristy. She was looking at him, scared to move. He began his story.

"Nurse Betty Gow, in her routine, puts baby Lindbergh to bed. Wrapping him up tight in his blanket and pinning it so he could not wiggle out. After Mrs. Lindbergh checks in on the baby, she goes on with her nightly bath." Jim paused and took another sip of his water.

"After Mrs. Lindbergh sinks into the tub, nurse Betty Gow goes back into baby Lindbergh's bedroom. She grabs the baby and walks over to the window. Bruno was waiting outside on top of the ladder. The window jams halfway open, so nurse Gow must slide the baby through without waking him. With both hands inside the window, Bruno takes the baby into his right arm. As his weight shifts, the ladder snaps, tossing Burno and the baby to the ground."

"Col Lindbergh heard the ladder break." Jim continued. "He thought it's coming from the kitchen, so he went over to investigate. The sound of the ladder breaking, and the baby's cry also awakens Mrs. Lindbergh, who had dozed off in the bathtub. She slowly climbs out of the bath, dries off, and dons a robe before going to the baby's room to check on him."

Tears began to fill Kristy's eyes as she listened intently to Jim's side of the story. This one was being told for the first time.

The truth.

"The FBI tried to blame Lindbergh's servant, Violet Sharp, for the crime. She was a tranquil person, and she loved little 'Lindy,' as she used to call him. Shaken up by the incident, Violet couldn't handle the blame and reaction from the public, so she committed suicide on June 10th, 1932." Jim looked at the floor.

"I'm sorry if I am scaring you, but I *know* how all this happened. I am not sure *how* I know, but I know." They continued to watch the show.

'There were two ransom letters mailed from Brooklyn, demanding $70,000 in cash for the safe return of the baby. But, there was no baby. He had been murdered. On May 12th, 1932, a delivery truck driver found a toddler's body in the woods partially buried in a shallow grave outside town. It turned out to be little Charlie Lindbergh. He had a massive skull fracture. Some monster had killed the Lindbergh baby.'

'America was in shock!'

Jim looked over at Kristy. "It was an accident. The baby died from the fall. They intended on giving him back after they got their money. The rickety old ladder could not hold the weight of them both. No one thought of that. Greed for money and a simple accident cost the life of that little child."

'The FBI tracked the ransom money to Bruno Hauptmann, who denied knowing anything about the kidnapping. After they investigated Hauptmann's home, the FBI found over $14,000 of the ransom money. He was tried and executed on April 3rd, 1936.'

Jim shook his head in disbelief.

"And the nurse gets away with it." He said in an evil tone.

"It was all her idea. She was the one who handed the baby to Hauptmann. Nurse Betty Gow took most of the ransom and hid it. Hauptmann was just too dumb to do the same. He grew up poor, and the money was burning a hole in his pathetic pocket. Some people believed he was innocent, but he wanted his piece of the Lindbergh pie just as much as the next person." Jim again looked over towards Kristy. He was expecting her to be ready to run. Her eyes were filled with tears as she continued to listen to Jim's side of the story.

"I know you do not understand. I don't even understand. But I do know that I am right. I saw it," Jim took a deep breath.

"You have to believe me, Kristy. That baby died by accident. Betty Gow was responsible for the kidnapping. Bruno Hauptmann disagreed with taking the baby but could not resist the money. What was going to be some easy cash ended up in a murder."

The Narrator started with the second story.

'Amelia Earhart, the first female aviator to fly solo across the Atlantic Ocean, had gone on to earn many awards and broke many records. On July 2nd, 1937, during her biggest mission, Amelia Earhart disappeared over the Pacific Ocean in an attempt to circumnavigate the globe.'

Jim watched, again hypnotically.

'Fran Noonan and Amelia Earhart departed Miami, Florida on June 1st. By June 29th, they were 22,000 miles into their journey. They had landed in Lae, New Guinea. On July 2nd, 1937, at midnight, Earhart and Noonan took off from Lae Airfield. The destination was Howland Island. The final approach to Howland Island using radio navigation was not successful. Fran Noonan had mentioned his concerns earlier in the planning, but Earhart would not listen.'

Commercial break.

"She didn't know how to work the new radio system," Jim explained to Kristy, almost like he was told by Amelia Earhart herself. "The antenna under the fuselage was too long, and Earhart didn't like the idea of cranking it back into the aircraft after each use, so she cut it shorter without telling anyone."

Jim got up and pointed to the television screen.

"See the tiny antenna? She cut it."

Kristy, listening to both stories-Jim's versus the TVs unfold. Jim's making more sense. She couldn't figure out how he could just come up with this information when Earhart and her story happened decades before Jim's birth.

The Narrator began:

'Earhart was approaching Howland Island and sending voice transmissions that were identifying her, but she was unable to hear the transmissions from below. By 6:14 am, calls came in stating Earhart and Noonan were 200 miles from their destination. Earhart tried whistling into the microphone, nothing. At 7:42 am, Earhart radioed that she was flying at 1,000 feet and was low on gas. She should have been over her destination at this point. The US Coast Guard Ship, Itasca, tried to send signals out to Earhart. In a last-ditch effort, they were using Morse code signals. Earhart acknowledged receiving them, but she was still unable to determine directions. She was truly lost. Somewhere over the Pacific.'

Commercial break.

"She heard the signals that night," Jim stated. "Earhart thought she was directly above Howland Island, so she descended the plane. The flight's transmissions were off. Earhart was 100 feet lower than she thought she was. She crashed into the Pacific just off the Phoenix Islands. Noonan was killed on impact." Jim looked over at Kristy, who was staring back in disbelief.

"How?" she asked. "How can you possibly know this? Did you study this stuff in history class?" Kristy's voice sounded confused. "How come I never heard you talk about American history like this before?"

"As I said before, I have seen things." Jim shrugged.

The Narrator continued his story.

'There was a massive search over the Marshall, Gilbert, and Phoenix Islands along with many others in the vicinity. Nothing ever showed up. No plane, no survivors. It was like The Electra-Earhart's plane had disappeared without a trace. Earhart's husband, George Putnam, funded his searches of these areas. He spent over 4 million dollars on searching the 150,000 square miles. There was no trace to what happened to Earhart and Noonan. But, theories remain.'

'He also came up empty-handed.'

'One theory was the Electra ran out of fuel, and Earhart had to ditch in the open sea. Aeronautical engineer Elgen Long and his wife Marie devoted 35 years of research into the 'crash and sink theory.

'Another was Captain Laurance Safford, who began a lengthy analysis of the flight during the 1970s. His research included intricate radio transmissions. He concluded. '"Poor planning, worse execution.

Earhart's mother convinced Putnam to undertake another search of the Phoenix Islands. Nothing emerged from that search.'

'In 1988, the search picked up around Gardner Island. But, it came up with nothing.'

'In 2012, a photograph taken in 1937 was enhanced and showed a blurry object sticking out of the water. But after 75 years, that object was long gone. With every tropical storm causing the plane to sink in the Pacific Ocean, slowly being lost forever.'

'In 1940, a skeleton was found on the island believed to be a woman. Others concluded they were from a male. There was some controversy about the skeleton and whether they were from a five-foot-five male or a tall white female from northern European ancestry. Since then, the bones have been misplaced and have never been found. A 2007 expedition to Nikumaroro Island found some artifacts of uncertain origin. They were very weathered but included bronze bearings, a zipper pull (possibly from a flight suit), and bones-inconclusive whether it was a human or sea turtle. All the pieces found around the islands were disproved as Earhart's. Sonars found a vessel that could have been the Electra's but quickly discredited as a small coral reef. All the evidence since 1937 has been deemed circumstantial.'

'Between all the searches, theories, and conclusions, one thing was definite. Earhart and Noonan were truly lost at sea, somewhere off Howland Island.'

The End.

Jim turned off the television and began to tell Kristy the rest of the story. The truth as he knew it.

"Earhart was running low on fuel, and she thought she was in line with Howland Island. Her transmissions were off, and she thought she had another 100 feet or so. She ends up crashing the Electra just off the coast of Garner Island. Noonan died on impact. Badly injured, Earhart survived. There was a small colony of indigenous people on the island. Some of the youngsters witnessed the crash and immediately ran out to the ocean's edge to investigate. They could hear Earhart screaming in pain. She had broken her leg near the hip. The elders rescued her before the plane sank, with Noonan inside. They nursed Earhart back to health. She had also suffered from severe head injuries and could not remember anything about her previous life or the flight. She lived out the rest of her life on the island. Amelia Earhart died at the ripe old age of 75 and was buried on the island."

Jim reached over and grabbed Kristy's hands.

"I know these things. I could know even more. Like where Carmen Potter is." He squeezed her hands gently. They were sweaty and shaking. "Please try to understand me, Kristy. I am trying to deal with this the best I know how."

"Rob is watching over that little girl, Kristy." Jim, sounding sincere, stared deeply into Kristy's eyes.

Kristy stiffens up, looking away.

Jim let go of her hands.

"I love you, Kristy. Please believe me. I will not hurt you. You have been there for me when I needed you the most," He smiled. "At this moment, I may not remember a whole lot of our lives together. But I have been told stories about us from the therapist, our friends, and my parents. I know it can't all be good, but I was told we did everything together. I do know what I feel for you now is real."

Kristy cleared her throat.

"Yes, you are right," She stated. "We were two of a kind. We loved biking together, long walks, and going to the movies once a month with Tom and Jenni. Other than us not being able to have children, our life together was perfect."

"Let's remember that life and move on." She got up and started her evening routine, trying to comprehend what just happened. Jim followed suit and put the glasses in the dishwasher. He followed her down the hallway. He watched her get ready for bed.

"What if that girl who was missing was our little girl?"

Kristy began to cry.

"I don't know, Jim. I just don't know." She slowly shut the bedroom door, leaving Jim to go to the spare bedroom where he had been sleeping.

22

Truth To Be Told

When Jim awoke, he headed to the kitchen, only to find Kristy already awake and showered. She was leaning over the kitchen counter, looking out the back window and sipping on her second cup of coffee.

"Good morning," He greeted her as he entered the kitchen. Kristy jumped slightly and turned around.

"Good morning, handsome," She replied, smiling.

"How did you sleep last night?"

Jim had started to walk over to pour himself a cup of coffee. He noticed Kristy had placed his medications next to his cup.

"I slept okay." He replied. "The sleeping pills help with that. How about you? You are up early."

Kristy turned her gaze out the window.

"I couldn't sleep last night. I have had a lot of things going through my mind since our conversation in the living room. I have a lot of questions." She took another sip of her coffee. "Last night has made me realize that something happened to you in that accident."

"I would like to know what is happening to you, Jim."

"I know this seems strange, but I can tell you one thing for sure." Jim paused as he poured his coffee.

"I told you, I know certain things that no one else could ever know. Also, Rob comes to me. He tells me more of what he has seen. After he does this, I am exhausted. It's like he sucks the energy from me." Jim walked over to where Kirsty was standing, pulled a stool up close to her, and sat on it.

"As I told you last night," He said in a strange voice, "I can tell you a lot more stuff. Ask me anything I can tell you. Prove to you what I know."

Kirsty could feel her entire body shudder and fill with goose-bumps.

What was he going to tell her? She wondered.

Jim leaned over the counter so that he could look Kirsty in the eyes. She diverted her stare and looked beyond him, avoiding eye contact. He took her hands and held them in his, lightly pulling on them, forcing her to make eye contact.

"Last night, you cried yourself to sleep. You prayed to God for me to get well. You asked God to protect you from me if I ever go crazy again. Honey, I would never hurt you. How can I prove this to you? Is there one thing you would like to know about your past?" His voice was unfamiliar, but his words came out mesmerizing.

Kirsty's mind raced. She started to blink away tears. The silence seemed to last forever. She finally brought herself to stare directly into Jim's steel-blue eyes. Her breath was shaking. She was shaking.

"When I was young, my mom and dad were killed in a car accident. My aunt told me that he was driving my mother to the hospital. I have dreams of being with them, but my aunt Darla who raised me, said that I stayed with her while they went to the hospital. She told me that my mom was not feeling well, and daddy was taking her in to see the doctor." She blinked away tears.

"My dream was so real, I swear that I saw my dad looking over at the radio, trying to put my mom's favorite station on when he went into a ditch and hit a tree."

Jim nodded.

"That was not a dream, Kristy. You were in the car. Your mom was crying in pain and asked your dad to put some music on to help her relax. Her favorite station didn't come in too well on the road between your house and town. He was trying to tune it in when the corner came up too fast. He couldn't make the turn."

Kristy does not move her stare. Her eyes overflowed with tears.

"Your mom was in labor with your little sister." He said, wiping away Kristy's tears. "Your parents didn't want you to know your mom was pregnant. The ultrasound showed that there was something wrong with the baby early on. The doctors didn't know exactly what, so your parents decided not to tell you until she was born. Just in case she didn't survive."

"Your aunt was trying to protect you. She didn't want you to know that you were in the car that night. Afraid that you might start to remember things. Remember seeing something awful. Your aunt was to meet your dad at the hospital and take you home with her until the baby was born," He continued. "Your parents died on impact. The doctors tried to save the baby, but she was too sick and wouldn't have made it either way."

"Her soul watches over you, Kristy. She protects you. Remember how you found that dime on the bed after you made it? That time right after your first miscarriage? That was her, Kristy, your sister. She was trying to tell you everything will be okay. I tried to tell you back then about the dimes. Remember? Well, it's all true, Honey."

Kristy broke down crying. No one could have known what Jim had told her. Kristy's aunt rarely talked about it and never mentioned a little sister. She doesn't even remember telling Jim about the dime. She didn't want him to know she didn't believe the story about the dimes. She was not a believer in ghosts, spirits, and hauntings, or reincarnation. But, Jim was a believer, long before his accident. Somehow, he knew about her parent's accident and the dime. He told her like it happened yesterday.

"Who told you all of this?" Kristy sobbed. "How long did you know this?"

"I saw this when I died. Rob fills me in with bits and pieces."

Kristy composed herself, finished her coffee, and walked over to the kitchen sink.

"I think we need to talk with someone about this." She stated. "Someone who can help us deal with it." She rinsed out her cup and put it in the dishwasher. She turned around to Jim, who was still sitting and staring at her. His eyes were filled with tears.

"I'm sorry if I hurt you," he said, stuttering through his words.

Kristy, concerned and scared, walked over and kissed him on the forehead. "That's okay, Jim. You have been through a lot in the past couple of months. Time will help heal all of this. I am going to stay with you and help you. I believe in you, and I still love you with all my heart."

Jim smiled pitifully.

They decide after breakfast to call up Tom and Jenni and have them come over to hear Jim's story. To help them understand what was going on in Jim's head.

Tom and Jenni were shocked when they heard how much Jim knew about this kidnapping.

Tom seemed as mesmerized as Kristy was when she first heard some of the stories. "People just don't know this stuff or even come up with such concoctions!" Tom blurted out.

Jenni cut Tom short.

"If my grandfather were alive, he would talk to you about this." She looked into Jim's woeful eyes.

"You see things and know things no one else will ever see or know. You talk to your Spirit Guardian. He tells you everything you want to know. He reminds you of what you saw while in Heaven," The corners of her mouth curve up to a smile. "That, my friend, is truly amazing! Try to embrace it, not scare it away, Jim."

"Like I told Kristy, you have a Weyekin. That means Spirit Guardian in Nez Perce. It's Rob," she said. "My grandfather rarely spoke of this as he only heard about it from his elders. You died in that accident, Jim. You and Rob died. His soul decided to cross over, but somehow yours wanted to stay. You have more to do here on Earth," She looked sternly into his blue eyes. Her eyes were as dark as ever.

"What did Rob tell you?"

Jim sat back staring at Jenni, frozen.

"It's okay. You don't need to say anything. It may be too early to be looking for that anyhow." She looked over at Kristy.

"How has he been at night? Has he been having nightmares? Blacking out? Those are all signs that the Weyekin is speaking with Jim."

Kristy looked at Jim. He was sitting silently, almost trance-like.

"Most of the time, he is like that-in a trance." She answered. "He takes medicine to help him sleep, so I haven't witnessed any nightmares or terrors."

They all sat in silence, watching Jim. He does not move a muscle, staring ahead.

Jim finally broke his stare, blinked, and turned to Tom.

"Those girls on the news. Carmen and Harper. I know what happened to them. I know all about them. Harper died just after the kidnapping. It was an accident." He then turned his attention back to Jenni.

"Carmen is alive. She is in considerable trouble. Those guys are dangerous," he paused. "I need to go to the police and tell them everything."

Jim, for a moment, forgot that his friend sitting in front of him was a police officer, and he was a detective. Tom just sat back and listened to what Jim had to say.

Jim started his story.

"The girls were just having a little fun before school started. The day was hot, and the beach was crowded. These men who ran into the girls on the beach were a little older. Harper didn't know that Carmen had been communicating with one of the men she had met on social media. The two of them had been texting and talking for months. They had planned this meeting, turning it into a double date—all this unbeknownst to Harper.

The four of them talked, swam in the ocean, and hung out for the day. In the end, they finally exchanged phone numbers. Like average teenage relationships start." Jim looked around. Everyone had their full attention on him, listening to every word. Especially Tom.

"Before the girls left the beach that day, they made plans to meet up with the boys that night. It would start with a trip to the movies, and who knows what else. At first, Harper was reluctant to go. Her parents kept a close eye on her and warned her about going with strangers. But, she finally gives into Carmen's pleas and promises of a fun time. One last hoorah before school began," Jim paused. "Those men had their own agenda."

Kristy started to get nervous. "Why don't I make some iced tea for everyone." She was hoping this would stop the rest of the story. She knew it couldn't be good. They all ignored her, focusing on Jim's story.

"The girls met up with the men from the beach." Jim continued. "When they pulled up in a big, dark gray van, with dark windows. Harper became a little nervous. Carmen was too excited to notice or even pay attention. She acted like she knew one of the guys. Like he was her friend. He kept telling her she was beautiful. The stuff she liked to hear. Carmen walked up to the window and talked with the men. Harper, staying back, wanted to run at this point. Carmen begged her to come with, convincing her that nothing would happen. That, if anything kinky *did* happen, they would leave. Harper reluctantly climbed into the van with Carmen close behind. The van's door automatically slid shut and locked. The girls were now trapped. Vanishing without a trace."

Kristy again interrupts. "I'm going to make some coffee and tea," She said in a louder voice, now shaking a little.

Tom got up and looked at Jenni, who had not moved since Jim began his story.

"Jenni, would you like some tea?" He asked her. "I know I would like to have some," Tom walked away from the table, forcing Jim to stop with the story for now. They all needed a little mental break.

Kristy made tea and poured four cups. Everyone gathered around Jim, anxiously awaiting the rest of his story.

"Well," Jim began again. "Once the van drove off, Harper started to question where they were headed and tried to open the van's door. That's when one man leaped into the back and bound the girls with duct tape. He then covered their heads with pillowcases. The van then rushed off. Neither of the girls knew where they were headed. Both wished they had stayed home that night."

Kristy took a long sip of her tea.

"I don't know if I want to hear the rest of this story." She stated. "I have been watching the news, and those girls have a big reward for them. I have been hoping they would be found before Christmas. Those parents look so pitiful each week, pleading with the kidnappers. Harper's dad is a millionaire and is offering a huge reward for her safe return."

Jim resumed. "Yes, and the kidnappers know that. Carmen was bragging to the one she met online about how rich her friend was. That was how they knew this was the right friend. Harper Bengston's friend."

"You see, Harper met one of the kidnappers several years ago while on a plane alone coming from London. She told him everything. He listened. He waited, he planned, and he knew when the time came." Jim's voice became malevolent, intimidating his listeners.

Kristy gathered all the cups and turned to ask Jim a question.

"So, how do you know about Harper dying? Or if she died?" She paused and waited for an answer.

"Rob told me. She and Carmen were separated. They decide, after a fight with the girls at the shack, to separate them. Harper was brought back to the van. She is being brought to the men's boss. The men from the beach took Harper in the van and quickly drove off. She had gotten distraught, as her gut instincts were telling her that this kidnapping might get even worse than it already had. She started to panic and tried to kick out of the van. When she did this, the van door popped open. Harper was wrapped in a sheet, some of it hanging off of her feet. As the door popped open, her feet fell out, and so did the sheet. As the sheet hit the gravel, the back tires caught it, pulling Harper out of the van onto a gravel road. The van was driving quite fast and slid sideways over the rocky gravel and on top of Harper's chest, crushing her. It happened at the same time as my accident with Rob. She was the girl that was standing next to me while I was trying to call Rob back. Her face was blurry, but I remember her smile."

Kristy and Jenni were in tears.

"Oh my God." Tom blurted out.

"Yes, Tom. Harper crossed over. She could have lived, but she didn't want the men to abuse her body. Harper didn't want that for her or her parents. So she decided to make a choice. You see, some people can make this choice. Harper was a good soul, and she had a choice. Her parents will never know. Carmen will never know. But,

I know, and I am telling you, so now you know," Jim looked at his hands. They were sweating.

Tom sat back in his chair, trying to comprehend Jim's story. He had been following this story on television like many others across the country. But, he and the people in this kitchen right now were told the truth. At least he thought, Jim's rendition of the truth. The story was being told like Jim was standing there himself. But, how could he have made any of this up? What would Jim have to gain? Why was he telling this story now? Was he somehow a part of the kidnapping? Tom shook his head and walked over to the window. There were a few snowflakes lazily falling from the sky. They came from Heaven, he thought. That's where Harper Bengston was right now, listening to her story being told by James Cavalier. Jim had met Harper in Heaven when he died in the accident. Jim had seen a part of Heaven very few people have ever seen. Tom had heard once that time did not exist in Heaven. That would explain how Jim knew so much when he didn't cross over. He just visited for a short time, Earth time.

An eternity in just a few Earth minutes, Tom thought. *He, Jenni, and Kristy only saw a small portion of Jim's world, and they were mentally exhausted.*

"The kidnappers put Harper's body in a big plastic drum out in the back of the shack. They pounded the lid on it. That is where you will find Harper." Jim's voice now sounded pitiful.

"I think that we should go to the authorities about this," Tom spoke up. "Maybe there is time to save the other girl."

They all looked at Tom like he was crazy.

"How are we going to explain how Jim knows this stuff without being involved?" Kristy asked. "I mean, if Jim goes to the station and tells his story to them, they'll think he is a suspect, or he might know the suspects!"

Jim's eyes grew big, and he started to look scared.

"I knew I shouldn't have said anything to anyone." He said as he stood up and walked over to the kitchen window. "But, Tom was right about Carmen. She was in danger. Those kidnappers were monstrous people." He turned around. "I just don't know what to do." He said in a worried voice.

"Well, I think if I took you to the station and explained our situation. If I could get someone to listen to us, we could save Carmen," Tom said, coming up with a plan. "I know everyone very close here, and so do you, Jim. I don't think they will slap the cuffs on you that fast. Hell, they would probably be happy to see you!" Tom got up and walked over to Jim. "Let's go to the station, you and me."

Jim shrugged his shoulders.

"We gotta start somewhere." He said and followed Tom out the door and into his car. The girls stayed back at the house.

23

The Station

It was early afternoon, and everything was quiet when Tom and Jim arrived at the station. One of the deputies was sitting at his desk on the phone. He hung up when he saw Jim with Tom.

"Hey, buddy," He greeted them, looking a little shocked to see Jim. "Holy crap! Where did you find this fella?" He asked, motioning towards Jim.

"How the hell have you been?" He asked as he reached out to shake Jim's hand.

Jim, looking confused, cannot remember this man. Looking around, he barely remembered this place.

His blank look at the deputy must have said it all. The deputy's smile faded, and he turned back to Tom.

"This is Deputy Timly." Tom introduces the deputy to Jim.

"He started right before you left for....." Tom looked over at Jim.

"You only saw him a couple of times before you left." Tom corrected himself.

Jim stared at the deputy, trying to remember something about him.

"What brings you here today? Showing Jim around town?" The deputy walked over to his desk, motioning for the men to have a seat. "Please sit, and we can catch up a bit. Can I interest either one of you in a cup of coffee?"

"Well, we come to see someone about a case that Jim may have some important information on," Tom replied seriously. "Maybe you and Chief Brandt can help us out."

The deputy pulled himself up and sat on the edge of the old office chair. Jim recognized the sound as it creaked under his shifting weight.

Odd, Jim thought. *This particular sound of all things to remember.*

"Exactly what is going on? Is it regarding that missing girl in Coeur d'Alene?" He looked over at Jim, who was looking around the room, trying to remember anything and everything, ignoring the men's conversation.

Right now, Jim's brain was fixated on trying to remember this place. A place where he must have spent a lot of hours, starting when he was a boy.

"No," Tom replied. "It has something to do with another case. Is the chief here?"

"Well, he is out on a late lunch with his wife. He should be back in about fifteen minutes or so. Let me get you two a soda at least, and we can catch up on things until he gets back."

"Sounds good. I would like a diet soda, and what would you like, Jim?"

"W-w-well, I would like a Sprite," Broken from his trance, Jim stuttered out an odd answer. He felt like he was getting a headache. His mind had been stimulated a bit too much already today. Now, he would have to answer to the Chief of Police of Bonners Ferry when he couldn't remember this guy's face from any stranger on the street? Jim was a bit uneasy.

"Can I get some aspirin?" Jim asked Tom. "I am getting a splitting headache."

"I'm sure we can get you something; let's go back to my desk." He said as he rose from his chair. Since Tom and Jim were partners, they shared an office. Since Jim's accident, Tom had not touched his desk or belongings. Jim froze just outside of their office. He noticed the bronze plate on the door.

Detective J. Cavalier

&

Detective T. Mason

Tom walked over to his desk and pulled open a drawer. He took out a bottle with some pills in it.

"One or two?" He asked Jim as he opened the bottle.

"It's getting pretty bad," Jim answered as he looked around the office. Pictures of Tom, Jenni, Jim, and Kristy adorn the wall between the two desks. One, in particular, had a beautiful mountain range in the background. The four of them were holding mountain bikes. Jim got closer, getting a better look at the picture.

"I have not seen pictures of the four of us since I've been home," he said as he studied the photograph. "I was told I loved to ride my bike around town. A lot." He looked over at Tom, who was leaning back in his chair with his feet propped up on his desk, holding out two white pills.

"Yes, buddy. You did love to cycle. You would go out every chance you got. Kristy loved it as much as you did. You would cycle to work as many summer days as you could. Sometimes I would join you. I miss those days, and I look forward to biking with you again someday soon."

"We will, Tom. Once I get my balance and my brain back." Jim said, walking back towards his desk.

"For now, I'll keep my feet on the ground. I don't think my head could handle any more bumps to it anytime soon."

Erik peeked into the office and handed Jim his soda. Jim swallowed the pills and turned towards Tom.

"I would like to spend a little more time in the office to see if anything jogs my memory."

"Sure, we have a few minutes before the chief gets back."

The small desk sat in the corner facing a window overlooking the parking lot. File cabinets surrounded it, and on top were stacks of papers. All around the room were signs of Jim's past life. His life before the accident. Pictures of him, Kristy, Tom, and Jenni hung on the walls in frames from each adventure they embarked on together. Then, one image in the back caught Jim's attention. It was a picture of Rob kneeling over a massive bear. He walked over to the picture. His stomach started to ache. Jim noticed some of the photographs had both Rob and Jim in them. He stared closely at Rob, studying him. Every smile, every stitch of clothing, every pose. Jim continued through all the pictures. One had two large elk in it. Rob and Jim looked like they had won the lottery. They were high fiving over the lifeless animals. He noticed another picture of the two on horseback, standing in front of a dead sheep with massive horns, giving a thumbs up. If only he could remember those moments in time.

"I'm gonna miss those days with you, buddy." Rob's voice rang in Jim's head.

"You and Rob were headed to Alaska for a moose hunt when you got in the accident," Tom explained in a sad tone in his voice. "I was staying back to cover a kidnapping case we had in Coeur d'Alene."

"Rob told me that he knows where that girl is, too," Jim replied in a dazed speech.

Tom looked at Jim like he was crazy. That girl had been missing without a trace. It would be a miracle to find her.

"Really?" Tom asked doubtfully. "Where is she then?"

Jim walked around his desk and sat in his chair. He picked up the picture in the frame of him and Kristy on their bikes in the sunset. Jim smiled. He vaguely remembered that ride. He set the photo down and attempted to open his desk drawer.

It was locked.

"She's in a house." Jim slowly stated as he lifted a clock made out of bike sprockets, revealing a key. He took the key and opened the drawer. Inside was a little dish, and in it was a tarnished dime. Jim picked it up and held it in the air.

"This is her dime."

Tom's heart skips a beat.

"Excuse me, sirs," the deputy interrupted.

"The chief is back in his office. I told him you guys were here, and he was anxious to speak to both of you."

As they made their way back to the chief's office, people started filtering back in from lunch. Jim and Tom were quickly led inside, and the door closed behind them.

"Chief, I know about the two girls missing from Myrtle Beach. The rich girl named Harper Benson and her friend Carmen Potter!"

"Really? Please fill me in as to what you know about this, Jim," The chief looked up from his desk and locked eyes with Jim.

Jim begins his story.

After many questions and stimulation from the chief, Jim began to see orange flashes with black shadows flashing back to orange. He realized he was starting to pass out.

Moments later, Jim started to wake up. Everything was blurry.

"We just need to get you home, buddy," Tom guided Jim out to his vehicle.

"The Chief will understand."

24

Taking it Easy

"*Hey, buddy!*" Jim could hear Rob's voice. "*What were you thinking! You can't just waltz back into your office and talk to your boss about some random kidnapping and not have any way to prove it!*" Rob's voice escalated in Jim's mind. "*I had to intervene!*"

Jim slowly opened his eyes; he could see Rob standing in front of him, his aura a bright blue-green. He realized now that Rob was the one who was making him blackout.

"*What do you expect me to do, Rob,*" Jim questioned as he looked around the empty bedroom. Empty except for Rob, himself, and the blonde-haired girl over in the corner.

Harper.

"*We have to come up with a plan first. Something to get the chief to trust in you. Some way of proving that you know how to find Carmen and the little girl from Coeur d'Alene!*" Rob suggested. "*Because there are many more girls, Jim. More girls are being picked up all across the country by this creep's thugs every day!*" Rob walked towards Jim, his aura fading, now with a faint orange glow swirling around it. "*We need to act as fast as we can. This case is so huge. You have no idea!"* Rob stopped in front of Harper, looking into her worried eyes. He smiled at her. *"Once we get them to believe you, we will be able to fly out and meet with the unit and give them some assistance. We need to act quickly, there is a ship leaving soon, and those girls will be on it!"*

"Ship?" Jim questioned Rob. His eyes were locked on Harper.

After a moment, Jim slowly started to come around, realizing he was sitting on his living room couch with Tom and Kristy looking at him. He closed his eyes again and took a deep breath.

He was drained.

"Are you okay?" Kristy's voice was wavering with concern.

"I want to go to bed," Jim said in a weak breath. "I'll be fine once I can lie down and rest. I am exhausted."

Tom helped Jim to his feet, and the three of them slowly made their way to Jim's bedroom. Jim sat on the edge of the bed and turned to curl up on his side. He was sleeping almost immediately.

Unnoticed in the corner of the room, a faint green glow with swirls of orange running through it.

****

Over the next few days, Kristy attempted to keep Jim quiet. She did not want him to end up back in the hospital.

I can't afford any more steps back. Kristy thought.

The only place he was allowed to go was to physical therapy. Then afterward, over to Tom and Jenni's cafe for a coffee and donut. That was it. Kristy stayed close by, making sure no one approached him or asked him questions to excite him.

Jim didn't argue. He didn't like when it happened that day at the station. The stimulation was just way too much too soon.

The only thing Jim kept worrying about, though, was Carmen. He could not keep his mind off of her. She was out there somewhere in a run-down shack, freezing, starving, and alone. The only one that could help her right now was him, and he was resting. It didn't settle right with Jim. But he knew that if he didn't relax and get better, he would not be any good at finding her or those other girls Rob had mentioned.

So, when Jim started feeling better, he convinced Kristy to call Tom and see what he thought about going back to see the chief.

Meanwhile, Tom had met with the chief and briefed him about what Jim knew. The chief wanted to meet with Jim as soon as possible to hear Jim's side of the story. He wasn't entirely convinced how Jim knew this stuff. Either way, they needed to get to the bottom of this.

This upset the chief. No matter what was going on right now, Jim might know something that could help the FBI. It was still an ongoing case. The story was still being run at least once a week on many of the news channels. Bradley Bengston's daughter and her friend were somewhere out there, as far as the chief knew. If Jim knew something about their whereabouts, he needed to tell the chief soon.

After Tom left the station, Chief Brandt decided to make a call to Jim's doctor.

Not too long after Kristy made a phone call to Tom, he showed up at her house. He was in uniform. The chief had sent him over to pick up Jim for questioning.

"The chief talked to Dr. Jones, and they decided that Jim had enough time to rest. There was an unsolved case that needed Jim's help," Tom relayed to Kristy.

Kristy was not happy seeing Tom arrive in his uniform and squad car.

"I am very sorry, Kristy," Tom sounded sincere. Kristy's eyes filled up with tears. "But, the chief gave me an order. I cannot refuse his orders, Kristy. He is my boss. I would be brought up on charges of insubordination and withholding evidence, and so would Jim. My hands are tied. It would be less traumatic if I took him in for questioning rather than someone else. Either way, Jim needs to tell the chief what he knows." Tom stood at the house's threshold, waiting for Jim to appear. He was waiting for Kristy to invite him in. Today, he felt like a stranger.

Kristy, not saying a word, gently swung the door open. She went to her bedroom to change and get ready to go to the station with Jim and Tom. Tom tried to persuade Kristy to stay behind, but she refused.

"I am not leaving him, Tom," Kristy stated boldly; her voice was shaking. "We both go, or we both stay. It's your choice."

Tom didn't argue. It was not worth it. Jim had to be questioned, and time was running out. The authorities in South Carolina needed to be informed of whatever information Jim knew. If this had to be done with Kristy, so be it. He stood just inside the doorway of the house, waiting patiently for Jim and Kristy to get ready.

Jim came out of the hallway bathroom and looked towards the front door, where Tom patiently waited.

"Hey, partner. How come you're all dressed up?" Jim started towards Tom.

"Jim, Tom is here to take you to the station for questioning. Your doctor said that you had had enough rest. They need you to tell your story, and then they are going to contact the department in South Carolina."

Tom held the door for them as they walked out to the car. They all get into Tom's cruiser. It was only a fifteen-minute drive to the station that had today felt more like hours. Deep down, Kristy knew that Tom was only doing his job. It still hurt her to have to do this. It was more for fear of damaging Jim's fragile mind. He had just started to seem more like his old self. She was not ready to lose him again.

"Kristy," Tom started to explain. "You know we need to find those girls. Jim had rested for a few days. They are running out of time."

He sighed. "Just think if you had a daughter that had been kidnapped, and someone like Jim could help her."

Kristy rolls her eyes as she rests her gaze out the side window. A light amount of snow blanketed the cold earth. She was thinking about what Tom just said. She couldn't possibly understand having a girl. Something she has longed to have for a very long time, let alone to have her taken away. But the idea of a loved one being kidnapped. Well, that did hit home.

Kristy's mind began to race with thoughts. *What if those girls were already dead! What if they think Jim took them? His alibi was driving with his now-deceased buddy off to a hunting lodge in Canada. Who would believe him that he didn't have anything to do with it? What if Jim blacks out again or has a full-blown seizure this time? What if he goes back into a coma?* Kristy started to feel uneasy. Jim reached over and took her hand. He somehow realized that she was beginning to panic. She looked up at him; he nodded and mouthed the words.

"It will be okay."

Kristy took a deep breath.

"It's okay, Tom," She answered. "You don't need to explain. You are just doing your job. It's just that I don't want Jim to get over-excited and blackout again. The doctor said that every time that happens, Jim's progression is set back. I just don't like the idea of this happening over and over again." She continued to look out the window from the back seat. Jim was sitting next to her, not saying a word. "Hopefully, everything goes well this time, Jim can explain what he knows, and we can go home."

At least that's what she hoped.

As they pulled up, the station was empty. The chief had ordered employees away from the station. They were ordered to stay quiet and not to approach Jim. It was for Jim's safety, as he didn't need any extra stimulation. The interrogation coming up was going to be enough stimulation. The deputies were only there in case Jim went crazy.

"Where is everyone?" Kristy asked, looking around. There were only two cars in front of the building and one squad car around the side. Not a soul outside.

"The chief ordered everyone away, except a few," Tom replied as he put the car into park.

They entered the station and were met by the chief and his deputy.

"Hello, Jim," The chief held out his hand. "You have lost some weight since I last saw you. How are you feeling?"

Jim looked at his hand for a moment. Then slowly reached out and shook it. Jim noticed that the chief's hand was massive and rough. He started to remember his scratchy voice. The chief was a big guy, about six-foot-six and 350 pounds, making Tom look small. His light blond hair was cut short to the point of almost baldness. He was covered in freckles. Jim looked at him, not saying a word. His recollection of this giant man with the big hands and rough voice standing in front of him smiling started to come back.

Kristy gently touched Jim's shoulder. He jumped, startled.

"Are you okay?" She asked. "We can wait one more day if you are not ready."

Jim cut her off as the chief shook his head 'no.'

"No, Carmen needs me. I need to do this. I should have done this the other day, but my damn brain didn't want to cooperate. Where do you want me to start?" He asked the chief.

"Well, everyone, please come into my office." The chief suggested, waving his hand to the left. The three of them entered and had a seat. The chief's computer was up on a live feed. There had been reporters around the clock at the Bengston house since the kidnapping; they had been slowly dwindling. Two were left.

Diehards, Tom thought, looking at the screen. He, too, had been following the case. Now, even more closely that he knew what Jim had told him.

"Well," the chief began. "We all know why we are here today. I was informed that you had some information regarding the two girls kidnapped a few months ago. Harper Bengston and Carmen Potter, is that correct?" He asked as he held out a recorder. It looked tiny in his large, thick hands. A little red light was lit, showing that the voice recorder was on. "Sorry, friend, but I need to record this entire story. It's protocol."

Jim took a deep breath.

"Where would you like me to start?" He asked.

"The very beginning," The chief replied.

"It was hot the day of the girls' kidnapping...."Jim began his story. It almost seemed unbelievable. He could barely remember his wife and coworkers by name, but he could describe the details of a kidnapping that happened on the other side of the country.

* *

"These predators also have the missing girl from Coeur d'Alene." Jim finished his story.

Looking shocked, Chief Joseph Brandt leaned forward in his chair.

"Wow," he crossed his hands and rested them on his desk.

"So, Harper Bengston, daughter of the millionaire, is dead? Does the same kidnapper have the Coeur d'Alene girl? What if you are wrong, Jim? What if those girls just ran away? We would be the laughing stock of the entire country!"

"I'm not wrong," Jim shook his head. "I have seen Harper. She and Rob have told me the entire story of what happened. She is scared for her friend Carmen, and she knows if I do not help her, Carmen will disappear forever. Right now, I am that girl's only hope! If we don't act fast, she will be gone forever! I can promise you that," Jim's eyes never left the chief's.

"Well then, prove it," The Chief demanded.

"Ok. Let me tell a story from your past? Something only you know. I can tell you anything."

The chief's heart skipped a beat, and he was not sure that he wanted to hear what Jim had to say. Not with everyone here, listening. He broke his stare and looked around the table.

"How bad will this be?" The chief's voice was trembling.

"They can leave." Jim nodded towards the others; his voice was deep and low.

The chief looked over at Tom. Tom stood up, opened the door, and led Kristy and the deputy out of the room.

The door closed behind them, and Jim started his story:

"You were thirteen when you saw your first dead body."

The chief stiffened in his chair. He knew where Jim was going with his story.

"You and your girlfriend were planning on hooking up that Friday after school. You were planning on losing your virginity to her. When she didn't make it to your meeting place, you went looking for her."

The chief interrupted Jim.

"Enough, Jim. I've heard enough."

But, Jim didn't listen.

"It was almost dark, and your bike light wasn't too bright. You didn't care at this point. You were so distraught when the girl never came. You were angry, and all you wanted to do was go home, cursing her name out loud as you pedal your bike home."

"Jim, I told you that I've heard enough!" The chief voice was getting louder.

Jim ignored the chief, continuing his story.

"As you are riding along the path, right before it crosses the road, you hear this grotesque groan. Your girlfriend was lying in a ditch. She had been raped and beaten."

The chief stood up, and he was now towering over Jim sitting across the table.

"Enough, I say!" His voice was shaking.

Tom opened the door to see what was going on. He saw the chief leaning over the table, sweating and shaking, holding his head down. Jim, like a statue, hadn't moved.

"Just, stop," The chief took a few deep breaths. "I fucking believe you. I haven't told a soul that I found her. I was so scared someone would have thought it was me! I just went home, not saying a word, and cried myself to sleep. I am haunted every day about that night. Thinking that if I had told someone, she would be alive today. She could have told them who her rapist was. Jesus Christ. I didn't need to relive that."

"I didn't think you would believe me if I were to tell you anything else. Please know that she forgave you. She understood why you left. It's okay, and her soul is okay."

Jim continued with his story about the investigation.

"As you know, right before my accident, I was investigating a case of a young girl that disappeared from her grandparent's house. That girl is still out there! She is one of many across the country that are being sold overseas in a human trafficking ring! Remember the number on the phone we could not identify? It was *his* number! The kidnapper!" Jim leaned into the table. "Why don't you call the Myrtle Beach police station and speak with their lead investigator. Ask them to pull all the girl's contact numbers from the phone they found. Let's see if that girl was communicating with the same guy. I bet the numbers match," Jim smirked.

"You may have cracked this case wide open!" Chief Brandt replied as he tried to comprehend how much Jim did know about this case. "This is just so unbelievable. I am having a hard time wrapping my head around it."

Jim broke his stare and looked around for Kristy, who was sitting next to him.

"Yeah, I hear ya. Try being in my brain these past few weeks." Jim could feel his heart begin to beat rapidly in his chest, the palms of his hands started to sweat. Kristy was his comfort zone. She reached over and touched Jim. He took a few deep breaths.

"It's okay, honey." She leaned over and whispered in his ear. "You can continue."

Jim ran his hands through his hair. They were shaking. He started to describe what he knew.

"On a red dirt road by the Georgia state line, there is an old, abandoned shack. It's off the road a bit, the driveway hidden from sight. If you didn't know it was there, you would drive right by it." The chief handed Jim a paper and pencil, and he started to draw a picture.

They watched in silence as Jim drew this shack. A shack where awful things had happened and where horrible things were still happening.

Jim slid the picture to the center of the table. He was finished with his story. The chief picked up the drawing, looking at it carefully.

"We need to contact the Myrtle Beach authorities."

"You can go home, for now." The chief said as he stood up from his chair. "Go home and get some rest. Things are going to start happening quickly, and you will need to save up your energy. I'm sure we will be flying out of here soon."

Once everyone left the chief's office, he picked up his phone and dialed Myrtle Beach's FBI department.

There was silence between Tom and Kristy as he brought her

home. Jim kept dozing off, exhausted from the stimulation earlier at the station. As Tom slowly pulled up the driveway in front of the garage, the motion lights turned on. Tom got out of the car and helped Kristy bring Jim into the house and to his bed. He barely stirred as Tom helped Kristy slide off his shirt and pants.

Jim slowly leaned into the middle of the bed and fell soundly asleep. Not bothering to try and get Jim under the blankets, Kristy didn't think he would wake up until morning anyhow. Tonight Jim needed his rest. If the FBI thought they had a break in the story, they might want to speak to Jim soon.

Kristy wanted to make sure Jim was prepared for that.

25

Syn's Plan

Syn planned to gather girls from all over the country. He figured that it would be harder for the authorities to track him if he stayed spread out. Syn only used his few trusted contacts that he had developed a business relationship with over the years. Once he found a girl, he would start the grooming process. When they were ready to run off or meet up with the person he pretended to be, he would send out one or two of his men. It was as easy as that.

Social media made this especially easy. No one ever came in direct contact with Syn. It was the perfect plan. He would arrange a drop-off point with his men.

Syn was always planning. If things didn't seem right, he would abandon the pick-up. Luckily for Syn, that only happened once. It was in a small town so far up north. No one would have ever suspected him. His timing had been off that week, and it happened to be some sort of firearm season. A ton of people with loaded guns entered the woods like something Syn had never seen! Around every corner on every dirt road, there seemed to be a truck parked or people walking. Everyone had a gun. It was almost like he was in a war zone.

Syn was almost to his pick-up point when he heard a series of gunshots. He panicked as he tried to turn around on the narrow road. Two men had walked out of the woods in front of Syn. They were covered in blood. He panicked and didn't know what to do at that point. So, he sped past them and the hidden barrel. Syn just kept driving until he came to a larger road that led him out of the woods and into a small town. He stopped at the small convenience store and gassed up. He left the area, stopping one last time to see the largest freshwater lake in the world. He would never forget it. A lake that was so large, no one could not see across it.

Syn weeded out all of the unwanted or desperate girls pretty quickly. He had been doing this long enough to detect suspicious activity on their social media sites. He would just drop, block, and erase them from ever finding him or contacting him. So many girls wanted to be liked, loved, or just to have someone listen to them. He didn't need the sketchy ones.

Syn kept a list of girls that he kept up in communication with. Mostly girls that had felt misunderstood and dejected by their peers. Who talked about running away to a better life.

Syn was drawn to these girls. He would begin by slowly grooming these girls, exchanging numbers, talking to them, and listening.

Those were the best kind of girls—the naive ones.

Then out of those girls, he weeded them down even more. He didn't need to be too greedy. Once he was pleased with his selection, Syn would arrange for the pick-up.

Syn couldn't risk getting caught. He continued to keep his identity hidden from his contacts like he had done all his life. So, he would arrange a drop-off point. One that he would find just far enough out of the city, so no one would hear the girl's screaming. First, he would watch the area, then set it up with a security camera and a hidden barrel. He would mark the location on GPS. When the time was right, he would then send it to his contact. They would bring the girl to the spot and stuff her into the large barrel. After Syn deemed the area safe, he would pick up the barrel with the girl in it and the camera. He would leave behind cash or drugs, or whatever the agreement was. He would leave that area and never return. One and done.

A quick trade. No one ever had seen Syn. That's the way he liked it.

Once Syn had the girl, he would bring her into the house he had on the outskirts of Charleston. The place he had been preparing for months. The house had windows that were painted and glued with curtains. All the doors had been sealed off, except the one leading to the garage. It made it easier to keep guard. The walls were made soundproof by adding extra layers of insulation and padding, then covering them with a false wall and paint. The house from the outside looked normal. Even inside the first door, it looked like an everyday home, except the back bedrooms. That was where he kept the nightmare in silence.

****

Syn looked over at the girl now sitting on his couch. She was his first abduction in the US. It was a fluke that she was even sitting there in front of him.

He considered her his prize.

She had reached out to him first. Syn immediately knew that she was a gullible, foolish little whore. All she was looking for was a friend to fuck while staying at her grandma's house. A friend to hook up with for a couple of weeks in late summer. A few months earlier, this girl had contacted Syn through one of his many profiles in one of his private groups. This group he had created long before he left China. Through this group, he was able to keep in contact with a few select teenage girls. He was getting to know them, getting them to trust him. Some posts he would not comment on. But this one girl. The one from Idaho. She was different. Desperate. Syn wanted her. He figured she would be an easy sell with her raging hormones.

Early on, when she first joined the group, he had investigated her profile. He created his profile of a guy from the same area her grandparents had lived. What a perfect idea! Looking at old pictures on her timeline, he could see her checked-in locations on her profile page. She made many trips to see them throughout the years. It was going to be too easy!

Syn's profile picture was what caught her eye, and it just so happens he was a guy. Nice looking and living in Coeur d'Alene! So, she decided that since she would be staying there in August, she would send him a friend request. Maybe hook up and hang out. Who knows what might happen to two hormone-raged teens. Syn waited a couple of days, scanned again through her profile before he accepted her request.

She was practically begging to be picked up. She only had two weeks in Coeur d'Alene with her grandparents, so Syn decided he would make it work.

That meant he would have to arrive in Coeur d'Alene a few days before her and familiarize himself with the city. He rented a room at the hotel under one of his assumed names and memorized everything about the little podunk town. It wasn't that hard to compare it to where he was from.

Syn took some pictures of the surrounding areas, something to prove where he was, which looked familiar to this stupid girl. Anything that would make picking her up easier. Like the abandoned playground just a mile or so down the road from her grandma's house. It was going to be the perfect meeting ground for them. Since she couldn't drive, she could just walk and meet him. The spot was perfect!

Syn snapped a picture of swing sets, which he had covered in red and pink rose petals. Sending the message:

I CAN'T WAIT TO SEE YOUR HOT ASS ON THIS ;)

Syn waited for a response. Hoping the girl recognized the area. He got an immediate response.

OMG!!! I KNOW WHERE THIS IS! IT'S NOT FAR FROM MY GRANDMA'S!! I CAN'T WAIT FOR YOU TO PUSH ME HIGH!

He smiled, looking at one of his phones.

This is going to be a piece of cake. He thought.

Syn and the girl started sending little texts and pictures back and forth. Like two teenage kids planning their first date. To hold hands, kiss, then who knows what. Her parents were only gone for two weeks, which meant they had to meet up soon to make the most out of their short time together.

Syn had to act fast.

I'LL BE HERE FRIDAY, MY PARENTS FLY OUT THEN, AND MY GRANDMA IS PICKING ME UP AT THE AIRPORT.

She gave Syn all the information he needed. He decided to check everything out before she arrived. He grabbed his keys and headed out the door.

Friday mid-morning, Syn found himself heading back to the airport. He needed to see this girl and what she was all about. He watched her plane slowly taxi up to the terminal. He stayed back unnoticed, waiting. It wasn't too long before she came rushing off the jetway, jumping into her grandma's and grandpa's arms.

She was cute, a little older than he thought, and she had no makeup on. Unlike most of her online pictures, where she was all painted up, wearing low-cut blouses. *Looking like a slut,* he thought. *It would be better if she were younger.*

He was glad he had saved those pictures she sent to him. They would be her selling point. They had gotten his attention. So, he didn't care what she looked like now, if she brought him money.

Syn didn't give a fuck much about anything else.

He watched them gather her suitcase and followed the three of them back to her grandma's house. He wanted to make sure that this was the place. They were unaware of Syn, from a distance, watching their every move. It was not long after she was in the car that the girl began to text Syn.

I'M HERE! FINALLY LANDED! HEADING TO MY GRANDMA'S HOUSE.

I know. Syn quietly watched from his car across the parking lot. *You're perfect and stupid.* He looked up from his phone and smiled as he replied to her message.

YAY! SYS (see you soon):

FOR SURE, WE CAN MEET UP TOMORROW, she texted.

HOPEFULLY, He replied.

Play hard to get. Girls liked that, Syn thought.

Early the following day, the girl began texting Syn. He didn't answer.

"*I just want to enjoy my fucking coffee first, bitch,*" He grumbled as he got dressed and headed for the nearest coffee shop. Ignoring her texts.

I should have just let one of the guys pick this one up. He thought.

As he sat in the corner of the coffee shop going through his private social group, his phone lit up with incoming texts from this girl.

WHAT'S WRONG?

U MAD?

I WANNA C U!

It worked. Syn chuckled.

NAH, JUST BUSY RN (right now)

TEXT YA LATER.

Now, leave me the fuck alone! I have another girl I'm looking at, a sad, lonely, desolate blonde. She needs me right now. Syn began his conversation with her, under yet another profile, on another cell phone.

He knew that he had to keep them separate. Right now, this girl needed his immediate attention. She was closer to the house he had in Charleston so that she would be an easier pick-up. Another one he would be handling on his own. He had to concentrate, making no mistakes. This girl was feeling abandoned by her family. Syn listened and gave her the advice she wanted to hear.

Later that night, Syn finally got back to the Idaho girl.

YOU THERE? He sent out a text.

SORRY I WAS BUSY BEFORE

SOMETHING UNEXPECTED CAME UP THAT I NEEDED TO TAKE CARE OF

I'M ALL YOURS NOW :)

She immediately responded:

YEAH I'M HERE ;)

AND WAS SAD N LONELY TIL NOW

Syn's phone rang.

"Hello." He answered in his best impersonation of a Midwest accent.

They talked most of the night. She wanted to see him and talk in person. He wanted to meet her also, but for different reasons.

Syn would tell her his plan. A plan that he had been working on since he started talking to her a few months ago. Unbeknownst to the girl, this plan would change her life forever.

Syn told her he would like to meet her at the park near her grandparent's house. After lunch, she would go for a walk. He would be waiting there for her. Then, they could get to know each other.

After all, they only had two weeks.

The following hours couldn't come fast enough for the girl. She had spent all morning straightening her hair and putting on her makeup. She wanted to look just perfect for him. Lunchtime with her grandparents went super slow. She ate as much as her nervous stomach could handle, then cleaned up the dishes. She was getting bonus points from gramma.

"Can I take Boo for a walk, granny?" The girl nervously asked.

"Of course, sweetie. Make sure you hang on tight. He likes to pull. He is not leash trained, ya know." Her grandma replied in a soft, soothing voice.

"Thanks, granny!" The young girl hugged her grandma tightly and quickly got ready for her walk.

Just before she left the house, she sent Syn out a text.

OMW (on my way)

Syn impatiently waited, pacing on top of the picnic table where he could get a good vantage point. He was just about to give up when he saw her walking up the road, turning into the abandoned park.

Walking a fucking dog. Really? He thought. *That wasn't part of the plan! What the fuck am I gonna do with this dog? It better be friendly.*

Syn *hated* dogs, mostly because he was afraid of them. Especially the big ones! He remembered some of the drug houses he went to in Russia. Those dogs had to be the meanest Syn had ever come across. The cartel needed them to be big and mean to their precious contents. This dog with the girl was big.

When the dog saw Syn, it began to bark, making Syn even more nervous.

The girl stopped and stood at a distance. She tried to keep the dog contained as it jumped at the end of the leash, barking at the man who was frozen on the picnic table.

She began to feel unsure of the situation. But it was too late, and she was already here.

The girl was quite surprised as she approached the guy.

Was this the guy she was supposed to meet? She thought. *He looked so much older than his profile picture.*

208 - SHANNON LEE

The girl started to get a little nervous. The dog could feel her energy and began barking again, lunging at the end of his leash.

OMG, Boo! Stop! You are making me scared! She thought as she cautiously walked up to the man. *He seemed more of a grown man than a teenage boy.* She thought. *What have I gotten myself into? It's too late to turn around. He has seen me.*

The girl took a deep breath.

"Hi." She tried to shout over the barking dog; her voice was trembling. "Sorry if he makes you nervous. He is pretty friendly, really."

She was finally able to settle the dog with a handful of treats. While the dog was eating its treats, she tied him to the picnic table. He stood more quietly, wagging his tail at the girl. He looked over at Syn and let out a deep, low growl. Syn, keeping a safe distance away from the mongrel, walked over to the swing set.

Once the dog was quiet, Syn sighed, smiling nervously at the young girl. She smiled back. Her makeup was flawless, her hair amazing. He noticed she was wearing one of her low-cut blouses under her jacket.

"Hi," Syn whispered and half-waved at the girl. "I was attacked by a dog when I was younger. They all make me nervous now." He continued in a low voice, not wanting to alarm the dog.

"Come over here and swing with me." He grabbed the swing.

The dog again growled and started to yip nervously.

Fuck. Syn thought. *Couldn't you have left the fucking dog home?*

"It was easier to get away telling my grandma I would take Boo for a walk." The girl threw over some more treats. "That's all I got." She looked over at the man sitting on the swing.

He looked so old. The girl pondered. *What should I do?*

He tapped the swing next to him. He had covered it in rose petals.

"C'mon over and sit," He encouraged the nervous girl. "I don't bite any more than that dog."

Besides, he thought, *he was not going near that damn dog.*

The girl took another deep breath. She could feel her heart beating in her throat. She wanted to run. But she didn't want to be rude.

Maybe this was a bad idea. The girl looked around. *How can I get out of this now? If I try to leave now, it will hurt his feelings.* She looked back at the dog, now more relaxed.

I'll swing for a bit, then go home. I'll chalk it up to a lesson learned: I'll delete this one from my contacts. It'll be over.

As she took a few steps closer to the man, she could smell his cologne. It smelled almost intoxicating. Looking at him now swinging, he didn't seem so scary. She forced a smile.

He smiled back.

This meeting was risky for Syn. He wore his sunglasses and ball cap, the glasses were large enough to hide most of his face, and the hat would shade the rest. He could not risk her seeing his entire face. This job was one he had to do himself, and he wanted to make it quick.

After talking for some time, the young girl began to relax. Syn gave her a slight push on the swing. He was touching her softly with each gentle push. Nervously, the girl stiffened with each touch. His cologne wisped through the air as she drifted up to him on the swing.

"It's okay," He whispered. "We can take it slow. I'm in no hurry."

He felt her start to relax as she began to tell him more about herself, where she lived, where her parents worked, her school, and her hobbies. Everything about her: he listened, pushing her gently.

Syn had always been a good listener.

Finally, Syn slowed the swing until the girl was stopped. He walked around to the girl's front side and put his hands softly on her thighs.

"I won't hurt you," he said softly. "We will take this at your speed."

She wrapped her legs around his waist, shocking him! He pulled his hands away, and she let go. At this point, he couldn't afford to scare her.

Sitting silently, she looked at the ground and started to shake.

"Would you like a drink? It will relax you,"

"Yeah, it probably wouldn't hurt," The girl answered, her voice still a little shaky. She stayed motionless on the swing as Syn walked to the trunk and grabbed a bottle of beer out of the cooler. The dog was now asleep under the picnic table.

"I've come prepared." He handed her a bottle while he took a long drink of his own.

"Cheers." She held up her bottle and started to drink, grimacing as the bitter beer washes down her throat. She tried to guzzle it quickly, stopping to cough and catch her breath midway through. Syn pushed at the bottom of the bottle, forcing her to finish it.

Gone. The girl thought as she threw the bottle over at the sleeping dog. It jumped and ducked further under the table.

Syn ran his index finger across her wet lips, tracing up the side of the girl's cheek. He kissed her softly on the lips. She began to feel numb inside as the fear rose through her body. There was something inside of her shouting at her to run away. That was when she realized it was a trap. She was unable to move. She started to breathe more heavily as he kissed her neck.

Oh, God, RUN! Run, you dummy. She tried to get off the swing but instead melted into Syn's awaiting arms. He held her tight, kissing her as she continued to feel the effect of the drugs.

In one last effort, the girl attempted to push Syn away. It was too late; her world was spinning out of control. The drugs had taken full effect. Her legs started to feel like jello. She fell into Syn's arms, her face pressing into his neck as she collapsed. He leaned in, grabbing onto her as she fell into him.

Within a minute, she was completely passed out. Syn picked her up and carried her over to his car.

The dog jumped up and started to whine as he watched the girl disappear inside the car.

"Shut up, you fucking mutt," Syn grumbled as he walked around the car.

The girl did not know that her drink was laced with something that would make her powerless. The girl tried to scream out, only to slur her words. Syn slammed the car door shut.

All of this was way too fucking easy. Syn chuckled to himself. *Except for that fucking dog barking!*

The dog barked louder once he no longer saw the girl.

Syn got into the car and drove out of the parking lot, the dog still barking.

The girl's cell phone started ringing. Syn rifled through the girl's shirt and felt the buzzing. He pulled the phone out of her bra.

'*I love my mom,*' Flashed across the screen. He changed the notification to ignore and turned the phone off. He then wiped it free of prints.

"Fuck." Syn cursed under his breath. He looked in the rearview mirror and saw the dog barking even crazier now, pulling at the leash. It finally frees itself and runs after Syn's car.

'*Fucking barking idiot,*' Syn whispered to himself as he sped down the highway.

He rolled down the window and threw the phone out into the ditch. The dog stopped and smelled the phone before starting back towards the car.

As he drove past grandma's house, he could see her looking out the window, down the highway from where he had just come. Little did she know, this was the kidnapper driving past her house with her granddaughter unconscious in the trunk of his car.

But, grandma never noticed the silver Impala driving by.

****

A few months earlier, Syn was finishing the house in Charleston. The room where he would be storing the girls was the only room completed so far.

He needed to have such a holding area for the girls, close enough to the port to get a large group of girls together and ship them out. But, most of all, he needed a partner. One he could depend on. One who would stay loyal, one who was already hooked on drugs and money. Not just on drugs, but sex, money, and dealing. That kind of trust would be hard to find.

Syn decided he needed to go back to Beijing to find his assistant. This kid, like Syn, lived alone on the streets. No one would notice him missing. He was perfect for what Syn needed! When Syn was finished with him, he would kill him.

No witnesses.

This guy was more than willing to help Syn. The promise of girls, drugs, moving to America, and lots of cash was too good to turn down!

The only stipulation was that he had to do whatever Syn wanted and keep his nose clean while working for Syn. That, or he would pay the ultimate price.

The guy couldn't turn this offer down. It was too good to resist.

26

Myrtle Beach

The chief made the first call out to the FBI agents, and after several transfers and repetitive statements, he finally reached the special agent leading the case.

She answered the call with a loud, boisterous voice.

"Special Agent Dulcey speaking."

"Hello, Special Agent Dulcey? It's Chief Brandt from over in Sandpoint, Idaho. I have one of my detectives claiming that he knows where your two missing teens are."

"How is that possible for your guy out in Idaho to know what is going on with my kidnapping case here in Myrtle Beach?" She continued, barely taking a breath. Her voice rang in the chief's ear.

"Did he know the girls, or did he have any contact with them?" Dulcey asked, not letting the Chief answer one question before she fired another one at him.

"If he knows anything about this case, we will need to bring him in for questioning ASAP." Her voice shrilled to the point that the

214 - SHANNON LEE

chief had to pull the phone away from his ear. He let Dulcey finish with her barrage of questions.

The phone, for a moment, was finally silent.

The chief began to tell Jim's story of how he and Tom were investigating a missing girl from Coeur d'Alene when Jim was in a horrific car accident that killed his best friend.

He told her that his detective had come into the station saying that he knew about the girls, how he had seen who took them, and knew where they were. He said that when he was in that accident and was pronounced dead, he had gone to Heaven. While there, he saw everything. Everywhere.

The only clue he could show for this was a contact number in the girl's phone and a sketch of an abandoned shack.

The number was not traceable. But the chief still read the number to Dulcey, hoping there might be a link somewhere. There was a long quiet pause on the other end of the line.

"Oh my God! The number matches perfectly to the number we have taken from the phone we found!" Special agent Dulcey exclaimed. "We just may have a serial kidnapper on our hands! I'll give you my fax number, and you can send me a copy of the sketch! I'll get working on this!"

The chief got a cold chill down his spine. The hairs on the back of his neck stood on end. There was a break in the case linking two kidnappings from different parts of the country. The best news was that they had a lead.

We may have a serial kidnapper on our hands! Dulcey's voice repeatedly rang in his ears.

"We need to get your James Cavalier out to Myrtle Beach as soon as possible!" She shouted.

****

Special Agent Dulcey was a headstrong person with an even more vibrant personality. One of her daughters was the same age as both girls. She was refusing to give up on them. She just had that hunch, bringing this story closer to her than any of the other cases she had been assigned.

Dulcey also was a devout Christian and very involved in her church. The same church that the Bengstons had attended. Their daughter Harper and her daughter Emily attended the same Sunday school. She had watched Harper grow up into a beautiful young, talented lady singing in the Church choir. Sundays haven't been the same since she disappeared.

Dulcey didn't like how that made her feel. Making her that much more determined to bring in James Cavalier to Myrtle Beach to help those girls come home! It also was the first case in her career that she had yet to solve.

The Bengston's had just started to come back to church after being absent for a few weeks. It was especially hard for Dulcey. She wanted to talk to them. But, she just couldn't bring herself to approach them.

Dulcey sat with her husband and kids; she could not even make eye contact the first time the Bengstons walked through the church doors. Everyone watched in silence as they walked down the aisle towards the front of the church, staring ahead and avoiding eye contact with anyone. Dulcey breathed a sigh of relief when they took their seats up close to the pulpit. The two families used to share a pew towards the back of the church. But, not anymore. Things were different.

Could she blame them? The thought ran through her mind. *So far, she has been a failure.*

The kidnappings had been hard on everyone involved. The longer the girls were missing, the worse the guilt haunted Dulcey. She had no answers for this sweet family.

Until today, when she answered the call from a Bonner County police chief stating he had some information regarding this case. Now, she wanted to talk with this Detective Cavalier as soon as she could. She needed to know where the girls were and who had them!

****

After she hung up the phone with the Bonner County Chief, Dulcey called her team members together for an emergency meeting.

Each detective was hand-picked by Dulcey to be on her team. It only took about half an hour for them to assemble at the station. They had the drive and the determination that was almost like her own.

But, Dulcey was about to push them to their breaking point.

She briefly told them all about the phone call from the Bonner County Sheriff's office in Idaho. She held up a sketch of a shack that was faxed over to her.

"Ok, gang. We have a lead, and it's coming in from the other side of the country! A kidnapping from Idaho that may have a link to ours. There is some sort of 'psychic detective' with a mutual phone number." Dulcey told them the story.

"The Bonner County Chief of Police in Sandpoint, Idaho, has called to inform me that one of his deputies had some information on our Bengston kidnapping case," She continued. "A few months ago, they had a kidnapping up there that this deputy had been investigating. Not long after that, he was involved in a horrible car accident that had killed his friend and nearly took his life. This detective had been hospitalized up until just a few weeks ago."

"Soon after he left the hospital, he presented to his chief in Sandpoint with some strange connections to our case. The most interesting being the contact number on their missing girl's phone. It matches one of the numbers that we cannot identify on Carmen Potter's phone. He also faxed me a drawing of a shack where the detective believes the girls are being kept. The deputy states he had seen the shack with the girls in it while in a coma. Guys, if he knows something, this could help us break this case wide open!"

"So, we are supposed just to believe that this guy had an epiphany while in a coma?" One of her deputies asked. "What if he and his friend were the kidnappers? Who is to say otherwise?"

"I have a gut feeling about this," Dulcey replied, trying to ease her team member's mind. Her faith in God was strong, and she had always listened to her intuition. That, she believed, was what made her the great detective that she had become.

She stood proudly at the table with the map in her hand. The sketch of the shack, along with several pictures of the girls, was laid out on the table. Dulcey set Carmen's cell phone on top of the pile. All of it for everyone to see.

Dulcey laid the office phone in the middle of the table and put it on speaker. She made a call to both the girl's parents and briefed them on the phone call from Idaho and what their next plan of action was. She also informed them that this lead might be the closest thing they have to locate the girls. She also told him that once she talked more to Detective Cavalier in person, she would again reach out to them. They were thankful for the call and would wait for any more information.

"We need to be on our A-game," She looked around and made eye contact with each of her staff members. "I know I have pulled you from your families and loved ones, but you know they are safe. The Bengstons and Ms. Potter don't have that right now. So, it's our job to do our best, if it takes hours, days, or weeks. We will bring back those girls. I trust that and know you all have it in you. You are my best, don't let me down!"

Dulcey pulled out a map of South Carolina and laid it across the table. She circled Myrtle beach and drew with a red pen the line where Harper Bengston lived and then where Carmen Potter lived. She connected that to where the girls lived and drew a line to Barefoot Landing.

Dulcey started the brief.

"We found a backpack with Carmen Potter's phone inside it. It had been lying behind a dumpster by Barefoot landing. It was weathered and had some water damage. Luckily it was in a protective case, which kept it mostly dry. The phone was cleaned thoroughly and charged. It had remained locked until earlier today. Our IT people, along with Carmen's mom, finally figured out the password." Dulcey looked around the table at her team of detectives. "Once we opened her phone, we found this." She throws a bunch more photos of the girls on the table, over the map. "There is also that number on the phone that Carmen had been in touch with for about six weeks. There were back and forth texts. This guy was communicating with Carmen for quite some time!"

"This person convinced her to give him her number after he friended her on social media. The texts go right up until they meet up on the beach! We believe there are two of them. The texts end when they plan on going on a double date. The odd thing is, Harper has no clue she is being set up on a date at all. Somehow Carmen must have persuaded her to go out with them to the movies. Somehow, Carmen's backpack with the phone inside was left behind. Lucky for us, some good citizens found it and brought it to the police station!"

"Just earlier today, I decided to send out a text to Harper's phone. Just to see what would happen."

A distinct chime came from Carmen's phone. Dulcey paused for a moment. They all watched as it buzzed across the table, its screen lighting up with text notifications from Harper's phone.

Harper's name flashed across the screen. They all looked at each other in shock.

HELLO? Read the text

No one said a word. They all just stared at the cell phone, frozen like mannequins in a department store window.

Dulcey picked up the phone and typed back.

HI.

IS THIS HARPER?

Everyone, still in shock, stared silently at the phone.

CLOSE

Dulcey types: CARMEN?

LOL

WELL, THEN WHO IS THIS?

Long silence. Minutes seemed like hours as they sat, staring at that pink phone laying in the middle of the table, the screen now black.

"Well, what the hell does that mean?" One of the team members asked out of frustration.

"It means that whoever has Harper's phone is not Harper." Another answered.

"It also might mean the kidnapper has Harper's phone!" Dulcey responded. "Either way, we need to find out who is on the other line, using Harper's phone." She picked up the phone and texted:

THIS IS THE FBI, WE HAVE COMPENSATED THIS PHONE.

YOU NEED TO TURN IN THAT PHONE IMMEDIATELY TO THE NEAREST POLICE STATION. IT IS WANTED AS EVIDENCE IN A FEDERAL INVESTIGATION.

She placed the cell phone on top of the photos of the girls.

THAT AINT GONNA HAPPEN came across the cell screen.

Dulcey gasped.

It's him! She thought, picking up the phone.

AGAIN, THIS IS THE FBI, YOU WILL BE CHARGED WITH WITHHOLDING EVIDENCE IF YOU DO NOT TURN IT IN!

There was a long silence. Dulcey could feel her blood pressure rising with every minute that passed by. Then, the pretty pink phone once again lights up, buzzing with an incoming text:

I HAVE THE GIRLS

I DEMAND A LARGE CASH REWARD FOR THEIR SAFE RETURN I KNOW THAT ONE BELONGS TO A MILLIONAIRE

Pause.

NO COMPROMISING ON THE AMOUNT OF CASH.

"Woah!" One of the lieutenants shouted out. "What the hell!"

They all had their focus on the pink cell phone in the middle of the girls' pictures.

"What should we say in response?" One of them asked.

Dulcey picked up the phone, opened the text, and looked around at her team. She made eye contact with each one.

"We're gonna try to keep the conversation going. It will help us find out what tower that cell is pinging from." She started to type:

WHAT KIND OF REWARD ARE WE TALKING ABOUT HERE?

"One question at a time." She stated. "We need to get that ping."

Minutes seemed like hours as everyone stayed motionless, staring at the phone.

Then, the answer came:

5 MILLION DOLLARS

IN CASH

Immediately Dulcey texted back:

Again, silence. Everyone was on edge. HOW DO WE KNOW THE GIRLS ARE EVEN ALIVE?

THEY ARE. GET YOUR MONEY TOGETHER IF YOU WANT THEM BACK.

No one around the table spoke a word. Dulcey continued to study the map. Some of the things just didn't make sense to her. She looked closely at the proximity of each location. It was all over the map.

Were the kidnappers trying to confuse them? Thoughts were racing through her mind. *Were they still in the area? When was the backpack dropped off?*

They needed to find out where that cell tower Harper's phone was pinging off.

WELL, WE NEED PICS FOR PROOF. THEN WE'LL TALK $$

Dulcey hit send.

"We need to get that damn ping," She grumbled. "Once we do, we can narrow it to exactly what area this sketch came from and where that shack is. The detective from Bonner County Sheriff's department has no clue exactly where this was. He just knew that there was an abandoned shack on a gravel road in the woods." Dulcey's voice was stern and serious. She picked through the stuff on the table and pulled out the sketch of a shack.

"We need to get that detective out here to help us visualize this. We need to know exactly where in the hell this place might be." She waved the sketch through the air.

A snap chime came upon Carmen's phone.

They all gathered around as Dulcey opened it.

It was a picture of Harper, scared, sitting in the back of a vehicle. Her mouth had been duct-taped, and she was wearing a white lace shirt.

It disappeared as fast as it appeared.

Then, another snap chime.

This time it was a picture of Carmen, she looked dirty, she

was wearing an oversized baggy black t-shirt, unlike something she would typically wear, and her hair was knotted up in a mess.

"There you go," One of them spoke up. "Photo proof that the girls were still alive. Let's go get these scumbags!"

"Not so fast," Dulcey interrupted. "There was something odd about Harper's picture. She was clean, her hair still made up, and she was still in the same clothes that she was in at the beach. Her face was puffy and bruised. It looked like she had been crying. That was the only thing out of place in the photo." She stood up and looked around at her team.

"If you all are too quick to jump to conclusions, you will fry this case," Dulcey's eyes were big with excitement. "We need to get together a plan to set up a meeting spot for this ransom exchange. I know that I have the best of the best here in front of me. So, we need to save those girls and bring them home!" She sat back in her chair. "We need just a few more texts to get a solid ping...

Carmen's phone went off again.

SO HOW ABOUT IT?

ARE THEY WORTH 5 MIL?

Dulcey took a deep breath. She typed in her response.

OF COURSE-NAME THE TIME AND PLACE

"Now we wait. The ball is in his court," she said, frustrated. They all sat staring at Carmen's phone.

"I have contacted Mr. Bengston," One of Dulcey's team members informed her. "He is going to contact his bank and try to get the cash together. We also have narrowed where the pings are coming from," She stated in a southern voice. Her eyes never left her laptop as she walked over to Dulcey and held the screen so she could see.

"The phone last pinged off a tower somewhere just outside St. George!!!" Dulcey shouted. "The kidnappers have not moved! They must be hiding out somewhere in the woods!"

"Well, then we need to contact the sheriff there. We should let him know we are coming once Detectives Cavalier and Mason land!"

"Detective, get a call out to the local police department in St. George!" Dulcey ordered one of her staff. "Let's get an aerial map of that area as well to see if we can spot the shack from the air."

"We will pick up the Idaho detectives at the airport in the morning, and they can brief us on the drive to St. George," Dulcey stated. "Was that call made out to the Charleston Sheriff's office yet?" She asked one of her team members.

"They are putting a team together for standby," He replied.

"I just hope the hell this detective from Idaho is right!"

Dulcey picked up the drawing of the shack and walked quickly over to the printer to make some copies.

"This is the sketch of the shack. Take one and study it. I want everyone to be familiar with this picture. Hopefully, when Detective Cavalier gets here, he can give us some more information on the kidnapper and this shack he drew." She studied the picture. "We need to get fully focused on finding these two girls before it's too late!"

"We are not going to announce it just yet, but there may be more girls! Girls from as far away as Idaho! We might be onto something big!"

A phone call came in for Dulcey. She immediately answered. It was the chief from Bonner County. After a few minutes, she hung up the phone.

"James Cavalier is on his way to Myrtle Beach," She informed her anxious staff.

"We will meet them at the airport in the morning. Then, we leave immediately for St. George! We cannot waste any time."

"Now, everybody goes home and gets some rest. We will have a long day ahead of us tomorrow!"

27

Flying East

Kristy received a call from Tom. He was at the station in the chief's office.

"They want to have Jim fly out to Myrtle Beach to help in the investigation," He paused, waiting for a reaction from Kristy. "They want me to bring him out there. If Jim solves this and reunites father and daughter, his name will be on every household television in the U.S.! It could be huge, Kristy!"

Kristy paced in front of the kitchen door, whispering on the phone, so Jim could not hear.

"I don't know, Tom." She sighed softly. "What if he has one of his episodes? I don't know if his doctor will let him go. I...I.just-"

"We have already talked with Dr. Jones and got the go-ahead to fly him out tonight." Tom interrupted. "We don't have much choice at this point, Kristy. It is a National FBI case, and Jim had the most recent lead with those phone numbers matching up. And what if he does have these psychic abilities!" He continued. "They want him out there ASAP, so he can lead them to the shack he drew. Hopefully, we can find those girls. It may become an extraordinary story, and Jim is at the front of it!"

Kristy was trying to let all this craziness absorb.

This all seems surreal. Kristy thought. *One minute Jim is recovering from a deadly car accident, and the next, he is involved in a huge FBI investigation!*

"It is now out of our hands. Jim claims he has some circumstantial evidence in this major investigation. We fly out in a few hours, Kristy! The Feds are meeting us at the airport and bringing us to an area where they think that shack may be located," Tom states. "We need to catch those scumbags before they kidnap anyone else!"

Kristy began to cry.

"I guess those girls need Jim's help, more than I need him here with me." She sobbed. "I'll let Jim know and help him pack. He has medications that he takes around the clock. You can't let him forget to take them, Tom. I need you to be responsible for Jim. He knows some of them and when he needs them, but you will need to help him out. He still is not one hundred percent, ya know."

"Yes, I realize that. Dr. Jones reminded me. I am on my way over there. Jenni is coming with me. She said she would stay with you."

"Alright. I'll start packing Jim's things," She replied. "See you in a bit."

She hung up the phone, looking over at Jim. He was looking back at her, realizing the conversation was about him.

"Am I in trouble?" He asked her.

"No, sweetie." Kristy shook her head. "The FBI in Myrtle Beach wants you to come out there and assist them in bringing that girl home. I hate the idea of you leaving me again. I worry about your medications and am scared you'll have a spell and blackout." She dried her tears. "I'm afraid you will end up in the hospital again, Jim. I don't know if I can go through that again."

She ambled back to the couch, buried her face into her hands, and cried. Jim walked over and sat next to her. He pulled her close to him, and she melted into his chest as he held her tightly.

He closed his eyes. Kristy felt soft and warm. Warm static electricity started spinning through his veins as he felt the butterflies in his belly. He didn't want to let her go.

"I have to do this. Those girls are going to die if I don't do something to help. Time is running out. I will be home before you know it."

After a few minutes, Kristy took in a big breath and let him go. She got up and started to pack Jim's suitcase.

"I know there are some little girls out there, a lot more scared than me right now. Jim, God picked you to go and rescue them." She walked over to Jim and held Jim extra tight. He kissed her and held her tightly.

Kristy noticed Tom and Jenni walking up the driveway. She went to the door and greeted them as they approached the porch.

"Hey, guys. Jim is almost ready."

Tom could see the worry on Kristy's face as she walked over to grab Jim's suitcase and backpack.

"The doctor is hopeful that Jim can handle this kind of trip. He gave me his cell number just in case we encounter any problems." Tom reassured her.

Kristy nodded. She understood why they needed Jim. She just wasn't ready to let Jim go.

"I do understand why he needs to go out there, Tom, and I do feel better that you are going with," Kristy replied. "I have your lovely wife here to keep me sane." She put her arm around Jenni and squeezed her.

"Well, partner, you ready to head East?"

"As ready as I can be, I guess."

Kristy hands Tom a small carry-on bag.

"I have all his medicine labeled. Jim knows how to take most of them. The calming pills are in there, as well. A full bottle. You might need those."

"Well, Jim." Tom started towards the front door. "Let's blow this popsicle stand. We have a plane to catch!"

"Be careful out there. You never know what you might get tangled up in." Kristy kissed Jim on the cheek before he walked out the door.

"I love you with all my heart."

Jim followed Tom to the car.

Boarding the plane was going to be simple. It was later in the day, and no one was around the tiny airport. Jim just sat in a nearby chair as Tom went through and checked them in. Once he was finished, Tom walked over and sat next to Jim.

"Well, buddy, we should be landing in Myrtle Beach in about seven hours." Tom looked at his watch.

"I have never been there," Jim replied. "I wonder what the weather is like this time of year." He blinked and turned to Tom. "Do you think we will find Carmen?"

"I sure the hell hope so," Tom answered. "Those little girls desperately need your help. I just hope we aren't too late." He took a deep breath, leaned his head back, and closed his eyes.

"Me too," Jim responded. "I still can see Harper sometimes when I close my eyes."

"She panicked. If she hadn't tried to escape and kill herself, she would have never met me in Heaven. Things would be way different right now!"

Jim continued his story as Tom listened. His eyes closed; he rested his head on the back of the chair. He was amazed at how much detail Jim knew about the case compared to how little the FBI knew.

But it was only up to a certain point. He didn't seem to know how the girls were right now. Tom thought.

Tom was still trying to grasp how Jim's visions had brought them together on a plane heading to Myrtle Beach.

A few minutes later, they began to board the plane. The first flight was short, about forty-five minutes. Neither man said a word to the other. Jim was going in and out of consciousness. Their stop between flights was brief, and then they were in the air once again. Their next stop was Myrtle Beach, South Carolina.

Tom retook his seat next to Jim, who was sitting by the window.

"So, can you tell me a little more about this kidnapping now?" He asked. "You can't start a story like the one back at the airport without finishing it."

Jim started where he had left off. Tom silently listened.

Jim told Tom details of the kidnapping through Harper's eyes. He talked about the kidnappers and the man they were working for—the details of Harper's death and Carmen's prison.

Tom didn't interrupt once. Finally, when Jim finished up his story, Tom opened his eyes and turned to look over at Jim.

"Why would anybody do this to a young girl?"

"It's all about the cash."

Jim and Tom sat the rest of the trip in silence, Tom still trying to process Jim's story.

Struggling to stay awake, Jim dozed off.

The stewardess collected their trash, and the two men relaxed. Jim fell sound asleep almost instantly.

They were both awakened by a jolt of turbulence. Jim let out a scream. Frightened, he started to become agitated, pulling at his seatbelt. He looked around, trying to figure out where he was, but nothing looked familiar.

"Where are we?" Jim cried out. "Harper? Come back, don't you walk away!" Jim looked frightened, not noticing that Tom was sitting next to him. His steel-colored eyes shifted back and forth. He reached down, pulling at his seatbelt, watching Harper slowly walk down the aisle of the plane.

She paused, turning back to see Jim trying to stand in his seat belt, his head bobbing like he was drunk.

Jim stopped struggling when he heard Harper's voice.

"Carmen is starting to give up. She is counting on you, Jim. You must hurry!"

"I am Harper. I am trying my best!" Jim struggles with his words, almost slurring them.

Another jolt, and Jim woke up. He looked around the plane, trying to comprehend where he was. Outside, it was dark. He could make out some tiny lights far below. The rain was freezing to the window of the plane.

Tom put his hand on Jim's shoulder.

"Hey, buddy. It's Tom," he said in a soft tone, trying to calm Jim. But Jim seemed distant. He was looking past Tom like Tom wasn't even there.

"NO!" Jim shouted, grabbing again at his seat belt.

The flight attendant notices Jim and comes over to assist.

"Sir, can I help you?" She asked hesitantly.

Tom shook his head 'no' at her and winked.

"I have this under control, ma'am."

"Please, sir. I don't want to alarm the rest of my passengers."

"We will be okay, I promise you." Tom's voice sounded reassuring.

The flight attendant backed up and turned around, telling each passenger that everything was okay.

"We're on a plane headed to Myrtle Beach. Jim, you need to look at me and try to calm yourself. You're scaring the other passengers." Tom never removed his hand from Jim's shoulder. "You're okay. I'm here with you, and you're safe. Take some deep breaths."

Jim began to focus on Tom's eyes as he slowly drifted back to reality.

Thankfully! Tom thought as he inhaled in a big sigh of relief.

"Tom! I dreamt I was back in Heaven with Rob! There was this most amazing light! And Harper was there. She talked to me through her thoughts. Harper told me that she is worried about Carmen, Tom! She said that the kidnappers were planning to move her to a house. They have girls from all over the country in this house! They even have that young girl you and I were investigating from Coeur d'Alene!"

Jim started to get more excited.

"These men are gathering up the last of the girls so they can start packing them to ship out overseas! There is a boat coming into one of Myrtle Beach harbors. Once loaded, it will take off with those girls, taking them far away from here. We need to hurry because once they leave the country, those girls will never be found!"

"My God! They're selling these girls to international traffickers! We need to figure out where they are before that shipment leaves the harbor!"

Tom couldn't believe what he was hearing. *How in the hell can Jim know all of this?!? What does he mean Harper has told him this?*

As much as Tom tried, he could not wrap his head around it. But, he knew deep in his heart that Jim wasn't making any of this stuff up.

Tom realized now that every time Jim told him something related to the story, the rest of it slowly started to make sense. Plus, now they may have found the Coeur d'Alene girl!

All Tom knew was that he could not wait until Jim could talk with the FBI directly.

The airplane started to descend, and soon they were on the ground in Myrtle Beach, South Carolina!

28

Moving Day

Carmen quickly lost sense of time. So, when the men came into her room to wake her, she didn't have a clue what time it was. All she knew was that it still appeared to be dark outside.

Last night was the coldest so far. She shivered most of the night, trying to keep warm. Her arms and legs were numb with cold. One of the men grabbed her sternly by the arm and dragged her out of the room. She noticed how powerful he was. His warm hands were rough, his fingernails dirty. She saw a gold ring with unusual markings on his middle finger.

It was only one of a handful of times that Carmen had left her prison since she arrived.

She glanced around the room. There were holes in the ceiling, and the windows were either broken or boarded up. Wooden boxes filled with guns and ammunition were piled high in the corner, and the old couch was still in the same spot facing the door.

Freedom was just on the other side. She thought.

Carmen's glance drifted back to the couch.

The last time she had seen Harper was on that couch.

Carmen can't stop staring at the little couch.

Maybe Harper and her family went on with their lives, slowly forgetting her! Maybe she made it home and was back in school, enjoying hot baths and cooked meals.

Hopefully, Carmen prayed.

The man pulled Carmen by her arm into the kitchen area. She noticed a table off to the left. On it was another pile of ammunition and cell phones. This room was much warmer than her room ever was. As odd as it was, it felt nice.

A second man entered the shack wearing a black hat and sunglasses. Carmen recognized him immediately. It was her online friend.

He had a full beard now.

He looked at Carmen, studying her from top to bottom. She started to feel uncomfortable. He walked over to the table and started loading the ammo in one large empty wooden box.

The man who had his harsh grip on Carmen shoved her towards the man.

"I am not getting in any vehicle with her," the man grunted. "First, she needs to get cleaned up and have some of this matted shit cut off her head." He tugged at Carmen's tangled curls. "She fucking reeks! Besides, if she goes overseas, they will want something a little cleaner than that."

He reached down and grabbed Carmen by the arm. She attempted to stand and keep up with him, but her leg muscles could not support her body. Carmen tripped and stumbled to the floor. The man didn't slow down, pulling on Carmen, her left shoulder strained from its socket. Just when Carmen thought she couldn't take any more pain, the man dropped her next to a large metal tub filled with water. Not warm, bubbly water like Carmen had dreamt about in the past. But water, nonetheless.

Her first bath in months.

After setting Carmen next to the tub, the man walked around to one of the kitchen cabinets. He opened one of the cabinet drawers and pulled out a pair of scissors. He laughed as he then walked over to Carmen and hacked at her tangled long brown curls. She started to cry. It didn't take long, and her once beautiful hair was all cut off. It was almost to her scalp.

"Take off your filthy clothes, pig." The man demanded in a rough Western accent.

Why? What was he going to do with her? Her heart started to beat harder. So hard, she could feel it in her throat. She tried to swallow, but she couldn't. She was frozen with fear.

"ARE YOU FUCKING DEAF, BITCH?!?" He screamed in her face, and she felt his warm breath on her cheek.

"Take your Goddamn clothes off and get in the fucking tub! You reek like a pig!" One of the men grabbed what was left of her panties and ripped them off. He grabbed what was left of her pink shirt and ripped it off, exposing her frail, thin body. She was breathing heavily, almost to the point of hyperventilating. The two men just stared at her as Carmen slowly began peeling off her filthy shorts. Carmen stumbled; her legs felt like rubber. She collapsed on the hardwood floor.

"Get up, whore!" The man's voice crackled in anger.

Carmen could smell stale cigarettes on his breath.

Carmen couldn't believe that these were the same guys from the beach. The cute guys were talking and having fun with her and her best friend. She looked away in shame, having difficulty believing these guys would do such a thing to them.

"Get her cleaned up," One of the men stated. "And no funny stuff! They pay more for the virgins! Syn will kill you if you take that from her." He walked out of the kitchen and over to the box of weapons on the floor. He picked them up and walked out the front door.

She was still sitting on the floor. The guy Carmen had been talking with on social media walked over to her. He grabbed a bar of soap and a washcloth off the table and shoved her towards the tub. She was still in disbelief. She couldn't believe that she was stupid enough to fall for this guy.

How foolish was I to believe he liked me, she thought. *Now, look at where I am. Alone.*

A simple boy crush that had turned into this mess

"Get in, bitch," He growled again at her.

Carmen sobbed.

He grabbed her this time by her short hair and pulled her toward the tub. She started to step in slowly. Impatiently, he gave her a shove on the back. Carmen lost her footing and fell into the freezing water face first. Carmen jumped up and let out a shriek.

"Shut your mouth up, or I'll stuff it!" He yelled at her, grabbing his crotch. She looked down and away.

Sobbing, Carmen sat back down in the freezing water, her eyes focused on her feet. Her nails were growing out, and the nail polish was almost gone. She started to rub her body to get the layers of dirt off. Her skin felt like sandpaper. The man soaped up the dirty washcloth and started to clean her backside. His hands began to wander slowly over her entire body. She stiffened up in terror as his hands ran over her body.

The guy let out an evil laugh.

"I can do other things and still leave you a virgin!" He whispered, making sure his partner didn't hear him.

There was a time not too long ago when she would have loved to hear him say those things. Now, it made Carmen shutter with fear. She kept her head down, not wanting to look the creep in the eyes. She didn't want him to know how scared she was.

Scared to death.

He filled a bucket of water.

"Tilt your head back, bitch." He demanded as he grabbed a handful of hair and pulled her head back.

"Your hair is disgusting."

Carmen gave in reluctantly. He dumped the entire bucket of water over her head and into her eyes. Carmen started to spit the foul-tasting water out of her mouth. She tried to grab the sides of the tub and steady herself.

"Sit still!" The man said as he began to soap her hair. The soap burned as it ran into her eyes. She closes them tightly. She was trying to mentally escape as the man's hands kept running over her body, touching her everywhere.

Just make him stop. Carmen thought. But, the torture seemed to last forever.

When the man finally finished with Carmen, he pulled her from the washtub. She felt violated. But she didn't have the strength to fight back.

"Now, get dressed, you little pig!" The man shouted, making Carmen jump.

Carmen quickly put on a pair of pants and an oversized black tee-shirt. She didn't care; it just felt good to be cleaned up and clothed again.

"Let's get going!" The second man walked into the room. He grabbed Carmen by the arm and led her outside.

It was just starting to get daylight out when they exited the shack and headed towards the van. There was a foul odor that hit Carmen like a putrid wall of death. She could not figure out what it was. She started to gag as she was pulled down the front porch steps.

She couldn't handle the stench. Her stomach was empty and started aching with sharp, stabbing pains as she began to heave.

She paused and started to dry heave once more. It was making her empty stomachache. The man tugged at her arm. To avoid any more pain, she picked up her pace towards the dark gray van. There, the guy from the beach was standing with the door open. He was smoking a joint.

"Wanna drag?" He offered the man holding Carmen. He quickly took a long hit and blew the smoke slowly into Carmen's face. She began to cough.

Both men started to laugh. They shared the joint, blowing the smoke in Carmen's face until it was gone.

She began to feel weird. *Very weird.*

With her brain a little fuzzy, Carmen reluctantly climbed back into the same van that had taken her and Harper from their happy lives in Myrtle Beach.

Where would they be taking me? Carmen wondered. *Maybe it's to be with Harper.*

Her shoulder was hurting. It felt like her arm had been ripped from her body.

The men climbed into the van next to Carmen and slid a pillow-case over her head. They duct-taped it tightly on her. She started to panic.

"HARPER? Where are YOU?!?" She screamed at the top of her lungs.

Immediately, the van's door was slammed shut. She felt an open hand come hard across her cheek, followed by intense pain. Her teeth dug deeply into her fleshless cheek, and she tasted blood.

After what had happened to Harper, the men decided to buckle Carmen in the back seat.

The man from the beach sat on the passenger's side, while the man with the funny accent sat behind the wheel. The van's engine rumbles to life.

"Let's get the hell out of here!" One of them shouted.

Even though she could not see anything, Carmen closed her eyes and took a few deep breaths, leaning her head onto the dark glass. Her cheek felt warm and swollen. Her head was now throbbing.

But she was now warm. She comforted herself. *For the first time in a very long time, she was warm.*

The van sped off. In it, two kidnappers and the young, beaten and terrified Carmen Potter.

29

The Briefing

Dulcey had questions. A lot of them. She wanted to talk with the man who drew the map and the shack where the two kidnapped girls were allegedly being held. The man who claimed he could lead them to that very same shack in the picture. The man who claimed to have died and seen Heaven. Who now claimed to be a psychic.

Detective James Cavalier.

As Jim and Tom walked off the jetway, they immediately noticed a short-statured woman pacing in front of their gait's waiting area. Dulcey immediately noticed the two men together and approached them.

Hello, Detective Mason and Cavalier?" She greeted the men. "I am Dulcey Higgens, Chief investigator for the FBI unit," She extended her hand out.

Tom grabbed her hand and gave her a firm shake.

"Hello, I am Tom Mason, Detective for Bonner County Sheriff's department in Sandpoint, Idaho, and this is my partner, Detective Jim Cavalier," He motioned towards Jim.

"He's the real reason we are all here today."

Still foggy from the flight, Jim shook Dulcey's hand. His grip was not as firm as his partner's.

"I'm pleased to meet you," She replied. "My team is waiting outside, and we are driving to St. George as soon as we leave here. We are wasting no time. We can brief everyone on the way."

"Do you two have any luggage?" She asked, walking hastily towards the baggage claim with Jim and Tom following close behind.

"No," Tom answered. "Just our carry-ons. We didn't have time to pack a large amount."

Dulcey turned suddenly and headed towards the terminal doors, where the black SUV was parked just outside.

She walked over towards the SUV and popped the back door open. The men stacked their belongings in the back and began to take off their jackets.

"The air was quite warmer here than in Idaho," Tom chuckled. "The jackets had to go."

"Well, let's get outta here," Dulcey ordered as she jumped into the driver's seat of the SUV.

"Ok, everyone, we need to focus. Time is running out!" Dulcey's voice rang throughout the vehicle.

"This is detective James Cavalier and his partner, detective Thomas Mason of the Bonner County Sheriff's office," She introduced the two men as they slid into the back seat of the SUV.

"As I briefed you before, Detective Cavalier has given us some crucial information about this case so far." She continued as she pulled out onto the highway heading south. "Now, Detective Cavalier said he has even more information for us. Jim, go ahead."

The team intently listened as Jim began his story.

He told them about Coeur d'Alene's missing girl and her mutual contact, linking his phone number to the Myrtle Beach case.

Jim went on about his accident and his buddy Rob dying, seeing him cross over into Heaven, time standing still. Jim briefed on the stories that flashed in front of him. He shared what it was like to have a glimpse of Heaven. Every soul had its aura made up of the most incredible colors one could only imagine. Jim described how people on Earth have a narrow field of vision. In Heaven, the mind opened up to let in all the colors of the aura. He talked about how he had seen Harper that night, standing next to him. How their auras melded together

He told them about his visions and talking to Rob and this girl with blonde hair, that she had told him things. Things that would help him save her best friend's life!

"Let me get this right," Came a voice from the back of the SUV. "These girls you talk about. They are all alive, right?"

Looking down at the floor, Jim shook his head and continued to tell them about each vision. His story brought them right up to Harper's death and the shack Carmen had been imprisoned in for the past two months.

Jim was sure Carmen was still there.

If they hurry, they might be able to save her!

"That is amazing!" Dulcey exclaimed. "So, what do you think those kidnappers are going to do with those girls?"

Jim looked at her eyes reflecting in the rearview mirror.

"These girls were either being ripped off the streets as runaways or propositioned online. They are groomed to gain the trust of strangers. Remember, most of these girls are naive and vulnerable. They are jumping in cars with strangers and hoping for big dreams. They are eagerly giving out their phone numbers and addresses to these people. These strangers! They did this without even thinking. They are trained to lie to their parents about where they are going.

Some just sneak out so they can meet up with these predators. These girls have no clue what is about to happen to them. They are about to see Hell up close and personal."

Jim paused, looking out the window. The SUV was silent. As the team tried to process everything that Jim had just told them.

"The shack I drew, how far is it from here?"

"I haven't a clue where the shack you drew is even located," Dulcey chuckled out loud. "None of my team members have been able to recognize it or the area. I have even put out an APB, but no hits yet. This state is full of backwoods country. We have everything from mountains to swamps. I don't think anyone has ever set foot on some of this land. But I do have something I haven't yet told either of you. My people were able to trace a cell phone ping from one of the girls on a tower outside of St. George in Dorchester County. I am in contact with the local sheriff there."

She looked back at Jim and noticed he was pale and sweating, staring straight ahead. She turned to Tom.

"Is your friend okay?"

Tom put his hand on Jim's shoulder. "You okay, buddy?" He asked.

Jim turned towards Tom's voice. He could see Harper. She slowly faded away into Tom.

"I am not sure," Jim replied slowly. "I think I might need to rest." He turned his head, looking out the shaded window of the SUV. Tom immediately handed him a bottle of water and a protein bar.

After a few minutes, Jim perked up. His color had come back.

Dulcey decided they should stop for a bite to eat. So, she pulled up to a small restaurant just off the highway. As they waited for their food, Dulcey pulled her laptop out of her briefcase.

"Okay, team. I have Google maps up, and here is St. George's County. The tower where we have traced the phone ping. We also have looked over the drawing Jim has provided, and this is where he thinks the girls are. The brush is so thick in that area, and we cannot find a shack-or any type of rooftop." Dulcey looked around the table.

"As I said, our office has contacted the sheriff in St. George. From here, we will drive over to the station and meet up with him. Hopefully, he can shed some light on this investigation. Maybe he knows where this cell tower is. Or maybe even where this shack might be!"

Dulcey handed Jim a pile of pictures, with the most recent ones coming off Carmen's phone. He started looking through them one by one. They were mainly of the missing Myrtle Beach girls. He could hear the girls' laughing in his head, their voices ringing in his ears like he was standing with them on the beach.

Jim's heart started to beat fast, and he closed his eyes. He could see everything from that day. Carmen and Harper on the beach, the two men they were communicating with, Barefoot Landing and the van. His visions faded to the girls in the shack, fighting to escape. Harper's death. Carmen, naked sitting in an old washtub filled with water. Jim's breathing became rhythmic. His heart began to beat even faster.

He could see Harper's green aura as she tried to put her hand on Carmen's shoulder. But she was jerked away and pushed into the tub. The water was freezing, and Carmen let out a cry. Jim jumped and opened his eyes. He looked around; everyone was frozen, watching him. He took a long drink of his water. His hands were shaking, and the sweat started to bead on his forehead and dampen his hair.

"Carmen is being moved. They have cleaned her up and changed her clothing."

There was whispering around the table. *Who was this guy, and how in the hell does he know this shit?*

The waitress brought their bill, Dulcey handed her a credit card, and she walked away.

"Continue," Dulcey's calm voice encouraged Jim.

"She has been put back into the dark gray van. The windows are black so that no one can see in." He explained. "They are taking her to a house in the city. A house that held the collection of girls until they shipped them out," he stated. "He has many girls."

The drive seemed long, as no one said a word for quite some time. Probably still trying to comprehend this surreal information.

Many thoughts were crossing everyone's minds. *What if this detective from Idaho was wrong? What if there was no shack? They couldn't find the shack on Google maps. Maybe it wasn't here. Perhaps this was a wild goose chase, and in the end, the Bonner County Sheriff Department would be the laughing stock of the Myrtle Beach community. Maybe the entire world.*

"Ok, we just need to get to St. George," Dulcey finally spoke up after a few minutes. "Meet the sheriff and find that shack!"

"I have seen the shack in my visions." Jim sounded confident. "Once we get closer, I should be able to find it pretty easily."

Jim held up a photo of Carmen and Harper on Myrtle Beach, the day of the kidnappings. This picture was from Carmen's phone. The two girls were taking selfies. In the background, there were two dark-haired men. He stuffed it into his shirt pocket.

30

The Kidnappers

As they traveled towards St. George, everyone was silent. Jim decided to tell them more of the story. More about the kidnappers, their motives, and their plans.

"These predators are the scum of this Earth." Jim began. "They prey on the innocent. They pick up runaways off the streets and promise them better lives. They seek out the depressed, convincing them that they will find unconditional love. By mental persuasion and promises, these monsters make their living by taking advantage of these young, innocent girls. When they have collected enough, they sell them or pimp them out on the black market. They are the most dangerous of the human traffickers."

"Those men from Myrtle Beach are all a part of this. They have traveled to the US from across the ocean. These people are working for someone who is much more malevolent than you can ever imagine. That someone has no emotional connection to these beautiful lives. He is in it for one thing, and one thing only. Money."

"I am not sure why he would take such a significant risk with this ransom request. Maybe this is our chance, people! Perhaps this time, he will trip up and make a precious mistake! We are going to be there to bring him down!

"What I didn't tell you about this predator yet, was that he had met Harper a few years ago on one of her flights to London. He sat next to her on the plane. She told him a lot about her life. She forgot about the run-in, but he didn't. He has patiently watched her for many years. Following her through social media, he watched her grow up. Until he finally decided that it was time to make his move. In the meantime, he made plans to take other girls to help solidify his income. As I said before, social media has made it more accessible.

"Teenage girls are naive and like to talk to someone who will listen and not judge. Some are lonely and misunderstood. Some have little or no friends. Some girls are left on their own to figure out life. That is where wrong choices happen. These kids have no adults in their lives to guide them in the right direction or encourage them to make better choices. Our predator plays it cool. He sits and waits patiently for the prey to come to him. Once the girl gets to the point of wanting to meet or run away, he pounces. He starts by offering them a taste of money, making it easy for them. With money comes drugs and the promise of money if they want to come with him. Giving these girls the impression of a better life."

No one said a word; they had everything they could do to process the information being told to them. Each wondered how Jim could know any of this. But, he kept on with his story, like he had heard about it first-hand.

"This man had flown a few of his contacts here from overseas. The only people that he trusted completely. These trusted contacts have never seen this predator in person. He liked keeping it that way. This predator would go into each town, scope it out and come up with a plan. From there, he would send in his men, one or two at a time. He would have no direct contact with them. That meant a lower risk of being identified."

"It's a sick game of cat and mouse that he plays," Dulcey spoke up, interrupting Jim's story. She could not listen to any more of this. It just made her more anxious about getting to St. George and finding that shack.

Jim ignored her. He knew her people needed to know what kind of monster they would be dealing with shortly.

"Our predator has started to become greedy. His new plan seems to be not just about trafficking but a kidnapping ransom request. That is something new for him. I'm not quite sure why he was doing this."

No one had told Jim about the ransom.

How did he know this? Dulcey thought

"It all started by finding the right girl, with the right parents. Harper had fallen, unbeknownst, into his evil web years before her kidnapping. She was informing this stranger of her wealthy life. It was then that he knew this would be easy money.

Our man had done his research until he had this family memorized. For years, he had watched their every move and day-to-day routines. He watched and waited like a lion to a gazelle. Once he had the valuable information he needed, he would make his move."

****

"A few years back, Bradley Bengston had just been made Chief Executive Officer of a regional financial institution. He had merged two major corporations in two different states and was finalizing plans on an overseas merger soon. The news had posted a beautiful picture of him, his wife, and his daughter at the top of every online corporate journal page. In one of the articles, Mr. Bengston mentioned how proud he is of his daughter Harper. She was being accepted to an elite boarding school in England this fall semester. Her grade point average had been the highest in the state for the past three years."

"Remember the accidental run-in on the plane years prior?" Jim's voice was slow and steady. "You see, our kidnapper had intentionally bumped into Harper Bengston on that plane from Englund. He made sure he had a seat next to hers. He had walked alongside Harper up to the terminal waiting area and sat across from her, making small talk. Then after a few minutes, he approached the desk and asked for a change in seats. Telling the check-in officer at the desk that he was her stepdad and their seats somehow got mixed up. Since she saw them come into her gate area together and they were both in first class, the woman didn't even question him."

"Once this predator had his sights on Harper, he did everything to know her more. Finding her social media account was easy. Then, he began to watch Harper's profile more closely. There were a ton of pictures of her and her best friend, Carmen."

"Carmen didn't post much online. Every picture and tag online were with her best friend, Harper Bengston. Carmen's timeline had a few posts, most mentioning her mom spending a lot of time working. Her expression of sadness from being left home alone was obvious. That made Carmen a target. She was lonely, sad, and a direct link to Harper and a hefty ransom."

Jim looked around, noticing some of his peers nodding in agreement.

"The two best friends were inseparable. They were as close as sisters. Harper was Carmen's only friend. The Bengston's included Carmen in everything the family did together. There were no secrets between them. Up until lately

It was the perfect setup. All our predator needed to do was get Carmen to convince Harper to meet up somewhere. A plan that was years in the making was now being constructed for execution."

"Carmen was always looking for attention. Lately, it didn't matter from who. She would do just about anything to get guys to notice her. That was perfect for our predator.

He worked diligently to get Carmen to trust in him. By setting up a double-blind date with Harper. He convinced Carmen to keep it a surprise, telling Harper that it was one last before being shipped to London. That would be the perfect setup for the perfect crime."

"This monster's full-time job became visiting the girls' profile accounts and getting to know their routines. Every tag, every check-in, and every time they were together had been noted and studied. He had finally come up with a perfect plan, an evil plan. That was when he decided to bring in the three men from Beijing. One was about to get to know Carmen on a personal level. It started as a private message request. In no time, numbers were being exchanged, and the texting had started."

That had become way too easy.

✳✳✳✳✳✳✳✳✳✳✳✳✳✳✳✳✳✳✳✳✳✳✳✳✳✳✳✳✳✳✳

"The kidnappers were younger looking than their stated age. They had been promised lots of money and drugs for every girl they could bring to him. These men were his reliable accomplices. The only men he could trust. The lure of drugs, money, and freedom made them all too eager to hop on a plane to America. They were addicts in every sense of the word, their boss controlling their drug. The men didn't look Asian at all. Both had dark hair, and their skin a golden bronze. Our predator used his smooth ways to convince Carmen that he was interested in her. He would tell her that she was the most beautiful person he had ever seen. No one had ever seemed interested in her like this before. That had made it easier for him. Craving the attention, all Carmen wanted was to have fun on a date with a guy and her best friend. This yearning for attention would cost Carmen dearly."

"This monster had become greedy. If Syn had stuck to the original plan and just took some girls and sold them overseas, he may just have gotten away with it. But, he wanted out, and 5 million dollars seemed to be his golden ticket."

"Even if Harper wouldn't have died, his plan may have gone off without a hitch. But that wasn't the case; an accident had taken her life. Now, they say things happen for a reason. I believe that. Because Harper's death happened at the same time I was in my accident. That was where she cried out for my help. She was sent to me from God. I am the only one that can find Carmen Potter and the others right now. Those girls are running out of precious time, and that's why we need to hurry."

Jim looked around. Everyone looked like they had seen a ghost, mesmerized by his story. They were still trying to wrap their heads around all this information.

"I have to save Carmen and those girls. It's my job; it's our job!

Jim looked back out the window. A small 'Welcome to St. George' sign passed them by on the side of the highway.

Thank God we are here. He thought.

31

Gaining Ground

As the big black SUV pulled up to the St. George's Sheriff's office, the Sheriff stepped out to welcome the group.

"Well, howdy y'all!" He greeted them. The sheriff was a very tall thin man with red, curly hair. He approached the group extending his hand out; Tom was the closest.

A real modern-day Andy Griffith. Tom thought.

Tom shook hands with him; he was not much taller than himself.

"Nice to meet ya. I'm Detective Tom Mason, Bonner County, Idaho." Tom motioned to his right, "This is my partner, Jim Cavalier."

Agent Dulcey stepped forward from behind Jim.

"Hi, I'm Special Agent Dulcey, and this is my team, Special Agents Butch, Andrea, and Mindy.

The sheriff took a step back and looked at the new arrivals.

"Welcome to St. George. I am Sheriff Brian Metsgaff."

The man had a deep southern voice. "We have prepared for y'alls arrival and want to help y'all get to the bottom of this here kidnappin'. I have room here. Y'all can brief us before we leave. That way, we can come up with a plan to go find this shack y'all been talkin' about. Why, may I ask, do you seem to think it's in my county? I've been sheriff in this here county for over 15 years. I've covered a lot of ground 'n chased delinquents en 'shiners all over these here woods. I'm pretty sure I would have seen something suspicious like a kidnappin'."

"Let's get inside so that we can talk," Dulcey remarked. "We have a map and a sketch of the shack."

The sheriff escorted the six of them into the little room. Waiting just inside the door were two officers from the county sheriff's office. They are here to assist Dulcey, Jim, and their team. They knew this part of the county very well.

"Mike, Robert, this is Detective Dulcey Higgens with the FBI, and these are her colleagues. They have come here from Myrtle Beach to investigate a kidnappin' here. We are going to assist these people as much as we can."

"I don't recall any kidnappin' in these parts." One of the men stated.

"Do you all recall that high-profile kidnapping of Bradley Bengston's daughter and her friend that happened a couple of months ago in Myrtle Beach?" Dulcey reminded them. Well, Detectives Cavalier and Mason here have flown halfway across the country to convince us that they have a lead in this case. Between a cell phone ping and this sketch, we ended up here, in your district of St. George." Dulcey placed some of the pictures on the small, crowded table. We believe that they may be hiding out in this shack here in St. George." She held up the sketch that Jim drew.

One of the sheriff's men spoke up.

"What do these detectives from Idaho know?" He asked. "What kind of link is there between the Idaho and Myrtle Beach kidnappings?"

Dulcey replied immediately.

"Detective Cavalier was investigating a missing teen case in Coeur d'Alene, Idaho. There was a mutual contact number on the phone from the missing Coeur d'Alene girl and the phone we found of Carmen Potter's. We have not said anything to the press in fear that the number will be disconnected. We have sent numbers to dozens of police stations around the country. What we found was astonishing! The number was connected to many missing girls from different parts of the country! That means we may be onto something big, like some sort of human trafficking ring!" Dulcey stated, putting her hand on Jim's arm. She looked up to him and winked.

"Detective Cavalier, I am wondering-as I am sure my partner is. How in the hell do you know these girls are in this shack? Why weren't these two detectives investigated as suspects?" He asked Dulcey. "They seem to know an awful lot about this here case. My suspicions are on them."

"Well-----" Dulcey started to answer but was immediately interrupted by Jim as he held his hand in the air.

"My alibi was that I was in a horrific car accident. I saw my best friend die in front of me. I, myself, flatlined a couple of times. I spent several weeks in a coma and several more in hospitals with numerous surgeries and daily physical therapy sessions. I had to learn how to walk, talk, and swallow all over again. I had no recollection of my life as a cop, my beautiful wife, or any of my friends and family."

"I had a near-death experience that day. I saw the 'light' everyone had heard about. I now know, and I have seen stuff you can't even comprehend. Some of it I could never explain so you could understand. I don't have the time or the energy to start explaining my entire story in detail again. All I can say is, I flew across this country last night to help rescue some scared little girls. I say girls because

I have seen many. Our main priority is to find the kidnappers and rescue those girls! What do any of us have to lose?"

Jim walked to an empty chair next to the table and sat. He pulled the picture he took from the Myrtle Beach police department out of his pocket and laid it onto the little table in front of him.

"I want everyone to take a long look at this picture." He pushed his seat back a bit as everyone stepped closer to better look at the picture. Dulcey picked it up and studied it first. She then handed it off, and one by one, they passed it around the room.

"That is Carmen on the right and Harper on the left. I have never met nor seen those girls before. I have only seen this picture an hour or so ago. But I do know who they are. Because of one little mistake, their lives have been changed forever. It all began with a friend request," Jim took a long pause and looked around at everyone listening and studying the picture.

"If you haven't noticed, I talk about Harper in the past tense. That's 'cause she is gone."

"Gone where?"

Jim looked over towards the voice.

"She is dead. Stuffed in a barrel behind that shack in the middle of nowhere." He responded without hesitation.

"You wonder how I know that? Well, I have seen her. When I stood watching my best friend cross over into heaven. She was there standing next to me." He picked up the photo that was now lying back in the middle of the table.

"Ok, now take another look at that photo." Jim's fingers tapped on two figures smiling in the background of the picture.

"Look closely at those two men in the background."

Dulcey took the photo up and looked at it more closely.

"Oh my God! They were right in front of us the entire time!" She exclaimed. Her voice rose in intensity.

Jim smiled and nodded.

"That is also a photo of the kidnappers. The faces of the two men you all have been looking to find. They have our girls. Plus, many, many more."

Dulcey passed off the photo once again. This time she had tears in her eyes. The picture showed how happy the girls were that day. They were enjoying the sun and water with two male friends. In the blink of an eye, all of this had changed. She wanted those men more badly than ever. It could've easily been her daughter that was kidnapped.

"Do you mind if I say a little prayer?" She asked. "I know it may be inappropriate for some, but I would love to say just a little blessing."

No one said a word as they all joined hands. The pictures and Carmen's phone lay in the center of the table.

In a passionate voice, Dulcey began her prayer:

"Lord, please be with my crew and me, protecting us on our mission and guiding us to those precious souls. Lord, please keep Carmen safe, and hold her in your hands until we can get to her. Please welcome Harper into your Kingdom, keeping her close by your side until one day reunited with all of her loved ones. In Your name, we pray in silence."

"Amen."

Everyone stood still, holding each other's hand and in their minds, praying for those lost souls that they may someday be found and returned safely to their families. They were praying for deliverance to end the kidnappings and murders. To finally end the horror of human trafficking that plagued the country.

They were interrupted by the familiar beep and vibration of Carmen's phone.

The screen lit up. The background picture was a selfie of both girls from the beach.

HOW ABOUT THAT 5 MIL? It read.

TIME IS TICKING...

Dulcey read the text and looked around the room. I'm gonna buy some time here. She sent out a text as she read it aloud.

IT'S STILL TOO EARLY. THE BANKS ARE NOT OPEN YET. WE WILL NEED TO COLLECT FROM 2 OR 3 DIFFERENT BANKS, THIS MAY TAKE SOME TIME. PLEASE BE PATIENT.

No response.

Dulcey took a deep breath.

"We are running out of time. We need to figure out where the hell that shack is." She turned to detective Metsgaff, holding his computer with Google maps already pulled up on the screen.

"Here is where we are," He pointed out. "And that's the tower where the pings are coming from." He moved his finger over a few inches. "I know a few roads over that way. I have seen that tower many a time on my patrol looking for moonshiners and such in that area." He smiled. "I think we have gained a lot of ground on these scumbags!"

They all left the building, the sheriff leading the way with his two men. He jumped in his squad car; the others filtered into the SUV.

"I'm riding shotgun with the leader, and you have no choice," Dulcey ordered as she jumped in the front seat of the squad car.

Number one, as I should be. She thought as she smiled.

"I reckon I'm in no position to argue with such a determined FBI Special Agent as y'all." The sheriff smiled as he replied in his broad southern accent. "You two, take the other squad car."

The two squad cars and the black SUV turned on their lights and sirens as they pulled out of the St. George police station. All were heading in the direction of the tower where the ping was last—speeding down the highway, past a little gas station, where a large dark gray van was gassing up.

But no one noticed the van.

They continued to drive about a half-hour before they turned off on a narrow blacktop road. The convoy continued a few miles until they came to a gravel road.

Shutting off their sirens but leaving on the flashers, they slowly drove towards the cell tower.

Its red lights were blinking like a beacon of hope.

Brian pulled up to the nearest part of the road next to the tower. He put the car in park and got out. The others followed, getting out of their vehicles. Jim emerged from the SUV, looking around. He was taking in the scenery, taking in the familiar smells and sounds. He could almost feel Harper there with him. Everything around him felt familiar.

"Well, Jim." Dulcey walked back towards where he was standing. "This is the tower. What are you thinking?"

"This is familiar to me. The smell, the noise, the atmosphere itself..." He paused, still looking around.

"She was here at some point," he said to Dulcey, who remained at his side. "The girls have been by this tower. Harper has told me about the strange blink it has."

They all look up at the tower over Jim's shoulder, this time paying attention to the red-light blinking.

Long red... long red... short red. Repeat.

How did Jim know this? The sheriff wondered as he let out a chuckle.

"Never noticed *that* before," He seemed a little shocked. Shocked that Jim pointed it out immediately like he had seen that light before. Except that this was the first time James Cavalier had ever been in South Carolina. Let alone standing just outside of St. George next to one of their outpost towers in the middle of the Boondocks. But Harper had seen it, and she told Jim. Jim knew that she was bringing them closer to her and closer to the shack.

"I think if we go this way," Jim pointed to the left of a small "Y" in the road. He looked up from the map and turned towards Tom. "I want to drive. I will go slow. I think I can lead us to the shack!"

Tom stiffened. He paused and looked over at Dulcey. Not sure what to say, he took a deep breath and slowly handed over the keys of the SUV to Jim.

"SLOWLY, partner," Tom ordered as they locked gazes for a few seconds.

Jim smiled and turned around, walking over to the black SUV and climbing into the driver's seat.

The rest got back in their vehicles and eagerly waited for Jim to lead them to this shack in the woods. The shack with the girls inside.

Jim slowly pulled back onto the road and headed away from the tower. After a few minutes, he slowed even more, keeping his gaze toward the East, back towards the cell tower. He then came to a complete stop. Tom and Dulcey were looking over the map.

The map was almost perfect! Tom thought. *Almost.*

"You are driving fine, bud. You don't need to pull over here," Tom said as he looked in the direction Jim was looking. He saw nothing. The underbrush was so thick that it was hard to see more than a few feet off the road.

"You have a road drawn on this map, but I don't see anything here. Maybe you're a bit off?"

Jim didn't respond. He pulled ahead a few more feet and got out of the SUV. Tom, at first, did not move. His gaze went from Jim to the map, then back to Jim. It was at the same time that he noticed the same thing Dulcey had. Tom jumped out of the vehicle and quickly caught up to his buddy.

"Holy shit," Tom stuttered out loud.

The rest of them had jumped out of their vehicles and were approaching the men.

"Why have we stopped here?" One of them asked, their voice staggering.

That's when they noticed it.

"Oh my Gawd!" The sheriff's voice rang out.

They all begin to move the brush. It became clear that there was a fresh set of tire tracks, completely covered. He reached out and pulled more of the brush aside. A very grown-in road was uncovered. They were all shocked at what they were seeing. There was a road that was hidden out of sight.

It was purposefully hidden and very well.

Tom looked over at Dulcey and the sheriff. They were smiling.

"Let's go get those bastards," Dulcey said as she started walking over to the cruiser. She climbed inside and slowly pulled up the hidden drive, the others following.

The road was extremely narrow and was long and winding. As the SUV turned the last corner, the road opened slightly, and on the right was the abandoned shack tucked beneath some giant trees. The underbrush grew up all around it. Each vehicle came to a stop lining the little, overgrown yard.

Dulcey pulled out the picture Jim had faxed to her from Idaho. It was like he had stood in front of that shack and drew it. She could not believe her eyes.

The shack was in deplorable shape. The front porch roof was decaying and falling in. Some of the windows were smashed in and boarded up. The tar paper was peeling off the sides.

The chimney was crumbling on a roof covered with moss and had only half its shingles poking out from under the bright green growth. It wouldn't have survived another year.

Jim turned off the vehicle's engine. The shack had no signs of life around it.

There was no movement, no noise, nothing. An eerie presence filled the air.

Maybe Jim was wrong. Dulcey thought.

Jim slowly opened his door and stepped out. He began to look around. There had been recent activity around the shack. What little grass there was, had all been knocked down, and there were tracks deep into the muck.

Special Agent Dulcey radioed back to the station, stating her whereabouts. The sheriff did the same, requesting backup. Their voices were the only noise that they could hear.

Jim and Tom walked towards the shack. Tom had his gun up and ready. The rest of the detectives were close behind with their guns out for backup. One of the sheriff's men readied his firearm as they approached the porch.

There was an awful stench emanating from the camp yard. It was almost unbearable. Everyone had to put their sleeves over their noses just to breathe. One of them stayed back, the smell too intolerable for him, and he started to cough and gag. Jim walked up the steps, both men on either side ready for anything.

He pushed the front door, and it opened with ease. One by one, they enter the shack. As Jim stepped forward, the armed men quickly scouted the inside.

The shack was recently abandoned.

Jim walked over and put his hand on the arm of the couch. Dulcey watched him for the longest time, trying to figure out what he was thinking. He closed his eyes, keeping his hand on the couch.

"The girls have sat here," He finally said, opening his eyes and looking around. His eyes finally lock in on a door off the tiny room. It had many locks on it. "And that's where they kept Carmen."

Dulcey walked towards the door. The sheriff followed her. Jim stayed back, hand still on the couch, watching. As they approached the door, they noticed five locks lining its frame. Just inside the doorway, they could see Carmen's prison. The stench emanating from the room was almost unbearable, smelling like pure ammonia mixed with methane. It made their eyes water. They slowly entered, their hands holding handkerchiefs to cover their noses.

Dulcey gasped for fresh air.

Jim finally came up behind Dulcey and peeked around her. He wanted to see what he already knew, what he couldn't describe—the awful smell of urine, feces, and rotten food. The stench was almost unbearable.

In the corner was a small mattress, covered with a urine-soaked, stained sheet that was rotten and full of holes. There were no pillows or blankets. In the corner, above the mattress, was an eye hook drilled into the wall. It was holding a chain that led to the bed. Attached to the other end of the chain was a bloody pair of handcuffs. It was clear that the room was used as a prison.

Where was Carmen? Dulcey thought.

Dulcey started to sob. She couldn't believe her eyes. If this was where Carmen was held, this had to have been hell. Here she was, standing there in a thick fall jacket and hat. Dulcey could not imagine how that poor scared girl felt. She glanced around the room, taking her watery eyes away from the rotting mattress on the floor over towards one of the buckets still filled with urine and feces at the other end. The room had been used as a prison.

A prison cell was cleaner than this room was.

In the kitchen area, they found the tub still full of water. On the floor next to the tub was a pile of Carmen's clothes. Jim recognized them immediately and picked them up.

"These are Carmen's," Jim said, holding the clothes up.

They were so dirty that they were hard to identify from the pictures.

Dulcey's eyes started to fill up with tears. This isn't good, she thought.

All of a sudden, they hear a shriek coming from the back door.

"Holy shit! Dulcey, you gotta see this!"

Dulcey broke her stare from Jim and looked over towards the door. One of her agents stood, with the door halfway open.

"You are not going to believe this!" She started to shake, her voice softly echoing inside the empty shack.

Dulcey walked toward the back door.

"What in the-------" Dulcey stopped in her tracks as she stared through the door out on the back steps. There was a smell of rotten flesh that hit her like a brick to the face. What in the hell could smell worse than what was coming from the bedroom in the shack? Immediately her hand went up to her face and covered her mouth and nose once again. Her eyes started to water as she held back from gagging. She had smelled that before, and she never forgot it.

Dulcey had smelled that stench before.

Jim managed to scoot past her when the smell hit him. As he pulled his sleeve over his hand to cover his face, he knew what the commotion was. He just had to see it for himself.

"Well, I think we found Carmen, Jim. We were too late." Dulcey sobbed through her handkerchief.

It was a plastic barrel, about fifty gallons in size. Someone had removed the lid. Jim noticed the platinum blonde hair poking up into the sunlight.

Harper. His heart sank.

"That is not Carmen. It's Harper's body," Jim's voice was somber. "Stuffed in a Goddamned plastic barrel." He knew that she had been there for a while.

"My God, it's all true!" Dulcey shouted out loud, stumbling toward the barrel.

They all begin to gather around the barrel, each of them covering their faces, trying not to vomit. All of them sobbing, staring at Harper's body.

"Where is Carmen, Jim?" The sheriff turned to Jim. "It's pretty obvious that she is not here. Did you tip someone off? What *do* you know?" His voice was sharp with anger.

Jim ignored the accusation. Feeling a soft hand on his shoulder, he looked around to see who it was. Jim could see a green wisp of Harper's aura circling him. It was her hand that he was feeling. Somehow, she was trying to comfort him. He closed his eyes, embracing Harper's touch, listening to her voice in his head.

Jim opened his eyes and turned to the sheriff. He was giving him an evil look.

"They were at the gas station that we drove by on the way here. They've already picked up another girl!"

The sheriff's face looked shocked.

"Are you for fucking real right now?" The sheriff raised his voice at Jim.

"I cannot predict timeframes," Jim disclosed. "I got you this far, didn't I?"

There were a few minutes of silence.

Special Agent Dulcey finally spoke up.

"Remember, do not touch any of the evidence!" She ordered. "We need everything here untouched until the forensics team gets here to investigate!" She turned and started to walk around the corner of the shack. "I am going back to the SUV to call dispatch and have them send a forensics team and medical examiner out immediately."

"I will call my team also." Sheriff Metsgaff stated as he followed Dulcey around to the front of the shack.

"No need to, sheriff," Dulcey halted in her tracks. "It is now our investigation!" She was still irritated with the way the sheriff spoke to Jim. Jim was the reason they were where they were in the first place.

The rest of the team followed, leaving Jim alone standing over Harper's body in the backyard.

Tom was standing on the threshold of the kitchen door overlooking the scene. He could see Harper's blonde hair poking out of the barrel.

He began to cry.

****

Dulcey was assisting the investigators as they arrived. Giving them what information, she had at this point. She began to feel numb. As if this all was not real. For almost three months, she had waited for this moment. To know what happened to those beautiful Myrtle Beach girls. She never thought it would end like this. Harper was dead, and Detective James Cavalier had known it all along.

Dulcey watched as the forensics team began taking pictures, asking questions, and finally moving the barrel with Harper's body inside. They would now take it back to the morgue and try to perform an autopsy.

She walked away towards the front of the shack, not looking back.

Carmen's phone vibrated in her pocket. She froze. Slowly, she pulled the phone out and looked at the message.

WHERE IS MY FUCKING 5 MILLION?!?

YOUR TIME IS RUNNING OUT!!!

Dulcey looked up from the phone, one of her detectives looking at her. She could see the stress on Dulcey's face.

"What's going on, boss?" She asked.

"I got another text. We need to hurry with that ransom money."

Dulcey pulled her phone out of her pocket and called back to the station.

"We need to get that ransom together," She demanded. "The kidnappers are getting impatient!" Her voice was getting louder with each word. "We are running out of time!"

Hanging up the phone, she sent out a text to Harper's phone.

WELL, WE HAVE THE CASH. WHERE AND WHEN CAN WE MEET FOR THE TRADE-OFF?

Dulcey walked over to the sheriff.

"I think we need to get a team and some officers on standby." She ordered. "I just got information that the cell pinged off a tower in Charleston!"

The sheriff looked at her, surprised.

"Let me radio my station and have them keep an eye out for that van!" He jumped into his cruiser and radioed back to the station.

Meanwhile, Dulcey sent out another text to Harper's phone.

WE NEED TO SET UP A PLAN ON WHERE AND WHEN TO MEET.

Jim and Tom joined Dulcey and the rest of the group.

"We need to get our shit together and head out to Charleston ASAP!" Dulcey looked over at Jim. Unaware of his surroundings, he was in a deep trance. She just stood still and watched him. She nudged Tom with her elbow; he was also noticing how odd Jim seemed.

Jim bent over to pick something up and put it in his pocket.

"I have a feeling that's where the kidnappers are heading." She exclaimed.

Jim could see Harper standing in front of him. He watched her intently, her aura a beautiful green. Her sad, blue eyes stared back into Jim's. 'Hurry, Jim. Please.' Her voice rang in his head.

Jim did not move or respond. It was almost like he was paralyzed.

"Should we interrupt him?" One of the agents asked.

"No, he will be okay. He does this quite often," Tom stopped her. "He will snap out of it shortly. But, he will need to rest when he does. It saps a lot of energy out of him."

Now that the forensics team had left with Harper's body, Dulcey needed to get her crew together and head to Charleston to find and capture those kidnappers.

She now had one mission. To go back to Charleston and find that dark gray van filled with girls.

32

Another Girl

Carmen was sitting silently on the van's middle seat. The men were talking to each other in a language Carmen could not understand. The van was now driving down the highway, heading to the next town. The van slowed and turned into a small gas station. They had stopped to fill up with gas and grabbed some snacks for the road. She sat quietly in the back as she heard the door slide open. One of the men got out and headed towards the little store. The other jumped out and walked around the van towards the pump. He started to fill the van. At this point, Carmen thought of running. With her head still covered, she wasn't quite sure where she was exactly. Carmen tried to move in her seat. That was when she noticed she had been buckled in.

Feeling defeated, she began to sob.

Carmen held her breath as she heard a whine quickly approaching. Her heart began to race. Here could be her last chance for freedom!

'Unbuckle and run! Go now, or you'll never make it!' Carmen could hear a familiar voice in her head.

Harper?

Carmen's breathing started to pick up. She began to fumble with the seat belt. Her hands were too weak to push the button down enough to release it! She panicked, pressing the red button repeatedly with all her strength, but it would not budge.

Dammit! She thought.

A bunch of sirens kept coming up the road towards the gas station. Carmen again grabbed for the buckle, feverishly pressing the button with her fingers.

Still nothing.

As fast as she heard them, the sirens faded away from the gas station.

Why did she ever go with strangers? Thoughts started to explode in Carmen's mind. *This guy she was talking to seemed so lovely. He seemed so interested in her. Why would he now want to hurt her? Why did she have to involve Harper? WHY?*

She could hear the men shuffling quickly toward the van. As they got in, she could smell the scent of beef jerky. Then, a rattle of a chip's bag and the crack of a soda can being opened. Her mouth started to water. It had been so long since she had a decent meal. She remembered the last hot summer day, drinking a soda with Harper. Her mind drifted back to the sweetness on her tongue, the fizzing of the soda as it ran down the back of her throat. She imagined the feeling of the ice-cold fluid filling her stomach. She tried to swallow; her throat was dry. Carmen's stomach started to cramp, and she doubled over. She knew that she would probably never get to taste a soda ever again. She was almost to the point of not caring. Carmen was giving up. After this long, how would anyone find her?

Were they still even looking? Carmen closed her eyes, not wanting to think about her life anymore.

The van pulled away from the gas station, heading opposite to where the sirens went. Carmen, feeling the warmest she had in a very long time, became very sleepy. Without fighting it, she fell sound asleep.

Carmen was awakened by a shove to the back, knocking her onto the van's floor. She didn't know how long she was asleep.

Carmen realized that she *had* been successful at popping the seatbelt!

If I had only known, she thought.

Carmen didn't know what was going on until she heard another girl's muffled screams, and the van started to shake.

She opened her eyes, the pillowcase still covered her head, and tape covered her mouth. Carmen slid back into the seat and sat up straight. She could hear the young girl crying behind her. She turned her head and started to mumble something. There was a stiff grasp on Carmen's chin, and a short shove as her head hit the window.

She was startled and didn't attempt to speak again for fear of being beaten. Her ribs never healed from the last time she thought she could get away. Occasionally, when she took a deep breath, she could feel a sharp pain over her right side. Carmen closed her eyes and drifted back to the ugly memories of the day her ribs got broken.

* *

Carmen realized she had been alone for the entire day. She didn't hear any voices for quite some time. Now it was nighttime, and she started to think that maybe the kidnappers had left her to die. Or perhaps they had gotten arrested or were going to bring Harper back to the shack. She couldn't understand a word they said to one another, so she barely knew at any one time what exactly was going on.

It was probably a good thing she could not understand what they were saying.

Sometimes the conversation would be about their next move. If Syn couldn't get his ransom money, they would have to ditch the first plan and just send the girls overseas. Or it would be about her friend, Harper, who was stuffed callously in a barrel out in the backyard. As her body began decomposing, the smell was getting worse and worse. It was almost impossible to go back to using the outhouse. It had become a daily complaint amongst the men.

Carmen, at this point, had no idea that Harper was dead. All she knew was that her friend wasn't with her anymore. She prayed Harper had made it home safe.

She prayed every day.

Carmen finally decided to try and break the window in the tiny bedroom. Then she could scream, or better yet, if she could just break those damn chains, she could run away! Carmen started gathering anything she could lift and tossing it at the window. When that didn't work, she grabbed the cuffs and began to work on them. Carmen pried at them, trying to pull herself loose from the wall. She had to take it in steps. From not eating a decent meal in weeks, she had become weak. So just standing for more than a few minutes was exhausting.

That day though, she was working on pure adrenaline.

Earlier, Carmen found a cement block in the corner of the room and had hidden it under the corner of her mattress. With all her might, she grabbed it and began smashing the wall where her chains were attached. Feeling herself getting weaker and frustrated, she threw the block at the window. The effort made her pass out from exhaustion, and Carmen fell to the floor.

A few moments later, Carmen began to awaken. The sunlight hit her in her eyes as it shone through a hole in the window.

She had broken the window! She slowly got to her feet and regained her legging. She looked at the chains still attached to the wall and pulled on them. They slid out of the wall and hit the floor!

Oh, my God, I am free! She thought! *Time to run!*

Carmen stared at the hole in the window. She needed to break out the rest of the glass without getting cut as she walked over to the corner of the room and picked up the five-gallon bucket. Gagging, she dumped its reeking contents out. Now taking a deep breath, Carmen regained herself and walked over to the window. She heaved the bucket over her head, slamming it into the painted glass with all of her strength. The window broke and fell onto the floor in pieces. The warm sun hit her on the face and chest! She inhaled the fresh air blowing into the small room. It seemed to give her a little more energy. So, she wasted no time as she quickly pulled out the broken glass shards from the window frame, trying to keep calm and avoid getting cut. With her last bit of energy, she pulled herself through the window.

That was when the smell outside had hit her.

What in God's name is that awful smell? She held her arm over her nose and mouth, looking over at the big plastic barrel walking in the opposite direction.

She stumbled as she quickly tried to enter the woods, crawling on all fours. She screamed out loud, as the pain in her knees became almost unbearable!

She heard her echo screaming back, bouncing off the trees. It almost sounds like an evil laugh. She gasped for breath; she was exhausted.

Damn it. Carmen felt defeated.

She laid with her face in the cool grass. Carmen noticed something shiny on the edge of the dirt road in front of her. She crawled over to look. It was a tattered rose gold necklace with a heart-shaped locket, squished in one of the ruts on the path. Carmen immediately recognized it as Harper's, but Carmen didn't know was that it had been ripped from Harper when she was run over several months ago. Carmen got a pit in her stomach. She picked up the dirty, broken chain and started to cry. Harper never took this locket off. Ever. Carmen opened it and looked at the pictures inside. One side was Harper's parents, and the other was a selfie of the two of them. Shaking, Carmen quickly shoved it into her pocket and tried to stand. She staggered into the forest and plopped on the damp, leafy ground. She needed a moment to catch her breath.

As she laid just feet off the road, she started to hear an engine in the distance. She stayed motionless, listening.

The van drove within feet of her as it headed toward the front porch of the shack. She did not move. The van came to a stop, and the men got out. They started to unload it. Each taking turns to carry several boxes and bags into the shack. Carmen's knee was throbbing from the fall. She stayed still; she didn't want to screw this up now.

Carmen waited for the men to go into the shack and shut the door. Then, she gathered up what strength she had and started to stagger deeper into the woods. Carmen heard one of the men shout from inside the shack in a foreign language. She didn't know what he said, but she knew he must have found the room was empty. Carmen tried to move as fast as her weak legs would carry her, stumbling and half crawling deeper into the woods.

The two men were running around the shack in a panic. One of them ran out of the shack and stood on the porch, scanning the woods. The other ran around the back, shouting in another language.

Carmen stumbled to her knees and silently started to cry into the soft ground. She was out of breath and out of energy. She rolled onto her back and laid still, heaving for oxygen.

This is it. She thought. *They are going to kill me; I'm for sure dead.*

But, as scared as she felt, she was determined to escape. Carmen stood up once again and started to run. That was when it all went dark. She passed out. It was probably for the best because what was about to happen was horror beyond belief.

Carmen woke up with a horrible headache. Every time she took a breath, it felt like a knife in her ribs. One of the men was kicking her repeatedly and shouting something foreign at her. The pain was so intense; she couldn't catch her breath. She noticed that she was back in her little room, chained to the wall, and bleeding everywhere. She closed her eyes, feeling the kicks to her back; she again blacked out.

I can't take much more, she thought. *God, please just take me.*

* *

Carmen opened her eyes. All she could see was white. *Was this Heaven?* She thought. Then, she could hear the men talking. She quickly remembered where she was. Far from Heaven, she was sitting next to her kidnapper. Carmen reached over and touched her rib. There was a hard lump, and it was still a little sore.

Healing fractures. Carmen thought.

Carmen started to cough. She couldn't help it. She gasped in a big breath, trying to hold it in.

That was when she heard a girl's voice coming from behind her.

"Hello?" the shaken voice called out. "Is anyone else-----"

Carmen heard a thud as the girl must have been hit and knocked out. One of the men was shouting the entire time.

Almost instantly after she heard the thud, Carmen felt a sharp pain in the back of her neck and hit down hard on the van floor.

Carmen stayed silent.

The young girl in the back seat awakened and started to scream in a high-pitched screech.

"NO talking!" One of the men screamed back.

The girl paused, just enough to see the shadow of a fist come at her. The hit almost knocked her out, slumping her over in the seat.

The van was now silent, traveling towards its destination. There was no need to draw any type of attention to them at this point in the game. They are so close to getting those five million dollars. This ransom they were about to collect was worth more than a dozen of these girls put together!

"Text those stupid Virginia Beach FBI agents and ask about the money again," One of the men paused to look at Carmen. She could not understand him. "Let's get an answer before Syn decides to call us again."

33

Charleston, South Carolina

Jim slept the entire drive to Charleston; he was exhausted. Emotionally drained, the rest of the crew kept silent as well. Tom silently prayed to himself that this nightmare would be over soon, so they could go back to their simple life in Idaho.

The black SUV pulled up under the canopy of the hotel. Dulcey and her assistant went inside to check into their rooms.

Jim awoke when he heard the door slam shut.

Blinking, he looked around and tried to acclimate to his surroundings. Tom didn't notice Jim right away. He was busy texting Jenni.

"The kidnappers are here in Charleston. They have started preparing to move the girls." Jim blurted out.

Tom jumped, a little startled as he looked up from his phone.

"What did you just say?"

"The kidnappers have been preparing to ship the girls," Jim repeated.

"Are you sure? Do you know what this could mean?"

"Yeah," Jim answered sleepily. "I do."

"I just hope we can find them before they are gone. Lord knows how many of these girls have already been shipped out of the country."

There was a long pause.

"I know where the van is," Jim broke the silence. "I have also seen a house in my visions. It has quite a few girls inside."

"What?" Tom put his phone in his shirt pocket and turned around in his seat. "Are you saying that you're having *more* visions? When did this start? I thought you only knew things up until the date you had supposedly died?" Tom sounded confused."

"It never goes away. It's hard to explain, and I don't understand it myself. I see Harper more now that we are in South Carolina. Harper and Rob were with us at the shack."

"I cannot recollect all of our conversations from these 'visions.'" Jim half-smiled at Tom and turned his attention out the window.

"I don't know all of the answers. Do you understand that?"

"Honestly, I have a hard time believing any of this, and I'm sitting right here witnessing it."

"Well, remember when we were all standing around the barrel behind the shack? Harper was there with her hand on my shoulder, comforting me, showing me visions of the other girls. It seemed like when I had a vision, everyone else disappeared, and the world turned dark," Jim turned and looked into Tom's eyes. "Like on the plane. I could only see my vision at that time. I haven't a clue what you or the other passengers were doing. It's like I have a blackout, but I can see everything else!"

"Those kidnappers have no intention of giving up these girls easily. They are way too valuable. If this ransom attempt fails, they will sell the girls overseas, trafficking them on the black market."

Tom nodded.

"The predator behind these heinous acts is one of pure evil. He is smart and well versed in this, and he has been at it his *entire* life. This man has collected enough girls now for his next big move. I just don't know why he would want to ransom the two of them. In one of my visions, I saw a large shipping container over at Port Charleston. It's filled with barrels. One for each girl." Jim ran his hand through his hair. "The ship that the container is scheduled to be put on is leaving port in a couple of days. If those girls are loaded up in those barrels successfully, they could be gone for good! The only thing we have that will lure him to us is that five million dollars!"

One of the agents interrupted Jim.

"We need to go inside, Jim, so you can finish telling the others."

After listening to Jim's story, Dulcey placed a phone call. She sent a patrol car out on the Port Charleston Piers.

Game on.

34

House of Girls

The van finally slowed to a complete stop, and the engine turned off. Carmen listened as the men talked to one another before jumping out of the van and opening the side door. She realized this was the end of this trip for now. She was the first to be pulled from the van.

The girl's heads stayed covered as they were led from an enclosed garage, through a foyer, and into a small house. They had no clue where they were, only of each other's presence. Almost as if they could feel the fear energizing from one another's bodies.

The house was warm. It almost seemed welcoming to Carmen, who had spent the last couple of months barely dressed in a run-down shack.

She took in a deep breath. The air was light, with a plethora of smells looming in the room, and it made her stomach ache with hunger.

The men led the girls into a small living room. It was quiet. The only people talking were the kidnappers in their native language.

Their conversations were whispered. In this room, Carmen could smell something different. It had a very faint smell of perfumes and body sprays.

The girls were thrown onto a soft couch, and their pillowcases ripped off their heads.

The duct tape still secured their hands, wrapping around their waist.

Carmen looked over to see the girl from the van for the first time. She had tears in her eyes, and her face was puffy like she had been crying for a while. The girl had blonde hair and blue eyes. She looked a lot like Harper with longer hair. Carmen studied the girl as her eyes started to fill with tears, wishing she could talk to her.

A dark man walked into the room. A black scarf covered his face and his eyes with dark glasses.

"What the fuck is this?" He shouted in a thick accent. Carmen looked over to see who was screaming. The man's voice was much deeper than the others, hoarser. He was dressed entirely in black. Even his hands were covered up with black gloves.

Who was this guy? Why was he so covered up? She wondered. Little did she know, he was the monster who was responsible for all this.

His name was Syn.

The two men shifted their glazes from Syn to Carmen. Her hair was chopped, and she was in baggy, filthy clothes.

"We haven't had time for this one. We were busy trying to pick up the other one for you." The man pointed toward the girl that came in with Carmen.

"Fucking clean her up and get her fed!" Syn walked out of the room. "She is worth nothing to me that thin and dirty."

The two of them took Carmen into the bathroom first to get her cleaned up. The warm, soapy water on her skin felt good. The sores on her backside stung when the water hit them. But, after a while, the burning stopped, and Carmen welcomed the relief. It was her first time getting clean since the washtub in the kitchen back at the shack, and it felt amazing. The warm water and lack of food slowly begin to drain her. All Carmen wanted to do at this point was sleep. She struggled to keep awake as she sat in the bathtub, letting the warm water run down her face.

Once she was cleaned up, she was given some clean clothes to wear. She donned them and walked back to the living room. The men had some food on a plate for her. Carmen gobbled it up.

Carmen had inhaled her sandwich so fast that she got a severe cramp in her gut. She doubled over and began to vomit on the floor.

"You son-of-a-bitch!" One of the men yelled at her.

"You have to eat slower, you dumbass!" He threw a roll of paper towel at her and a bottle of bleach cleanser.

"Your mess, your responsibility." The man walked over to Carmen, pushing her until her face was almost touching the pile. Carmen turned away, not because she was grossed out, but because she was afraid she might want to eat it up again.

After cleaning up her mess, Carmen was given another sandwich. This time cut in quarters, one piece at a time. This was much better. Carmen finished her sandwich and was handed a glass of water. It was not cold, but she didn't care. She drank it all and let out a huge burp.

With food in her belly and a warm room, carmen found herself once again bound up on the couch next to the blonde girl. Carmen did not say a word to her. She was content. The food and water had been the most at one time she had since she was kidnapped.

She thought about where she was and the shack from where she had come. She began to sob and slowly drifted off to sleep.

The men grabbed the blonde girl; she jerked her arm away and started to scream. It jolted Carmen awake.

One of the men grabbed the blonde by the hair and punched her in the face. With a grotesque thud, the girl hit the floor. She was out cold, and there was blood coming from one of her ears. The room again had become silent.

One of the kidnappers walked over to her and spat in her face.

"I'll show you how to behave right, you little whore!" He reached out to grab her lifeless body.

"Enough!" A sinister voice shouted from the doorway between the kitchen and living room. "She is worth the most to me right now!"

The man grumbled and walked into one of the small rooms of the living room and shut the door.

"I just got word that the shipping container is ready. We can start moving the girls out of here tomorrow. The barge leaves in two days." Syn addressed the other man in the room.

"Once all the girls are loaded, we can focus on meeting for the ransom. Simple as that! They have sent me a picture of the cash."

They both smiled at one another as Syn walked out of the room, leaving the man alone with the two terrified girls. He was the one Carmen recognized from the beach.

He opened his knife and started to cut the ropes that confined the blonde. He ripped the tape from the girl's mouth and hands. He began to cut away her clothes, revealing her naked body. Terrified, she started to scream, lunging away from the man. He grabbed her by the hair and pulled her back to him. He slapped his hand over her mouth. Holding her tightly against his body as she struggled, he was too strong for her to fight off. The blonde girl was in shock. She had never been touched by any man before.

"If you scream once more, I will knock your teeth out!" He whispered into her ear.

The girl started to cry and melted into the floor once again. The man dragged her by her hair into the bathroom and began to hack it off. Carmen could hear her crying.

"No! No! No!"

After cutting off the blonde's hair, he attempted to shove her into the shower when the girl turned and bolted again. The man had lost his grip as she ran like lightning out of the bathroom. The girl was fast. She had been a track star at her school.

The man was shocked at how fast she ran around the tiny living room. He ran at her, trying to corner her. She got to a door leading out front, only to find out it was locked. She then zipped around, leaping over Carmen sitting on the sofa. The blonde just missed one of the man's grasp as he swung his arm out at her. Instead, his hand caught Carmen on the cheek, sending her sideways.

The blonde girl made it to the second door and opened it. As she stumbled through the door, she quickly came to a halt. Inside the tiny bedroom was a bunch of girls, all about the same age. All bound up and gagged, sitting side by side on the floor. A man with a gun was standing next to the door. He jumped back, startled to see who busted into the room. The girl screamed at the horror. Instinctively, he smacked her in the head with the butt of his gun. The blow knocked her out once again. This time, she didn't move.

The girl was shoved out into the living room, as the door to the second room was shut immediately. None of the girls dared to move. They were too scared. They just stared wide-eyed at the door.

The man grabbed the girl by the arm again. This time he had a better grip on her. He pulled her limp body to the bathroom and tossed her into the bathtub. He looked over his shoulder only to see Carmen watching intently. He kicked the bathroom door shut. Carmen was left alone, tied up. She slumped over on the soft couch and fell to sleep. Oddly enough, this had been the best sleep she had had in a very long time.

About an hour later, the blonde girl walked out of the bathroom. Her hair had been cut short. From a distance, she looked like Harper. Her eyes were blue, glasses were gone, and that hair! She was dressed in a pink shirt and shorts.

Carmen recognized them. *They were Harper's clothes! The ones she was wearing the night they were kidnapped!*

The shirt was washed but still dirty across the chest.

What happened to Harper? Carmen felt a sick feeling in her gut.

The blonde was crying and shaking from shock. Tears streamed down her cheeks.

The man walked the girl over to the couch and bound her up next to Carmen.

"Maybe that will teach you not to run, you fucking whore!" He shouted at her.

The blonde sobbed and shook, gasping between sobs.

Carmen wanted to stare at the blonde but quickly realized she had been through enough.

It wasn't long after when the other man walked back into the room.

"Put them in the back so that we can have this room again to ourselves."

The men walked the girls to the back room, where they kept the others.

The large man standing at the door with the gun put his hand on Carmen's shoulder and pushed her into a sitting position on the floor along the wall with the blonde girl. Keeping her face to the floor, Carmen looked around the room. There were many girls. All of them were tied up. Her eyes moved from one girl to another, studying each one of them, scanning their faces for Harper.

Why would anyone want this many teenage girls? Carmen thought. *How did they all get here? What were their stories? Where were they from? What was going to happen to them?*

One of the girls had been pretty beaten up. She looked like she was here the longest. She kept her stare to the ground, not making eye contact. She was the thinnest, and by far, the weakest. She curled up in one of the corners by herself.

The other girls were leaning on each other for comfort and protection.

Carmen wondered if some of the girls had the same regrets she had. Like wishing they hadn't gotten in the van or accepted that strange online request. But, like Carmen, these girls were looking to fit in, too. They also wanted to find that special friendship, giving their phone numbers to a stranger.

That same special someone promised them money, security, and freedom from her parents. Then ultimately taking it all from them.

There was a thin, black girl in the corner to Carmen's right and a fair-skinned girl sitting right next to her. She had her hair dyed black with purple streaks in it. She had multiple piercings. Some had been recently ripped out. There was a variety of girls, ranging from the ages of fourteen to nineteen years. The youngest was cuddling in one of the corners with two redheads. She was about ten or so. Her beautiful bronze skin and dark hair contrasted against their fair skin. Carmen felt sorry for the young girl. She was so young compared to the rest. So much more innocent.

How did they lure her into their grasp? Carmen thought. *Did they use candy? Or puppies? Maybe they just grabbed her when no one was looking.*

Either way, she was waiting in this room for her destination like the rest of them.

What Carmen thought was unusual about the girl was that she did not sob or cry. Her large eyes were not showing fear. Like Carmen, she kept looking around at the girls. Maybe she was looking for someone. She was held close by the two in the corner. They looked alike and were dressed alike. *Twins.* Not as thin as the rest, but they had stunning features. They, too, silently wait with the others, fearing their fate as well.

Another one of the girls that caught Carmen's eye had sandy-colored curly hair. Delicate little freckles dotted her cheekbones and the bridge of her nose. Her rust-color eyes kept their stare locked on Carmen.

Directly across the small room from Carmen were two black girls. Their hair had been in tight braids and beaded but recently hacked off. One girl was bleeding; she had been cut with a knife. They also seemed to be watching Carmen, wondering if she was the last of them to come through the door.

Or would there be more? No one knew.

The last of the girls sitting to Carmen's left was halfway hidden by the large older man with the gun. He never moved; he just stared at the youngest girl. Her large brown eyes were staring back at him.

Carmen could hear the men in the other room discussing their strategy. In the same language as before. She noticed one of the older girls looking at her. Tears filled her eyes, tape wrinkling over her crying lips.

Carmen slid over and put her thin arm around the girl. The girl buried her face into Carmen's chest and sobbed. She was trying to talk, but Carmen could not understand her. The two girls held each other tightly. Carmen closed her eyes to pray. Little did Carmen know; the girl was also praying silently with her.

They both prayed for a miracle.

35

Long Night Ahead

As the room got darker, Carmen felt her eyelids getting heavy. Since her abduction, she has been clean, warm, fed, and not alone for the first time. It didn't take long before she quickly dozed off into a deep sleep. The little girl who was praying with her earlier had already fallen asleep. She was curled up next to Carmen. She was also warm, and the steady heave of her chest felt comforting.

Only two of the girls were not asleep. One was the blonde girl, the last of the girls to be abducted. She was sitting with her back to the wall, terrified. Just minutes ago, she watched the man who had been guarding the door pull the youngest girl out of the bedroom. She could hear the little girl whimper, muffled through the tape she had across her mouth. She did not try to fight. The girls were now left alone in the bedroom. The blonde girl took a deep breath holding her hands up to her ears and started to hum. She could hear the muffled cries of the little girl in the next room. She was unable to comprehend what was happening to that little girl.

The blonde girl looked over at the girl with the scars sitting next to her. She, too, was awake, crying. Her neck and cheeks had tiny scars that looked like giant chickenpox. The blonde kept staring.

It was then that the girl with the scars noticed the blonde's steady gaze towards her. She was giving the blonde a dirty look.

"What the fuck you lookin' at, bitch?!?" She blurted out. The duct tape was hanging, exposing most of her mouth. Spit flew out with each word.

"I am sorry," the blonde whispered back. "I.... I don't mean to stare."

"Fuck you!"

"Well, I----"

"They're not chickenpox! If that's whatcha think." The girl glared at the floor, giving the blonde the evil eye. "They are reminders. Every time my stepfather and his son would rape me, they burned me with their cigarettes. So, I wouldn't forget that they were in charge. After 40 burns, I had 'nough. I had to run away before 41. That's when I met up with *him*."

The girl with the scars took a long, deep breath.

"He.... he promised me he would help me get away from that hell hole. He had cash and a place to crash." She tucks her head between her knees, sobbing. "This was not what I thought was going to happen. I don't know which is worse, staying home, getting raped. Or this. I would have been better off on the streets."

Finally, the girl with the scars couldn't take it anymore as she heard the constant sobbing of the little black-haired girl coming from next door. She frantically started to work at her duct tape and rope bindings. She could pull them enough to free her hands. She quickly moved towards her bound ankles. She finished pulling off the duct tape that was hanging off her mouth. It tore some skin off the corner of her lip. The girl let out a faint cry but continued freeing herself.

The blonde girl started to feel the energy coming from the girl with the scars as she worked at getting herself free. Working together, they did not exchange words. Swiftly they went from girl to girl around the room. In silence, each girl freeing the next.

Occasionally, they could hear the little girl next door let out a scream. The blonde girl shuddered as she desperately freed the last girl.

Carmen and the girl with the scars circled, scanning the room, looking for a way out. There was one tiny window that had been boarded up. An escape wasn't looking good for them.

Carmen slowly opened the door to the bathroom. High on the wall was a small window covered with carpeting. Carmen and the girl with the scars began to claw frantically at the carpet. Surprisingly enough, it peeled off a lot easier than they thought.

"Hurry." A whisper came from the bathroom door.

The blonde-haired girl and the twins were standing guard just outside of the bathroom. They were the ones that could hear the men getting louder next door. Suddenly, a scream came from one of the men. So loud, they all heard it. The girls froze in fear.

Carmen stared wide-eyed at the girl with the scars. They both began pulling and working harder at getting the window free of debris so that they could open it.

"I don't know how much more I can take listening to that little girl next door!" The blonde stated.

Once they tore everything from the window, they could see a street light filtering through the dirty glass. The girls worked frantically at the painted latch.

Most of the girls were now crammed into the bathroom, except the twins and the blonde.

Finally, the lock broke from its window frame, leaving a perfect mold where it had laid over the years. Carmen reached out and pushed up the window. Surprisingly it moved well, just enough for the girls to be able to slide out.

"I'll go first," stated the girl with the scars. "I am tall enough to help pull you guys through on the other side."

"Okay," Carmen replied, cupping her hands like a stirrup for the girl's foot.

Carmen hoisted the girl with the scars up toward the window.

One of the twins could hear something coming from the other room and tip-toed toward the door. She pressed her right ear softly up to it and closed her eyes to listen.

The men had become silent, and she heard a slight rustling. The little girl was quiet.

Carmen was holding the girl with the scars up to the window's edge. She could see some of the scars up close. They look horrid. The girl lifted her leg to the ledge and quickly slid out the window. She hit the soft grass below and slowly stood up.

The scarred girl took in a deep sigh and looked around. She was free! Her heart started to race, as she could feel the fresh, cool air on her skin.

Watching the girl with the scars disappear out the window, the other girls all started to get a little anxious. Each was pushing one another to get closer to the window, to be the next one out! Carmen once again cupped her hands for the next girl's foot.

Just then, the blonde came back over to the group.

"I can't hear anything coming from the room next door!" She whispered in a panic. "What if they killed that little girl!"

One of the twins gave her a worried look and walked over to the door to listen for herself. Just then, the door popped open, knocking her to the ground! One of the guards was standing there, zipping up his pants. He looked around in complete shock.

"What in the hell is going on in here!" He shouted in a raspy foreign accent.

Another man came running in with a flashlight and shined it around. He, too, was shocked to find most of the girls stuffed in the bathroom, and they began screaming and pushing each other, fighting to get out the window.

Carmen tried to heave the little girl who prayed with her out of the window next, but the girl's fear paralyzed her. In one last attempt, the window broke from its hinge and smashed to the ground. The girl with the scars could hear the noise coming through the bathroom window. She turned and bolted as fast as she could towards the back of the house. She disappeared into the woods, not looking back.

Although exhausted, she could not stop running.

"For fuck's sake!" One of the men marched quickly toward the bathroom. The screaming girls began trampling over Carmen. Each was hoping to make it out the bathroom window. Overwhelmed, Carmen cried out in pain.

One of the men walked into the bathroom, pushing the screaming girls aside as his partner pulled them back into the bedroom and shoved them one by one against the wall. At this point, Carmen was so exhausted; she just crawled back into the bedroom. One of the men kicked her in the bottom as she passed him. Doubling over in pain, Carmen slowly made it back to her spot next to the wall. All the girls were standing, their backs toward the men.

One of the men took his flashlight, poked it out the window, looking for any escapee. He could only see the stillness of darkness as she shined his light across the wood line. He walked out of the bathroom and screwed the door shut. Feeling defeated, the terrified girls began crying.

The lucky one was the girl with the scars.

36

The First Move

"Let's start packing up some of the girls and get them the fuck out of here!"

Syn screamed out orders in his native language.

"This will take a few trips. Make sure to pick out the stronger ones to go first. I'll go and draw the shit up. They're gonna need something to keep them quiet until that crate gets loaded on the ship! We cannot take any chances. We are too close!"

This overseas sale was going to be huge, making Syn a whole lot of money. He had to make sure every girl in that crate made it to Binhai alive!

Binhai was the largest port city in Tianjin, Northern China. It was also the main maritime gateway to Beijing, where most of Syn's buyers would be waiting.

The girls would be picked up there and delivered to their owners. Some of Syn's customers had purchased one girl, while others had two or three. Syn did not know, nor did he care, what would happen to the girls once they left his hands. Why would he? He would have his money and would be out of here.

Then, there was the ransom! The icing on the cake! Five million dollars! Syn was so close now; he could taste it! He had big plans for this money—retirement far away from America.

The men started grabbing girls and bringing them to the kitchen. The rest stayed huddled together, hugging each other and crying. None of them were aware of what horror laid ahead. Terror flashed on every face as the girls were separated. One of the men tried to rip the twins apart. They begin screaming uncontrollably and clinging to each other.

"Leave those two go; they have been sold together." Syn's voice crackled out, again in a language none of the girls understood.

After the first group of girls was all loaded into the van, Syn walked over to the door. He glanced around the bedroom where Carmen and the rest of the girls were. One of the men had been standing at the doorway with a gun in his hand. He was watching as the others were being led out.

"I need to send a text to that damn FBI agent." Syn paced in front of the doorway. "I need to tell them a time and place." He looked at the light purple phone in his hand. The sparkles picked up every ray of light left in the room.

Carmen recognized it as Harper's.

He had her clothes and now her phone? Carmen started to cry. *This can't be good.*

"I'll be back for the girls," Syn stated as he turned to leave, making eye contact with Carmen for a split second.

His face remained covered, except his eyes, and Carmen looked directly into them. For a moment, she thought she saw red.

"Keep moving the girls. I'll be back."

Syn walked out of the house and into the garage, where he

jumped into his vehicle. With no lights on, he pulled out of the garage and hurried off towards Aiken.

Back to that fucking shack. Syn thought to himself.

Syn needed to text his plan for the ransom to the FBI. He knew that they might have a tracer on Harper's phone by now, so he decided to drive back to where he made the last contact with them. It was risky, but he also couldn't risk them finding the house just yet. So Syn headed back towards the shack.

He found the back road that led towards the shack, and he looked up to see the cell tower. He drove up past it, turned around, and pulled off to the side of the road. He shut off his car and sent out a text.

THERE IS A WAREHOUSE ON
JOHN'S ISLAND
NO COPS, NO SNIPERS.
JUST THE MONEY FOR THE GIRLS.
IF YOU TRY TO DEVIATE FROM MY PLAN
I WILL KILL THE GIRLS

Syn sat in his Jeep, looking at Harper's phone, waiting for it to light up, and watching in the darkness for vehicle lights. With no streetlights for miles, it would be easy to spot anything coming up the road.

After a few minutes, Harper's phone lit up.

OKAY! WE'RE READY! WHEN DO YOU WANT TO MEET?

Do you really think you are ready? He laughed to himself. *Idiots.*

****

Just after his first contact with Carmen, Syn knew he had to come up with a plan. If it were a ransom, he would need to come up with a drop-off and pick-up point. He also knew it had to be away from the Charleston ports. So, he began driving around and looking for a few decent options for the past couple of months.

Syn planned different scenarios and escape routes in his head as he drove through the backwoods near Charleston. Syn always made sure he was over-prepared for any situation. That was what kept him from being caught.

One of his favorite spots just happened to be a used car lot in St. George. The lot there was perfect! On the back wall was where all the used vehicles were parked. Just beyond that, a railroad track ran through. Syn knew the back gate was locked. He planned to take the lock off and replace it with an identical one he would purchase at Home Depot.

When he was finished, he would throw away the key.

Another spot Syn remembered was a warehouse property in John's Island just south of Charleston. It was just down the road from where he had purchased the van. He had driven the van to this area and parked it there to inspect it. It was secluded enough that he felt safe.

Syn noticed that there had been several storage buildings on this property. He drove around to one of the back warehouses. It was in the perfect area. It was huge and lined with many corridors that were stuffed with hundreds of storage lockers. He walked the isles inside the back warehouse, checking out each unit and its distance away from the door. He decided which ones he wanted and rented them as soon as they become available.

This had taken years.

Then, there was the little shack. Syn had driven up there for one last look around. He decided to put one of the barrels he had used for transporting the girls out back, just in case this became one of the drop-off spots. He had to be prepared for just about anything, plus he hated that drive.

He especially hated that shack. It reminded him of one of the places he stayed for a short time in Russia, just after his mom died. He was so scared and alone. He thought he had found a safe place with some poor Russian prostitutes. They offered him a warm place to stay and food. But in turn, he was forced to make money as well. You would be surprised at how much money an eight-year-old boy brought in.

That was Syn's breaking point. He vowed that he would take care of himself even if he had to live outside in the woods, alone. Poor.

****

Syn sent the text to Carmen's phone, and he waited.
OK TOMORROW NOON ONE PERSON
NO COPS, NO SNIPERS
JUST ONE PERSON AND THE MONEY
IF YOU TRY TO DEVIATE FROM MY PLAN
I *WILL* KILL THE GIRLS
Everyone remained silent. Dulcey looked around at Jim and Tom and the rest of the agents.

"Well, what do we say to that?"

"I think we should act like this is a perfect deal," Tom said. "We send them a text agreeing with everything he has in mind. We need to keep him busy, buying us time to find what that phone is pinging off. Hopefully, in the meantime, Jim will be able to lead us to the house. Then we can ambush the kidnappers before they know what is going on."

"Sounds like a good plan, unless anyone here objects," Dulcey addressed her staff. Nobody spoke up. "Good. We will go with that plan. Thanks, Tom."

Dulcey sent a text to Harper's phone:
I GOT IT. CASH FOR THE GIRLS. JUST ONE PERSON, ALONE.

HOW DO WE KNOW YOU WILL GIVE US THE GIRLS?

Carmen's phone lit up.

YOU HAVE NO CHOICE.

Syn started up his vehicle and sped off back toward the house. He needed to get back to the two money makers and get them ready for the exchange tomorrow!

The two men pulled up to one of the gates just outside the port. The guard was standing just inside the gatehouse, holding a clipboard. He smiled when he saw the van pull up.

"Head through gate seven, go to warehouse ten. You'll see your shipping container just inside the doors on the right. It's red." He handed over the clipboard with a shipping ticket and the crate information on it.

"I was told it was all ready, and you have the keys, right?" He asked the men.

The driver chuckled and nodded. He took the clipboard with the receipt and signed it. He handed the clipboard back to the guard along with an envelope filled with cash. The gate slowly rose, letting them through.

With the drugs working, the girls sat silently, stuffed in the back of the van. They silently pulled into the warehouse alongside the red shipping container, scanning the area. The extra cash in the envelope was to make sure the place was empty.

One of the men jumped out of the van and opened the door to the container. Inside were a lot of barrels—one for each girl. The tops were off. Everything was set and ready.

Thanks to Syn.

The men worked quickly at unloading the girls one by one. Each had been blindfolded and carried into their cylindrical prison. Once each girl was set inside, they were given one more sedative. Then, the tops of the barrels were quietly set back into place and sealed up.

When the men brought the last of the girls in, they would give them the remaining sedative, as this should be enough to last them through the trip.

One last thing before they left, the men changed the lock on the container door.

No one could fuck with it while they were gone.

37

Getting Closer

As the convoy of police vehicles continued to drive through the West end of the small Charleston suburbs, everyone remained silent, constantly on the lookout for anything that didn't look right.

Dulcey turned to look at Jim, who was staring out the window.

"Jim, not to put any pressure on you, but do any of these houses look like they may be the one we are looking for?"

Jim looked at her green eyes reflecting in the SUV's rearview mirror. He didn't answer. He didn't know what to say.

Slowly, she continued driving up the street.

He finally shook his head and turned back toward the window. He was desperately looking for anything that looked familiar. His eyes combed every single house, garage, and yard.

Then, on the left-hand corner of the street, a gas station caught Jim's eyes. A little carved bear was standing next to the front door holding a Welcome sign.

"That gas station over there. I have seen it before!" Jim exclaimed excitedly. The small convoy of vehicles slowly pulled up, driving through the parking lot. None of them knew what they were looking for as the cars pulled up alongside the station to regroup.

After they got back on the road, Dulcey received a call from one of her staff in Myrtle Beach. They informed her that Harper's phone's last ping had come from that same tower back by the shack!

"Really? This guy has us running in God damn circles!"

"A gray van just pulled out in front of me! On Genesee and Third!" There was silence as adrenaline-filled the air, waiting for a confirmation on the vehicle. "I am unable to see who is in the windows. They are too dark. But I can see a bunch of figures inside, so I'm moving in!"

They all listened to the radio, waiting. One of the squad cars began to pull out of the station.

"I am going in for backup."

"Whatcha waiting for, Special Agent? Let's go!" Tom hollered out to Dulcey.

Dulcey pulled out screeching tires as she followed the squad car ahead of them. They zoomed up the street, with their lights and sirens going.

Then, that's when they saw it!

The gray van! As they pulled up to the scene, the officers were pulling a man out of the van. He had dark curly hair. From this distance, he looked like one of the suspects. From the passenger's side, a woman and many children all started piling out of the van. The younger ones were crying and clinging to their parents and older siblings.

Jim lurched forward from the back seat the minute he saw the van. It was much lighter than the one in question.

"That is not the van!" Jim confirmed just a little too late. "Those are not the people we are looking for."

"Independent Baptists!" One of the officers called out to Dulcey and Tom as they pulled up. "We are releasing them."

As the officers apologized and explained their situation, the man nodded completely understanding. He had heard about the kidnappings and expressed his prayer to the men trying to do their job. He calmed his family, loaded them back up into their van, and slowly drove off.

"I guess we continue to look for the house." Dulcey turned to Jim. "Until we hear something different from the office."

The sheriff from St George nodded. "I agree. We wait until Agent Higgin's office calls us back with that gate number at the port. Until then, we wait and see. I think we should also send someone out to the shack." he added.

"We'll keep driving until Jim recognizes something. Hopefully, this does not take all night!"

LOADING UP

It was just before midnight when Syn made it back to the house.

"I need to get these two girls the hell out of here!" He exclaimed. "I have set up the exchange. You three keep loading up the rest of those girls before daylight! We need to get all those fucking girls to the harbor and into that container! Remember, that barge will be loaded and leaving first thing in the morning! I have the port guard still waiting at the gate for you two, so move your God-damned asses!"

He walked into the room and grabbed Carmen and the blonde. The blonde again tried to bolt, but Syn was too quick. He put his leg out and tripped the frightened girl. As she began to fall, he grabbed her by the arm, twisting it violently. This maneuver brought the girl to the ground as he maintained his grip on Carmen. He shouted something in Russian to one of the other men.

Syn shoved Carmen onto the floor; she was too weak to move.

One of the men handed him a syringe. He plunged it into the blonde's arm. Immediately, she started to waver.

Oh, God! He just drugged her! Carmen thought.

But before Carmen could react, she felt the needle go deep into her arm. Soon, she realized there was no possibility of escape.

It wasn't long before the whole world seemed fuzzy to her as well.

Carmen took a deep breath, trying to make sense as to what was going on around her. Her thoughts were becoming too fuzzy, and her entire body was beginning to feel like jello. The man in black held her frail body up with one of his black-gloved hands. He pulled her and the blonde through the garage, past the van.

Where were they going? Carmen couldn't pull away. Her leg muscles were like rubber as she tried to keep up with Syn.

Carmen stood beside the car as Syn buckled the blonde into the seat. She heard a familiar voice talking into her ear. Carmen tried to fight the sedative. But all she could do was slump up against the car. She struggled even to stand. Her head bobbing on her neck looked like the plastic dog's head in the back window of her grandma's sedan.

Carmen stared blankly as a faint green hue manifested from the darkness. It looked like Harper! Carmen tried to focus on the figure standing in front of her. She reached out with a weighted hand.

'Hang in there, Carmen. I have help coming!' Harper's voice echoed in her head.

Carmen was unable to react as the drugs started to take full effect. She tried to yell and fight it, but the drugs were too powerful. A low moan was all she could summon up.

Soon her eyelids, along with every muscle in her body, began to feel heavy. She slowly slumped over into her seat. She was being guided into the car by her kidnapper.

Syn finished buckling up Carmen and walked back into the

house. He texted his instructions into Harper's phone and handed it to one of his men.

"Don't hit send until I tell you to." He grumbled.

The man looked at the phone and nodded as Syn turned and walked out of the house. He headed up the street, stopping at the corner and turning on his headlights. He then proceeded west towards St. George.

Syn needed to make one last stop before he headed to the warehouse.

The used car lot in St. George was quiet. The row of vehicles along the backside of the fence was different, but they still had one thing in common.

Their doors were left unlocked.

Syn drove over to one of the vehicles. He pulled out the blonde girl and shoved her in the trunk of a sedan. He wiped everything he touched and drove back out of the gate. He stopped just outside of the gate and brushed his tire tracks up to the sedan.

Syn pulled out a new padlock and locked the gate, drove up the railroad tracks, and dusted his tracks once again before leaving. He then proceeded toward the warehouse, backing into a hidden driveway that bordered the warehouse lot. Turning the car's lights off, he slowly backed in alongside a garage and got out. He walked towards the back of the warehouse lot. Syn quickly darted past the streetlight he had previously shot out with a BB gun. Once next to the entrance, he pulled out his phone and sent a text to Aziz.

IN 5 MINUTES, SEND THAT TEXT

Syn then entered the warehouse and headed toward one of his storage units. He quietly slipped inside and locked it from within.

Now, here was where he would sit, patiently and quietly, and wait.

THE WAREHOUSE

Dulcey looked at Carmen's phone just as it went off. She read the text out loud.

"THERE IS A STORAGE PLACE SOUTH OF HERE IN JOHN'S ISLAND. THERE IS A WAREHOUSE ON THE FAR BACKSIDE. GO INSIDE, TAKE A LEFT. YOU'LL SEE A UNIT MARKED 17. IT IS OPEN. GO INSIDE, AND YOU'LL FIND A KEY TO A SECOND UNIT. TAKE THE KEY AND OPEN UP THIS UNIT, PLACE THE MONEY INSIDE THE SECOND UNIT WITH THE KEYS. WHEN YOU LEAVE, LOCK IT UP. BUT, BEFORE YOU DO, LOOK UNDER THE WOODEN BOX IN THE MIDDLE OF THE FLOOR. THERE WILL BE A NUMBER.

TEXT ME THAT NUMBER ON THE BOTTOM. I WILL GIVE YOU FURTHER INSTRUCTIONS.

DO NOT TRY TO FOOL ME. I HAVE CAMERAS ON YOU!"

She looked up at her crew.

"This is it! We need to send someone out there to patrol! ASAP! We also need to track that ping!"

Dulcey radioed back to the group in the vehicles behind them.

"Quick change in plans. We need someone to drop off the ransom! We have a drop-off location!" She jumped out of the SUV and walked over to the cruiser. One of her agents followed close behind. She explained the text to the deputies in the car.

"We need someone to go to John's Island with the ransom and drop it off." She looked inside the car. "We are also sending an unmarked patrol car there right now."

"I am assigning one of you to take the money and drop it off. The kidnapper wants only one person there. He said he has cameras set up. We can't take any chances. He has threatened to kill the girls if he sees anything suspicious!"

"Charlie, I am assigning you to go with the ransom and drop

it off." Before he could comment, Dulcey walked away towards the SUV.

Charlie slowly pulled into the empty parking lot in front of the warehouse. He radioed back to Dulcey as he drove towards the back. The lot back there was dark, as if there were no lights.

"Wow! That was fast!" She exclaimed. "We got notice that there is an unmarked patrol car in the area."

He drove cautiously, not knowing what was around the corner of the darkened lot—trying to look in all directions at once. He didn't like the idea of doing this alone, knowing his backup was hidden out of sight, even from him.

The warehouse in the back lot was huge. The agent drove to the main door and parked his car. He paused, looking around for a minute. Making sure there was no one in the area. He radioed back one last time to Dulcey.

"I found the door to the warehouse, and I am going in." Charlie reached up and turned on his body camera. He slowly opened the door and got out, standing and listening for a moment. His eyes shifted around the empty lot.

"Great. You should be alone, just go in and find locker 17, drop off the cash, and get that number to me. Move as fast as you can and get the hell out of there. Once you're done, let me know, and get back here ASAP." Dulcey ordered.

"Roger that." He replied and quietly shut the cruiser's door.

"I sure as hell am not gonna hang out here or slowly drive back to Charleston." He sarcastically mocked as he walked to the trunk where the cash was and pulled it out.

Looking around one last time, he headed for the warehouse door and opened it.

Inside it was also poorly lit. The motion lights turned on, one by one, as the deputy walked the empty hallways, looking for the locker number given to him. It took him about ten minutes before he finally found number 17. It was locked. Butch's heart started to pound as he looked around, scanning the area for a camera, or worse yet, someone to jump out of the shadow and mug him.

He tugged again at the lock. His hands were sweating, each breath shook. As he tried to calm himself, he noticed a white sticker on the safety lock. He looked closer and noticed they were instructions. They read:

The key was outside the main door, under the mat.

"*You have got to be fucking kidding me!*" He whispered to himself. "*Now, I gotta go back and get the fucking key!*"

Charlie turned around and walked back to the entrance. He saw a mat just inside the door. He cautiously lifted it and found a key taped to the bottom of the mat.

Bingo. He breathed a sigh of relief.

He quickly walked back to the storage locker, his footsteps filling the corridor's silent walls. He stopped again in front of the locker and effortlessly slid in the key. The lock popped open.

Thank God! All he wanted was to get out of here as fast as he could. He cautiously opened the locker door. A squeaky rumble echoed through the building as the door slid upon its tracks. He stood still, nervously watching for any movement inside the locker. Except for the little box in the center of the tiny room, the locker was clean and empty. He walked up to the box and carefully picked it up and shook it. There was a sound of something inside.

Another key with a number inscribed on it. *Jesus, this guy has me running fucking circles!*

He took the key out of the box and walked out of the locker, shutting the door. He quickly walked down the hall, looking for the locker number that was on the key.

Syn could hear the rattle of the lock echo through his storage unit. His heart started to race. He put his ear to the wall and listened.

304 - SHANNON LEE

The agent swiftly opened the lock and cautiously slid the door open. His heart beating fast, he looked inside the dark locker. The light does not come on in this one. He started to panic, thinking something was wrong. He paused. His heavy breath was the only thing heard. As his eyes adjusted to the darkness, he could see the locker was empty except for a wooden crate in the middle.

The agent fumbled for the flashlight on his belt and clicked it on. He took another big breath and walked inside, scanning the area for anything unusual as he approached the crate. It was empty. He flipped it over, looking for the code he needed to give to Dulcey. He then pulled the backpack off his shoulder and took the money out, placing it inside the crate. Then as instructed, he put the little box with both keys in it on the top of the cash.

The agent quickly walked out of the room, shutting and locking the door behind him. He continued to walk cautiously out of the warehouse and back to the patrol car.

Glad that was done! He breathed a sigh of relief.

As he walked toward his car, the agent looked around the small, abandoned parking lot. A shadow moving around a nearby tree caught his eye. He panicked and pulled his gun. Shaking, he remained quiet and watched for any more movement, not sure if he would have to fire his weapon.

Minutes seemed like hours as he strained his eye, looking into the dark over at the group of trees across the parking lot. His hands started to shake as the gun felt like a thousand pounds in his outstretched arms.

Suddenly, a black cat jumped from the tree and scurried across the parking lot.

Fuck. Charlie finally took a breath. He quickly holstered his gun and got into his car. He squealed the tires as he left the warehouse parking lot.

"I gotta get outta here before I fucking lose it!" He whispered.

****

Syn, sitting quietly in the adjacent unit, had heard everything.
Man, that guy talked to himself a lot. He thought to himself.

Syn didn't waste any time; he immediately pushed at the little door hidden on the back of his unit. It opened directly into the room with the ransom money in it.

Five million in cash sitting in that crate, and it was almost out of his reach! He had miscalculated the distance and the weight of the money. Besides, the door was only big enough for the crate. So, he pushed his arm almost beyond its limit. He kept sliding it across the floor until he caught the edge of the crate. This time it barely moved.

"*Fuck!*" He muttered. He didn't think the money would have weighed as much as it did.

He finally was able to hook onto the crate with his fingertips. As he pulled against the cold steel wall, he could feel the ligaments in his shoulder stretching and burning, almost to the point of causing Syn enough pain to make him pass out. He was like a raccoon with a crumpled piece of tinfoil.

Syn wasn't letting go of those five million dollars!

One final heave and the box slid next to the door. Immediately, Syn emptied the box into two backpacks. He slid the box back to almost the same place it was. He then shut the small door and sealed it with a few screws. Wiping everything he has touched along the way.

Syn carefully exited the building, slipping out the side emergency door. He had disabled the emergency alarm, so it made no sound. Syn quickly disappeared into the dark woods across the lot. He continued up the path to the hidden driveway. He quickly slid in behind the wheel and pulled out of the driveway, keeping his headlights off.

He glanced over his shoulder to see Carmen still buckled up, sedated. He chuckled out loud, pulling the back off his phone. He ripped the battery out and tossed it out the window. It landed into a drainage ditch. A few miles up the road, he tossed out his phone. It landed perfectly in some water, almost as he had rehearsed it.

* *

Once Charlie was back on the road, he radioed back to Dulcey. "The cash has been dumped off."

"Great! What was that number in the storage unit? I need to text it to the kidnapper ASAP so that we can get the girls now!"

Charlie told Dulcey what the password was, and she immediately texted Harper's phone.

38

9-1-1

"Now, we wait for a response from the kidnappers," Dulcey informed her men. "We also need to keep an eye out for any activity around that warehouse. We still have a car out there, and II gave them orders to update me with *any* strange activity. Now, if only I could get Jim to recognize the house or the van!" Dulcey turned and winked at Jim sitting in the back. He smiled at her and shrugged his shoulders.

They headed back over to the gas station and slowly drove around the block, keeping a lookout for the van.

No one noticed Jim staring blankly out the window. His eyelids had begun to flutter. He could see a green haze above the seat between him and Tom. Jim was in a complete trance, eyes locked on Harper's aura.

"Tell them where the other girls are, James. Harper's voice echoed in his head. *"Tell them about the storage crate over at Port of Charleston. The one inside gate seven,* warehouse number ten, the red crate."

Tom noticed Jim's strange behavior. The blank stare.

Just like what he did on the airplane. Tom thought as he sat and stared at Jim as his head began to sway. Tom watched, wondering who or what he was watching.

Suddenly, Jim's body started to jolt and twitch. His eyes rolled into the back of his head.

"OH My God!" Tom shouted. He lunged for Jim, reaching through Harper as her green aura wrapped around both, then slowly disappeared around Tom's head. "Jim! Are you okay?" Tom's hair on his arms stood on end as he felt the cool breeze sweep around the back of his neck.

That felt like something just walked over my grave. Tom thought as goosebumps appeared on his arms and neck.

Dulcey pulled over as Tom held Jim's limp body.

"Jim, you okay? Wake up, buddy!" Tom's voice got louder with each word. Tom slapped Jim gently on the cheek.

Jim blinked. Slowly he regained consciousness as his eyes focused on Tom's. He scanned the faces of the people in the SUV.

Harper was gone. In her place was Tom looking a little concerned.

"W....W... We need to turn around and go back up this street. Back north a few blocks. Th, Th, then turn right. We need to go up to. To the corner." Jim tried to speak. He had to pause and catch his breath.

"The house at the end of the street, on the right. The backyard is up against a hill." Jim gasped; his head was pounding. He knew that they were close. Very, very close!

Dulcey made a U-turn in the street.

They were only a block away from where Jim said the house was when a young girl dressed in dark clothing stumbled out of a patch of trees off the curb. She bounced into the side of the squad car and tumbled onto the street in front of the SUV. Dulcey slammed on the breaks. Afraid to look out her window.

"What in the hell did I almost hit?" She shouted. She put the vehicle in park and released her foot off the brakes. She slumped over the steering wheel, heaving deeply, slowly looking up, for fear of what she might see. She noticed a girl peeking over the hood of the SUV.

"Oh my GOD!" Dulcey shrieked, her voice ringing throughout the SUV.

"It's a young girl!" Her heart was pounding out of her chest!

Rob had warned me that she would be coming. Jim remembered *The girl with the scars! She was one of the kidnapped girls he said would find us!*

Dulcey jumped out of the SUV to see the poor girl now sitting in the middle of the street. She was crying uncontrollably.

"Help me! Help the others!" She screamed. Sitting, crumpled on the ground. She was desperately making eye contact with each person who approached her.

Dulcey knelt beside the girl as Jim stood over them. They both notice her scars, Dulcey's eyes fill up with tears. She put her hand on the thin girl's back. It was ice cold. Heaving with exhaustion, the girl jerked away.

"Someone dial 9-1-1," Dulcey ordered. "Tell them where we are, and tell them NOT to use their lights or sirens. We still do not want to attract any kind of attention to us!"

The SUV lights outlined the thin girl's silhouette. Dulcey could see what looked like burn marks on the girl's face and neck. Her eyes sunken in and bloodshot, tears were running down her face.

She was so thin. Dulcey's heart sank.

"Are you okay? I am Special Agent Dulcey. My team and I are here to find some missing girls. Do you know where they may be?"

"I got free!" The girl cried out. "I was the first to go out the window because I was the tallest!"

"But, the men heard us or something. They came bursting

through the door! The girls weren't fast or strong enough to push anyone else out! When I heard them hollering, I ran as fast as I could towards the woods. I ran until I fell in front of your vehicle! Please, those men are evil people! The rest of the girls are in danger!" The young girl stated, sobbing between breaths. Looking around frantically, she screamed out: "Don't let them find me!"

"How many men are there? Do you know what house it is? How many girls are there?"

"Um, ah...I think there are three...no four men. I'm not sure. There were maybe twenty or so girls and two more brought in a couple of days ago. I don't know where the house is. I.... I'm sorry...so sorry...." The girl's voice was shaking. "When I heard the men shouting from the window, I ran into the woods. I didn't look back. I just ran as fast as I could go! I kept running until I blacked out!" She took a deep gasp of air. "When I woke up, I began to run again! That's when I saw the cop car coming up the road and tried to stop it! I guess I didn't see your black SUV. I'm sorry, I abandoned those girls back there! I just left them! I am so, so sorry."

"It's okay, sweetie. You may have saved their lives! We will find them. We will rescue them."

"They talked about taking the girls somewhere," The girl informed them between sobs.

"Where?"

"I don't know; they speak in a different language sometimes. It kind of sounds like German or Russian, maybe." The girl babbled. "And the one little girl."

"Oh, God! One girl was tortured last night. We all could hear her screaming! We couldn't do anything to help her! I think they killed her! I am so sorry!"

"It's okay, honey. You're now safe. We will find those girls and bring them home." Dulcey helped the girl off the street, and they walked the girl to the SUV. She told them about how one of the men picked her up off the streets of Philly—promising her freedom and money. She talked about the cries from the little girl being tortured in the room next to hers. She described how they were drugged, beaten, and tortured.

The officers could only listen, dumbfounded. Jim began to recall some of the girl's story.

It was all true! He wasn't losing his mind! He thought.

This man was who Harper had been trying to tell him about! He listened to the girl intensely. The more she talked, the more he remembered! Harper's voice whispered through his mind. She was telling him about a scarred girl and how she would break free and find them!

They were closing in on the gap! Jim could feel the adrenalin flow in his body.

Within minutes, the ambulance silently pulled up next to them. The paramedics loaded up the girl and began assessing her.

One of the special agents climbed up inside the ambulance and sat beside the scared girl.

"I will stay with you. I will protect you."

"Please help the rest of the girls!" The scarred girl shouted out the closing ambulance doors.

Swiftly, they all got back into the vehicles and resumed driving up the street.

They approached the small house on the right. It looked like the others but tucked in a bit farther off the road. It was hard to tell in the dark, but the grass on the front lawn seemed quite long. The little gray house in question looked as if it were abandoned.

There was a garage attached to the house. So, if there was a vehicle in question, it could be hidden out of sight. They drove by slowly. Looking for any signs of movement.

Jim's eyes locked on the house. His heart began to beat harder as he heard Harper's voice echoing through his head rapidly. Describing the house, the girls, and the kidnappers.

Jim took a deep breath and tried to swallow, but the lump in his throat made it hard to do.

"That's the house I have seen in my visions! That's where he's been keeping the girls!" Jim stated, his voice crackled with excitement. The more he saw, the more he remembered, and the faster his heart raced!

"Some of the girls have been moved. They need to get them out of there tonight!"

"My God," Dulcey exclaimed, looking out at the little house, looking for any signs of life.

"It's just so damn dark!"

She pulled up past the house, turned around, and parked on the street. She got on the radio and told the car behind them about the place in question. That's when she realized what Jim had just told her.

"What do you mean, they have moved some of the girls? Where are they moving them, Jim?" She turned in her seat and looked directly into Jim's eyes.

"They are in a red shipping container at one of the warehouses at the Charleston Port," Jim told Dulcey in a calm, collective voice. "It's all starting to come to me now! It's a red crate in warehouse ten." Jim's eyes never left the little gray house. It was almost like he was on autopilot.

"Are you fucking kidding me right now?!?" Dulcey shouted at him. She immediately picked up the radio and called into her office. She requested a patrol to run surveillance through the Charleston Port shipping yards.

"Keep your eye out for a dark gray van, a red shipping crate, any young girls, or anything else that might be suspicious around warehouse ten." She exclaimed.

"Has there been *any* movement around that warehouse in John's Island?" She asked.

The radio for a moment was silent. Then, a rush of static came through.

"I haven't seen a damn thing since Detective Charlie left. Do you want me to go inside and check it out?"

Dulcey looked over at Jim. He shook his head.

"Don't do it," Dulcey sighed. "We can't risk going into that warehouse. Because if he finds out, he will kill those girls!" Dulcey ordered into the radio's microphone. "We just cannot risk that right now. Stay where you are and watch closely for anyone going in or out of there!" She commanded.

"Roger that." The static voice answered back.

Dulcey sent out a text to Harper's phone.

PLEASE DO NOT HURT THE GIRLS.

WE JUST WANT THEM HOME SAFE.

THE MONEY HAS BEEN DROPPED OFF.

I HAVE THE NUMBER YOU WERE LOOKING FOR.

One of the men read the text from Dulcey out loud and laughed.

OK-came the text. SEND IT

Dulcey turned off the SUV. She watched as the patrol car in front of them continued up the street and parked around the corner. Making sure it was out of sight from the house. Now it was just a waiting game. Within a few hours, daylight would be upon them. She texted the number that Charlie gave her to Harper's phone.

Harper's phone lit up with the number. The men smiled.

"They dropped off the fucking cash! And we are on our last load!"

"Text Syn so he can pick it up and drop off the girls. Our job here is almost done!" The man chuckled as he texted the number to Syn's phone and waited for a reply.

One by one, the officers started to fall asleep until the only ones left awake were Dulcey and Tom. She looked over and began to question Tom.

"So, how long have you and Jim known each other?" She whispered.

"Oh, about ten years or so. After I married my wife Jenni, we decided to move to Bonners Ferry. She is Nez Perce, from a tribe in that area. She wanted to raise our kids where she grew up in a traditional Native American way. And Bonners Ferry was a perfect little town. They were hiring at the police station 32 miles South in Sandpoint. I took the job as Jim's partner." Tom stared out the window into the dark street.

"We had our lives planned out perfectly. That was until we found out that we couldn't have children. I struggled to cope when we got the news. So, I confided with Jim one day. It was then that he told me that he and his wife had the same issues. After that, we connected and started to do more of the things couples in our predicament did. Jenni and I found a house in the same suburb as Jim and Kristy. We became close friends. We started to do everything together. From work and biking to backyard bar-b-ques. Jim is a great guy, and he is an even better detective."

"Has Jim always had visions like this?"

"No," Tom shook his head. "He always believed in the supernatural. But, he never described anything like this to me before."

"Do you think he is legit? I mean that he didn't have something to do with this?" Dulcey looked at Tom.

"Without a doubt, he is legit. Jim is the most honest man you'll ever come across. That is why I am here. I have believed in him from the beginning. He would never harm anyone."

Their conversation was interrupted by an incoming radio call from one of the officers at the warehouse.

"We did find a red crate where you said, over at the Charleston Ports. So, I called the Judge, and we are now waiting for a search warrant. Once it's in, we will be able to get the shipping information we need and be able to unlock it! I have a feeling that it's full of drugs, firearms." The voice on the radio crackled.

The radio had woken up everyone inside the SUV.

Dulcey looked around at her people, noticing everyone staring back at her. Except for Jim. His stare was concentrating out the window.

"You know what's in that red crate, Jim?" She asked in a firm, steady voice.

Jim slowly turned his attention from the window to Dulcey. He looked directly into her large green eyes, eagerly waiting for his answer. Somehow, she already knew what it was. She just wanted to hear him say it out loud.

"A bunch of girls stuffed in barrels."

A tear rolled down Dulcey's cheek.

For the rest of the night, everyone stayed awake. They sat in silence, watching for anything that may come from the house across the street. Things remained quiet for a very long time.

Finally, breaking the silence, a voice came back on the radio, startling Dulcey and her crew.

The Myrtle Beach station was calling in with a report.

"We got our warrant and are going over to the guard shack to obtain keys to the shipping crates in that warehouse." The voice on the other end crackled. "Oh, and the last ping from Harper's phone was off a tower in the city of Charleston! The very same tower Carmen's phone has been pinging off! It looks like you two are on top of each other!"

"He's in the fucking house!" Dulcey's voice filled the SUV.

39

Go Time

Just after midnight and working by flashlights, the four men inside the house began prepping the last of the girls for their move.

One by one, the girls were led through the living room, past the sofa where the little dark-haired girl laid motionless. She was naked and covered in blood. No one knew if she was dead or alive. Some of the girls let out a shriek as they walked by her battered body. That would embed a horrid visual into their memories forever.

Shipping girls overseas would be the men's first time, and the loading process went relatively smooth. Not making small talk, the men did what they needed to. But, it was their first time shipping this many at a time and working for Syn. They knew that they had to move fast. Syn would not have it any other way. When it came to crunch time, Syn became even more irate.

"Did Syn ever send you a text back saying he got the money? Where the fuck is he anyhow? This was his big job!"

"How the fuck do I know? He is probably waiting at the Port for us. Ya know how spotty the service is inside the warehouse there."

Discouraged with the absence of Syn's response, the men continued to load up the girls.

The cargo container that sat at the warehouse was being shipped out tomorrow afternoon. They needed to get the girls into the shipping container and drug up the others once more before the crate got loaded onto the ship. They had to give the girls just enough of the drug to keep them quiet. Too little of the drug someone might hear them, too much, and they may stop breathing.

That red crate was like a temporary prison. Like it had been before, it brought the innocent overseas to a place where an even bigger evil awaited. The girls' next journey would be one of absolute horror.

They were being sold across China, Russia, and the Middle East, bought by people for a lot of money and using the girls for various intentions. Prostitution brought in the most significant sales.

Within a year, most of these girls will have been beaten or drugged to death. None of them would be coming back. These girls' families would never know what happened to their sweet, innocent little girls. Those families would pray for a safe return of their precious babies that would never come.

* * * * * * * * * * * * *

Back at the Port, a locksmith was called in to open the crate. The officers continued to walk the isles of the warehouse. They remained on high alert, checking behind every container, examining every shadow. Backtracking whenever possible to make sure nothing was missed.

Then, one officer heard something. He stopped abruptly and held out his hand to silence his partner.

"You hear that?"

Tap.... tap...tap...scratch, scratch...tap....tap...

It was a faint, eerie sound as it echoed through the warehouse. It was so minute that the men had to concentrate on hearing where the sound was coming. They would take a few steps, stop and listen. A few more steps, listen.

"Rats," One of the officers said aloud.

Another put up his hand to silence him.

Tap...tap...scratch. Scratch...tap...scratch...

Finally, one of the men zeroed in on the red crate near the entrance. It was the only crate that they heard a noise coming from it. They all stood silently, listening. The noise was so faint that the echoing of the city outside bouncing through the warehouse almost drowned it out.

"I hope back-up comes soon with someone that can unlock this damn crate!"

An officer from the back walked up past the other two men and knocked on the container's solid steel wall. The sound reverberated through the empty halls of the warehouse, making some of the men uneasy.

"What in the hell are you doing?" His partner half yelled out.

"We might as well see if it knocks back. Who knows how long it'll take back-up to get out here this time of night."

Everyone was motionless, listening for an answering knock.

A few moments later, a return tap, not quite as loud, answered back in the same number of taps, just slower.

"Holy shit!" He exclaimed, jumping back from the crate.

Again, they exchanged taps. Tension began to build, heartbeats racing through each exhale as the officers listened in complete shock.

What in the hell was making that noise? They all thought.

One of the officers picked up his radio with trembling hands and called back to the station.

"You need to hurry with that back-up and locksmith! I think we've found something huge here!"

The tapping and scratching in the crate became a little more frequent and louder. Almost sounding desperate.

Tap, tap, tap, tap! Scratch...bump, bump.

Within a few minutes, two squad cars pulled up. Two officers got out of the vehicle, along with a warehouse guard. He was carrying a set of master keys. They eagerly entered the warehouse where the others had been waiting.

The guard walked up to the gate baffled, stared at the three locks.

"I have not seen these types of locks on a crate before. I don't think I have a key for it. Come to think of it. I have never seen more than one lock on any of these crates in the 20 years I've worked here." The guard looked through his keys but found nothing that would work. Someone had changed the locks, obviously hiding something valuable inside.

"I think we will need bolt cutters. Whatever's in this crate must be worth a helluva lot of money!" He looked back at the eager group of officers, giving them a confused look. "What in the hell is that noise coming from inside?"

"That's what we would like to know," Came back a reply, as one of the men walked to the squad car and reached inside the open trunk. He pulled out a pair of bolt cutters and walked back to the crate door. He handed them to the warehouse guard. The guard immediately cut through the locks.

"Just cut the damn thing off. We have the warrant."

"I just have never seen a lock quite like this before," He commented as he struggled to get the cutters in place. "What in the hell do you think is in there?" The locksmith paused as he asked the police officer standing over his shoulder.

"We are not quite sure." The officer replied. His hand was on his holster, preparing for what might happen next.

"Your job is to get this door open."

After the third lock was finally cut through and pulled off, the door finally opened. Inside, the crate was lined wall to wall with barrels. Each had holes along the top. At first, it was quiet. Then, the shaking breaths and occasional groans came from the dark shadows inside the barrels. They were human sounds!

"This is Sargent Rowland with the Charleston Port Authorities!" The officer hollered into the crate. His voice dulls within the enclosed walls.

The men could hear a faint voice from the shadows of the container.

"H-h-h-hello?" It was a girl's voice. It sounded shaky and weak.

"We have come to rescue you." Sargent Rowland replied.

"Oh my God, help us please!" Another girl's voice came from the darkness of the crates. The barrels came alive with the sounds of girls sobbing and begging to be freed.

"Holy shit!" One of the officers exclaimed as he reached for the flashlight. The light passed across the barrels. He could see small, frail fingers and hands waving out from the holes. Another officer picked up his radio.

"This is Sargent Rowland with the Port Authority police department. We found a bunch of kids!" His voice rang nervously over the radio in the SUV.

"Oh my God! They're kids stuffed in barrels inside of this shipping crate! I cannot imagine this right now! I think they are all young girls! Who in the hell would do this?!?"

Dulcey looked over at Jim and Tom. Tom's eyes were huge as Jim continued to watch out of his window. She began to say something when the fierce barking of a dog drew their attention toward the house.

****

It was still dark when a short, stout man emerged from the house next door. He was about to take his German Shepard for his usual morning walk. The same routine every day for the past three years.

Except for this morning, the dog was acting a little odd. The dog didn't want to take the normal left down the block. Instead, the dog began to pull at the leash and bark toward the abandoned house to the right. The man grumbled at the dog and pulled him back in the direction of their original path. It soon became a tug of war—man against the dog. The dog refused to budge. He began to pull at his leash; his barking became more and more desperate. This unusual behavior made the man feel uneasy as he attempted to pull back harder on the leash. The man tried to direct the dog away from the house. He lunged, pulling the man off his feet and across the driveway. Continuing to bark and lunge toward the abandoned house.

The barking dog continued to jump, biting at his leash, attempting to break free. He kept spinning and pulling until the man's face hit the ground. When he finally released his grip on the leash, the dog ran full force to the garage doors barking the entire time. Between spitting out dirt and grass, the man swore at the dog, yelling at him to retreat. But the dog didn't listen.

The officers watched the entire scene unfold in front of the SUV.

"What the fuck is this?" Someone in the back grumbled.

"I don't know, but if this fucks up our investigation, I'm gonna shoot the damn dog myself," Came a reply.

The German Shepherd ran back and forth in front of the garage door. He would sniff beneath it and bark wildly. His owner slowly got to his feet and began to stomp across the yard, half hollering-half whispering for his dog. The dog continued to bark and sniff the ground, running back and forth in front of the garage, occasionally stopping to scratch at the door.

Inside the garage, the two men just looked at each other as they listened to the barking dog on the other side of the garage door.

One of them started to panic as they heard a man's voice getting louder as he approached the garage.

"Keep calm," One of them whispered. "Just get into the van quietly. I am going to start it and pull out of here slowly. We have to get these girls the hell outta here, and we can't look suspicious!" He reached down and turned the key. The van rumbled to life.

The Shepherd dog hopped back but quickly returned to digging at the garage door, more furious now than ever! The man came to a complete stop like he had heard a ghost. Every day for the past three years, that house had been dormant. No one in the neighborhood ever noticed any movement near or around that house in years. Until now! Suddenly, the man could hear a vehicle from inside the garage start.

Frozen, the man did not move. He had even stopped calling for his dog. The dog kept his attention on the garage door, continuing to bark more and more frantically. He seemed determined to get at whatever was inside.

The driver of the van pushed the button to raise the garage door. The moment the garage door opened; the German Shepherd squeezed under it. They could now hear the dog barking over the van's engine as he entered the garage. He jumped at the window of the van, barking and growling, saliva and foam flying from his mouth, splattering the windows. The men looked at each other. Their eyes widened in panic at the size of the dog.

"What if it's the cops!" He exclaimed as he rolled up the window.

"If it's the cops, we go out shooting!" The driver exclaimed.

One of the men couldn't handle the stress anymore. He reached under his seat and pulled out his pistol. He shouted something as he pointed his gun at the dog bouncing in front of them. He pulled the trigger.

BANG!

The dog's owner was just about to holler again when he heard a single shot come from the garage. He dropped to the ground, pressing his face-first to the grassy dirt once again.

"Jesus Christ!" He groaned.

A single shot hit its target and silenced the bark. Shocked, the man laid on his stomach.

Holy shit, my fucking dog has been shot! He thought as he decided to jump to his feet, turn and run back towards his house, slamming the door behind him.

"What in the fuck are you thinking!" The driver yelled at his partner. His hands were still shaking as he kept a tight grip on the pistol.

"Just get us the fuck outta here!"

The garage door was finally up. It was still dark outside. The man cautiously backed up the van.

The dog's owner ran through his living room, startling his wife as he picked up the phone and dialed 9-1-1. He waited anxiously for the operator to answer. Peeking out of the living room window, he shut off the lights.

"What was that loud noise? What's going on, Joe? Where is Buddy?" The man's wife asked, confused. Her voice was shaking as she followed him to the window.

The man held up his hand, motioning for her to be quiet.

The 9-1-1 operator picked up.

"9-1-1, what's your emergency?"

"Hello," The man answered, his voice shaking. "My name is Joe Roberts, and my neighbor has just shot my dog. Hurry, my God! Please hurry."

Dulcey jumped as she saw the dog run toward the garage.

"What in the hell is this?"

They continued to watch everything that happened.

The garage door slowly kept rising, exposing what they could only hope to see. It was the dark gray van with blackened windows

that Jim had seen in his visions. It was idling patiently for the door
to open completely.

Oh, MY GOD, Jim was right! It was them! Everyone went on alert.

"Holy shit! A God-damned dark gray van is pulling out of the
garage! That mother fucker *was* right!" The sheriff in the patrol car
said to his deputy.

Every officer watched in astonishment as the van began to slowly
back out of the garage.

Immediately the sheriff got on the radio to Dulcey.

"I can see they are moving! Get your asses here! IT IS GO TIME!"
He shouted as he placed his patrol car in gear and squealed up the
street towards the driveway.

Still peeking out of his window, the neighbor began to describe
the van as it backed out of the garage.

That's when the big black SUV came speeding down the street,
while a cop car came from the opposite direction pulling towards
the van!

"Wow, you guys *are* quick! I don't think you need so many people
for a dog, though." He said sheepishly. "I'm safe in my house."

"Please stay in your house, sir," The 9-1-1- operator instructed the
man. "Whatever you do, DO NOT go outside!" She ordered. The
man didn't understand, but he listened to her and stayed on the
phone. He continued to watch out his window, telling her moment
by moment what was going on.

"Please get away from your windows, sir." The operator demanded.

The man slowly pulled his drapes and got on his knees. He continued to peek out the corner of the window. The operator could
hear the man's frantic wife shouting at him, asking him about the
noise and their dog.

The sheriff as he throttled his patrol car toward the unsuspecting van. Dulcey, driving the SUV, quickly approached the driveway from the other side.

The van stopped, patiently yielding for the oncoming vehicles to pass. Unaware of the patrol car coming in the other direction.

This did not happen. The sheriff slammed on his brakes, coming to a stop right behind the van. Another patrol car came speeding in behind with its lights flashing.

They had the van surrounded.

The sheriff opened the door to his squad car and began to pull his weapon. Two more squad cars were coming up the street with their lights flashing.

Dulcey, Tom, and the rest all jumped out of the SUV, guns pulled. Ready to fire at any minute.

Jim did not move. He buried his head between his knees as he sat still in the back of the SUV.

"FREEZE!" Dulcey screamed from behind the SUV's door. "FBI! GET OUT OF YOUR VEHICLE AND PUT YOUR HANDS IN THE AIR!"

With its windows shaded, it was impossible to see inside the van.

Dulcey's heart began to race. For months she had dreamed of this moment, not sure what to expect. Now, she was facing her worst nemesis. She was terrified!

As the police cruisers pulled up to a stop, they shined their lights onto the van. Desperately, no one could see inside its windows.

"There are girls inside that van!" Jim yelled to the officers. "We need to be careful!"

The van's engine roared, and it lurched forward. Dulcey immediately began to shoot. Three shots hit their target, finally blowing out the right front tire.

The sheriff opened fire on the engine until it started to smoke. They eagerly watched the front window, waiting for any type of movement.

The van revved up and lurched forward, jerking on blown tires across the front lawn. They again fired at the engine, this time disabling the van.

Another squad car came up behind Dulcey's SUV and pulled in front of the van.

Rat-a-tat-tat! A round of fire came from the van, sounding like an assault rifle. The bullets fill the window with holes, spattering blood on the inside of the squad car.

"GET OUTTA THE VEHICLE! NOW!!!" The sheriff shouted between gunshots. "YOU ARE SURROUNDED!"

Jim did not move. He could hear shots going off all around him. He noticed some of them hitting the SUV, shaking it as they came up against its tough steel doors.

The standoff seemed like it was going in slow motion. Shots were fired back and forth. Jim could hear Dulcey and Brian shouting at the men in the van in between gunfire.

Finally, one of the men jumped out of the driver's side and made a run for the house. Shots were fired. He stumbled as he made it back into the garage and disappeared into the shadows.

The other man continued to stand his ground, firing back at the squad cars, spattering them with bullets. Some hit their marks.

The man on the phone with 9-1-1 was baffled.

"I didn't think you needed to gun the men down for shooting my dog," He spoke into the phone. "It's a bit much, don't you think?"

The shots began to slow, but no one moved. The police officers used their vehicles for protection, watching for any movement that might come from the van—waiting to open fire once again—being aware that the girls were still in the van.

Seconds seemed like minutes, and minutes seemed like hours. The men inside the van and a random officer would exchange an occasional shot.

A blood-curdling scream came from the garage, followed by a

dog growling! A third man, who was cornered inside the house, tried to sneak out the back of the garage. The Shepherd dog grabbed him by the neck as he tripped over him.

Jim sat up and looked out the side of the SUV for the first time since the shots were fired. People were lying on the lawn and slumped over the squad cars. He slid out of the side of the SUV.

As the two more squad cars came screeching to a stop. Cops jumped out of their vehicle, and firearms were drawn, shooting back toward the van.

Finally, one of the officers fired a container of tear gas. It landed next to the van. More screaming came from deep within the van.

It was one of the girls as she started to awaken from her drug-induced slumber. She screamed as the tear gas hit her face, stinging her eyes. She noticed the broken glass and blood everywhere.

The crippled van sat silently as the sounds of screaming girls started to fill the air inside it. The shots have finally stopped, the last kidnapper ran out of ammunition.

"Stop shooting towards the van!" Jim screamed. "There are innocent girls in there!"

Jim looked around the front yard. It looked like a battlefield. There were bodies everywhere, some still moving, others dead.

There was a siren coming up the street, slowly drowning out the cries of the girls.

The German Shepherd's owner was still kneeling in his living room, peeking out his window, talking to the 9-1-1 operator—his wife, hiding under the kitchen table, crying into her apron. For Joe Roberts, it all started with walking his dog and ended with his dog being shot and the FBI in a standoff next door.

You cannot make this shit up. The man thought.

Dulcey, Jim, and the others began to approach the van. They could see a couple of shadows slowly trying to move towards the back.

"Keep on high alert!" Dulcey ordered. "Keep your firearms drawn!"

She had been shot as she reached and grabbed her bloody wrist. The pain was indescribable! She clenched her teeth but said nothing. She, too, wanted to see for herself what exactly Jim had been telling them. She, too, needed to see who was inside that van.

Slowly the officers, with their guns drawn, approached the van. It was starting to sway with the movement coming from inside. Shadows were seen within the cracks and holes through the dark windows.

Not knowing who was making the van rock with life, the officers kept their weapons drawn. Slowly, continuing their move forward toward the bullet-riddled van.

Suddenly, bloody fingers started to poke out of the bullet holes in the back of the van's windows! At first startling the officers, as they realized that it was the girls, they picked up their pace to the van's back door.

A few of the girls were almost fully awake. They were still fighting off the drug.

The officers could hear them screaming as they came up to the back of the van. Tear gas was stinging their eyes. The girls began clawing at the back window, smearing it with blood as they saw the officers approaching.

Tom reached towards the handle to open the back door. As he lifted it, the door burst open with the weight of the girls pressing against it. Some of the girls tumbled to the ground. They were covered in blood.

"It's alright, you are going to be okay," One of the officers reassured the frightened girls, helping them up off the ground. It was apparent that they were all underweight and freezing. Some of them are too weak to stand.

"Oh, My God." The dog's owner relayed this to the operator and his wife. "The van is full of.....Oh My God!" He stated, shocked. "They look like young girls!" He exclaimed! "Lots of them! Holy shit, this was happening *next door!*" She shouted into the phone to the operator.

The officers began slowly walking the girls towards some EMS workers. They meet halfway, taking the crying girls and wrapping them up in blankets. Carefully guiding them into the ambulance as more were pulling up.

Tom turned to head back to the van. He noticed the rest of the officers walking up as they slid the van's side door open to expose more girls. Some slowly tried to gain composure as they awoke from the drugs that they were given. Some still did not move.

As the ambulance with the first two girls slowly pulled away with its lights and sirens on, the EMS workers from the other ambulances grabbed their gurneys and headed towards the van.

Dulcey attempted to once again walk over to the van and inspect the area. She staggered as she started to pass out, slowly being lowered to the ground by Jim.

When she came to, she noticed she was strapped onto a gurney. She could see the EMS workers hanging IVs over her head as they started to push her towards the ambulance, where they worked swiftly to stabilize the bleeding coming from her shoulder. As she becomes more awake, she attempts to pull herself off the gurney.

"No, not this time, detective," A soft but stern voice stated. Jim pressed his hand gently on her shoulder. "You've been shot in your left shoulder. You need to go to the hospital to stop the bleeding and have it looked at."

At that point, Dulcey realized she was just too weak to get up and fight. She finished her job, and her adrenaline rush was over. God had helped her find His children by sending her detective

James Cavalier. She would never doubt His divine powers ever again.

The EMS workers shut the ambulance doors, closing her view of the van and the girls. Dulcey closed her eyes and felt the rocking of the ambulance as it drove off. Sirens were blaring.

It was finally over.

Jim turned and started walking over toward the battered van, where the girls had been bound up and stuffed inside. One atop of the other. As he approached the site, he realized what Harper had been trying to tell him. But this was incomprehensible. Some of the girls had been shot. Most were so drugged up that they didn't move quickly. Each was being helped out and sat next to the van to be examined by medical staff. They were triaging the ones in most need of medical attention.

When a new ambulance would pull up, the workers would assist the sickest girls up on the gurney. They would quickly secure them onto the tiny bed and wheeled them off and repeated it until every girl was out of the van and gone.

All but two girls made it. Bullet holes riddled their thin, battered bodies. They were sitting on two other girls' laps, just behind the driver's seat, unintentionally shielding them from wayward bullets.

Jim sat next to a familiar girl. As she slowly awakened from her drugged slumber, she began to cry. Jim noticed how emaciated and frightened the girl looked. He introduced himself and asked her where she was from and what her name was.

"I am Emily." The girl answered in a weak whisper. "I am from Skandia, Michigan. But, he took me from Coeur d'Alene, Idaho. I was staying at my grandma's house there."

It was her! The girl that he was investigating right before the accident! Jim froze for a moment.

Jim thought he would never know what exactly happened to her.

Now, here she was, sitting next to him on the lawn! He sighed in relief.

"I am James Cavalier, a detective at the Bonner County Sheriff Department in Idaho. I was working on your case back home, Emily. Your grandma's dog had pulled out of his collar and ran back home." He looked at the girl's tear-filled eyes and took a deep breath. She was the case he had been working on back home. She had brought Jim here.

"Without you."

The girl began to cry. Jim hugged her as her frail body shivered from the cold. She buried her face into his arms, and they both sobbed.

The girl from Idaho was missing the longest.

Jim held her frail body tightly.

"It'll be okay. You are safe now." He reassured her.

"I am so sorry I was so stupid to fall for him. Mom had warned me about this stuff happening all the time!" She continued to sob. "He was so nice to me, and he said I was pretty. No one has ever told me that. *I trusted him.*" She began sobbing even harder.

"He didn't seem like the type to hurt me. He wanted to meet me, especially when he found out I was visiting so close to him." She exhaled, sobbing.

Harper stood over Jim's shoulder, listening to the girl's entire story.

"All I wanted to do was have some fun! Maybe movies, the beach, or a hike somewhere. He didn't want me to tell anybody that we were friends! He said people wouldn't like the idea of us together. I began to think: Maybe he was right; no one would understand us. So, I kept our relationship to myself." As the girl began to tell her story, Jim could hear Harper's voice telling her story, using the exact words. Only she was telling Carmen's story.

"He told me things to make me trust him and want to be with

him!" The girl cried out; Harper's sobbing voice still echoed in his head.

"Every one of us, he lured into his grips!" She looked into Jim's eyes. She noticed they were filling up with tears.

"Don't beat yourself up, Honey," Jim tried to calm the upset girl. "Thank God I found you, Emily, or who knows how long this nightmare would have gone on. How many children he would have abducted?

Jim felt Harper's touch on his shoulder. He could feel her sadness wrapping around his heart, making it feel heavy. It was like a warm breeze followed by a cold chill going up against Jim's spine, melding into his heart.

Harper, you were sent to me by God. To help these lost souls escape. Thank you and thank God." Jim smiled.

40

Reunited

"We need to get some deputies out to that warehouse in John's Island!" Dulcey ordered her assistant.

"That's where the other girl is! That fucking kidnapper never responded to us!" She attempted to sit up in her hospital bed. The pain in her shoulder was too intense. She almost passed out as she fell back into her pillow.

"Yes, Ma'am. I will send someone right now!"

Dulcey's assistant walked out of the triage room toward the end of the hallway, where she could get a better signal to call back to the station.

Dulcey laid back, her mind racing with what-ifs.

What if we killed the kidnapper in which we have been talking? What if we never find Carmen? We will have no answers and no money for Mr. Bengston!

She pressed her nurse call button.

When the nurse got to Dulcey's room, she was getting out of bed—almost passing out from the pain.

"I gotta get outta here!" Dulcey ordered.

The nurse walked over to press the button on the wall.

"Not today, my friend." She smiled at Dulcey.

Dulcey's assistant walked back into the room. She seemed unable to look Dulcey in the eyes.

"I gave the station your orders. They will send someone into the warehouse. They also informed me that the officers have found Harper's phone." She sighed. "It was in the van."

Tears filled Dulcey's eyes.

"They also found a little girl dead inside the house. It appeared she was raped and tortured." The assistant's phone buzzed in her hands.

"I have no service in the room; I'll go answer this. I'll be right back." She quickly walked out of the room.

After a few minutes, she again entered Dulcey's room.

"The warehouse unit was empty. The money was gone. No signs of the girls or the money. It's like they just disappeared without a trace!" She exclaimed.

"He's just that God damn good," Dulcey replied in a melancholy voice. "We lost her, Mindy. We lost Carmen."

Her assistant walked over to Dulcey and sat alongside her bed. They both break down and cry.

Each girl was examined and questioned by Dulcey's team of FBI agents. Then, each waited to be picked up by their families, caregivers, or local foster care agencies.

Emily's parents were escorted from the airport straight to the hospital. They were so glad to get their baby girl back. Her mom couldn't refrain from hugging her thin, frail body and crying, telling her that her horse had missed her as much as they did. Emily held her back as tight as she could, feeling the warmth of her mom's body. Her mom's heart was beating in her ear, reassuring the girl she was now safe.

"I am so sorry, mama. I am so, so, sorry!" She was crying softly.

"I just wanna go home, mom." She whispered in a tired voice. "I want a hamburger, some popcorn, and a huge soda." Emily closed her eyes. "And ride Big John."

As the news began to leak out, the media sent their reporters to cover the story at the local hospital and the Bengstons' home, questioning them to see if there had been any news on their daughter or her friend.

The headlines read that a local FBI team uncovered a major human trafficking ring, rescuing many girls missing all over the country. The news stated that they had one suspect in custody, and he was being treated at the local hospital for dog bites to the throat. Once he was stable, he would be moved to an undisclosed location and arraigned.

Brad and Mary Bengston would get their phone call, too. Letting them know that they had located the kidnappers, and many girls were found. Unfortunately, Carmen and Harper were still missing.

They told them about the remains of a human body located in another rural area where the kidnappers had been. It was a female, and she was unable to be identified. There was a high probability that it could be their daughter, Harper. An autopsy will be conducted, and dental records obtained to find out the girl's identification. The remains had been flown to Myrtle Beach. In a few days, they should know if it was their daughter.

Brad hung up the phone, turned to his wife. With tears in his eyes, he told her the news. She melted to the floor, crying. The phone rolled out of his hand as he dropped to his knees to console his devastated wife. No money in the world could bring their daughter back to them alive. Bradley would have given up everything he had to have his girl in his arms right now.

As they both held each other, crying. Harper's spirit embraced them, her aura wrapping around them tightly. Mary felt a soft, cool touch of static rush through her body. Brad felt it, too. Neither mentioned it to the other; they just embraced the moment.

Their only daughter was gone. But her spirit would live on in everyone she knew.

Mary noticed a small, shiny object between the two of them on the floor. She picked it up and handed it to her husband.

They both look at his shaking hand.

It was a dime. The year on it was the year of Harper's birth. A sign from Harper that everything was okay.

41

Homeward Bound

The next few days consisted of interviews with local papers and television stations. Jenni and Kristy flew to Myrtle Beach to be with Jim and Tom. They visited Dulcey a couple of times while she recovered in the hospital. The bullet damaged no major arteries or nerves. Most of the girls had to stay overnight for observation and fluid hydration. Once stable, they were all released with their families and loved ones.

Jim had gotten a call from Brad and Mary Bengston. They wanted to meet with him and his partner in private, without cameras or reporters around. So Jim and Tom drove over to their home while Kristy and Jenni stayed back at the hotel.

The Bengstons showed Jim around Harper's room, her pictures, and her artwork. Harper loved to paint. One watercolor in particular interested Jim. It was a picture of a figure. He was painted orange. Green and blue clouds surrounded him. The man had no face; he was holding something up high above his head. It glowed like a green star.

Jim realized that he was looking at his aura, and the star was Harper. She knew. Somehow, she always knew. Her gift was to help others. She did this at the cost of her life. The end of a beautiful soul here on Earth. Jim was her vision. Her energy.

The flight home was a long-welcomed quietness for everyone. It wasn't just Jim that needed to rest. They all got some much-needed sleep. The plane's wheels hitting the tarmac jolted them awake. Slowly they all began to move, anxiously waiting for the plane to pull up to the jetway. One small connecting flight, and they would be home. An hour. Tops.

Tom and Jenni were sitting directly behind Jim and Kristy on the plane. They were happy that this was all over now, too.

No one talked about their ordeal.

****

Once home, Jim and Kristy grabbed a bite to eat and retired to their living room to rest in their recliners.

Jim looked at Kristy. "It seems like it has been a long time since we got to relax like this."

Kristy turned on the TV, and a true detective series came on the screen. The narrator starts to mention a mysterious letter. Jim's eyes brightened; he turned to say something to his wife. She shut off the TV.

"Not tonight, honey." She exclaimed.

"Where are the cards that were at the hospital? Let's read them."

Kristy looked at Jim. She had forgotten about the cards. They have been put away neatly in a shoebox in the hallway closet.

My God, I forgot about those cards! She thought.

"I have them, Honey." She responded. "They are in the hallway closet. I have a special card from Mrs. Jackson you should read. I wanted you to see it when you were feeling better. I guess now is the best time as any."

She got up and walked to the hallway closet and grabbed the little box on the top shelf. She stopped right before the living room and kitchen.

"Let's go to the kitchen table, where the lighting is better, and I will show you."

They both sat at the table and opened the shoebox. Inside were all the cards Jim received while he was in the hospital. There was a beautiful card in the shape of angel wings at the top of the large stack. It sparkled with iridescent glitter.

"That is the one from Rob's mom I was telling you about."

Jim reached in and picked up the card. "This is the one I remember seeing hanging on the corkboard at Sacred Heart!"

He slowly opened the card to read what was written inside.

Shannon Lee was born and raised in Michigan's Upper Peninsula. She has always been intrigued by the stories her grandmother passed down from the generations of living in such a remote place as the U.P.

Shannon enjoys kayaking with her Yorkie, Bindi, and camping throughout the vast wilderness of the U.P.

CPSIA information can be obtained
at www.ICGtesting.com
Printed in the USA
BVHW071047041121
620779BV00005B/53